Match Point

Match Point

KATHERINE REILLY

HEAD
ᵒᶠ ZEUS

An Aria Book

9 7 5 3 4 6 8

A catalogue record for this book is available
from the British Library.

ISBN (PB): 9781035911660
ISBN (E): 9781035911677

Cover design: Meg Shepherd

Typeset by SiliconChips Services Ltd UK

Printed and bound in Great Britain by
CPI Group (UK) Ltd, Croydon CR0 4YY

Head of Zeus Ltd
First Floor East
5–8 Hardwick Street
London EC1R 4RG

www.headofzeus.com

For Kim

Thank you for believing in me

Prologue

Today is going to be a better day.

That's what I keep telling myself as I open yet another brown envelope, pull out the book inside and place it on top of the pile that's getting steadily higher on my desk. We get sent dozens of books from publishers for review here at *The Daily Journal* every week, and as the culture features assistant, it's my job to get them all out, pile them up and line them on a trolley so that the books editor can scan the spines and select the ones she wants to read and feature.

Worryingly, this is one of the most interesting aspects of my job.

Not that I'm complaining. I know I'm lucky to be working at a newspaper at all, and when I moved to London last year, I genuinely didn't think I'd be able to land any kind of role in the media, so I should be grateful to be here, piling up books and fetching tea and coffee. It's just, I did hope that maybe I'd get to be a bit more involved in the creative side of things and, as I'm turning twenty-nine this year, I do sometimes wonder whether I should be in something higher than what is essentially an entry-level job.

Take yesterday for example. My only pressing job was to book a table for my editor, Harvey, at The Ivy for a lunch meeting today, and then I spent the rest of my valuable time organising the books we received that morning by colour of spine and then taking online quizzes about which dog breed suits my lifestyle the best, which Disney character I'm most like, and which 'oos celeb is my perfect match.

I learnt that I should own a Norfolk terrier, I have a lot in common with Meeko – the racoon from *Pocahontas* – and, should I ever find myself single again, it wouldn't be a bad thing for me to bump into Chad Michael Murray. Which is all very useful information, but I didn't exactly wake up this morning full of motivation, knowing that I'm contributing to society in a helpful way.

So, that's why I'm filling myself with positive thoughts today, and as soon as I'm done opening these books, I'm going to write a list of things that I can do that will be useful for my career, like how I need to email the arts desk again, just to double-check there's still no designer jobs going there, or how I should start applying for roles at galleries and publishers that have a strong graphic novel output. I can't let myself get comfortable here. If I want to work in art then I have to actually *do something about it*.

Yes, good. Strong motivational thoughts. Already things seem better.

'Flora, Harvey wants to see you.'

I glance up from my growing book pile to see Basil, our intern, hovering next to me whilst scrolling through his phone. He sounds irritated that he's had to make the journey of a few metres from his desk to mine to deliver the message. The floppy-haired twenty-year-old son of one of Harvey's golf buddies, Basil has been at the newspaper for just over a week, here for 'work experience', though so far he has yet to do any real work. He spends most of his time on TikTok and accompanying Harvey for long lunches.

'Thanks, Basil,' I say brightly, determined to be full of optimism.

He shrugs and slinks back to his desk, slumping down in his chair without breaking eye contact with his phone the entire time. My heavy eye-roll is caught by the sports journalist Iris, who is talking through a layout with someone nearby. At first, I feel embarrassed that someone saw me do that behind his back, but when Iris smiles at me conspiratorially, glancing at Basil and echoing my eye-roll, I'm relieved, grinning back at her.

Iris is one of the only people I can stand here at the newsroom – mostly because she's the only journalist who bothers to give me the time of day. Despite the fact we work in different sections – her in sport, and me in the culture corner – we still hang out in the kitchen sometimes, making coffee and giggling about our stuffy, pretentious colleagues or diva sport celebrities she's interviewed. We've been for lunch a few times too, which, although it might not be a big deal for her, really means a lot to me. Since I haven't been in the city that long, I don't really have any proper friends in London. It's nice to feel like I have someone I can talk to.

We're very different. I was intimidated by Iris at first: she's confident, smart, quick-witted, and mesmerisingly beautiful with dark hair, delicate features and striking green eyes. She's also very stylish and sophisticated, always dressed as though she's going for an important lunch meeting at Sexy Fish in Mayfair, the sort of woman who walks in a room and all heads turn towards her. I, on the other hand, tend to be reserved and cautious, wrestle daily with my unruly wavy blonde hair, have a wardrobe of mostly faded T-shirts and ripped jeans, and I sort of slink into a room hoping I won't be noticed.

Still, we click. I guess opposites attract.

When I get to Harvey's desk, I clear my throat and say, 'Basil said you wanted to see me?'

Without looking up from his screen, Harvey holds up a finger, signalling at me to wait until he's done with the email he's writing. I try to suppress a smirk. This is *classic* Harvey: to demand someone come talk to him and then make them wait. He loves to feel important and remind his employees who's in charge here.

Harvey is a sixty-something pompous arsehole who shouldn't be the culture editor of a national newspaper because he doesn't appear to know anything about film, art, music or theatre. Unfortunately, he did know all the right people to land the job. The fact that he sent an intern a few metres across the room to say he wanted to see me instead of just getting up and walking over here himself sums up the man.

'Right, that's done,' Harvey says finally, pressing send and then swivelling in his chair to face me. 'Flora, let's go into a meeting room.' He pushes himself up from his chair. 'Basil, give me five minutes and then we'll go for our lunch.'

'Great.' Basil nods, scrolling through his Instagram. 'I've been swamped all day.'

I glance up at the clock on the wall. It's eleven thirty.

Walking over to one of the free meeting rooms, Harvey opens the door and gestures for me to enter.

'Take a seat,' he says, letting the door shut behind him and looking out across the newsroom. The meeting rooms are essentially a row of glass boxes to one side of the room, so everyone can see into them. Harvey strokes his chin thoughtfully before shoving both his hands in his pockets and turning to face me. He exhales.

'Flora, I'm afraid we have to let you go.'

I blink at him. 'I... sorry?'

'I'm sure you're aware of the sorry state journalism is in these days,' Harvey continues brazenly, taking his hands out of his pockets and resting them on the back of the chair opposite to lean forwards. 'Cuts have to be made. You only joined us last year and, well, you know how it goes. Last in, first out.'

I stare at him in disbelief.

'Are you... *firing* me?' I manage to croak.

'No, of course not!' He recoils, shocked. 'We're making you redundant.'

Hot tears prick at the backs of my eyes as his words sink in. Yeah, this may not be my dream career, but it's still my *job*. I've done everything the role required. I can't believe they're getting rid of me. Harvey literally had a four-hour lunch the other day,

4

which I know he expensed. I've never expensed anything. How am *I* the cut that's going to save them money?!

He clears his throat, shifting uncomfortably. 'Nasty business, all this, but necessary. HR will want to go through all the particulars with you. I want to personally thank you for your... adequate work the last few months. I'm sure you'll succeed in whatever you do next and if ever you want to go for a drink so I can give you some pearls of wisdom...' he pauses, his eyes roaming down to my chest and back up again '...my door is always open.'

Oh my God.

Is he hitting on me WHILE he's sacking me?

'Anyway—' He coughs, turning to look through the glass at the clock – it's now eleven thirty-four. 'I'd better get going for my lunch meeting. Any questions, send me an email and we can get it all straightened out. In the meantime, off you pop to HR and they'll be able to help with the next steps. Sorry, must dash.'

He hesitates as he reaches the door and turns to look at me, taking a deep breath. 'Flora,' he begins in a softer tone, and for a moment I think he might be about to say something nice. 'You did remember to book The Ivy for me and Basil today?'

Still in shock, I find myself nodding, my mouth too dry to form any words.

'Excellent,' he says, perking up. 'I can't get enough of their Malaysian prawn curry. It's awfully good. You must try it, should you ever get the chance.'

And with that inspirational parting advice, he leaves the room.

'Trust me, Flora, they are going to rue the day they let you go,' Iris is telling me as I glumly unlock the door to my flat. 'I know it seems shit right now, but try to focus on the fact that you never liked this job anyway. You are going on to bigger and better things – I know it. It may not feel like it now, but this is a good move for you.'

It was nice of Iris to insist on accompanying me home after I cried all over her shoulder in the office toilet and then continued to moan at her about my pitiful career on the train from Waterloo to Wimbledon, where I live with Jonah in our rented one-bedroom flat. When I agreed to move to London with him, I didn't have a clue where to live because I didn't know the city well, but it turned out he'd already chosen Wimbledon. All his friends live South West, so I guess it made the most sense. I was the one who found this flat, though – as soon as we set foot on Lingfield Road for the viewing, I knew it was where I wanted to live.

Leading Iris into the living room, we find the TV is on. Jonah must have forgotten to switch it off before he left this morning. He's left it on Eurosport, streaming the Australian Open. One of the players is yelling something angrily at the umpire.

'Kieran O'Sullivan,' Iris says dreamily behind me, looking over my shoulder.

'Who?'

She nods at the tall, dark-haired guy gesticulating wildly at the umpire. 'The Irish tennis player. Hot-headed and ever so *hot*.'

'Oh yeah, I've heard of him.'

We watch as he whips his cap off his head and throws it on the ground in frustration, eliciting a chorus of boos from the crowd.

Iris folds her arms. 'He's an interesting player to watch when he gets it right. Intense, moody, sexy.' She lets out a wistful sigh, adding under her breath, 'I could watch him all day long.'

'Is he this bad-tempered in person?'

'I wouldn't know – he doesn't do interviews. He used to, back when he started out. He got to the final of the Australian Open pretty young and suddenly everyone thought he was going to wipe the floor at the other Grand Slams, but it never happened. He's made it to a lot of semi-finals and finals, but never quite got his hands on those big trophies.' She shrugs. 'He seems to avoid journalists now.'

'Maybe that's a good thing,' I remark, as he's given a warning from the umpire.

Peeling my hat, scarf and coat off, I start looking for the TV remote, growing more and more frustrated at not being able to find it. I always leave it in the exact same spot on our glass coffee table, but Jonah tends to toss it down wherever, even though I've asked him countless times to put it in its correct place.

'I love this room,' Iris remarks, as I slide my fingers down the side of the sofa cushions. 'Your painting is so beautiful.'

I glance up at the pink cherry blossom art covering the entire back wall around the fireplace and mantelpiece. Inspired by a similar design I saw in a movie, I painted it the week we moved in to make the flat feel more homely and personal. Jonah kept grumbling about the fact I was putting all my spare time into decorating, which could wait, rather than unpacking essential boxes, but I disagreed. Moving here was daunting. When I walked into the flat, I needed to feel at home.

'Don't get too attached,' I mutter. 'We're painting over it.'

She frowns, bewildered. 'You're *kidding*.'

'Jonah— sorry, *we* think making the room a cream-white would make it a bit more sophisticated.' I finally find the remote beneath one of the throw cushions. 'Aha!'

I turn off the TV.

That's when we hear it: the loud groan from the bedroom. A man's voice. Jonah's voice. I freeze. The sound is followed by a woman's moan. Iris stiffens.

'That… that can't be…' I whisper, trailing off as a lump forms in my throat.

My heart thudding against my chest, I tiptoe over to the bedroom. Iris follows me and comes to stand at my side, gripping my arm in solidarity. The woman's voice floats through the door again.

'Oh yes! *Yes*, Jonah!'

The colour draining from her face, Iris clasps her hand over her mouth.

'Flora,' she whispers through her fingers, her eyes glistening with pity.

I grab the handle and turn it, pushing the door and letting it swing open.

There on my bed is my next-door neighbour Zoe, stark naked, straddling Jonah as he lies on his back, his hands gripping her grinding hips.

At first, I just feel numb, like my brain doesn't quite understand that what I'm seeing is real and so there's no need to process it. But as the reality of the situation sinks in, the searing pain in my heart sends my body into shock.

I let out a low, feeble whimper.

Jonah lifts his head and sees us. With a panicked expression, he lifts Zoe up and flings her away from him, sending her toppling off the side of the bed and onto the floor with a yelp. If it wasn't such a sickening scenario, it would have been funny. A sitcom audience would have laughed their fucking heads off at that bit. But this isn't a fictional scene. No one is yelling 'cut', because this is real life. This is actually happening.

'Flora!' Jonah squeaks, cupping his dick with his hands. 'What are you doing here?'

His eyes dart about the room as Zoe's flushed, startled face pops up at the side of the bed and she reaches to wrap herself in our duvet that must have been cast aside earlier.

Cut. *Cut*.

My head spinning and vision blurring, I reach to steady myself on Iris before collapsing into her arms as my legs buckle out from beneath me.

CUT.

I

SIX MONTHS LATER

'Are you sure about this?' Iris asks on the phone, while I place a pair of high-waisted denim shorts neatly at the top of my bag. 'Four weeks is a long time on your own.'

'Iris, I've never been more sure about anything in my life,' I insist, putting her on speaker and balancing my phone on top of the pile of books on my bedside table while I carefully fold some pretty floral dresses. 'Four weeks on my own is just what I need.'

'The Lake District is so far away.' She sighs. 'Can't you work on your graphic novel here in London? That way we can still hang out. All my other friends are married or have babies, and, as much as I love them, I need *you*. Who else is going to drink into the night with me and dance wildly on tables?'

I snort. 'When have we ever danced on tables?'

'We might do if you stayed in the city. London in the summer is wild.'

I chuckle, pressing my dresses neatly down into my case. 'It's only a few weeks and then I'll be back to dance on all the tables you want. The whole point of this is for me to get out of the city and take some time for myself.'

She sighs, her tone becoming soft and serious. 'Flora, don't be annoyed by me saying this, but I'm worried about you. I get that a change of scene can help spark creativity – and I'm all for you getting a break – but I don't want you to go all that way and find yourself feeling... lonely.'

Hanging my head, I press my lips together. In the last six months, Iris has become my closest friend and I can understand why she's saying this. It's not like I've been in the best place since Jonah moved out. Safe to say, I was a total mess for a while. I'm not exactly proud of how I handled the break-up: begging Jonah to stay when he was the one who cheated was a dismally low period of my life that I'd rather forget.

Despite all the red flags, all his cutting comments and neglect, I'd naively convinced myself that he was *it* for me. The One. We'd been together three years and I'd left my friends and my PA job in Norwich for him. I'd moved to London, where I knew no one, and made every effort possible to fit into his life. I'd somehow stopped caring about what *I* wanted; everything was for him, whatever made *him* happy. I willingly made it that way. And suddenly, when it all fell apart on that fateful day in January, I found myself with no job, no friends and no Jonah.

My whole world had crumbled into nothing.

Except for Iris. She's been at my side through it all. I'm lucky to have her – she may be a new friend, but she's turning out to be the best one I could have hoped for. A lot of my older friendships waned when I started dating Jonah. He didn't get on with my small group of school friends. Whenever I organised to see them, he'd moan about having to come along, and if he did then he made it clear he was doing so reluctantly. Knowing it might cause tension between me and Jonah made me less inclined to organise to see that group and my efforts dipped dramatically. By the time I left for London, it felt as though we'd drifted apart and I'd become closer to Jonah's theatrical mates.

But since the break-up, none of his friends have spoken to me. When it came to choosing sides, I never even got a look-in.

Having lost the majority of my connections to Jonah in one fell and very painful swoop, there's been one that has been cruelly impossible to shake: my next-door neighbour. When we broke up, Jonah wanted to immediately move out of this flat and into a house-share in Clapham, but in spite of the memories he was leaving behind, there was something about this place that I couldn't say goodbye to. I'd fallen for Wimbledon, and couldn't imagine being anywhere else in London, so I chose to stay. But moving on became a lot more difficult with Zoe coming and going all the time.

Unfortunately, I live next to the human reminder that, as I'd always feared, I was never good enough for someone like Jonah. Zoe, on the other hand, is impossibly perfect. She's tall and willowy with glossy brown curly hair, razor-sharp cheekbones, plump lips and big brown eyes. Her nails are always manicured, her make-up is flawless, and she works in fashion PR, so she dresses impeccably every day. I've never seen her look bad. Not *once*. Even when taking out the bins, she still looks like an off-duty model.

And on top of all that, she's nice. Well, I thought she was. She was very friendly and funny when we used to bump into each other. I thought we'd struck seriously lucky with our neighbour – you hear some rogue stories about London. But since the incident, we haven't spoken. She tried to apologise on the day, but Iris told her to get the hell out of there and to never speak to or go near me again. She seems to have taken that advice very seriously, which is probably a good thing. But it doesn't matter, I know Zoe's there and every time I catch a glimpse of her gliding off to work, I'm reminded of what I'm not.

Still, things are getting easier. The debilitating ache that made itself at home on my heart for the first few months after Jonah moved out has almost completely dissolved. I miss him less every day and it's helped that I've kept myself busy with temp PA work. It's paid much better than my brief fling with journalism and has helped me to keep up with the rent on this place now that Jonah isn't contributing anymore. Of course this is London, so I still had to get in touch with my dad to ask for financial help with the rent, which was mortifying.

'He's happy to pay the whole year of your rent,' his personal assistant, Andy, had told me chirpily down the phone. 'We can make that transfer to you today.'

'No, no, *no*,' I'd said sternly. 'That's kind of him, but I just need a loan for the next couple of months while I find my feet. I'll move somewhere cheaper once our lease runs out, but for now, if he—'

'Okay, and… there. That transfer is done,' he'd interrupted. 'If you wouldn't mind emailing to confirm receipt, we'd appreciate it. Now, is there anything else I can help you with today?'

'I… uh… okay, wow, thank you, but I'll just transfer most of that straight back, because as I said, that's really nice but I didn't want him to cover—'

'You are so welcome, Miss Hendrix. Is there anything else you need?'

'Uh… I'd like to thank him, if that's possible?'

'I'm afraid he's in back-to-back meetings today, but I'll be sure to pass on the message.'

'Oh, okay. Thanks. Maybe he could call me when he gets the chance.'

'Absolutely. Have a great day and thank you for your call.'

My dad didn't call, but he did message a day or so later to check I'd received the money, which is something.

Despite what I said, it has been a relief to have the money in my bank account for now. I'm still determined to pay all of it back, because I really don't want to have to rely on my dad for anything. And now an opportunity has arisen that is too good to turn down: the Wimbledon tennis tournament is approaching and flats in the area are in hot demand. I've made a KILLING by letting out the flat through an agency: these next four weeks are paying for three months' rent at least. The prices are madness, but, hey, I'm not complaining.

It's perfect – my flat is in a great location and I was able to note in its description that the flat upstairs is currently empty, since its occupant, Mrs Perry, has taken a once-in-a-lifetime trip to travel around Asia for three months, so whoever stayed here wouldn't need to worry about noise. It got snapped up immediately. I guess there must be seriously devoted tennis fans out there willing to pay whatever it takes to live in Wimbledon and soak up the atmosphere.

To be fair, it is pretty cool around here at this time of year. Wimbledon Village really comes alive – there's a great buzz as people from all over the world descend upon this corner of London. All the outside areas of the restaurants and bars are flooded with people chatting and laughing in the sunshine, and the village itself looks idyllic with hanging baskets everywhere overflowing with bright, colourful flowers and all the shop windows compete to have the most extravagant tennis-themed display.

But the best thing about it is that it's given me the nudge I needed to leave London for a bit and rent a cottage in the Lake District where I'm finally going to start work on my graphic novel. It's *perfect*. My grandmother on my mum's side lived in Keswick and some of my most treasured memories are from when I'd go stay with her for a few weeks in the summer. Every now and then, we'd go off exploring and find a quiet spot away from the tourists – I'd sketch and she'd paint using watercolours.

During my teen years, it was an escape for me from the turmoil of living with Mum. Grandma knew what was going on with her and what I had to deal with. *Everyone* knew. Mum was what they call a functioning alcoholic when I was little, able to go about her daily routine without drawing much attention to her drinking problem, but she couldn't sustain that way of life for long and by the time I was fifteen, her addiction had complete power over her.

It's not like I could go to my dad for help. By then he was living in New York with his new heiress wife, Camila, helping her with her expanding property empire. But I had Grandma. She would come down and stay with us a bit when she could; she helped out in the holidays by whisking me away to the Lake District, and she also passed her artistic genes down to me. She was the only person who believed I could make it – neither Mum nor Dad, for different reasons, noticed I was even interested in art.

When Mum died after I'd left school, Grandma came to stay in the Norwich flat to help me sort all the admin with the funeral and then she helped me find my own place, away from the sad memories. Dad did check in and he did his best to be there for me in the only way he knew how – by offering financial help – but it was Grandma who I depended upon for everything else. It was only when she passed away a few years later in my early twenties that I realised I was on my own. That's why Iris is wrong. I won't feel lonely in the Lake District, even if I don't meet a single soul for the next four weeks. It's the only place I've ever felt unconditionally loved.

'You don't need to worry, Iris,' I assure her earnestly now. 'I am going to have the best time. It will be peaceful and quiet and inspiring. This is *exactly* what I need.'

'What you need is a sexy man between your thighs.'

I burst out laughing. '*Iris!*'

We're interrupted by my doorbell. I frown in confusion, checking the time on my phone. It must be a delivery, although I don't remember ordering anything.

'I have to go – someone's here,' I tell her. 'I'll speak to you later.'

'Okay, message me when you're on your way!'

We hang up and I slide my phone into my pocket, before hurrying into the hallway and swinging open the front door. Except it's not the postman.

Standing on my doorstep is a tall, broad-shouldered guy in black jeans and a white T-shirt that shows off his tanned, muscled arms. He's wearing a cap low over his face, so I can only glimpse his full lips and hint of dark stubble along his chiselled jawline. When he lifts his head, he fixes me with piercing sapphire-blue eyes framed by bold, dark eyebrows.

I inhale sharply as I instantly recognise him.

It's Kieran O'Sullivan. As in, *Kieran O'Sullivan* the famous tennis player and world-renowned arsehole. I knew he was tall, but wow is he *tall*, maybe six foot four, and breathtakingly handsome. If he hadn't made it in tennis, he surely would have been a good fit for a Calvin Klein advert with his perfect bone structure and smouldering eyes. What the HELL is Kieran O'Sullivan doing on my doorstep? He doesn't look lost. He looks impatient, as though I'm the one who is in the wrong place.

He scowls, a signature look for him.

'Are you from the agency?' he asks impatiently with a soft Dublin lilt.

'Y-you're—' I begin, stammering.

'Yes, I'm Kieran, nice to meet you,' he says dismissively as though it's not nice to meet me at all, it's a damn inconvenience.

And then he marches into my flat.

Kieran O'Sullivan casually walks past me and into *my home* as though he owns the place. I'm so bewildered that I just stand aside and let him pass, as though it's completely normal for a stranger to wander in off the street and enter your home without any form of explanation. As he brushes by I'm hit with a musky sandalwood scent combined with a strong whiff of stale alcohol. He disappears into the living room and the mirror on the wall opposite shows that my mouth is hanging open. I quickly shut it.

Before I close the front door, I poke my head out and look both ways down the road to check if he was running away from paparazzi or something and ducked into the nearest house, but the road is empty. He's come on his own.

I take the opportunity to check my reflection – I wasn't expecting to bump into a tennis star today. I comb my fingers through my hair, attempting to tame the waves, and run a finger beneath my eyes to make sure the mascara I clumsily applied this morning hasn't smudged. I didn't put on any foundation this morning and my freckles are on full show, made more prominent by the sun we've been getting in London recently. I notice the pair of gold hoop earrings on the hallway table next to the vase of fresh flowers I arranged this morning – I put the hoops there yesterday on purpose so I wouldn't forget to bring them on my trip. Quickly putting them on, I check my reflection one last time and then scurry towards the living room.

By the time I make it in there, I find to my surprise that Kieran has already kicked off his shoes, leaving them strewn on the rug, and is lying across my sofa, clumsily rearranging the cushions to make himself more comfortable.

He glances up as I walk in and frowns. 'I'm sure I can get myself acquainted with the place. You don't need to hang around. Thank you.'

I gape at him. 'I… I'm sorry, um, can I ask what… what you're doing here?'

'I appreciate I'm early,' he grumbles, removing his cap and tossing it on the floor. 'But I didn't think it would matter. Do you know if there's any paracetamol here? I meant to buy some on the way.'

'P-paracetamol?' I stammer. 'Uh, sure, there's some in the medicine cabinet.'

'Great, if you could get me those with a glass of water, I'd appreciate it.' He grimaces, plumping up the cushion behind his head before resting back against it and closing his eyes. 'I have a bad headache.'

I blink at him. 'I'm sorry, I'm confused.'

He runs a hand down his face and peers through his fingers at me. 'I can get it myself, but I'm not feeling my best and I just thought, as you're already up…'

His sentence trails off. He looks at me pointedly, as though waiting for something.

'Um. Okay. I'll get you some,' I say, bewildered.

'Thanks,' he says gruffly before shutting his eyes again.

Turning away from him, I shuffle into the kitchen and pour a glass of water. As I shut the tap off, I take a moment. It's obvious what's happened: he's got the wrong house. It's not that surprising that a tennis player would be in Wimbledon a couple of weeks before the tournament – he'll be gearing up for it here with his team – but I can't quite understand why he's acting as though I'd be expecting him.

Grabbing the paracetamol, I return to the living room to find he's now sat back up and has buried his head in his hands, groaning loudly. His phone buzzes in his pocket and it looks like it's a real effort for him to get it out. He sees the caller ID, mutters something under his breath, and ignores the call, setting his phone aside.

I approach, holding out the paracetamol, and placing the glass down in front of him.

'Thanks,' he grunts without looking up at me, breaking two painkillers out the foil.

'No worries. Um, I don't mean to be rude, but can I just ask again why you're—'

'Ugh.' He gags after taking a swig of water to wash down the tablets, before peering at the glass, looking offended. 'What the fuck?'

'Is there something wrong with the water?'

'It's not exactly Evian is it,' he mutters.

My cheeks flush in mortification. I guess I shouldn't be surprised that a professional athlete like him is used to the finer things in life, but it's rude of him to be so open with his displeasure. I cross my arms defensively.

'No, sorry, it's tap,' I tell him.

With a pointed shudder, he places the glass down on the table next to the coaster. Not *on* the coaster. NEXT to it. *Who is this guy?!*

That's it. I've been polite enough. It's time to get some answers.

'Excuse me, but why are you here?' I ask bluntly.

He frowns at me. 'I didn't think it would be a problem that I'm early.'

'But I'm not expecting you.'

'Well, I wasn't expecting *you*,' he mutters, looking me up and down. 'As I said, I appreciate you greeting me but I can see everything's in order, so you can go.'

'Why would I go?' I ask, putting my hands on my hips. 'I live here.'

'No,' he says, narrowing his eyes at me. 'I live here.'

I stare at him. Oh God. This is bad. Kieran O'Sullivan is clearly having some kind of episode and has convinced himself that he lives in my flat!

As he rises to his feet, eyeing me suspiciously, I take a step back from him.

'You're not from the agency, are you,' he surmises.

'What agency? No, I'm not from any agency.'

'Who are you? How did you know I was staying here? Did someone on my team tell you? Who? How did you get in?' he asks rapidly, his voice strained and sharp. 'Who told you I was staying here?'

'I didn't… no one told me anything!' I stammer, unnerved by the flurry of questions. 'This is my flat! You don't live here, *I* live here!'

He hesitates. 'This is your flat.'

'Yes!'

'As in, you didn't mean you're staying here, you meant you *live*-live here.'

'*Yes*,' I say, staring at him wide-eyed.

'Ah.' His expression softens with relief. 'I think I understand the confusion. You've rented out your flat for the next few weeks, right? Yeah, I'm the one who's renting it.'

I'm too stunned to speak for a moment.

'Huh?' I blurt out eventually.

'I've rented your flat,' he repeats, reaching up to rub at the nape of his neck. 'I thought you were from the letting agency.'

'You… you've rented my flat,' I say in disbelief. '*Really?*'

He nods, slumping back down on the sofa.

'Are… are you sure?' I check.

'Yep,' he says wearily, nodding at the cherry blossom on the wall. 'This is the place.'

I pause, attempting to wrap my head around the fact that

it's not a tennis fan who will be living in my house, but Kieran O'Sullivan, a celebrity.

'Sorry I'm early,' he says, making himself comfortable again while I stand frozen to the spot. 'I know I'm not meant to be here until five, but... I was at a loose end.'

His phone rings again. I can see from the Caller ID that it's someone named Henrietta. He glances at it, but doesn't move a muscle, letting it ring out.

'You're staying here,' I say out loud as though that might help my brain to accept the fact. 'That's... wow.'

He presses his lips together, looking uncomfortable. 'Yeah, look, I'd appreciate it if you didn't tell anyone that. I don't want the press swarming the place.'

I realise he's looking at me expectantly.

'Oh. Sure. Of course. I won't say anything to anyone.'

His frown deepens. I can tell he doesn't believe me.

'Promise,' I add quickly, though I appreciate that doesn't mean much to him. He doesn't know me. 'Anyway, I hope you'll like it here. I wasn't expecting a player to rent it. It's quite small, but it's a great location. Near to Wimbledon Village, so a good atmosphere. Although I guess you'll be too busy to really appreciate that. Busy playing in the actual tournament...'

My nervous prattling trails off. He's sitting with his hands clasped together on his knees, staring straight ahead at the wall, his brow furrowed. Everything about his body language is screaming that he's uncomfortable with my presence. He's making me feel unwelcome in my own home.

'Uh... if you have any questions, though,' I continue, 'or need anything—'

'I'll talk to the agency,' he cuts in brusquely.

I'm taken aback by his interruption. 'Right. Okay.'

'I've got everything I need, so you're free to go.'

Funny how words can say one thing, but everything else about the way you say them can make them mean something else. His words may make out that I'm 'free to go', but there's nothing about his tone or demeanour that's giving me a choice in the matter. He's not even bothering to look at me. His body is angled carefully so he's almost got his back to me. His voice is sharp and stern, like a pissed-off teacher dismissing an enthusiastic, pestering student.

This guy is telling me to fuck off.

And you know what? He may be a tennis star, but this is my house. According to our terms, he isn't due to arrive here until this evening, yet he's strolled in here without any kind of meaningful apology, kicked off his shoes without putting them on the shoe stand, ignored the coasters, and is now making out as though *I'm* the one at fault. That's not fair and I'm not going to let him make me feel this small. I've been nothing but polite to him.

'The flat isn't available until five o'clock,' I state, putting my hands on my hips and lifting my chest. Yeah, that's right, *Kieran*. I'm power-posing at you. 'So, while I finish packing and sorting the flat out, *you* are free to go.'

His eyes flash with irritation as he finally makes the effort to look up at me. His jaw tightens and the lines on his forehead deepen as he stares me down. I refuse to be intimidated, holding his eye contact. Neither of us say anything. The silence is deafening.

My phone starts vibrating with a call in my pocket, and I reluctantly tear my eyes from his to check who it is. It's the number of the holiday let company through which I've booked my Lake District cottage.

'I have to take this,' I tell him curtly, spinning around and marching out the room towards the kitchen to take the call.

'Hello, Flora speaking,' I say, the irritation that's built from Kieran's rude behaviour fizzling away at the thought of the quaint cottage awaiting me in the Lakes.

'Miss Hendrix, hi, it's Hailey from Simply Cottages. You've booked through us for your stay this month in Keswick?'

'Yes, hi! Are you calling about where I'll be able to find the keys when I arrive tonight? I think it said in the email that someone would—'

'I'm so sorry, but I'm afraid we have a problem with the cottage you've rented,' Hailey interrupts, her voice strained. 'You will no longer be able to stay there.'

My heart drops. 'But... I'm meant to be arriving tonight for four weeks!'

'I know, I'm so sorry. It's completely out of our control.'

'What exactly is the problem? Because I don't need anything fancy and I'm sure whatever it is could be fixed. Or if there's just a leak or something then maybe I could still—'

'The roof has *completely* caved in.'

I pause. 'What?'

'It's a nightmare,' she whines, exasperated. 'It's booked out for the entire summer. I'm so sorry about this. You'll receive a full refund of course and I'll send over all the details regarding that in an email—'

'Whoa, whoa, hang on.' I take a deep breath. 'Hailey, I have to come to the Lake District. Is there somewhere else I can stay? Surely you have another cottage. You can't just cancel my booking at the last minute and not offer a replacement.'

'It's the height of summer, our busiest time of year. We don't have anywhere available. I can only apologise.'

'You don't understand, I *have* to leave my place!'

'Let me ask my manager to speak to you and I'm sure we can not only offer you a full refund now, but a discount on your next booking to make up in some small part for the inconvenience. I'm just going to put you on hold.'

'Hailey, I—'

I'm interrupted by a crackling noise followed by classical hold music. Closing my eyes in despair, I slump against the counter and run a hand through my hair. *This can't be happening. This can't be happening. This CANNOT BE HAPPENING.*

I jump at the sound of the front door slamming. Creeping out the kitchen, I peer into the living room to find it empty. I breathe a sigh of relief. Kieran must have seen sense and decided to come back later. At least I've got that jerk out my hair.

'Miss Hendrix?' Hailey says, coming back on the line after a couple of minutes.

I grip the phone tightly. 'Yes, hi, I'm here.'

'My manager isn't available to talk right now, but he's going to give you a call to offer a full explanation and answer all your questions. Once again, we apologise for this inconvenience and hope this won't affect your booking with us again in the future. Thank you for your understanding.'

She hangs up.

Now what am I going to do?

2

This isn't how it's supposed to go. I'm supposed to be getting away from London so I can finally feel in control again, start feeling like I'm doing something with my life rather than wasting away in a flat on my own with no real job and no purpose in a city where I have no friends other than Iris. After a terrible start to the year, this was supposed to be the turning point. I needed this escape. I was going to come back to the city feeling refreshed and excited for whatever lay ahead. With my graphic novel underway, I was going to apply for jobs at art galleries and publishers, jobs that I'd feel passionate about. I had a plan.

And now it's gone to shit.

I let myself have a moment or two to wallow, moving my half-filled case and lying face down across the bed to scream into my duvet, before I tell myself to get my arse up and start looking for somewhere else to go for the next few weeks. There *has* to be somewhere else I can go in the Lake District – there's always last-minute deals, surely I'll be able to snag one.

Setting my laptop up at the kitchen table, I start looking up other companies that rent houses in Keswick, but everything I find is completely booked up for the summer. I widen my search, but have no luck. No cottages, no apartments, no suitable hotel rooms available across the next four weeks. Pushing my laptop back, I groan, folding forwards and resting my forehead on the table. This is a disaster. A complete and utter disaster.

Choking back tears, I know the one person who I need to talk to right now is Iris.

It's strange to think that our friendship is still relatively new. When Jonah left and I could barely leave my bed, let alone the house, it was Iris who came over uninvited and sat with me while I cried, who listened to me talk over and over about my heartbreak and stroked my hair and said everything was going to be okay. She ordered me expensive takeaways that I could only pick at, too upset to eat, but she never made me feel bad about how much money and food I must have wasted. She kept coming over whenever she could to check in on me. At my absolute lowest, she made me feel less alone.

That meant everything.

I've always tried to pretend like I don't mind not having a family I can depend on. When I was at school and I'd go round to friends' houses and see how much their mums and dads did for them, I'd tell myself that it was good to be responsible. I was proud to be self-sufficient and cook for myself because my mum wasn't there when I got home and I had no idea where she was or who she was with. It was a good thing to learn how to take care of myself. I would be the one who had the advantage in life when we left school and were sent off into the big wide world. That's what I told myself.

I *almost* believed it.

And while I'd had a lot of anger at my father for leaving me with Mum when he knew about her growing addiction issues, I'd learnt to handle it, thanks to therapy. I'd learnt to communicate my anger and I'd learnt to forgive him. Things are fine between us, we just don't have anything in common and he's emotionally distant from me. On the rare occasions we talk, it's stilted and dry, neither of us ever saying anything important. But I was grateful to him for offering me financial help when I really needed it. That was his way of showing he cared, and I accepted that.

This year has felt like a test. I know you shouldn't depend on someone else as much as I did with Jonah, but when you don't have family, you want to create one and that's what I thought we were doing. He was everything to me. I desperately wanted to be everything to him, so I accepted his finely tuned criticisms, and resolved to be what he needed, no matter the cost to myself. His ultimate rejection was earth-shattering. I've never felt more worthless and undeserving. That's why Iris would never fully understand how much she helped just by being there. Just by checking in and letting me know that *someone* cared, that was the glimmer of light I needed to pull me back from misery to see sense and regain a determination to put one foot in front of the other and carry on muddling through.

Slowly, I've spent the last six months finding myself again. I've looked after myself, bought nice clothes and products, had my hair and my nails done when I wanted. I started listening to the feel-good pop songs that Jonah always sneered at, and those songs made me feel so happy and uplifted that I would physically shudder at the thought of being with someone who could be so miserable, pompous and try-hard that they would loudly dismiss and demean such joyful music. Life is too short to be so pretentious.

I've proudly got to the stage where I want to try to create my comic book. Jonah made it clear that I didn't have what it takes, but he's been wrong about so many things that I was hoping he might be wrong about me. I can't give up on this now, not when I've come so far. I need to make this work and even though it looks like everything is falling to pieces, I don't want to give up quite yet.

I just need someone else to tell me that too.

Iris answers after the first ring.

'Hey, Flora,' she says brightly, music and people chatting in the background. 'Are you on your way already?'

'It's all gone wrong.'

'What? Hang on. I can't really hear you, one second.' I wait as she moves and the noise in the background dims. 'Sorry, I've headed out to the pub for lunch and it's busy in that beer garden. What did you say?'

'The roof collapsed.'

'WHAT? Oh my God, are you okay?!'

'Not this one. The Keswick one.'

'The which one?'

'The cottage in Keswick that I rented,' I explain through sniffles. 'The roof collapsed and they can't put me up anywhere else. I tried finding somewhere new to book, but there's nowhere available.'

'Oh no! Oh, Flora, I'm so sorry. You were so excited. That's awful! What are you going to do?'

'I don't know, but I have to leave my flat. Now I have nowhere to go.'

'Don't panic, we'll sort something. Surely you can speak to the agency and they can let whoever has rented your flat know that there's been a problem and they can't stay there anymore,' she suggests.

I hesitate. I wish I could tell her that it might be difficult to tell a famous tennis player that he hasn't got anywhere to stay while competing in Wimbledon anymore, but I promised Kieran I wouldn't tell *anyone*, and as much as I trust Iris, I stick to my word. There's no point in telling her about him anyway – it's not like she'll get the chance to meet him. I'll tell her after the tournament.

'I don't know whether that's an option,' I say, keeping it vague. Propping my elbow up on the table, I rest my chin in my hand. 'This is such a bad start.'

'It's not brilliant luck admittedly,' she concurs, 'BUT this does not mean your break is cancelled. Flora, there are so many places in England you can escape to for a few weeks to work on your book.'

'But you know that I wanted it to be the Lake District.'

'I know, but there are other places just as beautiful,' she says gently. 'You can go to the Lake District another time – like when you write the sequel to your bestseller debut!'

'I wish,' I mutter wistfully.

'Flora, you cannot let a collapsed roof ruin your plans. This is a tiny hiccup. I was worried about you going all that way on your own anyway, so maybe this is Fate's way of telling you I'm right and you should listen to what I say.'

'Uh-huh.' I smile into the phone. 'Go on then, what should I do?'

'You will get your cute butt out the door, go get yourself a delicious crisp glass of rosé in the sunshine somewhere, and enjoy scrolling through the last-minute deals for countryside retreats, preferably ones that aren't hours away from London. That way I can nip and see you if you'll let me.'

I sigh. 'A glass of rosé in the sun does sound tempting.'

'Off you go and call me when you've booked somewhere new. And remember, you don't need to stay in just one place the entire time so don't feel down if somewhere you like is only available for a small chunk of time – book it and find somewhere else for the next chunk. If need be, you can come crash on my parents' sofa in between.'

I find myself nodding along to her instructions. 'Okay. You're right. A new plan.'

'An *exciting* new plan,' she emphasises. 'Everything happens for a reason.'

'I am going to go book somewhere else,' I declare, rising to my feet.

'Yes, you are. Call me when it's done!'

'Will do. Iris, you're the best.'

'Well aware of it.'

We hang up and with a fresh wave of determination, I grab a bag for my laptop, pick up my sunglasses and keys, and march down the hallway and out of the house. Stepping out into the sunshine, I take a deep breath of fresh air and slide my sunglasses on.

'Time for a new plan,' I announce to no one.

Setting off in the direction of Wimbledon Village, I keep a lookout for an empty table outside one of the restaurants and bars – Iris's explicit instructions were to drink a glass of rosé in *the sunshine* – but everywhere is heaving with people. When the weather is this nice, all of London is outside. Teetering dangerously close to being in a bad mood again at yet ANOTHER stumbling block in my plans, I do my best to keep my cool and head to The Dog and Fox pub in the hope of finding a seat somewhere in its outside space – I am only one tiny person, maybe I can tag on to someone else's table.

Grabbing a glass of wine at the bar, I head out to the beer garden. As expected, most of the tables are full, but there is one towards the back that looks empty, until I get closer and see that there is someone seated at the end of the bench. They're on their own, scrolling through their phone with a pint of lager in front of them. I assume they're waiting for someone else, but hopefully they won't mind me perching on the end.

'Excuse me,' I begin with my sweetest smile, 'could I sit—'

'No,' he grunts before I've even finished my sentence.

I've realised who it is. His cap is down over his face; that's why I didn't recognise him straight away. *Kieran fucking O'Sullivan.*

3

Lifting his head cautiously, Kieran peers up from under his cap and starts.

'You,' he frowns, adjusting his sunglasses and sitting up straight. 'Did you follow me?'

'No!' I bristle, my face heating at the suggestion. 'I had no idea you were here! I thought you'd left!'

'I did leave. I came here.'

'Yes, thank you,' I snap. 'I realise that now.'

'What are you doing here?'

'Not following you. I... something came up and I need to do some research. I thought I'd get a glass of wine in the sun while I did so. What about you? What are *you* doing here?'

'The place I rented isn't ready yet.'

I note his pint of beer and raise my eyebrows pointedly. 'I thought you had a bad headache,' I mutter. 'So bad you couldn't get your own paracetamol.'

His jaw tightens. 'Hair of the dog.'

Pressing my lips together, I make a decision. I resolutely plonk myself down on the other end of his table and reach for one of the flimsy cardboard coasters, setting my drink on top of it before pulling my laptop out of my bag and opening it up in front of me. I pick a bit of fluff off my keyboard.

He watches me in silence.

'What are you doing?' he asks in a low, sullen voice.

'I'm having a drink and doing some research,' I inform him haughtily, logging onto the Wi-Fi and taking a sip of my drink.

'I meant, what are you doing at this table?' he clarifies through gritted teeth, and it gives me great satisfaction that I'm bothering him.

'You're on your own and so am I. There's plenty of room for both of us to sit here.' I perch my sunglasses on top of my head so I can see my screen properly. 'I'd already ordered my drink so I need somewhere to sit while I drink it.'

'You can't just sit down when you haven't been invited.'

'That's funny, because I distinctly remember you waltzing into my flat when *you* hadn't been invited. You even had a little lie-down on my sofa.'

He shifts in his seat. 'That was a misunderstanding. You're being purposefully rude.'

'As opposed to how *charming* you were to me, once you realised your mistake,' I say sarcastically.

'I may have been a bit thrown by the confusion,' he says defensively, scowling at me. 'But I wasn't rude.'

'Really? Tell me, Kieran, what's my name?'

He hesitates. 'Why is that—'

'Surely anyone with an ounce of manners might have thought to ask the person whose house they intruded upon, the same person who kindly got them some water and paracetamol, what their name was,' I say innocently, tilting my head at him. 'Or did I miss you asking me that during all your grovelling apologies?'

He inhales deeply through his nose, the muscle in his jaw twitching. He can't answer.

HA.

'Yeah, I didn't think so.' I return my attention to my laptop, typing into Google search, pressing return and then reaching for my glass of wine.

After a good minute of silence, he clears his throat.

'Fine,' he grumbles. 'Maybe I should have asked you your name. And apologised.'

'M-hm,' I say, keeping my eyes on my screen as I scroll down the search results.

'I'm sorry for intruding—' He waves his hand, gesturing for me to finish his sentence.

'Flora.'

'I'm sorry for intruding, *Flora*.'

I nod in acknowledgement of his apology.

'I'm Kieran,' he adds.

'You said.'

I hear a small sound emit from his throat, a sigh of exasperation maybe, before we fall into silence. Out of the corner of my eye, I see him take a sip of beer, glance at me one more time, and then get back to his phone until one of the members of staff comes out with a pizza for him that he must have ordered before I arrived.

I block him out mentally and zone in on my task: come five o'clock, I have to be out of my place and on my way to somewhere new. But as my glass empties, my level of hope sinks along with it. Finding somewhere remotely nice in the UK that's reasonably affordable and available at this late notice is an impossible task.

A movement at the other end of the table distracts me momentarily. Kieran's finished his food and is getting up to leave. As he passes by, I glance up, expecting him to say goodbye or *something*, but he doesn't. He leaves without a word.

Fine. Whatever. Good riddance.

Chewing my thumbnail, I start scrolling through my phone contacts. *Someone* in there has to be able to help. I start feeling desperate as I near the bottom of my list. I don't know that many people here in London – the only person in this city I'm close to now is Iris and she's currently living with her parents after her landlord kicked her out with just a month's notice. I know she offered it as a backup but I can hardly rock up at their house in Fulham, asking to take the sofa for four weeks. Secondly, the whole point of this was I was supposed to get *out* of London.

A glass of wine is set down in front of me.

'I didn't order—' I begin, but stop talking when I look up to see it's Kieran towering over me.

'I felt I owed you a drink as an apology,' he says, with no

attempt at hiding the resentment in his tone. With another pint for himself, he returns to his end of the table.

'Oh. Thank you. That's… nice.'

He doesn't say anything, sliding his Wayfarers back on and turning away from me to watch the passers-by. I roll my eyes at his back. I'd rather he didn't buy me a glass of wine at all than get it for me so reluctantly. I appreciate the gesture, but it hardly feels sincere.

Obviously that won't stop me drinking it though – as far as I'm concerned, it's a free glass of wine. I take a sip and am pleasantly surprised to discover that he ordered a much nicer rosé than I selected. I think this is the expensive one.

Right, back to my research. I try to keep in mind what Iris said and work out whether I can stay in one place for a bit and then move on to another, but even with more flexibility I still face the same problems. The nicest, most suitable places are either completely unavailable or at absurd prices at such late notice.

As I continue to hit one disappointment after another, I huff and sigh, before giving up completely and, with a loud whine, I bury my face in my hands.

'Could you… could you stop doing that?' I hear Kieran ask. I break my fingers apart to peer at his irked expression through the gaps. 'People are looking over and I'd rather they didn't.'

I let my hands drop down to the table to glare at him. 'Oh, I'm sorry that my misery is so inconvenient for you.'

He looks unimpressed. 'Excuse me for wanting a bit of privacy.'

'Yeah, you're really Mr Incognito in your cap and sunglasses,' I mutter, rolling my eyes. 'A cap is *literally* part of a tennis player's uniform.'

'Uniform?' he repeats with a hint of a smirk.

It's the first time I've seen him edge near a smile. Of course it's a conceited one.

'Sorry, sports kit,' I scoff. 'You know, if most people saw

someone in a crisis, they would ask what's wrong, not tell them off for whining too loudly.'

'I didn't tell you off, I politely asked you to stop. The minute someone recognises me, I don't get to relax. I wouldn't expect you to understand,' he says bitterly.

'So someone might ask you for a selfie. What's the big deal?'

'They might ask for a selfie if they're brave enough to come over, but they don't ask for permission to take pictures and videos of you from their tables. It's impossible to relax when you know you're being watched and recorded.'

I sigh, irritated. As much as I dislike him, he may be making a tiny bit of sense.

'Fine,' I relent, resting my fingertips back on my keyboard. 'I get it. I won't do anything more to draw attention. I'll leave after this drink anyway, okay?'

He nods sharply. My fingers still, I stare blankly at my screen. I have no idea what to type into the search engine next. I'm not sure I can bring myself to look through any more holiday sites. As I accept my failure, I close my eyes in despair.

Kieran coughs and then mutters something so quiet, I don't hear it at first.

'Sorry?' I ask, turning to him reluctantly, ready for the next criticism. Maybe I'm shutting my eyes too loudly or perhaps I'm drinking my wine too slowly.

'What is the crisis?' he says softly, his brow furrowed.

I blink at him, pressing a hand on my chest. '*My* crisis?'

'You said you were having a crisis,' he reminds me impatiently.

I raise my eyebrows at him. 'Are you asking me if I'm okay?'

I can't see his eyes behind his dark lenses, but his tense expression is giving me *just get on with it* vibes.

'Okay, well, to be honest, I have nowhere to go for the next few weeks,' I inform him. 'The roof of the cottage I'd booked in the Lake District has collapsed, so I can't go there anymore, and I can't find anywhere else at this late notice.'

He watches me pick up my glass of wine and swill it before taking a large gulp.

'You're worried about finding somewhere to go on holiday,' he says slowly, as though he's unsure of the problem. 'There are plenty of places in the UK. You can find somewhere.'

'Yes, but I have very specific requirements,' I say defensively, already questioning why I bothered to share my problems with someone so obnoxious. 'I can't book just anywhere.'

He takes a drink of his beer and then shoves his hands in his pockets. 'All right, what are your requirements?'

'It has to be somewhere in beautiful, tranquil countryside with at least one lake or a body of water, and it needs to preferably be available for four weeks, as I don't really want to flit about the place, I'd like to feel still and serene on the inside, too. And it can't be too expensive, and I don't want to go to a hotel, so it has to be some kind of cottage, flat or house, but one that's not too big as I'm going on my own.'

He stares at me. I stare back at him.

'Those *are* specific requirements,' he finally admits.

'Exactly. Which is why, I'm sorry, but unless there's some kind of miracle and a cottage in Keswick comes available in the next few hours, you're going to have to stay somewhere else for the tournament.'

'Sorry?'

'The flat may no longer be available,' I clarify, taking another sip of wine. 'I appreciate that it's an inconvenience, but surely someone like you can—'

'I'm not moving,' he interjects sternly.

I falter. 'But, you may have to. We may not have a choice.'

'*You* don't have a choice but to rent the flat to me like you agreed to, since I've paid for it and we entered into a contract,' he responds calmly. 'I'm sorry that your holiday has fallen through, but that's not my problem.'

I stare at him in disbelief. 'Are you... are you serious?'

'I've rented that flat fair and square. You'll need to find alternative accommodation.'

'But… you're Kieran O'Sullivan! You could stay anywhere!'

He winces. 'Please shout my name louder,' he hisses sarcastically, glowering at me. 'I'm not sure the people in *Australia* heard you.'

'There must be a hundred fancy hotels or mansions you can stay at,' I argue, ignoring him because his comfort is the least of my priorities right now.

'I don't want to stay in a fancy hotel or a mansion,' he shoots back.

'Why the hell not?'

'I have very specific requirements.'

I narrow my eyes at him. 'Really.'

'Really.'

I fold my arms. 'Go on then. What are *your* specific requirements?'

He takes a slow sip of his drink before setting down his glass and launching into his answer: 'It can't be a hotel room, because that's too impersonal, and it has to be a flat, not a house because that's too big when it's just me, but there needs to be a garden or at least some kind of outdoor space. It also needs to be a maisonette, so I don't have to share a front door with anyone, and it needs to be close to the All England Lawn Tennis Club and the Village so I can get a drink when I need one. Most importantly, if there's somewhere available on Lingfield Road, I'll be staying there and nowhere else. Non-negotiable.'

By the time he comes to the end of his list, my mouth is hanging open. Firstly, I'm bowled over by the detail of his answer, having only been treated to short, snippy remarks from him so far, and secondly, there is NO CHANCE that that was all real. It can't be. It's too ridiculous. Tennis players take part in tournaments all over the world, he surely can't find places that match those *exact* requirements every time he plays. He's just trying to be difficult.

'You made that last bit up,' I blurt out accusingly.

He shakes his head. 'Nope.'

'So, you're telling me that despite the fact that you could stay anywhere in London that you like, you refuse to move out of my one-bedroom flat because it's on Lingfield Road?'

'Yes,' he confirms. 'Oh, and the wall art.'

'Sorry?'

'The cherry blossom wall art in the living room. I like that.'

I stare at him, baffled. 'Okay, I'm flattered you like my work, but Kieran, if Lingfield Road is that important to you for whatever reason, then maybe you can see if anyone else who lives there would like to rent their place out to you. The flat upstairs is empty. We can get in touch with Mrs Perry and see if—'

'What do you mean your work?' he asks, his eyebrows pulled together.

'Huh?'

'You said you were flattered I liked your work.'

'Yeah, because you said you liked the wall art,' I explain impatiently. 'Did you hear what I said? I really think if you asked around—'

'*You* painted the cherry blossom?' he interrupts.

'Yes!'

'Are you an artist?'

'No. Well, I want to be. I mean, that was kind of the whole point of me going to the Lake District. I wanted to start working on my graphic novel there. That's why it's so bad that the cottage has fallen through – literally,' I murmur, running a hand through my hair.

'Artists can work from anywhere.'

'Yeah, well, this artist can't,' I snap. 'I need to be in the Lake District. How did we get onto this? I think we should focus on the problem of where you're going to stay.'

'Where *you're* going to stay,' he corrects firmly. 'I've already been very clear that I'm not moving.'

'It's my flat!'

'You rented it out to me.'

'You can stay anywhere!'

'I don't want to stay anywhere else,' he says through gritted teeth, glancing nervously at the table behind me as the volume of my voice rises in conjunction with my growing anger at this unreasonable, stubborn prick.

'Why is Lingfield Road so important?'

'Look, there's got to be someone you can stay with—'

'There's not.'

He takes a deep breath through his nose. '*Okay*,' he says in a strained voice, once he's done with his pointed breathing. 'Then I'm sure you can find somewhere else that's suitable for an aspiring artist, even if it's not the Lake District.'

'It needs to be the Lake District,' I insist, even though I've spent the last hour researching other areas. But he's being so rude and unreasonable, I'm instinctively being as difficult as possible. 'That's the only place I'll be able to work on my book.'

'Come on, you're making an excuse,' he says, swivelling in his seat to face me properly. 'If you want to start drawing your graphic novel, you should start. You don't need to be in the Lake District. That's ridiculous.'

I clench my fist, my blood boiling. 'No it's not.'

'What is it about the Lake District that you just *have* to have to start your book?' he asks angrily, throwing up a hand, growing more animated as our argument escalates.

'I don't know, Kieran, how about silence, tranquillity, beautiful lakes and breathtaking mountains for a start?'

'That's what a true artist needs to create a graphic novel, is it? Lakes and mountains.'

My face flushes with heat. 'Yes! They are inspiring! I want to be inspired!'

He snorts. 'That's officially the stupidest thing I've ever heard.'

Fuck you, Kieran O'Sullivan.

Before I have a chance to think about what I'm doing, I stand up, pick up the rest of my glass of wine and throw its contents right at his face. With droplets of rosé dripping off his cap and down the lenses of his sunglasses, he splutters in surprise.

Everyone in the beer garden turns in our direction.

I calmly put the glass back down, pick up my bag and leave.

4

I may have ever so slightly overreacted.

But you know what, I wasn't going to sit there and let some overpaid dickhead tennis player laugh at my dream just because he doesn't get it. It may sound stupid to him, but it's not stupid to me and he had no right to make me feel like an idiot.

Plus, I really don't like him.

When I get home, I'm still raging. I slam the front door shut behind me and stomp into my bedroom to chuck my laptop bag on my bed before letting out a loud 'ARGH' of frustration. I pick up one of my scatter cushions and mean to chuck it across the room, but it sort of plops down in front of me. Breathing heavily, I stand there for a moment with my hands on my hips. Then, with a heavy sigh, I pick up the cushion again to put it back in its place. *Fuck's sake.* I'm so pathetic, I can't even throw things in anger.

I slump back on my bed, burying my head in my hands.

I feel so lost. How many times can you keep getting knocked down before you give up trying to get back up? Maybe I need to accept the fact that I'm not an artist. Jonah always said it would make it easier if I did. The most infuriating part of today is that I'm not completely convinced Kieran O'Sullivan wasn't making sense back there. I mean, that's why I got so defensive and chucked my wine at him, right? There are artists all over the world who are able to create work without being in any one specific place. Most of them do it around day jobs and chaotic family life. Here I am with no responsibilities, no dependents, but not one ounce of inspiration. I have time, but no ideas.

And what am I still doing in London? There's nothing for me here anymore. Maybe I don't belong here, as hard a fact as that is to swallow. I can still vividly remember the first day I moved to Wimbledon, and instantly fell in love with it. I love the vibe of the place; I love the pubs, restaurants and shops; I love the Common – I love that it feels like its own community. I remember that buzz I got the first time I walked through the Village, thinking that this was the place for me. Jonah and I were going to be happy here. I was going to stick out a media job and land a book deal, and we'd sit on the Common with our cans of Pimm's in the summer and laugh and talk and be happy, just like everyone else you see lounging in their couples or groups across the grass.

But look at me. I'm not happy. I'm on my own and I'm failing. Constantly. I can't even book a fucking holiday without the whole thing going up in flames. Maybe it's time to accept that London hasn't worked out. Maybe I need to—

The doorbell rings.

I snap my head up. It can't be Kieran. He wouldn't come back here.

Would he?

I cautiously get up and scurry along the hallway to look through the peephole. Wearing his now-damp cap, Kieran O'Sullivan is lurking on my doorstep, his moodiness exuding through the door and into the flat. I watch him reach up to press the buzzer again impatiently, glancing around him. God, what is wrong with him? He is paranoid. There's literally no one else on the road.

'What do you want?' I ask through the door.

He steps closer to speak, keeping his voice as low as possible. 'I'd like to talk to you.'

'I don't want to talk to you. Please go somewhere else,' I tell him curtly.

'Flora,' he says through gritted teeth as he rests one arm on the door and leans into it. 'I would really like to speak to you. Please can you open the door.'

'You can speak to me where you are.'

'Not properly. Anyone could overhear,' he says, checking over his shoulder.

I don't say anything, stepping back and folding my arms.

'*Please*,' he says in a strained voice.

Steeling myself, I open the door, taking him by surprise. He stumbles forwards, regaining his balance and then striding in. He stops in the hallway, taking off his cap and turning to face me while I shut the door behind him.

'What did you want to say?' I ask breezily, passing him to move into the living room.

'I wanted to ask you why I'm standing here covered in rosé,' he begins, as he follows me and lingers in the doorway. 'Do you have *any* idea what you've done?'

I frown at him. 'So you're not here to apologise.'

He gives me a puzzled look. 'I don't apologise unless I know what I'm apologising for. Otherwise it would be insincere.'

'How noble.'

'I specifically asked you not to draw attention to me,' he says, his blue eyes blazing as he tosses his cap on the sofa, running a hand through his hair. 'You threw your drink all over me in front of everyone. Do you know what happened after you left?'

I shrug.

'I was *mobbed*,' he growls.

With a pointedly bored sigh, I pick up his cap and squeeze past him back into the hallway to hang it on one of the coat hooks.

'Do you know how annoying it is to have people ask you for a selfie when you've just been covered in wine?' he continues, watching me curiously as I stalk back into the room. 'I had to be rude and fob them off to get out of there.'

I mock gasp, placing a hand on my chest. '*You* had to be *rude*? Inconceivable.'

He cocks his head at me, narrowing his eyes. 'I would rather have stayed under the radar.'

'I would rather you hadn't insulted me,' I reply haughtily, busying myself by plumping up the sofa cushions that he flattened earlier.

It's not completely natural to me to be this confrontational and although I think I'm doing a pretty good job at holding my own, I'm still finding the conversation a bit unnerving so I need to do something with my hands. Also, he has the most intense eyes I've ever seen in my life and he won't take them off me. Not in a good way.

More like, if looks could kill, I'd be breathing my last.

'How exactly did I insult you?' he wants to know.

'You made fun of me.'

'No, I didn't.'

'You called me stupid.'

'No, I *didn't*.'

'Kieran,' I say, straightening and putting my hands on my hips, 'are you seriously standing there and telling me that you don't remember the exact words you spoke to me in the pub just now? You're going to deny it?'

'If you think I called you stupid, then you misunderstood my meaning,' he argues. 'And I apologise if I said it clumsily, but I didn't mean to call you stupid. I was saying that what you said was stupid.'

'That's the same thing.'

'No, it's not.'

'Yes, it is.'

'No, it's not!' he repeats crossly, his nostrils flaring and his voice rising. 'You are not stupid if you say a stupid thing. People say stupid things all the time. For example, saying that you have to be in the Lake District to create art is a stupid thing to say.'

'You're insulting me all over again!' I point out, throwing my hands up. 'I shouldn't have let you back in. Why don't you go somewhere else?'

He takes a step forward. 'I can prove to you that what you're saying is stupid.'

I glare at him. 'How?'

He jabs his finger in the direction of the cherry blossom artwork across the wall behind the TV. I pause, turning to look at it. I don't know what I was expecting him to give as an explanation, but I wasn't expecting this.

'There,' he says, studying me. 'I'm guessing you didn't drag this wall all the way up to the Lake District to paint that.'

'That's... different,' I stammer.

Exhaling, he lowers his hand to his side again. 'All I was saying is that people make excuses all the time because they're scared of putting themselves out there. If you want to draw a graphic novel, Flora, you can do it anywhere.'

I continue to stare at the wall, perplexed. He sighs and turns away, getting out his phone and sitting down on the sofa to read through it. I suddenly feel weirdly vulnerable, as though he's seen through me. Folding my arms across my chest self-consciously, I swivel to face him, jutting out my chin defiantly.

'Still, you shouldn't have been so mean,' I state, although it sounds petty and childish out loud.

'You shouldn't have thrown your drink at me,' he retorts without a moment's hesitation, as though he was ready for me to say that and had already prepared his answer.

I shift my weight from one foot to the other. 'Fine. Unlike some people, I'm big enough to admit when I'm wrong.' He lifts his eyes to me in mild surprise. 'The throwing of the drink was a little... unnecessary. I should have, instead, explained to you why I was upset.'

He presses his lips together and takes a deep breath, his chest rising slowly, his gaze fixed on me the whole time. I wait for him to say something. He doesn't.

'Aren't you going to apologise?' I prompt impatiently.

'I already did,' he claims.

'*Excuse* me? No you didn't!'

He frowns at me in confusion. 'I said just a moment ago that I apologise if I said it clumsily and I didn't mean to make you feel bad.'

I open my mouth to protest and then realise that... he's right. He did say that, right before he made his point about my wall art, but I was too pent up with irritation and anger to hear and appreciate it.

Damn it.

'Oh yeah,' I mutter. 'Okay. Fine. Thank you. I accept your apology.'

Going back to his phone, he quirks a brow in satisfaction.

'There's no need to look so smug.'

He ignores me completely and I roll my eyes, moving to slump down on the other sofa. I feel exhausted and I still have to work out what I'm going to do about the next few weeks. Kieran's phone rings and I glance over to see him frown at the caller ID and ignore it.

'You can answer her; don't mind me,' I say absent-mindedly, chewing my thumbnail. It's a habit that I gave up years ago, but it returns when I'm stressed, like a nervous tick.

'It's fine, I'd rather...' He pauses, tilting his head at me. 'How did you know it was a "her"?'

'I assumed. Why, am I right?'

He doesn't say anything but the muscle in his jaw twitches.

'I'm right, aren't I,' I say brazenly. 'Henrietta. You should answer her calls. She obviously needs to speak to you if she keeps calling.'

'Not that it's any of your business,' he begins in a deep and even voice, 'but I'd rather not speak to her right now.'

'Why? Are you worried she's going to be cross at you for leaving her place this morning without saying goodbye?'

His eyes widen in shock. I feel a rush of pleasure at being the dominant one in this conversation. Up until now, he's seemed so superior and conceited, it seems like an achievement to put him on the back foot for once.

'How did you know that?' he asks, the creases on his forehead deepening in concern. 'Did you read it online somewhere?'

'No, I took a guess and you just confirmed it for me,' I tell him primly. 'It doesn't take a genius to work it out. You rock up here way too early in clothes that you were clearly out in last night, hungover and stinking of booze, and you keep ignoring calls from a woman.'

He scowls. 'All right, Sherlock. Very clever.'

His phone starts ringing again and I roll my eyes. 'I *know* it's none of my business, but at least message her if you're not going to pick up,' I suggest. 'Maybe she thinks she did something wrong. If she didn't, it's not fair to leave her worrying, and then she'll stop pestering you with phone calls. A win-win situation.'

'I'm not… she didn't do anything wrong.' He sighs, stroking his stubble thoughtfully. 'What we have is casual. She knows that.'

'So why did you feel the need to creep out this morning?'

'I didn't want the paps to see me leave. They're often around her building first thing. I wanted to get out of there before they arrived.'

I nod, intrigued. 'So she's famous, huh. What does she do? Would I know her?'

He doesn't answer.

'Whatever,' I say, sighing impatiently. 'Don't be a dick, just message her and explain the thing about the reporters. If she's famous, she'll get it, won't she.'

He picks up his phone begrudgingly and starts typing before glancing up at me, looking uncertain. 'Did you say I stink of booze?'

'Oh. Uh… yeah. But I think the rosé has made it worse, to be fair.'

He can't help but smile at that, and I catch a fleeting glimpse of his dimples. I would say that I hadn't noticed them before, but I actually think he just hasn't smiled properly in front of me until now. They completely change his face, making it softer and more appealing. But they appear so briefly before his blank expression returns, I'd question whether they genuinely exist.

When his phone rings again, I groan, throwing my head back and looking up at the ceiling. 'Just pick up. She's obviously upset.'

'It's not her,' he tells me, before actually bothering to answer his phone. 'Hi, Neil.'

I bring my head forwards again, noticing his expression darken as he listens to whoever Neil is on the other end. His eyes flicker at me.

'Yes. It was a misunderstanding. I can explain when I see you,' he says with an edge to his voice. 'How bad?' As he listens to the answer, he presses his lips together so tightly into a thin line, they almost disappear. 'Okay. Fine. Don't bring Nicole in yet, just you for now.' He pauses to listen again and shakes his head. 'No, just you, Neil. I mean it. I don't want the whole team here. Oh, I'll need some fresh clothes. Yeah, Tori has my stuff. It's due to arrive here at five, but I'll need something before then.' He looks at me pointedly. 'Apparently I don't smell too fresh and I'd like to shower.'

He hangs up and sighs heavily, bowing his head for a moment.

'Everything okay?' I ask.

He inhales and types something into his phone. At first I think he's rudely ignoring my question and is back to messaging Henrietta, but then he rises to his feet and comes over to me, holding out his phone so I can see his screen. I take it from him to look at it properly.

It's a string of reports on social media, the majority of them displaying the same clip: a video of me and Kieran talking to each other in the beer garden of Dog and Fox, before I stand up furiously and chuck my drink all over him.

'Oh my God,' I whisper, scrolling in horror. The re-posts and comments are endless.

'You should be flattered,' Kieran remarks drily. 'A drink throw so good, it's gone viral.'

5

The photographers arrive in a trickle. At first there's just one guy with a camera round his neck, lurking on the pavement nearby, and then another one arrives, greeting him like an old friend, and then another and another until there's five or six out there. It's only been a couple of hours since the wine-throwing clip was uploaded online and already they've tracked down where Kieran is staying. It's creepy.

'You need to stand back from the window,' Kieran tells me crossly for the hundredth time. 'They'll see the blinds move.'

'I don't understand how they worked out where you are!' I exclaim, dropping the blind. 'How do they *know*?'

'Because people tell,' Kieran says bitterly. 'One of your neighbours must have seen me and spread the word. Probably when you wouldn't let me in and insisted we talk loudly through the door. It wasn't exactly subtle.'

'Oh, so this is my fault?' I huff, glaring at him.

'You did throw the wine and then refuse to open the door. I warned you at the pub that this would happen.'

'You are unbelievable,' I snap, as I start moving back and forth across the room. 'And I do *not* mean that as a compliment.'

'I didn't think you did.' He watches me march away from the window and back again, chewing my thumbnail. 'Can you please stop pacing? It's irritating.'

I narrow my eyes at him. 'No, I will not stop pacing, Kieran, thank you very much. Because of your fan base out there, I'm cooped up in here and I can't just sit around while people talk about me online.'

'The paparazzi are not my fan base,' he informs me in a low, cutting voice, glancing instinctively at the window. 'If anything, they're the exact opposite. Waiting to tear me down at the first opportunity.'

'Have you seen what they're saying about *me*?'

'I told you not to look at your phone,' he says a little softer than usual, a hint of something apologetic in his voice. 'It's better to ignore it.'

'They're calling me an "unknown blonde"! And your "new lover".' I grimace, cringing at having to say it out loud. 'Why would they say that?! We only just met!'

'You threw a drink at me. Not many people would do that to someone they don't know.'

'You made me cross!'

'I know.'

'I don't normally throw drinks at people! In fact, that was my first time!'

He sighs, rubbing his forehead and shutting his eyes for a moment. There's an increase of noise and commotion outside and Kieran snaps his head up.

'That will finally be Neil arriving,' he announces, pushing himself up off the sofa and heading out the room to get the door.

When it opens, I can hear the reporters shouting over one another with their persistent questions: 'Neil, *can you tell us what happened at the pub?*'; '*Who's Kieran's new girlfriend, Neil?*'; '*Are you worried that this will affect his performance at Wimbledon?*'; '*Is it serious? What's her name, Neil?*'

The door shuts and their voices are silenced. I press a hand over my mouth. This is mortifying. Absolutely mortifying. I've got a couple of missed calls from Iris, and I know that she must have seen it by now and recognised me from the video. It won't be long until a lot of people I know will do the same. God, why did I have to throw that wine at him and make a spectacle of myself? Why did I lose my temper? Why did I let him get to me?

I blame Kieran. If he hadn't been so rude, none of this would have happened.

At that moment he comes back in the room followed by Neil, who Kieran has explained is his coach. If I'd seen Neil walking down a street, I might have thought he looked familiar but I doubt I would have been able to place him. When Kieran said that Neil Damon would be coming over to help with some damage control, he seemed confused at my blank expression and repeated his name as though that might help. *Neil Damon*. I told him it was ringing a bell, but I'd need some help. Looking a little perturbed, he reminded me that Neil Damon was a famous American tennis player, now retired. He won Wimbledon twice.

Neil is much shorter than I expected. I assumed all tennis players were muscled giants, but Neil is about five foot eight. He's good-looking, with dark greying hair, soft brown eyes and a stern expression. For some reason I thought he'd be wearing a tracksuit, because in my head that's just what tennis coaches wear, but he's in an expensive-looking tailored suit and tie, with a leather bag slung over his shoulder. As he enters the room, I smile timidly at him. He does not smile back.

'You must be Flora,' he says gruffly.

'Hi, it's nice to meet you.'

He studies me for a moment. I fiddle with the hem of my crop top.

'Nice to meet you too,' he says icily. He holds out the bag to Kieran. 'The change of clothes you requested. Sorry I couldn't get here sooner. Have you spoken to anyone?'

Kieran shakes his head. 'Just you.'

Neil turns to me. 'And… Miss Hendrix?'

He looks at me expectantly. I glance at Kieran, confused.

'She hasn't spoken to anyone,' Kieran answers. 'I don't think.'

'That's something. Makes things a little easier if we take

control of the narrative. Not exactly the start I had in mind for your tenure here, Kieran,' Neil scolds, his tone clipped.

Kieran tenses. 'It wasn't mine either, Neil. The news stories aren't accurate. Flora and I met today and... there was a miscommunication at the pub.'

'Yes, well it looks a lot more intimate than a mere miscommunication,' Neil seethes, moving to the other side of the room. 'What message do you think this gives your competitors, hm? I thought you wanted to be a serious threat this year.'

'I don't need a lecture,' Kieran snaps. He glances at me. 'This isn't the time to talk.'

'Uh... why don't I leave you guys to it,' I suggest, making my way through the middle of them so I can exit the room. I stop at the doorway to appeal to Neil. 'It really was a miscommunication. I'm sorry it happened.'

Neil doesn't say anything, staring at the floor with a tense expression. I take the hint and hurry out, shutting myself away safely in the bedroom. *Shit.* This is bad. My day has officially gone from terrible to fucking disastrous. As if I didn't have enough to worry about, I'm now a *meme*. I lean back against the door and close my eyes, wondering if I should consider never leaving this room again. I could just curl up under the duvet and wait there for all these problems to go away. The paparazzi will leave, Kieran and Neil will leave, the meme will eventually disappear, and I can go back to being a nobody.

My phone vibrates and when I see that it's Iris, I decide to pick up. I've ignored her long enough.

'Hey,' I answer quietly.

'OH HI,' she cries so loudly, I have to hold the phone away from my ear momentarily. 'You FINALLY decide to pick up.'

'Yeah, sorry, it's been... busy.'

'Flora, what the FUCK?! Why is there a video of you on social media throwing a glass of wine in the face of Kieran O'Sullivan?'

I dig my teeth into my bottom lip.

'Uh... that's not me?' I attempt pitifully.

'Yes it bloody well is,' she counters breathlessly. 'Do you know him? Why wouldn't you tell me this? What is going on?'

I take a deep breath. 'Okay, off the record?'

'Fuck's sake, Flora, obviously off the record. When do we speak ON the record?'

'Good point.' I rub my forehead with my free hand, a dull ache forming on one side. 'You know how I rented out my flat for the next few weeks? It turns out that it's Kieran O'Sullivan who has rented it.'

'You're joking. You're JOKING. Is this a joke?'

'No. It's not.'

'Oh my God!'

'I know. He arrived here earlier than he should have done and so he left, and then you know how you told me to go to the pub? I ended up at the same one he'd gone to. I wasn't stalking him, though. It was by accident.'

'Okay...'

'Then we got into an argument and I threw my drink at him.'

'Flora! I mean, I would say I don't believe you, but I've seen the bloody evidence online! This is madness. Kieran O'Sullivan! What's he like?' she asks eagerly.

'You know how everyone thinks he's a dick?'

'Yeah?'

'He's a dick.'

'Ah. Hence the wine throwing.'

I nod, gripping the phone. 'Iris, there are reporters outside my door.'

'Shit. They found you quickly. Not surprising though. The video has gone viral and they're good at their job. Have you spoken to them?'

'Obviously not. I want them to go away as soon as possible. I don't want people thinking I'm Kieran O'Sullivan's latest conquest,' I mutter, grimacing. 'It's so embarrassing.'

'I don't know, Flora, maybe that's a good thing.'

'You *what* now?'

She giggles. 'Can you imagine Jonah's face when he sees this? Fucking idiot, he's going to lose his head thinking you're dating a world-famous tennis player. And the tennis player in question happens to be sexy as hell.'

I chew on my thumbnail. I can't pretend like it hadn't crossed my mind that Jonah might see the video. It was, in fact, one of the first thoughts I had when it started spreading across the internet like wildfire. I couldn't work out if it was a good or a bad thing that he might be left under the impression that I'm dating Kieran. I guess it's a good thing so long as he doesn't think I'm throwing the wine at Kieran's face because I'm being dumped by him.

'Flora, you still there?' Iris checks.

'Yeah, I just... I'm trying to get my head round how to play this.'

'No-brainer. Let the world think you're an item. Better that way in the eyes of your tragic ex-boyfriend and your landlord.'

I hesitate. 'My landlord?'

'Yeah,' she says, as though it's obvious. 'You don't want him thinking you've rented out the flat to a tennis player, right? I thought you said to me a while ago when you were first thinking about renting out the place for the tournament that you weren't sure if that was allowed in the terms of the lease. Did you ever check?'

My blood runs cold. 'Uh.'

'Okay, look, if the paparazzi are already at your flat, then the cat's out the bag. They'll photograph Kieran leaving or coming home at some point, and if the landlord sees, he might put two and two together. Better for him to think that Kieran's your boyfriend. You don't want to risk him kicking you out.'

'Iris,' I squeak, my throat constricting, 'I have to go.'

'Okay, but don't ignore me! I want to hear about what happens!'

I promise her I'll keep in touch and then hang up, my heart

hammering against my chest. Shit, shit, *shit*. I hadn't even thought about my stupid tenancy agreement! HOW had I not thought of that?! I don't want to lose this flat, not yet. It's the one place I feel safe right now.

Spinning around, I swing open my door and hurry into the living room. Kieran is nowhere to be seen and Neil is lurking by the window, typing furiously into his phone. He glances up at me, unimpressed, as I walk in, then returns his attention to his screen.

'Hi,' I say briskly, my hands growing clammy, 'where's Kieran?'

'He's taking a shower,' Neil says distractedly. 'I know we don't have the flat until five, but since you two are already so well acquainted, we thought it would be all right.'

'I need to speak to him,' I say, ignoring his pointed remark.

He grunts in response, his eyes fixed to his screen.

Frustrated, I go to the bathroom and knock loudly on the door. 'Kieran? Kieran, you have to leave.'

No answer. With an impatient huff, I hammer my fist against it.

'Kieran, I know you're in there! Did you hear me? You have to get out!'

'I'll be five minutes,' he calls out, irritably. 'I'm about to shower.'

'No, I don't mean you have to get out the bathroom,' I hiss, trying to keep my voice down so Neil can't hear me. 'I'm talking about the flat. You have to go.'

'Why?'

'Because you have to,' I seethe, glancing down the hallway to the living room door. 'I'll explain, but I can't through the door.'

'Why not? You made a point of making me talk through the door earlier.'

OH MY GOD. There are so many tennis players in the world. Why does the one renting my flat have to be the most INSUFFERABLE one of all?! Attempting to remain as collected and calm as possible, I glare at the door.

'Please,' I say through gritted teeth.

As painful as it is to say out loud, the right word does the trick. The door swings open so suddenly that I stumble forwards, catching myself and regaining my balance by grabbing hold of the side of the doorframe. Kieran is standing in front of me shirtless, holding a towel round his waist. Stunned into silence, I stare shamelessly at his insanely muscular bare torso, my eyes roaming down his solid tanned chest and perfectly sculpted abs.

I swallow.

'What's wrong?' he asks impatiently.

'Everything okay in there?' Neil calls out from the living room.

'Yes, all fine thanks,' I squeak in a much higher-pitched voice than normal, stepping into the bathroom and shutting the door behind me. Kieran looks bewildered.

'What are you *doing*?'

'I don't want Neil to overhear but we have to talk,' I whisper, trying to keep my eyes firmly on his and not let them wander downwards, no matter how tempting. 'There's been a problem and I appreciate you don't want to leave but you definitely need to find somewhere else to stay for the next few weeks. Sorry.'

He sighs, lifting his eyes to the ceiling. 'I told you before I'm not leaving. I can help you find somewhere else to go if you like, but—'

'No, it's not that. There are going to be photos of you staying here in the press.'

'So?'

'So, if my landlord sees, he might think I've let out the flat for Wimbledon, which is against the rules of my lease.'

He stares at me, his brow furrowed.

'But you *have* let out the flat for Wimbledon,' he says eventually.

'Yes, I'm aware of that, thank you,' I seethe, going to lean casually on the heated towel rail and then flinching when it instantly burns my hand.

Realisation dawns on him and his eyes widen with interest. 'You broke the rules.'

I glare at him, heat rising up my neck at being caught out. 'I wasn't *sure* of the rules. It might be fine, but I don't think it is. Do you know how high rent is for this place? I'm temping at the moment; cash isn't exactly flowing in. It's not like he'd be affected by someone else crashing here for a few weeks! He'd get his rent on time as usual so I didn't think it would be a problem. I didn't think he'd ever find out.'

Kieran listens to my rambling with a set expression, no hint of compassion.

'So, when the tabloids run the photos of me coming in and out of the house, you're worried he'll see those and work out your con,' he says slowly.

'It's not a con! I'm not some kind of criminal mastermind.'

'But you are committing a crime.'

My mouth drops open in disbelief. 'It is not… it's… I… you…'

He arches a brow and a hint of a smile plays across his lips. I exhale in fury.

'You are so *mean*,' I hiss.

'Don't worry, I don't plan on ratting you out to the police,' he says coolly. 'But I'm afraid I won't be giving up the flat. I like it here on Lingfield Road.'

There's a knock on the bathroom door and I freeze at the sound of Neil clearing his throat from the other side. Kieran's eyebrows shoot up.

'Kieran? Miss Hendrix?' he says, sounding uneasy. 'Are you… both in there?'

My head held high, I open the door. Neil's eyes scan from my fixed smile to Kieran's current state of undress. His jaw clenches.

'I don't mean to interrupt,' he says, his voice clipped and cold.

'It's fine, we were… talking,' I stammer, glancing at Kieran who remains unfazed. 'I'm afraid there's a problem.'

Neil frowns. 'What is it?'

'Kieran can no longer stay here,' I say bluntly. 'He'll have to find somewhere else. Sorry about the mix-up, but there's nothing I can do. I have to stay in the flat.'

'What happened?' Neil asks, puzzled.

'I… uh… well, you see… I…'

'The roof of Flora's holiday cottage in the Lake District collapsed and she has nowhere to go,' Kieran cuts in. 'I was just telling her that we could help her out. Find her a nice hotel room or something, right?'

Neil eyes Kieran suspiciously. 'I suppose.'

'Perfect. That's decided then,' Kieran concludes.

'No, I don't want a hotel room,' I tell Neil, trying to remain as polite as possible in front of a legendary Wimbledon champion, but already bristling at Kieran's attempt to take control of the situation. 'I have to stay here. Kieran, *you'll* have to leave.'

'Why do you *have* to stay here, Flora?' he asks, acting confused, knowing full well I don't want to admit the hiccup about my lease in front of Neil.

'Because this is my *home*,' I say through gritted teeth. 'Why can't you go stay in a luxury hotel room yourself? Surely that would be much more suitable accommodation for a Wimbledon competitor.'

'I'm afraid that I've already outlined to you why that's not possible,' he states simply. 'I won't be leaving here. That's final.'

'Then we have a very big problem, because I won't be leaving here either,' I retort.

'You can't kick me out. I've already paid the full let and you needed to give me much more notice, legally.'

'Well, you can't kick me out because I live here,' I clap back, my blood boiling.

'Then, it looks like we're both staying.'

'Fine!'

'Fine. We're both staying,' he states.

I blink at him. 'Wait, what?'

'You know what,' Neil interjects, his eyes darting between the two of us, 'let me have our lawyers glance through the terms and conditions of the lease and—'

'No need for that,' Kieran says, while my breath catches in panic. 'She can have the sofa.'

Neil looks at him, forcing a nervous laugh. 'I'm sorry, Kieran? I don't think I heard you correctly.'

'No lawyers,' Kieran states firmly to Neil. 'For now, if neither of us can leave, Flora can stay on the sofa until we work out a better solution.' He turns to address me. 'However much I'd like to be chivalrous, I think while I'm training for Wimbledon I should sleep on a mattress. If at all possible, I'd like to compete at the biggest tennis tournament in the world without a cricked neck.'

I gape at him. Neil is doing the same.

'Good, that's settled,' Kieran says calmly, gesturing to the door. 'Now, if you both don't mind, I'd like to take a shower. The smell of rosé is making me feel a bit nauseous.'

At a loss as to what else to do, Neil and I file out of the bathroom in silence. Kieran shuts the door firmly behind us and moments later, we hear the sound of running water. We stand in the hallway, both deep in thought. Neil eventually saunters off towards the front door. He turns to shoot me one last venomous look and then leaves, temporarily filling the flat with the frenzied sound of the paparazzi waiting in great anticipation to find out what is going on here.

Although that really is anyone's guess.

6

Have you ever been woken up by a blender? I have, and I can confirm that it is not a pleasant way to be roused from a deep slumber. On the first morning of mine and Kieran's bizarre living arrangement, the loud and abrupt whirring makes me sit bolt upright on the sofa and clutch my heart, wondering what the hell is going on and whether someone is drilling roadworks in the middle of my home. As my brain comes into focus and I realise what's going on, I reach for my phone on the coffee table and check the time.

You have got to be KIDDING.

Throwing off the duvet, I push myself up from the sofa and march to the kitchen where the door is wide open. Hovering next to the blender, Kieran is already dressed in his sports gear, his eyes bright, his hair dishevelled. He notices me and arches his brow. I'm too tired and cross to care that I'm standing in front of him in my baggy Snoopy T-shirt and a tiny pair of blue pyjama shorts that I shrunk in the wash, so they're more like pyjama hot pants.

'It's six thirty in the morning,' I croak, my voice yet to warm up.

He frowns and then shakes his head, gesturing at first to his ears and then to the blender. 'Can't hear you,' he mouths.

'I said, it's SIX THIRTY IN THE MORNING.'

He turns the blender off. 'Sorry, what was that?'

I narrow my eyes at him, clenching my teeth. The day has barely started and this guy is already giving me jaw-ache.

'I said, it's six thirty,' I repeat as calmly as possible. '*What are you doing?*'

He busies himself with finding a glass and pouring his drink into it. 'I'm making a fruit smoothie. Do you want one?'

'What? No,' I huff, pushing my hair back from my face. 'I want to go back to sleep like a normal person!'

'All right,' he says, turning round and leaning back on the counter as he takes a gulp of his drink. 'Go back to sleep.'

'I won't be able to now! You've woken me up with your blending!'

He tilts his head at me. 'Not a morning person, then.'

'No one is a morning person when they've been woken up by an angry machine!' I hiss, gesturing to the blender while he glugs his drink. 'Next time, shut the door. It's called being considerate! It's called *manners*.'

'If you were in a hotel, you could sleep in as long as you like without being disturbed,' he says casually, lowering his glass as his tongue runs along his top lip. 'You could have a nice long lie-in, order breakfast in bed—'

'I'm not leaving,' I cut in, folding my arms. 'I know what you're trying to do and it won't work. I told you, I have to stay here otherwise I risk losing the flat altogether. You're the one who's caused this mess. If you're not happy, then *you* should leave.'

'I'm not trying to do anything,' he claims with a shrug, finishing the rest of his drink and placing the glass down in the sink. 'I'm perfectly happy. You're the one complaining.'

He goes to leave, his arm brushing against mine as I stand back to let him through the doorway.

'Ew! Why is your arm moist?' I grimace, wiping mine pointedly.

'I'm sweaty from my run.'

'You've been on a run *already*?' I ask in disbelief. 'What time were you up?'

'Early,' he calls back over his shoulder, heading towards the bathroom.

'Wait, whoa, what are you doing? I need the—'

He slams the bathroom door behind him and I hear the click of the lock turning before the shower is turned on. Then he starts humming. Not singing, *humming*.

What a prick.

My bladder aching, I flip a finger at the bathroom door and then hurry back to the sofa, plonking myself down and pulling the duvet back over me so I can at least stay in the warmth until he's done. How has this happened?! My head still feels in a complete spin about this entire situation.

Last night, I decided to google Kieran just to get a better idea of the person I will be living with for the next few weeks and it did not give me much comfort. I was too tired to do a deep dive into his life, but from his recent stint in Germany where he played in the Halle Open, an ATP grass-court tournament held in mid-June at the same time as Queen's here in London, there's a load of photographs of him emerging from a big bash just two days before the tournament began with a hot German model on his arm, bleary-eyed and yelling at the press as he ducked into a car.

He wouldn't be my first choice of housemate, I have to say.

He's taking his time in the bathroom and I know he's doing it on purpose. The ache in my bladder is becoming unbearable. When His Royal Highness finally emerges from the bathroom, I sprint down the hallway and practically throw myself at the toilet, barging him out the way as he struts out topless, with his towel around his waist. He feigns surprise as I shut the door quickly behind me.

I can practically hear him smirking on the other side of it.

Just before I shower, I notice my reflection in the mirror. *Oh dear*. My hair is completely dishevelled – not in a sexy way – and I didn't do the best job at removing my mascara last night, so there's hints of a dark smudge under both eyes. And as much as I love my Snoopy T-shirt, I'm not sure it's my best look. Groaning, I reach for my make-up remover and cotton pads to wipe away the remaining traces from yesterday's coverage, and then strip down to get in the shower. It's not until I'm out that I realise I didn't bring any clothes with me into the bathroom, so I'm going to have to go out there in my towel to retrieve some. Whatever. He feels confident to wander around in his towel, I shouldn't have any qualms in doing the same.

Clutching it tightly around my body, I open the door and slink out into the hallway, padding into the living room and bending over to grab some clothes from my case. I haven't yet unpacked my Lake District bag and I'm still working out where to put all my stuff while Kieran's here. I'm rummaging around my things when the doorbell goes.

I straighten, clutching a pair of neon pink knickers.

Before I can dart back to the safety of the bathroom, Kieran is at the front door and has swung it open. 'Come in, guys,' I hear him say.

Guys? GUYS?! What guys?!

Still grasping the knickers, I stand frozen in a panic, praying that they walk straight past the living room and down to the bedroom. *Please don't come in here. Please, please, please, please—*

'Oh!'

Three men, including Neil, have strolled into the living room and are now staring at me with their mouths open. Coming in behind them, Kieran follows their line of sight and starts. His eyes widen as he suppresses a smile. The heat rises up my neck and through my cheeks. I stare back at them like a deer caught in headlights.

I remember the knickers in my hand and drop them. By some cruel twist of fate or maybe because God hates me, they land on top of the coffee table rather than behind it.

The four men glance down at the splayed-out knickers and then back up at me.

'Hi,' I squeak, giving them an awkward wave. 'Sorry, I didn't realise... I didn't know people would be arriving this early.'

Neil presses his lips together, turning to Kieran, who looks infuriatingly smug.

'Are you ready?' Neil asks in a strained voice.

'Yeah, let me grab my bag,' he says, disappearing into the hallway, followed by Neil.

'Where should I leave the equipment, Kieran?' one of the other men calls after him.

'There in the living room is fine,' comes the reply.

He nods and the two men set to work retrieving a load of fitness equipment from the hallway that they start piling up in the middle of the living room floor: resistance bands, mats, foam rollers, a giant gym ball, long agility belts, a huge stand of dumbbells and finally, a large purple bean bag. Since they're blocking the door, I stand there in my towel, helplessly watching this all unfold.

'Bean bags sure are good for fitness. Trying to get out of one is a calorie-burning challenge, am I right?' I joke with a forced laugh, attempting to break the ice.

The two men share a confused look. They don't answer. My face is fully on fire now.

'All done?' Neil asks, coming back with Kieran in tow.

'All done,' one of them reports.

'Let's go then,' he says, before turning back to address Kieran who is lingering in the doorway, inspecting all the gym equipment. 'By the way, there are a few reporters back and lurking outside, but the car is waiting for you on the road.'

His expression souring, Kieran nods sharply and pulls on his cap.

'Oh,' one of the other men says, turning to look at me, 'I don't know if you'll be in today, but someone will be dropping by this morning to set up the PlayStation.'

I blink at him.

He gives me a thumbs up and then follows the others out the

room. The front door swings open and there's a flurry of noise from the reporters when they notice Kieran, before the door shuts and I'm left standing alone in my towel in peace. Trying to convince myself that that wasn't as embarrassing as it felt, I glance at my phone to check the time.

It's only seven thirty, but it feels like I've been up for hours.

I exhale, closing my eyes. This is going to be a long four weeks.

'There's a sniper on the ridge, get behind cover!' Kieran yells into his headset. He's nestled in his bean bag on the floor in front of the PlayStation now connected to my TV, gripping his console and pressing the buttons at an alarming rate. 'Okay, let's push the team in this building. I'll go through the front door and you cover the back. Get a grenade through the window! GO! GO! GO! Ah I'm down! He's one shot, he's one shot! Ah, fuck's sake.'

As he groans in disappointment, I tap Kieran on the shoulder. He tilts his head up to look at me and reluctantly lowers his headset to sit round his neck.

'Would you mind keeping it down?' I say, my voice strained. 'You're not an *actual* general in an *actual* battle, okay? *Call of Duty* is a game. You don't need to bellow at your fellow troops. No one is going to really die, so let's tone it down a notch, yeah?'

He looks back to the TV, pulling his headphones back up over his ears. 'The sound effects are loud. I need to communicate with my team.'

Attempting a few deep, calming breaths, I tap him on the shoulder again, a little harder this time. He turns his head slowly towards me, his eyes narrowing. He pushes one of his headphones very slightly back behind his ear.

'Maybe you could turn the sound effects down, so you don't have to shout over them,' I suggest, like a teacher trying her best to be patient with an ungrateful little shit of a child. 'I'm trying to read my book.'

He gives me a forced smile, as though he gets it. I nod gratefully and go to sit back down, while he adjusts his headset.

Kieran's been out most of the day training and returned this evening smelling like chlorine, heading straight to shower before taking over the kitchen to make a paella that he ate in about five seconds flat. It's been nice having the flat to myself all day, but even though he wasn't here, he's made his presence known. His workout equipment takes up so much of the space in the living room that it makes it look cluttered and messy, which has been stressing me out, and I've tripped over those fucking resistance bands about five hundred times.

I've noticed he's also left loads of his products in the bathroom, and while I approve of all the fancy stuff he uses that smells very nice, I moved it all neatly into a little box for him on the edge of the bath, only to find that after his shower this evening, he left the bottles scattered carelessly all over the place in there.

Now he's back, the mood in the flat has dipped and I'm trying to accept that he's going to spend time in the living room, even though, technically, he's barged into my bedroom to play his stupid little game. I'm not going to go and sit in the bedroom to read, so the least he can do is keep it down. Settling back into the sofa cushions, I set down my chamomile tea and open my book.

Moments later, I'm disturbed again.

'The ring is closing, get in, get in!' he cries, as I lower my book in disbelief. 'Ah, okay, let's push this team. Go left, go left! No, what are you doing? Don't do that! I said go left!'

My jaw clenched, I glare at him before picking up a cushion and throwing it at his head. He turns round in surprise, looks down at the cushion and then back up at me, grabbing it and tucking it behind his back.

'Thanks,' he grunts, settling back onto it. 'That's much better. Right, lads, stop playing trash and listen to my instructions so we might have a chance at winning.'

I hate him.

*

Awoken by that BLOODY blender again, I storm into the kitchen and stand in the doorway until he notices me. Glowering at him, I wait for him to turn it off.

'Morning, sunshine,' he says coolly, focusing on pouring his drink.

'I asked you to *shut the door*,' I remind him, my blood boiling.

'My mistake. I'll remember tomorrow. That hotel room is still an option, you know.'

I stare at him, baffled. 'Doesn't it bother you that I'm here? Why would you want to live in a small flat with a stranger rather than an amazing hotel?'

'I could ask you the same question.'

'I don't get you,' I say, massaging my temples. 'Why won't you *leave*? What is so special about staying on Lingfield Road?'

Without saying anything, he finishes his drink and stalks past me out the kitchen.

'And do you really need all that gym stuff here taking over the whole place?' I ask, bristling as I follow him towards the bathroom. 'Don't you literally spend the whole day working out in a gym?'

He turns, leaning against the doorframe of the bathroom. 'I play tennis, too.'

'No shit.'

'I also swim in the afternoon.'

'Thanks for the details. If you're doing all that, *why* do you need a gym here?' I emphasise, rolling my eyes.

He shrugs. 'I might need to do stretches or drills here sometimes.'

'Okay, then could all the equipment live somewhere else until those times come?'

'No.'

I glare at him. 'Do you *ever* compromise on anything?'

He looks pensive. 'Yes.'

'But you won't compromise on this.'

'No.'

Taking a deep breath, I run a hand through my hair. 'You're really fucking annoying.'

His jaw twitches, his eyes flickering down my blue lace cami top and back up again. 'Where's Snoopy?' he asks, his brow creasing.

'What?'

'You were wearing a Snoopy T-shirt yesterday.'

I glance down at my pyjamas. 'I changed.'

He nods, his expression thoughtful.

'I liked the Snoopy,' he says, and then he steps back and shuts the door.

I stand still as he turns the shower on. I'm too confused to move. Did he just give me a compliment? No, he must have been making fun of me. Although, he didn't sound like he was taking the piss. If anyone else had said it, I would have thought that they were being nice. But as it's him, it must have been an insult. Maybe it was a backhanded compliment. Maybe he was saying he doesn't like what I'm wearing now. Anyway, why does he care? What was the point in him telling me he liked the Snoopy? He *can't* have liked the Snoopy.

Can he?

What sort of mind games is this dickhead playing?

That night, Kieran stands in front of the TV with his arms folded.

'Where is it?' he seethes.

'Where's what, Kieran?' I ask innocently, turning the page of my book.

'The *PlayStation*,' he growls, the lines on his forehead deepening.

Not saying anything, I press my lips together, reading the same sentence over and over, not a word of it going in. I'm too invested in feigning ignorance to concentrate.

'Flora,' he hisses, rubbing his forehead, 'it's been a really long day and I'd like to relax. Where have you put it?'

I shrug. 'I've also had a long day and I would like to relax with my book.'

My day has actually involved walking to the shop to get a coffee and a croissant, applying for two administrative jobs in the City that I don't want, and watching a few episodes of *Friends*. But he doesn't need to know any of that.

Kieran, on the other hand, I happen to know has probably had a fairly bad day. He's been in the headlines again thanks to the actress Henrietta Keane, who, I now assume to be THE Henrietta who's been phoning him. She went to a party last night and spoke to a showbiz reporter who was also in attendance. The main article led with:

'He's sad, untrusting and his heart is closed – that's why I dumped him': Henrietta Keane dishes the dirt on Wimbledon hopeful Kieran O'Sullivan.

Other publications have picked it up too, so it's being splashed about everywhere, along with plenty of commentary from 'friends close to the family' who, apparently, think it's appropriate to give their opinion. I don't disagree that he's cantankerous and downright annoying to live with, but I do feel a bit sorry for him. It can't be fun for exes to splash things like that about, whether they're true or not.

But I don't feel sorry enough for him to give him his PlayStation back without getting what I want first. Out of the corner of my eye, I can see him watching me intently.

'Please,' he sighs eventually, 'can you tell me where you've hidden it.'

I tear my eyes away from the page to look at him. 'If you promise to keep your voice down when you play your battle games, then I'll tell you where I've *tidied* it.'

Our eyes seem to be locked in a battle of their own, refusing to budge or back down.

'Fine,' he says, breaking away and lifting them to the ceiling.

'You promise?'

He holds up his hands. 'I promise.'

I nod to the wooden chest that is up against the wall next to the bookshelves. He opens it and takes a moment to look down into its contents, before pulling up his precious PlayStation and headset.

'Pretty stupid not to look in there, Kieran,' he mutters to himself, as he kneels on the ground to get it set up again. I chuckle lightly at his comment and he hears, glancing over. I notice his expression soften a little, before he returns to sorting out the wires.

The next morning, I'm surprised to find that I'm not woken up by the blender, but by the loud chattering of the paparazzi who have arrived to gather around the gate. Rubbing the sleep out of my eyes, I peer through the blinds and see them all congregated together. Even though they can't see me, I give them a dirty look.

I get up to head to the bathroom and see that the kitchen door is closed. I hear the sound of dull muffled whizzing behind it, and I smile to myself. Looks like being tough with the PlayStation last night helped matters. Deciding to repay his kindness by exiting the bathroom quickly so he can shower before me, I plod back into the living room to find him standing next to the sofa, holding his smoothie.

'Oh, hey. There are reporters out there so I would—'

'Your phone went off,' he interrupts, his voice sharp. With a thunderous expression, he pointedly glances to my phone sitting on top of the coffee table. 'I came in here and I saw it ringing on the table. I saw the name flashing up. It was Iris Gray.'

I frown at him, folding my arms. 'Okay. Kieran, why—'

'You're talking to a journalist,' he states angrily.

'What? No, I—'

'I know her name, Flora. Iris Gray is a sports journalist. Why would you be talking to her? Why would her name be saved in your phone? Are you feeding her information about me? Is that what's going on? Is that why you won't leave?'

I stare at him, bewildered. 'No!'

'I should have known,' he mutters, shaking his head, pained. 'I should have guessed that you'd sell your story.'

'I would never—'

'Was it you who told the press where I was staying? What has Iris offered to pay you? Has she—'

'Bloody hell, Kieran, no one is paying me anything!' I cry, throwing my hands up in exasperation. 'I would never sell a story, okay? Not everyone is out to get you!'

He stares at me, the muscle in his jaw twitching. His eyes are frantically scanning my expression, trying to work out if I'm telling the truth, but I can tell he remains unconvinced.

'Iris is my best friend,' I tell him firmly. 'We used to work together. We're *friends*. She doesn't print gossip-type stuff anyway. Check her columns, you'll see she hasn't written anything about you the last few days. She's only interested in the tennis! You can speak to her yourself if you don't believe me.'

Frowning, he keeps his mouth shut, his lips still and straight.

'Kieran,' I continue, taking a step forwards, 'I don't blame you for seeing her name and jumping to that conclusion, but I swear it's not what it looks like. She's my friend, who happens to be a journalist. Sometimes she calls me to check in on her way into work, which is probably what she was doing then. You can trust her. And… you can trust me.'

His eyes drop to the floor. I don't move, watching him closely.

'I should go shower,' he says eventually, storming out the room.

Grabbing my phone, I curl up on the sofa underneath the duvet and quietly wait for him to get ready. I'm irritated that anyone would think I'd do something so low as to sell my story, but I also feel sad that that would be Kieran's first thought. I guess Henrietta Keane hasn't exactly helped his paranoia.

When the bell goes to signal Neil's arrival, Kieran leaves without saying goodbye, opening the front door to an eruption of noise from the paparazzi. Once I've heard his car pull away and the road return to normal again as the reporters scatter, I get up and go into the kitchen to make myself a coffee.

That's when I notice there are two smoothie glasses in the sink. One that's empty and has clearly been drunk from, and the other on its side, its contents slowly oozing out across the basin. It takes me a moment to realise that's why he was in the living room in the first place. He was bringing me a smoothie.

7

When I spot Iris, she's emerging from the flower shop in the Village with a pretty bouquet of colourful summer blooms. She notices me strolling towards her and she throws her head back and laughs, before holding them out to me.

'Busted!' she cries, throwing her free hand up in the air. 'I was going to show up to our dinner with these for you as a surprise.'

'You got me flowers?' I gasp, as she hands them over and I admire them. 'Why?'

'Because your trip fell through and I wanted to cheer you up,' she says with a shrug. 'Don't get all smushy on me, it's not a big deal.'

'But it *is* a big deal!' I exclaim, before I pull her into a hug. 'That's so thoughtful and lovely. I can't remember the last time anyone bought me flowers. Thank you.'

'You're welcome, now let's go eat,' she says, looping her arm through mine and dragging me towards an Italian restaurant we've booked. 'I want to hear all about you flashing your knickers at your hot new housemate and his coach.'

'I didn't *purposefully* flash my knickers at him,' I remind her, lowering my voice as a man we pass gives me a strange look. 'I told you, I sort of just dropped them and they happened to land on the coffee table. It was mortifying.'

'I bet he loved it.'

'He loved me embarrassing myself, I'm sure,' I mutter.

We arrive at the restaurant and are shown our table, a nice

one by the window so we can watch all the people strolling by. With a week and a half to go to the tournament, a buzzing atmosphere is growing in the Village with purple and green – the official colours of the tournament – decorations everywhere you look, and tennis-themed displays filling all the shop windows. Everyone seems to have got in the spirit of things and it's hard not to feel excited about it all, even if you're not that into tennis. It doesn't matter that the sun has been hiding away today and it's been grey and cloudy despite it being the end of June, it still feels like summer here in Wimbledon.

Once we've given our orders and our wine has been poured, Iris takes her glass and sits back, taking a sip of her drink. 'So, how's the art going? Have you made a start?'

'Not exactly. I'm easing myself into it.'

She gives me a pointed look.

'I know, I know,' I sigh. 'I just didn't picture myself starting the book whilst still in Wimbledon, that's all. I thought I'd be drawing in a haven of peace and instead—' I gesture out the window where a group of tourists are taking selfies with the giant tennis racket and ball display right outside the restaurant '—I'm surrounded by chaos.'

'So use your art to escape it,' she suggests, tilting her head at me. 'You're so talented, Flora, you can do this. You just need to believe that. I really think that starting your novel is going to be good for you.'

'I wish I knew how to start it. How do you get inspired to write?'

She shrugs. 'I don't think that I'll be much help. I watch sport.'

'And that gets you fired up at your keyboard, huh.' I chuckle.

'That's what does it for me.' She watches me curiously. 'You never know, maybe watching a spot of tennis will do it for you, too, especially now you're besties with the tennis player ranked number forty-three in the world.'

'Sure, we're besties. We're really bonding through having nothing in common and our constant bickering over the shoe stand.'

'The shoe stand,' she repeats, confused. 'What are you talking about?'

'Oh, nothing,' I sigh, tapping my nails on the table. 'He leaves his shoes strewn across the hallway for everyone to trip over on their way out or in. I swear he leaves them out on purpose because he knows it annoys me.'

'You still think he's trying to get you to leave?'

'Maybe. Or maybe he's just this irritating in real life.'

'Well, you might want to give him a bit of a break today,' Iris points out, grimacing. 'Did you see the cover piece on *Sports Now* magazine?'

I frown. 'No, why? Is it about Kieran?'

'Not exactly, although it might as well be. It's an interview with Chris Courtney. You know him right? Fairly big name in tennis, currently number eighteen seed for Wimbledon. He won a couple of Grand Slams in his twenties – the Aussie Open and the US Open – but then lost his footing a bit. But he's been playing well recently and got to the semi-finals of Queen's. He's gunning for Wimbledon, the one he really wants. According to him, this year is his year.'

'Good for him. What's that got to do with Kieran?'

Iris places down her glass and props her elbows on the table to lean towards me. 'The interviewer asked him who he sees as the biggest threat to him this tournament and Courtney of course lists a few of the big names – Sovák, Jensen, Bissette – and then he can't help but take a jab at Kieran O'Sullivan.'

'Isn't that a flattering thing, if he sees Kieran as a threat?' I check, impressed.

'That's not exactly how he brings him up. No offence to Kieran, but he's unseeded. He may have a few ATP titles under his belt from a while ago and he's made it to a lot of the Grand Slam semi-finals and finals in his time – but it's not like he's a big name in the sport at the moment.' She hesitates. 'He's become better known for his flaring temper and boozy nights out in the lead-up to Grand Slams than his actual performance in them, which is a shame. I've always liked his style. A real natural.'

'Okay, so why did Courtney say he was a threat?'

'That's my point. He doesn't. Courtney lists the threats and then he adds that players like Kieran should accept when their time is up, while players like him can continue to face the next generation with any success.'

My jaw drops. 'Ouch! Bitchy.'

'Right?' Iris rolls her eyes. 'The interviewer didn't even ask anything to warrant that answer. But any opportunity for those two to take the other one down, they'll take it, especially if it brings them into the public eye again – and Courtney has certainly achieved that today. His quote has been picked up by all the nationals.' She hesitates. 'Although, maybe that's not a fair judgement about Kieran anymore. It's been a while since he made any public remark about Courtney.'

'Why do they hate each other so much?'

Her eyes widen in shock at my question. 'Come on, Flora! You must know the history between those two. Courtney is O'Sullivan's nemesis.'

'I didn't think people actually had those.'

'In sport they sometimes do,' she says with a shrug. 'They can't stand one another. Look, I don't think what Chris Courtney has said is in any way classy, but this could be a good thing in the run-up to Wimbledon. Kieran didn't do badly at Halle – he reached the quarter-finals – and he's still got some fight in him. I think he could take some of the youngsters if he really wanted to. He just needs a kick up the butt. Maybe this comment from Courtney will help ignite something in him again before he considers retirement. Maybe he'll want to prove Courtney wrong.'

'You think he'll be that affected by something Chris Courtney says?'

'Uh, yeah!' She straightens, looking at me strangely. 'Didn't you hear what I said? Courtney is his enemy. On and off the court. Kieran's ex-fiancée ended up marrying him.'

I pause, my glass halfway to my lips. 'You *what*?'

'Yeah, you must remember it. Kieran was dating this actress and they were engaged and everything. Then they broke up, she started dating Courtney and they got married soon after. It was a pretty big scandal at the time,' she informs me.

'Fuck. No wonder Kieran hates him.' I take a gulp of my drink. 'Now, I feel a bit sorry for him.' Placing my glass down, I exhale, shaking my head. 'I hope you're right and Kieran does decide to prove him wrong on the court. He has been training a lot.'

'Yeah?' A sly smile creeps across Iris's lips. 'He's looking in good shape, is he?'

I narrow my eyes at her. 'Stop it. Don't look at me like that.'

'Like what?' she asks innocently, before shooting me a mischievous grin.

'Like *that*.' I laugh.

'What? Like it hasn't crossed your mind.' She arches her brow. 'You're living in the same flat, he's unbelievably sexy, you're unbelievably gorgeous, you're both single... I'm just saying, it could happen. It would make a good anecdote at least.'

'Jesus, Iris, a good anecdote,' I repeat in disbelief, running a hand through my hair as my cheeks flush with heat. 'It *won't* happen. Firstly we can't stand one another, and secondly, I'm hardly his type. He dates models and actresses, people who are in the public eye for a reason. I'm... unnoticeable.'

'Oh shut up.'

'*You* shut up.'

She grins at me. 'He's seen your underwear already, who knows what might happen next?'

'You're very annoying,' I huff, staring at my drink as I fiddle with the stem of my glass, twisting it between my fingers.

It may have flitted across my mind once. Or twice. The possibility of it. But in a complete fantasy world where he's actually a nice person to be around. I would be lying if I said that he wasn't attractive, because look at him. He's obviously beautiful, and I've seen him topless in a towel and you'd have to be dead not to wonder how it feels to run your hands up over the smooth curves of his arms and along his broad muscled shoulders. Anyone would want to know what that feels like.

That's not my fault, that's just... science.

Yeah. That makes sense.

'You're blushing, Flora,' Iris remarks.

'I'm blushing because of *you* and what you're saying, nothing to do with him. Trust me, it's really not like that between us.'

'For now,' she says, taking a triumphant sip of wine while I roll my eyes, relieved to see our food arriving, which provides the perfect opportunity to steer the conversation away from Kieran O'Sullivan.

That night, I wake up to the sound of someone trying to get in through the front door. I sit bolt upright at the loud thump, followed by the wiggling of the door handle. My heart in my throat, I swing my legs out of bed and freeze as someone shoves themselves against the door with some force. Jumping to my feet, I'm about to rush to bang on Kieran's bedroom door and demand he get his tennis racket at the ready to threaten the intruder with, but I'm stopped by the repeated rings on the bell, followed by vigorous knocking and then the loud, slurred voice of Kieran himself coming from the other side.

'Flora?' he says through the letter box. 'Helloooo. Anyone at home?'

After checking that it is him through the peephole, I quickly turn on the light and open the front door. He practically falls through, having been leaning against it. Stumbling past me into the hallway, he regains his balance and then bursts out laughing, slumping against the wall and knocking the mirror so that it swings dangerously.

'Kieran!' I gasp, steadying the mirror and then closing the front door. 'What are you doing? What time is it?'

'Late,' he confirms, before giving a *who-cares* shrug. 'Or early. One of the two.'

He stinks of booze and he looks dishevelled and sweaty, his forehead moist, his hair sticking up messily, his eyes red and glazed.

'Sorry, I seem to have lost my keys,' he says, his words coming fast and slurred. 'Oh hang on.' He reaches into his pocket and pulls out his set of keys, staring at them in amazement as he jangles them from his fingers. 'Well, what do you know? Here they are! I swear they were not in there before. Lucky I found them.'

'God, Kieran,' I say, noticing the time on his watch. 'It's almost three in the morning. Don't you have training with Neil first thing?'

'Probably. But whatever – it's cool,' he insists, pushing himself off from the wall and zig-zagging his way down the hall and turning into the living room.

'I'm not sure he'll see it that way,' I mutter, following him nervously. 'I think you need to go to bed.'

'Neil is always cross at me about something, so it's no big deal. I can't please him, I can't please *anyone*.' He chuckles, although I don't know if anything he's said is funny. Slumping down onto my makeshift bed, he kicks off his shoes and rests his head back against the cushion. 'Didn't you read the news today? I'm a washed-up loser who is setting myself up for disappointment yet again. It's all good. You know what they say?'

I raise my eyebrows at him, unimpressed. 'No, what do they say?'

'It is what it is,' he says, nodding gravely. '*That's* what they say.'

'Okay, you really need to go to bed,' I decide, chewing on my thumbnail. 'I'll get you some water, yeah?'

'None of that tap shite. Get me the good stuff.'

Leaving him laughing to himself, I go to get him a bottle of

Evian and when I return he's squinting at his phone screen as an unsaved number calls.

'You need to get that?' I ask haughtily, passing him his water and picking up his shoes to carry them into the hall and place them neatly on the stand.

'Nah, it's someone I met tonight at the pub. She's very nice and all, but—' He shrugs. 'She's not for me.'

'She's not a model or not famous enough?' I mutter, placing my hands on my hips.

He snaps his head up to glare at me. 'What does that mean?'

'Nothing, sorry.'

I wave my hand to dismiss it, wishing I hadn't said anything. I honestly don't know where it came from. Not only is it absolutely none of my business, but he's too drunk and it's way too early in the morning to go into this.

'No, come on,' he challenges, sitting himself up properly. 'You think I only date certain women, is that it?'

I shrug. 'I don't know, Kieran. I'm sorry, it was an offhand comment. I didn't—'

'You don't think very highly of me. You've seen pictures of me in the press and you think you've got me all figured out, that it?'

'No, Kieran. I can't figure you out at all. You've been training really hard and now you've gone out and got pissed. Neil is going to kill you.'

'Especially when the video of me yelling starts circulating.' He sighs.

I wince. 'You yelled at someone?'

'A guy followed me into the toilet with his phone in my face asking me questions about Courtney,' he says, his voice venomous. 'So I told him to fuck off.'

'That... actually seems fair.'

'I needed to blow off some steam tonight,' he mumbles, unscrewing the lid of his water and taking a couple of glugs. 'Tomorrow, I'll be fine.' His phone rings again. He declines the call, inhaling deeply through his nose and turning to look at me.

'By the way, it's not because she's not famous enough. In fact, she's an influencer of some kind with, like, a million followers.'

'Kieran, you really don't need to—'

'She thinks I'm someone I'm not,' he states, his eyes moving from me to stare straight ahead at the cherry blossom art. 'And while sometimes it's fun to lean into it, play the part and enjoy that kind of—' he flays his hand around as he searches for the word '—misplaced admiration, I didn't feel like pretending tonight. She was fun, though, her and her friends. They were a good laugh. I needed that.'

Watching him as he swigs glumly from his bottle, his shoulders slumped forward, any lingering irritation at being woken up by this drunken idiot fizzles away into sympathy. He seems a bit… sad.

'I'm sorry about what Chris Courtney said about you,' I offer gently.

He shrugs. 'Everyone's thinking it. Why shouldn't someone say it?'

'That's not what everyone thinks.'

He presses his lips together, exhaling through his nose. 'You don't know.'

'I know what my friend Iris Gray thinks,' I counter, folding my arms. 'She thinks you have what it takes and she's usually right about most things.'

Turning to look at me again, his brow furrows like he's trying to process what I've said but it's taking him a bit longer than usual.

'She thinks that a comment like that from this Courtney guy might help fire you up a bit for Wimbledon,' I continue.

'Huh.' He lifts his eyebrows. 'And what do you think?'

'Me?'

He nods. 'You. Flora Hendrix. The stubborn neat-freak artist who always smells nice and wears a Snoopy T-shirt to bed. What do *you* think?'

I can't suppress the bubble of laughter rising up my throat at his comment about my scent. My eyes falling to the floor, I shake my head as I giggle and then when I look back up at him, I find him smiling at me. A soft, earnest smile, as though he's pleased with himself for making me laugh.

'I don't know much about it, Kieran, but I think you're working hard and if Iris thinks you have what it takes then I do, too. And,' I add, arching a brow, 'I think Chris Courtney is a bit of a wanker for saying something like that to a journalist.'

He nods slowly. 'He *is* a wanker.'

'I also think you really should get to bed. You have to be up in, like, three hours.'

'Yep. You're right, you're right.'

Pushing himself up off the sofa, he stumbles a little as he gets to his feet and I dart forwards to grab his arm to help him balance. Glancing up as he leans on me, I find my face inches from his, his searing blue eyes flickering down to my lips.

'You know, Flora,' he says slowly, peering down at me, 'you're a very interesting person.'

'Yeah? Thanks,' I say, guiding him towards the bedroom with his arm resting around my shoulders.

'I'm sorry for yelling at you about the journalist. I know now she's your mate.'

'That's okay, forget about it.'

'I mean it, I'm sorry. I find it hard to trust people.'

'Honestly, Kieran, it's fine,' I assure him as we reach his doorway.

He unhooks his arm from around my shoulders and turns to face me. 'I don't want you to hate me, Flora Hendrix.'

I blink at him. 'I don't... I don't hate you.'

'Good. I don't hate you.'

'Okay. Well, I'm glad we got that cleared up,' I say, breaking into an amused smile as he spins round and stumbles towards the bed. 'Are you going to be okay?'

'I'll be fine,' he says, sitting down on the edge of it and then falling backwards on top of the duvet, closing his eyes with his hands clasped over his chest. 'Thank you.'

I stay a moment in the doorway, my eyes locked on his Adam's apple as he swallows, unable to resist the temptation of shamelessly admiring his neck.

'Flora,' he says suddenly without opening his eyes, but making me jump out of my skin, heat flushing through my face. 'Are you still there?'

'Uh… yeah. I'm just about to go. Did you want something?'

'I just wanted to tell you that I like the cherry blossom art you did on the wall.'

I smile to myself, leaning against the doorframe. 'Good. I'm glad.'

'It makes me feel serene,' he continues with his eyes closed, his voice lowering, his breathing getting heavier. 'Like everything will be okay.'

I can't think of how to respond, so I don't. Instead I wait a beat until his breathing becomes soft snores, and then I quietly close the door, leaving him to sleep it off. Plodding back to my sofa, I get back beneath the duvet but despite the time, I don't feel so tired anymore. You always want your art to make someone feel something. Anything. I didn't know if I really had the ability to do that, but from what Kieran's just said, maybe my art does have that power after all.

No more excuses. Tomorrow, I'm going to draw.

8

I can't imagine looking forward to training on a hangover is much fun, but having your coach rant at you all morning on top of that must make it even worse. Put it this way: I do not envy Kieran today. When I glanced into the kitchen earlier, he was sitting at the table with his head in his hands, sipping from a new bottle of water every now and then, listening to Neil who is still pacing up and down the kitchen tiles so loudly, I can hear the slap of each footstep from here in the living room.

'You do realise that you've given him exactly what he wants, don't you?' Neil snaps. 'He knew this is what you would do if he talked about you – send you into a tailspin. Well, congratulations, you've strolled right into his trap.'

'It wasn't just what Chris said, Neil,' Kieran responds, his voice low and hoarse. 'I fancied a bit of a night out. Is that a crime?'

'It might as well be. You are training for Wimbledon, which, in case you haven't noticed, is in a week and a half. It's not just your time and effort you're wasting when you pull a stunt like this, Kieran, it's your team's, too. Or do you not care about us?'

'Of course I care.'

'Yeah, you have a funny way of showing it.'

'I made a mistake. I'm sorry.'

'Fuck's sake, Kieran, you say that every time. "I'm sorry, I've disappointed everyone". It's the same old fucking record. One of these days, you need to wake up and realise that you don't have many chances left. Do you even want this? Wimbledon?'

Kieran groans. 'Of course I want it! It's all I've ever wanted.'

'Then fight for it! Stop telling yourself you don't deserve it and throwing in the towel before you've even given yourself the chance. You act exactly how they want you to act. Why? You're better than this. I wish you'd see that.'

'Sometimes it's hard to keep believing,' Kieran grumbles.

I hear Neil let out a heavy sigh as the pacing stops, then comes the sound of chair legs scraping across the floor. He must have taken a seat at the table. I clasp my coffee mug, straining to hear.

'Kieran, if you don't really believe that you might be able to win Wimbledon, then why are you here? Why do you keep coming back?' Neil asks in a softer voice.

'I don't know. Maybe I just like routine.'

Neil laughs gruffly. 'If you liked routine, you wouldn't be a fucking tennis player. You'd have stopped travelling all the damn time and settled down.'

'That doesn't sound too bad.'

'Yeah? Then go ahead and give up. You have the money. You have that place in Dublin that's empty most of the year. You have the flat in Florida. You always said you wanted to retire here at Wimbledon. So go on, sell those flats and buy your dream house here in the Village to sit around in and read the paper all day if that's what you want.'

It's silent for a moment and then Kieran quietly replies, 'I want the Wimbledon trophy first.'

'Yes, you do,' Neil says, satisfied. 'And when you win it – *when*, Kieran – you can go after all the others. If you would only stop feeling sorry for yourself and start believing that you have as much right to be on Centre Court as anyone else. You've got the talent, Kieran – haven't I always said that? It's your mind that needs the work.'

Kieran sighs. 'I'm sorry about last night, Neil.'

'Not as sorry as you're going to be when I'm running you round that court in half an hour. Come on, get your bag and let's go. You can sweat it out. We'll get you one of those fucking green juices and you'll feel back on top of the world.'

'Nicole can't be happy about the video doing the rounds online. He followed me into the toilet, Neil. He was telling me I was a loser like Chris said. He got me riled up.'

'Forget it. We move on, okay? No distractions. Only tennis from now on.'

'Got it.'

I hear the chairs being pushed back as they stand up and I quickly pretend to be on my phone. Neil passes the living room doorway first, without looking in, stopping at the front door to warn Kieran there's a couple of reporters outside looking for a comment on his big night out yesterday.

'Guess I asked for that,' Kieran grumbles. 'Hang on a second, Neil.' He steps into the room and I look up from my screen as though I'm surprised he's still in the flat and I haven't been listening to every word they've spoken. 'Hey, Flora, you okay?'

'Yeah, fine. You?'

'I've been better.' He hesitates, fiddling with the cap in his hand. 'Sorry about waking you up last night. And for any drunken ramblings.'

'Don't worry about it. You were fine.' I offer him a reassuring smile. 'You were quite funny, actually.'

'Yeah? In a good way? Or in a I-should-bow-my-head-in-shame way?'

I pretend to think about it. 'Hmm. A good way.'

The corner of his lip twitches. 'Phew. That's a relief.'

'Kieran,' Neil states sternly, 'we're already late.'

With a small apologetic smile to me, Kieran puts his cap on and lowers the visor before following Neil out of the flat. As the car pulls away and the barrage of the questions from the paparazzi come to a stop, I take a moment to look at the cherry blossom artwork on the wall. You know, it really is quite good.

Putting my mug down, I get up to go shower. I've got a big day ahead of me. It's time to start my story.

*

My story SUCKS.

I've spent a whole day trying to work out what I'm doing and it's all a complete shitshow. WHY do I still think I can do this? I can't even start the fucking thing! I've tried storyboarding, but my feeble attempts with Post-it notes made me feel more depressed than before I started, so I screwed all those up and threw them in the bin.

After googling 'ways to get over writer's block' online, I made several cups of tea and then went for a long walk this afternoon, but that turned out to be shit advice. All the tea did was make me need to pee loads and when I was walking around Wimbledon, I saw bright, happy people who looked like they had places to be and were walking with purpose, unlike me, aimlessly wandering about with no destination, an eerie parallel to my life in general. It only served to remind me how London is filled with successful people who know what they're doing, while I continue to fail at everything.

I allow myself a bit of wallowing when I get home and then I realise that the best way to get drawing might be to actually try drawing. I've tried plotting, but maybe I'm one of those authors who the story just comes to while I go. After searching high and low through the living room, I realise that all my art supplies are in the bedroom, tucked away out of sight on top of the wardrobe.

Taking a deep breath, I cautiously open my bedroom door, nervous to see what state Kieran has left my room in this morning. It's actually not as bad as I thought it would be, although there are clothes strewn across the floor, and his attempt at making the bed is embarrassing. He may have half-heartedly thrown the duvet back into place, but he hasn't smoothed out the wrinkles, fluffed the pillows or placed the scatter cushions back on top. And I see the throw has been kicked off and left in a crumpled pile on the floor. I was expecting it to smell bad in here, like stale booze, but I'm pleasantly surprised – the window is open, so it's fresh and airy, with a subtle hint of his cologne hanging in the air.

It's a nice scent, sandalwood and citrus I think.

Resisting the urge to snoop through his stuff while he's not here, I pick my way across the floor. I feel guilty being in here without his permission. I have to respect that while he's paying to stay here, this is his room – my quarters are the living room – and I don't really have the right to come barging in here whenever I like. But I really do need my art stuff to start my book, so I'm sure he'd understand why I felt the need to trespass.

Standing in front of the wardrobe, I hitch up onto my tiptoes and try to reach the top but it's no use. The bed is too far from the wardrobe to use for a step up, so I have to go get a chair, and I place it carefully down on the carpet.

Climbing up onto the seat, I steady myself by gripping onto the sides of the wardrobe, the chair creaking and wobbling beneath my weight, its legs shaky on the soft, uneven carpet. I'm suddenly regretting insisting Jonah and I buy this rickety set of chairs from a second-hand furniture shop. It doesn't feel sturdy, but my art pad and box of pencils are now in view. I let go of the wardrobe to reach up and the chair jerks beneath me. I yelp, pressing my hands against the cupboard door to find my balance again. I exhale loudly.

'Easy does it,' I say out loud to myself, moving much slower this time and only removing one hand from the wardrobe to reach up over my head. My fingers grasp round the pencil box and I pull it forwards, before grabbing it properly and carefully tossing it behind me onto the bed.

'One more,' I tell myself.

Stretching up again, I can't grab onto the sketch pad as easily as the pencil box and I have to go up on my tiptoes, reaching even further so that my cropped T-shirt rides right up, exposing my stomach. Eventually, I brush the corner of my sketch pad with my fingertips. Using my forefinger and thumb to pincer it,

I drag it over and above my head, but I'm too enthusiastic and drop my heels back onto the seat of the chair with too much gusto. The art pad comes flying over my head and the chair wobbles forward dangerously beneath me. In trying to balance, I instinctively lean backwards.

I gasp as I slip and tumble into empty air.

But instead of landing on the floor, I fall into the strong arms of Kieran, who has appeared out of nowhere and rushed forwards just in time to catch me.

'Are you okay?' he asks, his voice raspy and urgent.

He has me locked in his grip, his arms wrapped tightly around my waist, his hands linked across my stomach beneath the hem of my T-shirt. My back is pressed against his broad solid chest, which is rising up and down with each heavy breath.

'I'm fine,' I breathe, my heart hammering from both the fright of the fall and the thrill of the catch. 'Thank you.'

He takes a few moments before he loosens his grip. I turn in his arms as he releases me, so that I can look up at him. I'm so close that I'm able to fully appreciate the long dark eyelashes that frame his eyes, and how defined the slants of his cheekbones are. My breathing shaky and shallow, I grip onto his strong forearms and lean back against the wardrobe. As his eyes travel down my face to my mouth, his throat bobs as he swallows.

Heat flushes up my neck.

My phone vibrates in my back pocket, buzzing loudly pressed against the wardrobe door behind me and jolting me from the daze.

He drops his arms.

'What were you doing?' he asks crossly, his forehead creased as he takes a step back and rights the chair. 'You could have hurt yourself.'

'I forgot that my art stuff was in here,' I explain, dropping down to pick up the loose pages of my sketch pad that scattered across the floor when it fell. 'I couldn't reach it.'

'Next time, wait until I'm back rather than risk breaking your neck.'

'Sorry, I shouldn't be in your room.'

As I gather the paper as quickly as possible, he leans over to pick one of the pages up. It's a sketch of two people in an embrace – a fair-haired man in a tux tipping back a red-haired woman in a ball gown. She is gazing up at him, her hand cupping his face.

Blushing, I swipe it out from his grasp and slip it into the middle of the pile I'm carrying, hidden from sight.

'Did you do that?' he asks, a glint of curiosity in his eyes.

I shrug. 'A while ago.'

'It was signed "Flossie" in the corner.'

'Oh. I was "Flossie" growing up and that's what my grandmother said should be my artist name. I like it but, you know—' I shrug. 'No use having an artist name and no art.'

'Flossie. I like it. It's a nice name.'

'Hm.'

'The sketch is good,' he says, looking genuinely impressed. He peers over my shoulder at the drawings in view on top of the pile. 'What are these for?'

'Nothing, I was messing around,' I say quickly, clutching the pages against my chest so he can't study them any further. 'How was training today? I take it you survived?'

'They're drawings of people,' he continues, ignoring my questions and frowning in confusion. 'I thought you were into landscapes, like the Lake District.'

'That's *where* I want to draw, not *what* I want to draw.'

'I see.' He gestures to the sketches I'm holding. 'So, even if you were just "messing around", what was that story about?'

'Oh, nothing. As in, these aren't part of a story. They were random sketches. They're nothing.'

'They don't look like nothing.'

I sigh. 'I like sketching characters – people – and I've always wanted to write a romance. But my ex-boyfriend pointed out that most people want superheroes and action from a comic book, not a romantic narrative. So—' I shrug, bowing my head '—these were just doodles. No one else was supposed to see them.'

He watches me curiously as I blush under his scrutinising gaze.

'You should draw what you want to draw,' he says simply.

'Not if I want to become a successful graphic novelist. I need to create something that will sell.'

'Who says a romance won't sell? This ex-boyfriend of yours?' He lifts his eyebrows. 'What was he, some kind of professional artist himself?'

'He was an actor and musician. I mean, you won't have heard of him,' I add, flustered. 'He hasn't made it yet as such, but he hasn't been out of work. He's done a bit of theatre. We met in Norwich, when he was touring a play there. That's where I'm from.'

'And this actor slash musician knows a lot about the graphic novel market.'

'He had a point. When you think of comics, romance doesn't spring to mind.'

'What about *Heartstopper*? And Jack Kirby created a romantic comic book series before he came up with the Captain America character. I can't remember what the series was called, but it will come to me.'

I stare at him, my jaw dropping to the floor. 'You mean, *Young Romance*.'

He clicks his fingers. 'That's it.'

'You like comic books,' I blurt out, nerves fluttering at the thought.

'Yeah,' he says, smiling warmly at my reaction. 'Big fan. Why do you look so surprised? I'm allowed to like things outside of tennis.'

'I know, but I… I didn't have you down as a comic book nerd.'

He strokes his chin with a bemused expression. 'Nerd might

be pushing it. But I enjoy graphic novels. That's why I feel quite confident telling you that your ex was talking... well, quite frankly, a load of shite. It's no wonder that you haven't been able to start your story yet – you can't write something that doesn't come naturally to you. If it's a romantic story that you want to tell, that's the one you should be writing.'

'I don't know,' I murmur. 'It's a competitive industry and Jonah said—'

'What?' Kieran cuts in, something like anger flashing across his eyes. 'What else did this guy say to stall you?'

I bite my lip. 'He didn't want me to get my hopes up. I didn't do an art degree or anything. He said he didn't think I'd practised my craft enough to make it. In other words, I wasn't good enough.'

Kieran's jaw twitches. Tipping his head back for a moment, he murmurs something under his breath that I don't quite catch.

'What did you say?' I ask, frowning.

'Nothing.' He gestures at my drawings. 'These look very good to me. I don't know much about art and so this may mean nothing to you, but I've only caught a glimpse at those characters and I want to know more. I want to know their story.'

'Thanks.' I hesitate, before adding softly, 'That means a lot.'

I bring my eyes up to lock with his and there's something about them that seems different. They've softened somehow. Usually his steely stare is cold and guarded, but here, in this moment, it's soothing and warm. I've forgotten how much this guy riles me; instead I'm lost in the gentle, swirling blue of his eyes.

He averts his gaze and the spell is broken.

'Sorry, for being in your room,' I say hurriedly. 'Thanks again for saving me. I'll... um... go.'

I scuttle out, returning to the safety of my sofa. But later that night, I find that I'm smiling to myself when I think about our exchange.

Kieran O'Sullivan likes my drawings.

9

I'm supposed to be drawing, but all I can think about is the strength of Kieran O'Sullivan's arms locked around my waist and how it felt to be cocooned by his body yesterday. He's so tall and broad and solid, I felt small and safe tucked into his chest, even if it was just for a few seconds. And I could have sworn there was something about the way he looked at me when I turned round in his arms to face him, an intensity that wasn't there before.

Okay, maybe I saw what I wanted to see.

But whenever I let my mind drift back to that moment – which, I have to admit, is roughly every ten seconds – a warm tingling sensation swirls through my body, sending my heartbeat into overdrive.

He did say I smelt nice, too.

I twirl the pencil round in my fingers, biting my lip. The open page of my sketchbook in front of me on the kitchen table remains blank. I sigh, annoyed with myself for wasting another afternoon. I toss the pencil down and slide my laptop across to me, typing in Kieran's name to Google search. I want to know more about him.

Ignoring the recent articles, I click on his Wikipedia page, focusing on the sections detailing his background and personal life, rather than the long paragraphs about his tennis career. The section about his background is fairly vague. He obviously doesn't like to talk about it publicly. I scan through how he grew up in Dublin, his parents divorced young, and he and his older brother, Aidan, were coached by their father, Brian. Aidan was an extremely successful young tennis star, but passed away at the age of twenty. There aren't many details about his death, but the largely accepted story is that it was drug-related.

'Oh my God,' I whisper, pressing a hand over my mouth.

From the section about his personal life, I learn that, just as Iris told me, Kieran was briefly engaged to British actress, Rachel Wallace, in his twenties but they broke up two months into their engagement and she subsequently dated and married Australian tennis player Chris Courtney. Apparently, it's also well known that Kieran and Chris have a long history of professional rivalry on the court – soon after Aidan died, Kieran faced Chris in the final of the Australian Open, having already beaten the world number one in the semis, a match that catapulted Kieran into worldwide fame overnight. The final was a highly anticipated match, since Kieran was only eighteen years old. Chris won three sets to two. Kieran broke his racket during the match and was fined.

Three years later, Chris played Kieran in the semi-final of Wimbledon, but Kieran had to forfeit during the match due to injury. Rachel Wallace was watching that match, sitting with Kieran's team. A year later when they faced each other at Wimbledon again, she was sitting amongst Chris's entourage. Kieran lost in three straight sets.

'Ugh,' I say out loud, my heart sinking for him. *Brutal*.

Since his break-up with Rachel, Kieran has been linked to several female public figures but hasn't had any serious relationships, and there's a note about his work with a mental health charity for young people. It also details that his father coached him up until he was twenty-six, when according to various sources, Kieran sacked him. They didn't speak for a long time after, although there have been reports of a reconciliation more recently.

Delving a little deeper into my Kieran snooping, I find an article from an Irish newspaper about the O'Sullivan brothers, published just after Aidan's death. It begins by saying that Aidan's death is not just an unbearably painful tragedy for the family, but a terrible blow to the world of tennis. '*Something of a tennis prodigy, Aidan was widely considered to be one of the brightest and most promising young talents in the sport,*' it reads. '*There is no doubt that with his electrifying raw talent, exceptional abilities and unwavering determination, Aidan O'Sullivan had an extraordinarily successful career ahead of him.*'

I gaze sadly at the accompanying photograph of Aidan beneath the paragraph. Tall, dark, strikingly handsome, he looks like Kieran, although with a slighter frame, gentle brown eyes and longer hair than his brother. Below that photo is another – one of Aidan and Kieran together when they were teenagers. They're standing on a tennis court with an older man, who the caption tells me is their father. Brian is talking at them and while Aidan is looking intently at his dad with a serious expression, Kieran is glancing away, laughing goofily at something in the distance. I read on to the next part of the article:

His younger brother, Kieran, is another remarkable tennis player, but is more emotional and volatile on the court. While he has displayed more flair in his style, Kieran has faced criticism for lacking the control that was so early mastered by his brother and often displayed amongst the top players today.

Although competitive on the court, the brothers were close off of it and Kieran will be suffering the loss of his beloved brother keenly. We can only hope that he won't retire from the sport himself in the wake of this tragedy, for then tennis will have lost two of its brightest stars.

As I come to the end of the article, I realise that a tear is sliding down my cheek. I brush it away with my finger, leaning back in my chair and exhaling audibly. Returning to the other search results, I can only find one big feature interview with Kieran and it's from years ago. In fact, when I check the dates, I realise that he gave it just a few months before his brother died. It's from a glossy weekend magazine of one of the national broadsheets and runs with the headline: *"I will win Wimbledon before my brother does" – Kieran O'Sullivan on why he's the one to watch.*

A lump rises in my throat as I scan through the piece, my eyes drifting over the quotes from Kieran that talk about why he's determined to prove to the world that he's not going to linger in Aidan's shadow, but will be the brother to be remembered. Aside from tournament press conferences, this looks like the last interview Kieran ever gave.

I'm reflecting on the sadness of it all when the doorbell goes.

Maybe Kieran has actually lost his keys for real this time. My heart pounding, I slam my laptop shut and jump to my feet, embarrassed that he's returned when I'm in the middle of researching him. I hurry to get the door, catching sight of myself in the hallway mirror, my cheeks flushed pink, my eyes bright with excitement.

'Pull yourself together,' I whisper strictly at my reflection.

Just because he caught me when I fell from a chair and said nice things about my art does not mean I should completely lose my head. One good thing does not cancel out all the horrible things that have come before. Okay, so he's maybe not as bad as I thought he was, but still, this guy has been rude and conceited since the moment we met. Plus, let's not forget the kind of women he's used to dating. He's hardly going to look twice at someone like me when he has influencers and models throwing themselves at his feet whenever he pops down to the local.

Saying that, there's no harm in checking that I look nice when he's around. I quickly run my fingers through my hair, smiling guiltily at my reflection – I purposefully took my time perfecting my make-up earlier in anticipation of his return.

With a deep breath and what I hope to be a casual, nonchalant smile, I swing open the door. My heart drops.

'Jonah!' I gasp, recoiling.

A smirk stretches across my ex-boyfriend's face as he lingers on my doorstep. Thanks to his reflective aviators, I can see my wide-eyed shock at his appearance. He lifts his arm to push his hair back from his face, his leather jacket squeaking as the fabric moves. It's a hot day, but he loves that jacket. Paired with the blue faded jeans he's wearing today, he looks like he's stepped off the stage of *Grease the Musical*, which he may well have done – I haven't been keeping track of his career recently and have blocked him on all social media.

'Hey, you,' he says softly.

My stomach knots at such an affectionate term.

'What are you doing here?' I ask bluntly.

'Can I come in?' he asks, peering to look beyond me into the hallway. When I hesitate, he cocks his head. 'You're not going to be awkward about this, are you? I'm just here to pick up some things, Flora. No need to make this into a big deal.'

As he whips off his glasses and swaggers past me into the flat, I'm hit by an overpowering wave of cologne that makes my throat tickle. I've always felt that smell is the most powerful way to evoke a memory, but this is a new scent to the one he wore when we were together. It doesn't make me miss him, it almost makes me gag.

When I join him in the living room, I find him scanning the place curiously. His eyes trace across the workout equipment, the colour-coordinated book spines on the shelves, the unused three-wick candle in the middle of the coffee table, the throw folded on the arm of the sofa, eventually landing on the PlayStation sitting beneath the TV.

'A few changes in here,' he says, quirking a brow. 'He's making his mark, I see.'

'So, what stuff did you want to pick up?' I ask, trying to sound cool and collected while my skin crawls with discomfort. 'I can't think of anything you've left here.'

He slowly turns to face me, inhaling deeply. His eyes drift down to my cleavage and back up again. I regret wearing a tight-fitted V-neck top today with my high-waisted black denim shorts. I fold my arms across my chest self-consciously.

'You look good, Flora,' he says gently. 'How have you been?'

'Great, thanks. You?'

He nods slowly. 'I've been good. Busy. Lots of theatre gigs.' He hesitates, before adding quietly, 'I've missed you.'

I clench my jaw, saying nothing.

'You didn't reply to my messages,' he comments.

'I didn't have anything to say.'

'I was hoping we'd stay friends,' he says, a pleading glint in his eye.

I clear my throat. 'What things did you think you'd left here? If you tell me what you're looking for, I can let you know if I've seen them.'

He watches me curiously. 'You don't even want to talk to me a little bit, Flora? Come on, we were together three years. I know things ended badly, but…'

He trails off, before giving a weak smile. 'You're right. I don't deserve you being nice to me. I just hoped… I don't know.' He takes a deep breath. 'I guess you haven't been missing me. I was surprised how quickly you moved on. Did you meet Kieran O'Sullivan after I left or did you know him before?'

I narrow my eyes at him. 'Excuse me?'

'It seems that he's moved in with you very quickly and I know you, Flora,' he says, fixing me with an intense stare. 'I *know* you wouldn't let yourself get caught up in a whirlwind romance. You're too smart for that. So I figured you've known this guy for longer than six months. When Zoe told me that she'd seen Kieran O'Sullivan going into our flat, I didn't believe her but then I saw the stuff online and I realised—'

'You're still in touch with Zoe?' I ask quietly, my blood turning cold.

'Yeah,' he says, the corners of his lips twitching up. 'We've always been friends. You know that.'

I desperately blink back tears, caught out by how much that

stings. I am not attracted to this man anymore – I know that. But his betrayal and its consequent humiliation still has the power to make me feel like an absolute fool. I have managed to persuade myself that he and Zoe would never speak again after what they did to me. How naïve. And now here I am standing in front of him months later, unwittingly duped all over again.

'Zoe and I, it's not serious,' he assures me, his eyes brightening, feeding off the fact that I've shown I care. 'Nothing like what we had together. And I don't know what's going on between you and Kieran O'Sullivan, but if ever—'

'It's really none of your business, Jonah,' I croak, feeling like someone has gripped my gut and twisted it sharply. 'Did you come here to get your stuff or quiz me on my life? Because you gave up all your rights to know anything about me when you shagged our next-door neighbour.'

He winces, his gaze dropping to the floor.

'I know I have no right to check on you,' he admits gently, looking genuinely pained. He's a fucking good actor. 'But I can't help it. I still care about you.'

'Jonah—'

He takes a step forwards and I instinctively stumble back.

'I know that I'm the dickhead here,' he states, his brow creased with determination. 'I don't deserve your forgiveness. What I did was wrong. But feelings don't change overnight. When you love someone, they become a part of you. I haven't shaken you, Flora. I'm not sure I ever will. And if someone is taking advantage of you, I want to know.'

I balk at his suggestion. 'What are you *talking* about?'

He raises his eyebrows, as though we both know what he means. 'Kieran O'Sullivan? Really, Flora. He's a notorious dickhead and word on the street is he picks up and drops women willy-nilly. You can't think he's genuinely serious about you.'

Did he just say 'willy-nilly'?

Bloody hell, the fact that I ever let this guy inside me makes me feel sick. In fact, I'm glad he said it. It bats away any doubts that might come crawling in with his clever manipulation and reminds me of what I've come to realise the last few months: Jonah is not the person I want to be with. I am no longer powerless in his grip.

I straighten, lifting my chin defiantly.

'You don't know anything about Kieran O'Sullivan,' I assert.

'Maybe,' he shrugs, his expression softening, 'but I know you. I know you're kind and generous and you see the best in people. That blinds you to their agendas.'

'The way I was blinded to yours?' I note, quirking my brow.

He sighs impatiently. 'I've apologised, Flora. I'm human. I made a mistake and I've held my hands up and admitted it.'

I snort, taking another step back from him. 'I caught you with her *in our bed*. It didn't take much to admit it.' I run a hand through my hair. 'Look, we've already been through this and I don't want to do it again. It's over and we've both moved on. Please get your stuff and go. If you tell me what you're after then I will try to find it for you, but I'm pretty sure nothing of yours is left here.'

His eyes flash with irritation.

'Fine,' he snaps. 'If that's how you want to play it, then so be it. Guess we're going to be petty exes after all.'

I roll my eyes. A few months ago, his poor opinion of me would have had me reeling. I would have been desperate to win back his approval, for him to think I'm nothing less than wonderful. But fuck him. I've wasted years of my life trying to please him.

'I'm here for my garlic press,' he states.

I blink at him, a snigger pulling at my lips. 'Sorry?'

'My garlic press,' he repeats, glowering at me. 'I know you're not a cook, so maybe you need me to explain what it looks like.'

'I think I'll manage. Anything else?'

'Not that I can think of.'

I leave him to make my way into the kitchen. As I start rooting through the drawers, I hear his footsteps behind me and out the corner of my eye I see him wander in and stop abruptly at the table, staring down at my sketch pad and pencils.

'You're drawing,' he states.

'Yep.'

'I thought you'd given up.'

I close one drawer shut and open another. 'Nope.'

He laughs lightly. 'Okay. That's interesting.'

Don't take the bait. Don't take the bait. Don't take the—

'Why is that interesting?' I snap, straightening.

He holds up his hands, a smirk playing across his lips. 'Whoa, Flora, no need to get defensive. I'm pleased you're drawing again – you're good at it. It's what you did when *we* first dated. It's... sweet.'

'Sweet,' I repeat, staring at him in disbelief.

'Yeah, that you're giving it a go again. Yes, it's a tough industry and, okay, so you're a lot older than most artists trying to crack through into this market and you don't have the experience or qualifications, but it's sweet that you're... trying. I'm glad our break-up has given you the time to take up your hobbies again.'

I can't think what to say. My throat seems to have closed up completely and no words are forming. He's watching me with an earnest smile, his poisonous words seeping under my skin, reducing me to a small, hopeless idiot.

'Who's this?'

Kieran's voice pulls me back. He's standing in the doorway to the kitchen in his shorts and hoodie, his hair wet and dishevelled from a swim. He looks from Jonah to me, his forehead furrowing in concern as he takes me in. I realise that I have unwillingly folded forwards in an unattractive hunch, winded by Jonah's speech, my hand gripping the side of the counter as though it's holding me up. My knuckles have turned white.

Jonah steps towards him, holding out his hand.

'Hi, mate,' he says breezily, 'I'm Jonah.'

Towering over him, Kieran glances down at his outstretched hand and arches a brow dismissively, as though bemused Jonah would presume he'd shake his hand. Jonah snorts, dropping his arm to his side.

'Okay, fine. It's like that, is it. I guess she's told you about me.'

'I've never heard of you,' Kieran states flatly. 'I did overhear what you were saying as I came in, though, and I'm not one for shaking the hand of a guy who likes to bring other people down to make themselves feel bigger.'

Jonah looks confused. 'Look, I don't know who you think you are, but you have obviously misunderstood whatever it was you overheard.' He chuckles, turning to me. Kieran fixes him with a cold stare. 'Flora knows me, don't you, Flora? She knows I wouldn't say anything to upset her.'

'You should go, Jonah,' I tell him, my voice wobbling, betraying my nerves.

'Fucking hell, what is this?' Jonah says, cackling with laughter. 'I just came here for my garlic press. It's not a big deal.' He looks Kieran up and down with a sneer. 'You don't need to go all macho on me, mate.'

'She said you should go, and I'm not your mate,' Kieran growls.

Jonah sighs breezily, but I can tell he's unnerved. Kieran is a lot bigger than he is. His fists are clenched, his eyes are flashing with rage and his large frame takes up most of the doorway, blocking Jonah's exit.

'Okay, I've got it, whatever,' Jonah mutters, rolling his shoulders back and lifting his chin. 'I didn't realise my presence bothers you, Flora. I thought we were adults and had moved on, but guess I read the room wrong. You should have said earlier if you wanted me to go. You didn't need your bodyguard to come do the honours.'

Kieran exhales with frustration, his jaw twitching. As he flexes his fingers, I can tell that he's trying to control his simmering anger.

'It's time to leave, Jonah,' Kieran reminds him with an intimidating stare.

'All right, all right, keep your panties on. She's all yours, mate,' Jonah snaps, moving to slide past him, before muttering under his breath, 'Go to town on my sloppy seconds.'

It's a fateful mistake. In one swift movement, Kieran grasps the lapels of Jonah's jacket in his fists, hauls him up and slams his back against the fridge so hard, it wobbles dangerously. Pinned to the fridge, Jonah gasps as Kieran looms over him.

'*What did you just say?*' Kieran seethes, leaning into him.

'Kieran, don't!' I blurt out, rushing forwards and grabbing his arm. 'He's not worth it. Trust me.'

Exhaling through his nose, Kieran's eyes remain locked on Jonah's, which are wide and panicked. I squeeze Kieran's arm. He takes a step back and lets go. Jonah gulps audibly as Kieran narrows his eyes at him.

'Don't *ever* disrespect her like that again,' Kieran says in a voice so deadly cold it makes Jonah shudder. 'Now, get out.'

His cheeks flushed pink, Jonah checks the lapels of his leather jacket and, shooting me a furious parting glance, marches out the kitchen. His footsteps thud down the hall and we hear the door slam so hard, it makes me jump. Kieran and I stand in silence, until he turns to me and puts his hands on his hips.

'I could use a drink,' he grunts. 'What about you?'

My heart racing, I lean against the counter.

'Yeah,' I breathe, breaking into a grateful smile. 'A drink would be great.'

10

'So tell me,' Kieran begins, sitting back and looking at me curiously, 'what exactly is it that you saw in that Danny Zuko wannabe?'

Sitting on the opposite end of the sofa to him, I take a sip of wine before answering. 'He was very sweet and charming when we first met.'

'Yeah, he seems a real catch. How long were you together, if you don't mind me asking?'

'Three years.'

'That long?' Kieran's eyes widen in shock. 'How is that possible?'

I sigh, swirling the liquid round my glass. 'I don't know. I put him on a pedestal, to be honest. He was so charismatic and funny, always the centre of attention and life of the party. I felt lucky to be with him. He chose me when he could have had anyone.'

'He *made* you feel that way,' Kieran comments with disgust. 'He knew you were out of his league, so he made you feel small so you'd think you couldn't do better.' He shakes his head, before muttering, 'I'm glad you finally saw the light.'

I grimace. 'Actually, I didn't.' I take another gulp while he watches me. 'He dumped me after I caught him cheating on me.'

Kieran tilts his ear in my direction as though he didn't hear me correctly.

'I know, I know,' I sigh, shaking my head. 'Pathetic, isn't it.'

'It's not pathetic,' he states, frowning at me. 'It's frustrating.'

'Yeah. When I look back on our break-up, I almost don't recognise the person I was then, you know? It's weird. I was so desperate for him to stay with me and now I really don't know why.' I take a more measured sip of wine. 'Anyway, I'm sorry about today. I didn't think he'd... I have no idea why I even let him in.'

'Maybe because you trusted him to act like a decent person,' Kieran says in a low voice, looking troubled.

'Stupid of me.'

'Kind of you,' Kieran corrects, his steely blue eyes locking with mine and making my heart flutter. 'That's never a bad thing. It was his mistake to think he could treat someone like that in their own home.' He raises his own drink to his lips. 'Let's hope he doesn't make that mistake again, for his sake.'

'I'm sure he won't, thanks to you.' I give him a wry smile, adding earnestly, 'Thank you. I'm embarrassed that you had to step in.'

Kieran frowns at me. 'Don't be embarrassed. It was my pleasure to put that prick in his place. Neil wouldn't be best pleased if he found out, mind you, so maybe we keep the incident between ourselves. After the other night, I'm meant to be lying low.' He hesitates. 'Let's hope Danny Zuko doesn't go running to the press to tell his sob story.'

'And admit that he got his arse kicked by you? Unlikely,' I assure him. 'He may be desperate for publicity, but surely not that desperate.'

'You'd be surprised.'

I bite my lip, tapping my fingernails on the outside of my glass. 'I'm so annoyed with myself. I wish I hadn't let him get to me today.'

'He knows exactly what to say to hurt you,' Kieran murmurs, his eyes dropping to his hands and glazing over. 'It takes time to put up a shield to that, especially when it's someone who knows you so well.'

With his head bowed, sadness radiates from him and I catch a glimpse of something vulnerable and bruised beneath his shield. It reminds me a little bit of how he looked when he came home drunk and he sat in that exact spot, staring at the cherry blossom art, lost in his thoughts.

'You sound as if you know how that feels,' I say cautiously, taking a gamble.

He stiffens, glancing up at me. I offer him a small smile, willing him to speak.

'My father likes to put me in my place,' he says eventually, holding my gaze. 'Constant, cutting comments that chip away so lightly you don't even notice the gaping hole they're creating. It's a clever form of bullying. Removing all your power to build up theirs. It can fly under the radar for quite a while.'

I swallow, my heart in my throat. 'I'm sorry, Kieran. That's awful.'

'It's all right,' he tells me. 'With the help of a very expensive therapist, I've learnt to deal with it and see it for what it is. He takes his anger out on me, I take my anger out on the court. Both of us are in pain.'

'Is that... because of Aidan?' I ask softly. 'If you don't want to talk about it, then—'

'No, it's fine,' he says earnestly, rubbing the nape of his neck with his free hand. 'Yeah, to put it simply, a lot of our anger stems from losing Aidan.'

'I'm so sorry.'

'It was a long time ago.' His brow creases before he glances up at me. 'You know much about him?'

'Aidan? Um... no, not really. I know he was a tennis player, too.'

'Much better than me,' he says wryly. 'That was always the way since we were kids. He was the one destined for glory. Dad told me that before he died, and he continued to tell me afterwards. It felt wrong to carry on playing after we lost him, but it gave me purpose to get up every day.' He knits his eyebrows together thoughtfully. 'In the end, tennis saved me.'

I smile warmly at him and I think it catches him off-guard. He frowns uneasily, as though he's suddenly realised what he's talking about. He knocks back the final dregs in his glass.

'Top-up?' he asks, getting up.

'Sure.'

He goes to the kitchen to get the bottle while I shuffle down the sofa to put his glass on one of the coasters. When he returns, he notices, filling my drink and making a point of finding a new coaster on which to place the bottle.

He nods to the three-wick candle set in the middle of the table. 'Do you ever light that thing? Or is it here for show?'

'Iris bought it for me when Jonah moved out and I'm yet to light it.'

He gives me a strange look. 'What is it that you're waiting for?'

'It's just so nice, I kept thinking I'd save it for a special occasion.'

'I used to do that with wine. I'd refuse to drink the expensive stuff and then I realised that I was denying myself the good stuff that was left forgotten on the rack. It seemed… stupid.'

'You're right. It is stupid. I don't know what I'm waiting for.'

He arches a brow. 'You want to light the candle?'

'Yes,' I state firmly. 'I want to light the bloody candle.'

He breaks into an unexpected grin, his dimples appearing and making my stomach flip. 'Great. I like a good candle. Where can I find a lighter?'

'There should be one in the kitchen drawers, in the cutlery one I think.'

He disappears again and I smile to myself, nestling back into the cushions. It strikes me that it's strange to be spending the evening talking to Kieran O'Sullivan over a glass of wine and a three-wick candle, but it's even stranger how it doesn't feel strange at all.

'Got it,' Kieran announces, waving it in one hand and holding something else up in the other. 'And look what else I found.'

I peer at him. 'Is that a garlic press?'

'This not what your one said he was here for earlier?' he checks, bending over to carefully light the candle. As he leans forwards to click the lighter, my eyes linger on the tanned skin of his arms and how his bicep strains against the fabric of his T-shirt. I'm reminded of how it felt to be locked in those very arms, pressed against his warm, solid body, and a flurry of tingles races through my body, covering my skin in goosebumps.

'Uh yeah,' I say, swallowing. 'That's true. God.' I close my eyes, pressing my forehead into my palm. 'He couldn't have come up with something better than a garlic press?'

'It's a sophisticated apparatus,' Kieran remarks, pretending to examine it carefully as he takes his seat. I realise we're sitting much closer since I moved up his end of the sofa to sort his glass out on the coaster and didn't shuffle back. If I were to twist to face him properly, our knees would be touching. 'I can understand why a pretentious shite like him would make the journey here for it.'

'He really is a pretentious shite,' I concede, my repetition of his phrase highlighting my clipped accent in comparison to his Dublin lilt. 'I once went to a party thrown by his castmates, and while I was there I was going on about him being a great songwriter. When we got home, he said that he was embarrassed I kept calling him a "songwriter", because it sounded too basic. He asked if, in the future, I could refer to him as a lyricist or musical poet.'

Kieran splutters on his sip of wine, leaning forwards and thumping his chest. Giggling, I bite my lip as he finishes coughing and looks up at me.

'You're kidding,' he wheezes.

'I wish I was.'

He bursts out laughing. I haven't seen this before. God, he's beautiful when he laughs like that, his eyes creasing, his dimples on full show. His whole face transforms with pure joy. Suddenly it's all I want to do for the rest of the evening. Make this man laugh.

'Musical poet. Wow. That guy.' Kieran shakes his head in disbelief. 'I don't understand how you ever listened to the misguided opinion of some... pompous arse like him.'

'It's easy to believe someone's opinion about you when you already think it about yourself,' I reason, twirling the stem of the glass around in my fingers. 'If no one supports you, you can easily convince yourself you don't have what it takes.'

He sits back, watching me. 'What about your family?'

I hesitate. 'Uh, my grandmother was supportive. My dad, not so much.'

He raises his eyebrows. 'You're not close with him?'

'He left when I was young and he's more invested in his new family. He lives in the US and we catch up every now and then, but our relationship is a bit stilted. We don't really know how to be around each other. He's all right, but it's always very formal.'

Kieran frowns, shifting in his seat. 'And your mum?'

I drop my eyes to my lap. 'She died when I was nineteen.'

'Oh shit, Flora, I'm sorry.'

'No, it's fine. Well, I mean, you know, it's not fine. Anyway, thank you.' I take a deep breath. 'She had issues with alcohol. It was hard. She wasn't a bad person, but she did some bad things. We weren't that close in the end.'

He nods. We fall into silence. He's wearing a concerned expression and I feel guilty that my reluctance to talk about Mum has brought our flowing conversation to a standstill. It's been nice to see Kieran relax a little.

'Why do you play so much PlayStation?' I ask suddenly, noticing it.

'It stops me from thinking about tennis,' he answers simply.

'You think about tennis that much, huh?'

'Quite a bit.'

'Are you thinking about it now?'

The corners of his mouth twitch. 'You just brought it up, so yeah. Do you play?'

'Tennis? No. Not really. I like ping-pong though.'

'Yeah?' He looks impressed. 'I'm quite good at ping-pong.'

I roll my eyes. 'Obviously.'

'It's actually a very different skill to tennis,' he says defensively.

'Uh-huh. Sure.'

'It is!' he insists.

'Kieran, stop trying to make out as though you're talented at two sports. You're talented at one sport, it just so happens you can play on a big court and on a mini one.'

'This just sounds like you're too chicken to face me.'

'*Excuse* me?'

He shrugs, a hint of amusement across his expression. 'It's okay. You can admit that you're scared. It would be like saying you're too scared to take on a professional polo player in a game of croquet – I can understand you'd feel intimidated by me.'

'I'm not intimidated by you.' I narrow my eyes at him. 'Are you challenging me to a ping-pong match?'

'If you were brave enough to play, then why not?'

'Oh, I'm brave enough. Fine, if we happen to come across a ping-pong table in the future, I will happily play you.'

'Good. I look forward to it.'

'Me too.'

We take a beat, and as I swallow, I notice his eyes flicker down to my mouth. I part my lips, before his gaze returns to meet mine and suddenly the air feels different, charged and exciting. When he looks away, he frowns uneasily, taking a sip of wine.

'This is really nice wine,' I remark, flustered, desperate to cut through the silence. 'Much nicer than the stuff I usually have in my fridge.'

'I'm glad you like it. It's a Sancerre.'

'Expensive. Are you into wine?'

'A little.'

I hesitate. 'Can I ask you a question? It may sound insulting at first, but I'm genuinely curious.'

He quirks a brow, relaxing a little. 'Intriguing. All right, what is it?'

'Are athletes supposed to drink when they're playing a big tournament? I just thought you'd be on this huge health drive, no booze allowed kind of thing,' I say hurriedly. 'But then here we are tonight, and then you were out the other night...'

'Yeah, it's probably not the smartest tactic. But hey, I've done all that health-drive stuff before. When I was younger and I was taken seriously, I was very strict. It didn't work out for me, so I got to the stage where I didn't see the point in denying myself a drink every now and then.'

I frown at him. 'What do you mean?'

'If it's the lead-up to the tournament and I feel like a glass of wine or a pint at the pub, then I'm not going to say no to—'

'No, I meant, what do you mean when you were young you were taken seriously?' I clarify. 'That sounds like you're insinuating you're not taken seriously now.'

'Oh. Well, I'm getting on now. I haven't done badly recently but I'm not such a big name in the sport anymore. I'm probably going to retire this year.' He cocks his head, unsure as to why I'm looking at him so strangely. 'I'm not expected to win.'

'But... don't you want to win?'

He blinks at me. 'Yeah, everyone wants to win. I've had enough chances, though, and whenever I got close...' he pauses, his brow creasing as he tries to find the right words '...I kept losing.' He drops his eyes and adds so quietly it's almost inaudible, 'Aidan would have kept winning.'

And suddenly, for just a fleeting moment, I once again catch a glimpse of a different Kieran to the one the world is presented with on court. With his shoulders slumped forward, his eyes gleaming with sadness, he seems defenceless and fragile. He's lost and alone in his thoughts, a boy who has had to carry a crippling weight of expectation and grief on his shoulders for years.

When he clears his throat and lifts his head, the boy is gone.

'So, in answer to your question, I allow myself the small pleasure of a nice glass of wine or a pint down the local, because why not?' He plasters on a smile and takes a sip of his drink, forcing his voice to be carefree and upbeat. 'When I lose at Wimbledon, I can blame it on the Sancerre.'

'Who says you're going to lose at Wimbledon?'

My direct comment catches him by surprise. He raises his eyebrows, stunned into silence. I stare right back at him with all seriousness.

'Flossie, let's be honest. I've never even got to the finals here before.'

I shrug. 'So?'

'So, I have to be realistic. No one thinks I have it in me to win.'

'*You* did,' I correct him.

'What?'

'There was an interview you did years ago. You said you would win Wimbledon.'

His expression darkens, his eyes glazing over with pain. 'I was a young brat,' he says, his voice low and strained. 'I had no idea about anything. I shouldn't have done that interview. The stuff they printed about what I said about Aidan... it was taken out of context. I didn't mean—'

'Kieran, I'm not talking about what you said about Aidan,' I say, leaning forwards, my knee grazing against his as I shift and sending a jolt through my body. 'I'm interested in what you said about *you*.'

He stares at me, his jaw clenched.

'Just because you haven't done it before, doesn't mean you won't win now,' I assert, not sure when I became an expert on professional competing but probably somewhere between my last gulp of wine and now. 'The way you spoke in that interview, I believed you.'

'You think... I still have it in me to win?' he asks quietly.

'Do you?'

Taking a deep breath in, he sips his wine.

'This is Wimbledon, right? Anything can happen,' I remind him.

He lowers his glass, his striking eyes sparkling at me. And then he breaks into a smile, a small one but it's so genuine and hopeful and inviting, that it makes my heart somersault and my breath catch in my throat. *Those dimples*.

It's not until much later in the evening when we've gone to bed that I realise what is niggling at the back of my brain. He called me Flossie.

I liked it.

11

I don't know how to act around Kieran. Something feels different now, and when we're together, I feel constantly on edge and aware of every single movement either of us make. In the week leading up to Wimbledon, he's not around so much due to his training, treatments and team discussions I guess, and I keep looking for excuses to be busy and get out the house in an attempt to stop my mind aimlessly drifting to Kieran and how he looks when he's only wearing a towel. I'm not going to lie, it's very nice to think about, but it's stopping me from focusing on anything else at all.

I've tried to lose myself in my art, but all I've managed to do this week are meaningless doodles – nothing with substance. I spent a whole afternoon sketching this picture of two figures lying next to each other by a lake, her head resting in the nook of his neck, her eyes closed as he gazes down at her. It's a nice, peaceful scene, but what's the point in it? There's no story to it; I have no idea who these people are or what they want. It's a picture of nothing.

I've been for dinner twice with Iris this week, and I even went to the cinema on my own one night despite it being one of the hottest days we've had this month. I thought I'd go watch a romance in the hope of getting some inspiration for my book, but I sat there in a near-empty theatre watching a movie about two people who are all wrong for each other falling in love, sweating my butt off because the aircon was broken and thinking about Kieran and his strong sexy arms the whole bloody time.

I'd really love for the weather to make up its fucking mind. The organisers of Wimbledon must be on the edge of their seats, wondering how on earth it's going to play out for them this year.

On the Friday before the start of the tournament, Kieran walks in to find me pinging one of his resistance bands against the wall in exasperation. In the middle of swigging from his water bottle, he stops abruptly in the doorway of the living room, taking in the pushed-aside coffee table and one of his mats rolled out on the carpet. His eyes travel down my dark green sports bra and leggings and back up again. My skin heats under his gaze, my pulse quickening as his mouth parts ever so slightly.

'What are you doing?' he asks quietly, studying me.

'I'm attempting a workout,' I admit, flicking my loose ponytail back from my shoulder. 'But it's not going well.'

He nods to his resistance band now lying on the floor across the room.

'You know you don't use that like a catapult, right?' he asks, a bemused smile playing across his lips.

'I know.' I lower my eyes to the floor, folding my arms across my chest. 'I was frustrated.'

'I see.' He leans against the doorframe. 'Sketching didn't go well today, then?'

'I still haven't started the book,' I mutter, disappointment shrouding my heart. 'It's been almost two weeks and I still don't have a story. I can't... I can't seem to focus.' I decide not to elaborate on why that may be, burying my face in my hands. 'Argh, what am I doing? I've basically wasted two weeks when I could have been working and earning. What is wrong with me?'

A few moments later, I feel the warm grip of his fingers wrap around my wrists, encouraging me to lower my hands and as I do so, I look up into his eyes as he stands right in front of me, my breath catching in my throat.

'You haven't wasted this time, Flossie, it's all part of the process,' he insists gently, his hands still holding mine, oblivious to the effect his touch is having on me as my heart races and my mouth runs dry. 'I know that you're organised, but you can't schedule when you're going to have a good idea.'

I swallow, forcing myself to look up into his eyes.

'So, what do I do?' I ask helplessly.

He lets go of my hands and takes a step back, tilting his head and looking at me thoughtfully. 'You need to find an outlet for that frustration and let your mind clear.'

'Okay. Any ideas? What do you do when you need to calm and clear your mind, like before a match?'

He shrugs. 'I don't do anything.'

'What? Surely you do something. What's your pre-match ritual?'

'I don't have one,' he insists, chuckling at my obvious bewilderment. 'I just go out and play.'

'That's it? Nothing for luck? No superstitions? I thought that was standard for people in sport.'

'Not for me.' He arches a brow. 'I feel like I've disappointed you.'

'You have a little,' I admit, making him laugh. 'It's a bit boring not to have *anything* cool that you do before you walk on to play a game at Wimbledon. I think that needs to change, Kieran. I'll think of something.'

He points his finger at me sternly. 'I'm not doing any kind of jig.'

'Yes, thank you, Kieran, I'm aware you're not actually a leprechaun.' I roll my eyes, thrilled to see his shoulders shake with laughter. 'It will be something a bit more chill and subtle than that. Something that calms you, but also gears you up.'

'Sounds necessary. In the meantime, let's focus on your current predicament. How can we help get your creative juices flowing?'

'We?'

He nods. 'I happen to have a bit of time off this evening, and I have an idea that could help both of us.'

'Really. What might that be?' I breathe, my mind jumping to somewhere it should DEFINITELY not be going.

He slides past me to go to the chest in the corner of the room, giving me a moment to break out from whatever spell he seems to be able to hold over me now and collect myself. When I turn round to see what he's up to, he's opened the lid of the chest and is peering inside. He looks over his shoulder and grins at me.

'You lied to me,' he accuses.

I frown. 'About what?'

'You said you were into ping-pong, not tennis.'

'Yeah?'

He gives me a look and reaches into the chest to dig around a bit before he pulls out a tennis racket, spinning the handle round in his grip. 'Then what's this?'

'That's old. I'd forgotten it was even in there! I played a little back at school, but I don't play anymore.'

He looks unconvinced. 'You told me you moved here last year.'

'So?'

'So,' he begins, walking across the room to stand in front of me with the smug smile of a detective in a murder mystery, right before they give their big reveal, 'if you don't play anymore and don't intend to, then why would you bother to bring your tennis racket all the way from Norwich to London barely a year ago?'

I open my mouth, but I can't think of a retort. *Damn it.*

He peers down at me. 'How about a game?'

I dissolve into a fit of laughter. 'Seriously? You want *me* to play tennis with *you*?'

'Why not?'

'You're Kieran fucking O'Sullivan!' I point out, aghast. 'I can't play tennis with you. It would be absolutely humiliating. I'm average at best and you're a professional, world-ranked player. There would literally be no point.'

'Go on, Flossie,' he chuckles softly. 'I'll go easy on you, I promise.'

He reaches up to tuck a loose lock of my hair behind my ear and my breath catches at the touch of his fingertips lightly brushing across my skin. I dig my teeth into my bottom lip and his eyes drop to my mouth.

Oh my God.

His hand lingers a touch too long at my cheekbone, before he swallows and blinks, as though he's been on autopilot and has suddenly realised what he's doing. He drops his hand quickly and pulls back, clearing his throat.

'What do you say, then?' he asks, going back to studying the racket. 'Fancy giving it a go? You never know, it might be exactly what you need.'

'All right, fine. If anything, it will at least be a good laugh.'

He breaks into a relieved smile. 'This will be fun.'

'You need to run for the ball, Flossie,' Kieran instructs. 'Not watch it bounce by.'

'You did that drop shot on purpose,' I accuse him, jogging to fetch the tennis ball from the back of the court.

We've come to the outdoor tennis courts in the park – for one terrifying and ludicrous moment on our way here, I did wonder whether he might be leading me in the direction of the All England Lawn Tennis Club and I panicked at the fact that not only was my standard nowhere near the levels they'd expect from members there, but I had also just thrown on an old baggy T-shirt over my workout gear and some scruffy trainers before we left. I didn't look Wimbledon-ready.

The courts were busy, but we arrived as a pair were leaving, and managed to bag one. So far, no one has noticed that they're playing on a court along from Kieran.

'Yeah, I do every shot on purpose,' Kieran calls out and I can hear him rolling his eyes. 'It wouldn't be great tennis if the shots I played were all by accident. You've been bolting around this court brilliantly; you could have got that one if you'd tried.'

Picking up the ball, I spin round to glare at him. 'I wasn't expecting it.'

'Again, kind of part and parcel of tennis playing: you don't know what shot your opponent is going to play. You have to be on your toes, ready for anything. Like this.'

He arches forward at the hips, his feet shoulder-width apart, knees bent, his weight on the balls of his feet, bobbing side to side.

'You see?' he calls, spinning the racket handle round and round in his hands. 'I'm energised, I've got momentum on my side, whatever you bring at me, you can see I look ready for it, right?'

'I can see you look like a twat,' I mutter.

'I heard that!' he shouts. 'Here, come to the net. I want to try something.'

I allow a smile as I make my way across the court towards him. This has been a lot more fun than I was expecting and there's something extremely thrilling about a professional tennis player praising your forehand.

We started nice and easy, and he's now begun to up the ante as I've got more into it, sneaking some annoyingly good shots in there. It was also quite sweet when he cautiously asked me if I'd like him to give me some pointers or if I'd rather he just shut up and let me get on with it. I think he was trying to make sure I didn't think he was being all pompous, but I assured him that I'd happily take advantage of a free tennis lesson from a pro.

And I would never have expected this, but Kieran O'Sullivan is a pretty good teacher. He's so much more relaxed in this environment than when he plays professionally, which I guess is an obvious thing to say because he's not competing here. But I get the feeling that I'm not the only person getting something out of this session. It's like something in him has lit up – he's at ease, his eyes bright and invigorated, and he's joking and laughing. The world doesn't get to see this silly side of him. He's having a really good time, and, sadly, I don't think it's anything to do with me.

I think he's having a lot of fun coaching.

'Okay, so you know what I want to see more of, Flossie? Your aggression,' he says, meeting me at the net and folding his arms across his chest.

'I don't have any aggression.'

'Yes, you do,' he counters. 'Everyone does. You're playing too nice. I want you to find your fury and take it out on the ball.'

'I really don't have any upper body strength. I'm more of a casual tennis player. You know… I'm dainty and elegant.' He smirks and I give him a pointed look. 'I *am*.'

'Sure, but you're also fiery and powerful.'

'Where did you get that?' I mutter, raising my eyebrows.

'We're going to do some warm-up volleys and then I want to see you smash the ball when I feed the lob, okay? Get your racket back early so you can judge the flight of the ball properly and you want to hit it with your arm outstretched at your highest point.'

'Fine. I'll give it a go.'

'Show me that aggression. You'll feel great afterwards. It relieves tension, boosts morale. You'll feel empowered.'

'If you say so. But—' I say, narrowing my eyes at him '—if I miss all these lobs and feel like even more of a loser, you owe me a drink.'

'Okay. And if you do walk away from this feeling empowered, then you owe me one.'

'Deal.'

That's fine by me. Either way, I'm having a drink with Kieran, and that makes my chest tighten and my hands tingle. I shake them out, doing my best to give him a cool smile as I walk backwards from the net.

'Ready?' he checks, once we're both in position.

'Ready.'

We start with some soft, easy volleys and then he gives me a warning nod before sending the ball up high in a loop towards me. I watch it drop and then I hit it down. It plops near his right foot. He watches it bounce and dribble away down the court.

He turns back to face me, arching a brow. 'That was…
terrible.'

'It was dainty!'

'Let's go again.'

After another well-positioned attempt, but lacking in power,
Kieran puts his hands on his hips and gestures for me to come
meet him at the net again. I tip back my head and groan,
preparing myself for either a lecture or a pep talk.

'Why can't you just accept that I'm not the sort of person
who can smash a tennis ball?' I query, picking at the grip of my
racket. 'I'm not competitive; I don't have the fire in me that you
do.'

'Yes, you do,' he insists, his eyes boring into mine. 'And I know
that, because on the day we met, you threw a drink at me.'

I hesitate. 'I was having a bad day and you really pissed me
off.'

'I made you angry.'

'Yes, you did.'

'What else makes you angry, aside from me of course?' he
asks with a sly, secretive smile, as though he knows something
I don't.

I shrug. 'I don't know.'

'Take your time. Think about it.'

Plucking nervously at the strings on my racket, I eventually
let out a heavy sigh. 'The way Jonah made me feel about myself.
That he has this ability to say things that reinforce my own
doubts and flaws.'

'He makes you feel small and powerless,' Kieran says in a low,
understanding voice.

'Yeah. But I can't blame that all on him. I guess it's hard to
have confidence and self-esteem when my dad left me, and Mum
was too caught up struggling with her own demons to notice
what I needed.' I hesitate, frowning at him. 'Is this becoming a
strange kind of therapy session?'

His lips twitch into a smile, his expression softening. 'Tennis can be therapy to me,' he admits, glancing across at the other people playing on the courts down the way. 'When I feel in control on the court, it helps.'

He's doing that thing again, offering me a glance at the weary, vulnerable guy hidden behind a carefully constructed brash and conceited reputation. It makes me want to leap over this net and hold him, and tell him that it's okay.

'And when you smash a ball,' I say calmly, 'it reminds you that you're not so powerless after all.'

He tilts his head at me. 'You want another go?'

'Yes. I do.' I nod vigorously, pumping myself up. 'Lob the ball. I think I've got this.'

'Okay,' he says, pointing his racket at me. 'I know you do.'

We move back to our starting points and this time I feel determined and focused, bending my knees and holding my racket steady. Kieran feeds the ball. Guiding the ball with one arm as it soars up into the air, I wait for it to come down in front of me, slightly to the right of centre, and I reach up with all my might, bringing my racket down on top of it with all the force I can muster.

The ball smashes down on his side of the court, bouncing just inside the singles line and flying out of play. It's a beautiful, powerful shot. And it feels *great*.

His mouth hanging open, Kieran lifts his hands in the air and whoops loudly, causing others to look in our direction. I burst out laughing, running a hand through my hair.

'That was INCREDIBLE!' Kieran cries, tucking his racket under his arm so he can give me an enthusiastic round of applause. 'Flossie, that smash was perfect. You'd have a hard time returning that one, let me tell you.'

'I can't believe I made that shot,' I breathe proudly.

'I can,' he says, his eyes twinkling at me, the creases around them deepening as his warm, sincere smile widens. 'I knew you had that in you.'

12

I'm waiting for him to come home. *Literally* waiting. Checking the time on my phone excitedly, sitting up straight whenever a car drives past. Finally, one slows and comes to a stop, before I hear a car door open and shut, and his bounding footsteps up to the door. As his key turns in the lock, I jump to attention, ready for when he appears in the room.

'Hey,' he says warmly, before he notices the pricey bottle of wine and the two glasses set out on the table next to the flickering candle. He glances up at me curiously. 'You lit the three-wick. What's the occasion?'

'I wanted to thank you for helping me with the tennis lesson yesterday,' I say, hoping I don't sound as nervous as I feel. 'Is this okay, or should you not be drinking two days out from Wimbledon?'

He doesn't say anything, his eyes flickering down to the neckline of my dress.

I've actually been in a T-shirt and pyjamas all day, but I put this on half an hour ago in preparation for his arrival. It's a blue and white mini summer dress with a sweetheart neckline and spaghetti straps. A lot of skin is on show and I've always felt sexy and confident in it. I want to feel that way with him because of what happened last night before we went to bed – it was such a small gesture, it may not have meant anything, but if there's a chance that it did... I guess, I want him to know that it meant something to me.

Last night, after we'd both got ready for bed, I was getting a glass of water in the kitchen, and he came into the room. Usually, he might say goodnight, but yesterday was different. Yesterday, he came over to where I was standing by the sink and leant towards me to kiss me softly on the cheek, just a centimetre from the corner of my lips. He pulled back, but kept his head dipped to look straight into my eyes.

'Goodnight,' he'd said huskily.

'Night,' I'd managed to whisper, my heart in my throat.

He'd lingered there for a moment and then frowned, before turning and leaving the room. It was only once he'd left the kitchen that I'd exhaled, steadying myself on the edge of the sink, my legs shaking. I had tossed and turned on the sofa most of the night, unable to stop thinking about him, a warm tingling sensation spilling through my body.

Up until a week ago I was under the impression that he was a short-tempered, uncompromising, ill-mannered stubborn prick who couldn't use a coaster. But his walls are crumbling, and hidden behind them is a carefully guarded softness. He's proven to be kind and thoughtful. Within these walls, he's not so distant; he's observant and encouraging. The more I get to know him, the more I think the world has got him wrong.

I also think last night, he wanted to kiss me. And I wanted to kiss him back.

So that's why I've put on this dress.

'You look...' He swallows, removing his cap and running a hand through his damp hair. 'That's a nice dress.'

Just the reaction I was hoping for.

'Thanks.' I smile shyly, wilting under his gaze.

'I'm going to shower,' he says slowly. 'Then, we'll open that bottle. Okay?'

'Okay.'

He takes a beat, standing still in the doorway with his brow furrowed, his eyes pensive. He eventually leaves and, as I hear the shower turn on, I take a few deep breaths, trying to steady my heart rate. He must only take a few minutes to shower and change, but it feels like forever. By the time he reappears in a shirt and jeans, I've rearranged the coasters on the coffee table too many times to count.

Kieran joins me on the sofa and I pour him a glass of the red, handing it to him, before sorting one for myself. Neither of us say anything for a moment. The room feels charged and electrifying. I can sense him watching me as I lean forwards to place the bottle down, before swivelling on the edge of the seat to face him, tilting my glass towards him.

'Here's to feeling empowered on the tennis court. *Sláinte*,' I add, way too proud of myself for a quick google of how the Irish say 'cheers' before he got home. I practised the pronunciation and everything.

'*Sláinte*,' he repeats with a knowing smile, clinking his glass against mine and taking a sip. He emits a sound of approval and I breathe a sigh of relief. I'd had to ask the shop assistant for help in picking a bottle suitable for a sophisticated palate.

'How was your day?' I ask, hoping to sound breezy, but my voice is a lot higher-pitched than usual.

'Tough. But I played well today.' He takes a large gulp of wine, before glancing at me. 'I told Neil I had an extra training session with you yesterday, which must have helped.'

'You're welcome. If you need any tips, you know where to come.'

He almost smiles, fighting to keep a straight face. 'I also informed him I'd be introducing a ritual to my pre-match routine, I just didn't know what it was yet.'

I sip my wine. 'I'm glad he's on board.'

'I wouldn't go that far. He told me to stop talking shit and focus on the game.'

'Sounds like sage advice. Did he ask about how our living arrangement was going?'

'He asks every day.'

'And what do you tell him?'

His eyes lock with mine. 'That, so far, it's fine.'

I nod, taking a drink. He follows suit. I press my lips together. He taps his knee with his finger. I have another large gulp. *God.* I can't remember the last time I felt this nervous. I feel so alert, fizzing with energy and apprehension. I'm so painfully aware of every move either of us makes, I can't relax. My mind is racing. I wish I knew what he's thinking.

'I have to tell you something,' I blurt out.

He tilts his head. 'Okay.'

I bite my lip, unable to fight an excited smile. 'I started my book today.'

His eyes brighten and he leans forward, resting his elbows on his knees, his hands clasped around his glass. 'You're kidding.' When I shake my head, he breaks into a wide grin, his dimples sending my heart into a sequence of somersaults. 'Hey, congratulations. You had an idea?'

'It suddenly came to me.'

'It was the tennis. I knew it would help.'

'I started storyboarding and working out the characters, and I had a couple of scenes in my head that I had to sketch even though I haven't finished plotting.'

'Can I see them?' he asks eagerly. 'The sketches you did today.'

'No. Not all of them.'

His smile drops. 'What? Why not?'

'They're early sketches, first drafts! They don't mean anything yet. You'll have to wait until the book is finished.'

'It takes a long time to create a graphic novel – that could be a year from now,' he says slowly, frowning at me.

'Patience is a virtue,' I tease, before shooting him a sly grin. 'I did, however, think you deserved a sneak preview since you've been so integrated into the artistic process, so, I set aside one panel for you to look at. You want to see?'

He downs the rest of his wine and gets to his feet. '*Yes.* Where is it?'

'It's in the kitchen.'

Putting down my glass next to his and, standing up, I reach

for his hand, interlacing our fingers, and leading him out of the room. It feels so instinctive to take his hand in mine that I don't really think about how forward it is to do so until I notice his warm hand grasp mine tightly in return. I should feel apologetic for taking his hand so brazenly, embarrassed even, but I don't. He stays close behind me as I walk the few steps into the kitchen. I release his hand to turn and gesture to the sketch waiting for him on display on the table. He stops still, taking it in, before he moves to press both hands down either side of the page, leaning forwards to properly examine it.

It was the first panel I drew this morning, before I'd even thought of a story to go with it. It's just a rough draft of what it could be, there's no colour, but I'm proud of it all the same: it's a single framed box and in it you see the back of a young teenage boy wearing a hoodie and shorts, with headphones resting round his neck and his hands in his pockets. He's standing alone, looking out across a neglected tennis court in an empty public park, the net frayed, the lines faded. In the distance, the sun is setting.

The caption in the box above the character's head reveals his inner monologue:

It saved me.

I nervously wait for Kieran to react, studying his expression as closely as he's inspecting my sketch. He hasn't said anything. His breathing is slow and heavy. His jaw twitches. My stomach is twisting itself in knots from nerves. I can't wait any longer.

'What do you think?' I ask quietly. 'Do you like it? You inspired it. I was thinking about our chat yesterday on the court and how tennis can be therapeutic, and then I kept thinking about what you said to me the other day, about how tennis saved you after... after losing Aidan. I couldn't shake it.' I hesitate, digging my teeth into my bottom lip, the doubts creeping in. 'Maybe... maybe it's too personal. I don't want to make you feel as if I've intruded on how you feel. If you don't like it, it doesn't have to go in the book, it was just—'

'I like it,' he says, his voice cracking.

'Really? You do? You're not just saying that to be nice?'

He pushes himself up from the table, straightening and turning to face me. His eyes catch the light and I see that they're glistening. He fixes them on mine and steps towards me, closing the gap between us. He's going to kiss me. I want him to kiss me. *Please kiss me.*

I tilt my head up towards him, my breathing shaky and shallow.

'It's... perfect,' he says in a low, steady voice, reaching out to brush his fingers along my cheekbone, tucking my hair behind my ear, just like he did the other day.

But this time, he's not apologetic.

Cupping my face in his hands, he dips his head and presses his mouth to mine. His lips are soft and tentative at first, and I hear myself sigh as I close my eyes and melt into him, relief and elation flooding through my body. I reach up to wrap my arms around the back of his neck and his hands slip down to my waist to pull me closer to him.

The kiss grows deeper, his tongue caressing mine making me feel dizzy. He was holding back at first, but now that I've reciprocated, he's revealing how much he wants it and I'm returning the favour. He wants this; *I want this*. A growling noise comes from the back of his throat and my breath catches at his sudden urgency. I'm desperate to savour this moment, how he tastes, how his body feels pressed up against mine, but I'm hungry for what's next. I can feel him hard through his jeans, pushing against my stomach.

Giddy with excitement and anticipation, I find myself smiling against his lips. Keeping his brow pressed to mine, he breaks the kiss to briefly look at me, his eyes ablaze as he breaks into a grin, his dimples sending my heart into a frenzy.

No more waiting. I draw his mouth to mine again, feeling a thrill of satisfaction in my stomach as he leans into me, kissing me harder. I almost lose my balance and stumble backwards, but

I'm caught by his warm, strong hands that have been roaming freely over my back before they drop to my thighs. In one swift movement, he lifts me up onto the table without breaking the kiss.

Fuck, he's strong. He's so strong.

My legs naturally wrap around his waist, his hands moving my dress up, scrunching the hem around my hips. My thighs feel cold as his hands desert them to move to the small of my back, his muscular arms holding me in place. He runs his lips along my jaw and down my neck, my skin burning beneath them. I tip my head back and inhale sharply, arching my hips into him and causing him to let out an involuntary groan of pleasure, his warm breath tickling my collarbone and covering my skin in goosebumps. When he comes back up to claim my mouth fervently again, he nips my bottom lip.

I swear to God that one tiny nip makes my whole body shudder. My nipples are hard beneath my dress and there's a pulsing ache between my thighs. I want him closer.

Instinctively I tighten my legs around Kieran's back, causing him to groan again into my mouth, while his left hand slides up my back to find its way to my hair, grasping it with a gentle, exhilarating tug.

No one has ever kissed me like this. I've never felt so wanted, so needed.

His lips leave mine again to graze back along my collarbone, his fingers helping to clear their path by pulling at the shoulder strap of my dress and letting it drop over my shoulder. It's a signal and I respond by slipping my hands beneath his shirt, digging my fingernails into the skin of his hips, etching them along to the bottom of his spine. I can feel his erection twitch against me and I widen my knees, opening myself more fully for him.

Kieran lets out a low shaky breath against my skin. '*Christ,* Flossie.'

His mouth traces lower and I gasp at the feel of his stubble on my skin as his lips trail the low neckline of my dress. All the while his thumb is sliding closer up my legs, trailing and teasing suggestively along the top of my thong. I bite back a moan as he circles my clit through the lacy fabric.

'Do you want—' he begins, lifting his head to look into my eyes, his voice raspy and strained.

'Yes,' I answer before he can finish the question because for fuck's sake, *please*.

He leans back in and kisses me again, his lips demanding and urgent. I feel like my own lips are bruised and swollen, but I can't stop. I just want more.

'You have no idea,' he says between breaths, his thumb slipping beneath the fabric of my damp underwear. 'You're all I think about. All I fucking think about.'

My head tilts back and my hand curls instinctively around the nape of his neck, as I bite my lip and—

The doorbell goes.

We freeze, locked together, our breathing rasping and heavy in unison.

'Ignore it,' he whispers, but he doesn't sound convinced, and when it rings again and he rests his forehead in defeat against my shoulder, I realise that he must have been expecting someone.

Kieran steps back away from me and I slide off the table, letting my dress fall back down my thighs and nudging the strap into place over my shoulder. Reality sets back in and I immediately feel self-conscious. What just happened?

'That will be someone from my team,' Kieran says in a low, regretful voice. 'I... forgot. They said they'd come over later to... talk. Strategy and stuff.'

I nod, my cheeks flushing. 'Right. Of course. Sure. That makes sense.'

'I'm sorry.'

'Don't be,' I assure him, folding my arms across my body.

The bell rings again. Ignoring it, he sways towards me and his hand curves softly around my hip. Kieran looks at me searchingly before leaning in and kissing me, deeply and slowly, sending another delicious wave of heat rippling through my body. This kind of kiss could swear me off all other kisses from anyone else ever again.

As he pulls away, his hand lingers on my waist. His throat bobs, his hungry gaze searing into me and making my skin prickle, before he turns to leave the room. He didn't need to say anything, I understood everything from that silent exchange.

This isn't over.

13

Iris is already waiting for me at the café when I cross the road. Sitting at one of the outdoor tables in the sunshine wearing a red playsuit with tan strapped wedges, her dark hair swept over one shoulder accessorised with huge sunglasses and bright red lipstick. She looks like she should be on the set of a 1950s Hollywood movie. She's sitting back, sipping her coffee and people-watching with no idea that the whole street is watching her – men are double-taking as they stroll past, so distracted that they stumble into the chalkboard propped up on the pavement advertising the Wimbledon-themed speciality coffees.

She sees me and sits up straight, waving me over excitedly.

'How are you?' she asks, getting up to pull me into a hug as I approach. She smells like an expensive delicate floral perfume. 'I got you a flat white.'

'Perfect, thanks,' I gush, taking the seat opposite her.

She slides her sunglasses down her nose to peer at me over the top of them. 'Don't you look pretty. Your butt in those shorts – I'd kill for your figure.'

'Says the woman with those pins,' I remark, glancing down at her long slender legs, her ankles neatly crossed under her chair. 'You're sending the Village into meltdown.'

'Oh stop it, you,' she says with a dramatic sigh, before breaking into a grin. 'Isn't this weather glorious? If it stays like this tomorrow, it will be the perfect start to the tournament. God, I love it here in Wimbledon at this time of year. The atmosphere is unbeatable, don't you think?'

'I do,' I agree, taking a sip of coffee. 'There's nothing like it.'

'It's so exciting and fun. You can feel it in the air.'

She's right, the Village is buzzing with anticipation for tomorrow as it readies itself for the influx of people about to descend on this small south-west corner of London, the rest of the world watching eagerly to see who will be crowned the Champions of Wimbledon. Even someone actively against sport would be hard pushed not to get caught up in the joy and charm of it all.

And with the sun shining, everything seems that bit better. The flowers are blooming perfectly, the bar and restaurant fronts are bathed in a sparkling golden glow, and everyone seems to be in a good mood. I'm hit by a wave of gratitude to be sitting in Wimbledon right now with my best friend watching the world go by. We spend a moment quietly taking it in. We watch a group of friends taking it in turns to get photographs next to the shop that's covered its entire wall in purple and green flowers; we laugh at the dog walker trotting by with dogs all sporting some Wimbledon tennis neckerchiefs; and we can't help smiling at the kids on their way home from a party blowing bubbles, trying to pop them as they float up into the air, blown out of their reach with the gentle breeze.

'How fucking mesmerising are bubbles?!' Iris blurts out.

'They really are!' I agree enthusiastically. 'I was seriously entranced there.'

'We need to go get some bubbles after this. I've never felt more relaxed.'

'Me neither. Bubbles. What a revelation.'

She chuckles. 'Ah, I'm so grateful to be out of the office the next couple of weeks to cover the tournament.'

'The office is that bad?'

'Ugh.' She wrinkles her nose. 'It's worse than ever. I don't think I'll have a job much longer, if I'm honest. I'm trying not to freak out about it.'

'They wouldn't get rid of you,' I say sternly, lowering my cup.

'You're the best writer on the sports desk. I saw you launched your Wimbledon blog on the paper's app. Last year it was a huge hit, and this year will be the same.'

She shrugs. 'Other people can write that, Flora. I'm not indispensable.'

'But you *are*.'

She gives me a grateful smile. 'Unfortunately the powers that be don't always think the same way we do. Anyway, it's fine. All I can do is keep working my arse off and hopefully they'll keep me on for a bit longer.'

'If they let you go, then it's proof they're absolute idiots.'

'They already proved that with you, darling.' She tips her head back and sighs, adjusting her glasses as she squints into the sun. 'All this overtime is doing nothing for my love life, though. And I haven't had time to look for a flat, so I'm stuck with my parents for a bit longer.'

I grimace. 'How's that going?'

'Fucking awful,' she says bluntly, making me laugh. 'I hear them fighting all the time and then whenever I enter the room, they go all quiet.' She hesitates. 'I think something is going on with them, but they won't tell me. They treat me like a child still.'

I shrug. 'Natural for them to want to protect you.'

'Whatever, I need to move out ASAP. Now, enough about my boring life, let's talk about you.' She picks up her cup to take a sip. 'How is Kieran? Nervous about tomorrow?'

'I think so, but it's hard to tell.' I pause. 'We almost had sex last night.'

Iris sprays her coffee out all over the table, coughing and spluttering, thudding her chest with her fist. I giggle, passing her a napkin.

'Flora!' she cries, dabbing at her mouth with the napkin and then whipping off her sunglasses to stare at me accusingly. 'What the fuck?!'

'What?' I shrug innocently.

She throws her hands up. 'You let me sit here and talk about

WORK and my PARENTS when you and Kieran O'Sullivan *almost had sex last night*? Why the fuck are we talking about anything else?'

'Keep your voice down, please,' I hiss, glancing nervously at the passers-by.

'How did it happen?' she asks eagerly, putting her sunglasses back on and leaning across the table towards me. 'Tell me everything.'

'I don't know. We had a glass of wine and then... I don't know, it got heated.'

'Oh my God, this is amazing,' she squeals. 'Look at your face. You've gone all shy! Fuck, Flora, do you *like* him?'

I bite my lip. It's one thing admitting to myself that I can't stop daydreaming about him. A warmth pools in my stomach when I think about him and I love how he makes me feel, somehow shy and confident, excited and terrified, all at the same time. It's like I'm only scratching at the surface of his character and I'm desperate to know more. I like that he's started to open up to me. I *really* like how he kissed me. But to say any of this out loud makes it real. And if it becomes real, then the chance of getting hurt becomes real, too.

'I don't know,' I answer eventually.

Iris leans back in her chair with her arms crossed, a knowing smile spreading across her face. 'Uh-huh. So what happens now? You live in the same flat. Are you two going to, like, be together?'

'It was one night,' I remind her, placing my cup back down in its saucer. 'And we were interrupted by his coach. We didn't get the chance to talk about it. Plus, I don't want him worrying about... stuff like that. He needs to focus on Wimbledon.'

'That's true. I hear it could be his last hurrah,' she remarks, before giving me a hopeful look.

'You're not getting anything out of me. Take that journalist hat right off.'

She shoots me a mischievous grin. 'You know, you're genuinely glowing. You've got to give it to me, Flora, I predicted this. I said this would happen. And there is only one bed in that flat.'

'I've been on the sofa the whole time.'

'Yeah?' She snorts as she lifts her cup to her lips. 'Let's see how long that lasts.'

When Kieran gets back from training that evening, he's not alone. His whole entourage has accompanied him back to the flat and Neil is talking at him from the moment they step through the front door to when Kieran places his bag down on the floor next to the sofa in the living room. Kieran offers me an apologetic smile as I glance up from the sketch pad resting on my crossed legs on the sofa. Just the sight of him makes me feel giddy.

'You need to keep focused, Kieran. I don't know where your head is at today,' Neil is saying, before he follows Kieran's eyeline landing on me. 'Ah.'

'Hi, Neil,' I say brightly.

He frowns, putting his hands on his hips. 'I didn't realise you were in here.'

'That's okay, I can leave,' I offer, swinging my legs down to get up as his team start filing into the room.

'No, Flossie, you don't need to move,' Kieran begins, holding up his hand. 'Sorry, I should have warned you that a few people would be here; they just need to run through a few things if that's okay.'

'Of course. I'll go to your room and work in there. It's really no problem,' I assure him with a smile, dodging around the physio who has come in carrying a massage table.

Picking my way across the room under his gaze, I pop into the kitchen to grab a drink before I get out of their way and find his nutritionist in there, filling up our fridge.

'Would you like some Evian?' she offers, glancing at the tap water in my hand and gesturing to the crate of bottled water by her feet.

'I'm good, thanks,' I say, smiling to myself as I recall Kieran's aversion to tap.

He's such a diva, I think affectionately.

Tucked away in the bedroom, I'm so engrossed in my sketching that I don't notice the flat has fallen quiet an hour or so later until there's a soft rap on the door and Kieran comes in with a sheepish expression.

'Hey,' I say, noting his hoodie and pyjama bottoms, 'you've had an outfit change.'

'Slipped on something comfortable after the acupuncture,' he informs me, rubbing the back of his neck as he leans against the doorframe. 'I'm sorry about that. I feel bad that you had to shut yourself away in here.'

'Don't feel bad; I was really happy to draw,' I assure him brightly, getting up and moving across the room to the door. 'How did today go? How are you feeling about tomorrow? Confident?'

He shrugs. 'As confident as I can be. Neil wants me to spend the evening watching some videos to analyse my play.'

'Sounds fun.'

'Doesn't it,' he says drily.

'I… uh… I have something for you.'

He arches an eyebrow at me. 'A gift?'

'Sort of,' I answer, reaching into my back pocket to pull out a bottle of bubbles that I picked up from a shop on my way home from seeing Iris.

His forehead creases in confusion. 'Bubbles.'

'Do you remember blowing bubbles as a kid and being completely mesmerised by them to the point where you didn't care about anything else, you were just looking at pretty little bubbles floating through the air?'

He doesn't look convinced. 'Uh. I guess. Although I don't remember feeling that poetic about them.'

I roll my eyes at his teasing. 'It hit me today. Blowing bubbles is perfect for your pre-match ritual! It's calming and sweet and it focuses the mind. Here.' I lift his hand and press the bottle into his palm. He closes his fingers round it. 'Before you go on court, if you're nervous, you blow some bubbles and it will help you feel better.'

'You want me to sit in the men's locker room at Wimbledon blowing bubbles,' he clarifies. 'It will sure give the other lads a laugh.'

'Which is also relaxing! Laughter is therapeutic, reduces stress, boosts endorphins,' I list cheerfully. 'I am telling you, Kieran, we have found your pre-match *thing*.'

'Bubbles,' he repeats with a sigh.

'Yes,' I confirm. 'Bubbles. Personally, I think you should keep that bottle on you at all times. If you're really in trouble during a match, you can even blow bubbles during the breaks when you switch ends.'

He narrows his eyes at me, scrutinising my expression to check I'm being serious.

'Flossie,' he begins, sliding the bottle of bubbles into his pocket, 'if you ever see me on a court at Wimbledon blowing bubbles then you'll know I've officially lost it.'

'I'll know you're doing everything you can to win,' I challenge. 'And that would make me proud of you. Plus, you know, I'll get a little thrill from it.'

He quirks a brow. 'You'll get a thrill from my international humiliation.'

'No,' I sigh. 'It would be exciting to see you using this gift I personally gave you. I'll know you're... you're...'

I trail off, his intense gaze wiping the entire English language from my brain.

'You'll know I'm thinking of you,' he finishes for me, but his voice is uncertain and hopeful, as though he's not sure that he's got the correct answer.

There must be something in my eyes that tells him that's exactly what I want, because suddenly his mouth is on mine. He's kissing me as desperately as I'm kissing him, my back pushed up against the doorframe, one of his arms propped over my head, the other behind me, his hand pressing against the small of my back as I arch into him. My fingers slide into his hair and he lets out a low moan as his demanding tongue finds mine, heat pooling between my thighs at every stroke.

Oh God, he's so hot, so *fucking hot* and everything about him sends me into a dizzying spin of desire. How solid and warm his body feels pressing into mine, the way he smells so clean and musky and masculine, the way he's kissing me so roughly like he needs this as much as I do, maybe more. His hands are roaming everywhere, over my shoulders, splaying down my back, stroking the curve of my hips, teasing across my thighs, cupping my arse, back to my hips, his fingers digging into my skin.

'You're driving me *insane*,' he says through ragged breaths, leaning into me and kissing a path along my jaw. He doesn't need to tell me that. I can feel him hard and throbbing against my hip. I want him so much it makes every nerve ending tingle, every inch of me ache. But a small, niggling voice at the back of my mind fights back.

Pushing against every instinct in my body, I pull away from him. And it's torture.

'We shouldn't,' I whisper, hating myself as his nose nudges mine, looking for more. 'Tomorrow is so important, Kieran. You're playing in Wimbledon.'

'Fuck Wimbledon,' he growls, kissing me again.

He's making this so difficult. It's physically painful to bring this to a stop.

I force myself to turn my head away from his. 'No, don't say that. You've worked so hard for this. I'd never forgive myself if anything we did impacted how you play. Please, we have to stop. You need to be focused. And you have all those videos to watch.'

He exhales with frustration, his hands still gripping my hips, his fingers beneath my top, burning into my skin. Resting his forehead against mine, he swears under his breath.

'I want to,' I emphasise huskily, 'but it's important that you rest. We can't risk it.'

I don't know how but I find the will to step out of his grasp and he lets his hands drop to his sides, leaning back against the doorframe. He sighs, lifting his eyes to the ceiling.

'I'm sorry,' I say, tucking my hair behind my ears.

He shakes his head. 'No, you're right. I need to be on top form tomorrow. Don't want to wear myself out tonight. Besides, I've waited this long. I can wait a bit longer.'

I swallow, blushing. 'I know. I've been thinking about this all day.'

'That's nothing,' he says, bringing his eyes down to meet mine. 'I've been thinking about this since the day we met.'

14

I have so many butterflies flitting around my stomach I can't eat. I honestly don't know how Kieran possibly handles these nerves – if I'm feeling like this when I'm not even a player, how must he be feeling when he's the one about to step out on court any moment? The Wimbledon Championships just seem so DAUNTING. Seven rounds over two weeks: first, second, third, and fourth round, then quarter-finals, semi-finals, and lastly, the final. How are these players not completely exhausted by the time they get to the final?! They get, like, one day break between their matches during that first week. I've looked it up and, as Kieran is playing today, the first day of the tournament, if things go his way and he keeps knocking his opponents out, he'll be playing Monday, Wednesday, Friday, Sunday this week, and then Tuesday, Friday, and the final Sunday next week.

That is a LOT. I'm tired just thinking about it.

Also get this: you get paid £55,000 for reaching the first round of Wimbledon. Even if you get knocked out that first match, you get that money in your bank account. And it keeps going up from there; you get more prize money for each round you get to. That's just one tennis tournament in the year.

WHY am I not a professional tennis player?!

Although, the nerves are enough to put me off. When Neil came to collect Kieran this morning, he told me that he would be playing on Court Seven, which isn't being broadcast with the main coverage on BBC One, but I'm able to live-stream on iPlayer. That was pretty much the extent of our conversation while he waited in the living room for Kieran to get ready to leave. Neil is definitely suspicious of me. After I'd finished offering him every variety of drink available in the house – of which there are quite a few, thanks to Kieran's nutritionist – and he'd politely declined all of them, he stood by the fireplace looking at his phone while I sat down and pretended to look at mine. Out of the corner of my eye, I could see him glancing at me every now and then with his brow furrowed, as though he was trying to work me out.

Kieran and I had an awkward goodbye thanks to Neil's presence. If Neil hadn't been there, I would have hugged him or *something*, but because he was watching us like a hawk, all I could do was smile at Kieran and say, 'You've got this,' before he was ushered out the door. I hope he remembered to bring the bubbles in his tennis bag.

Perched now on the edge of the sofa, I take a deep breath as I watch him and his opponent walk out on court. I feel a swell of pride at knowing him. I can't believe I've *kissed* this man. My heart sinks as Jonah's voice flits across my brain, reminding me that there must be a few women who have felt like this when Kieran O'Sullivan walks onto the court.

You can't think he's genuinely serious about you.

This morning, I put on a Wimbledon podcast that had an Irish commentator on it while I made a cup of tea, and when Kieran's name came up, I stopped what I was doing to listen, standing still in the middle of the kitchen floor. '*Kieran O'Sullivan has talent, but he's never quite lived up to his potential*,' the presenter was saying in exasperation. '*If you want to win Wimbledon, you have to be controlled mentally, but he's too volatile. He's just not a level-headed guy out there. He's had many chances and he's always bottled it. But hey, he's a lovely player to watch... when he controls his temper. Maybe he'll surprise us this year. But honestly? I'm not holding my breath. John, what do you think?*'

I switched it off.

Then, I sat down at the kitchen table. I opened my pad to a clean page, selected a pencil from the tin and I started sketching.

Before I switched on the TV to watch Kieran's match, I actually managed to finish a draft of the panel I'd hoped to complete today, so I feel like I've accomplished something.

Ever since the story idea sparked into my head, it's as though the characters have invented themselves without much work from me. They're driving the plot themselves and every now and then, I'll find myself sketching something about them that takes me a little bit by surprise – sometimes that alters the plot I'd planned a little – but that's okay. I'm happily losing myself in their story every day, learning about them as I go. I can't describe the feeling I get when I'm drawing. I'm not sure you can even call it a feeling. It's more of a state, a contented haze that I get to enter from which the rest of the world is completely shut off. I haven't found this place in a long time and I was scared I'd never get to retreat to it again, but recently I can't stop stepping back into it whenever I get the chance.

Even if this story goes nowhere, even if it doesn't become the graphic novel I'm hoping it will be, I'm so grateful that it's taken me this far. It may sound strange, but when I'm sketching, I know I'm doing what I'm *meant* to be doing.

I wonder if that's how Kieran feels when he plays tennis.

At least with my chosen art form, I can enjoy it alone without anyone else muscling in on it, but I guess you don't have that luxury in sport. Kieran's opponent in the first round is a young Swiss guy, Alex Berger, who, according to my googling, has a killer serve. 'Power, power, power' is how the article described Berger's style, which sounds mildly terrifying and, from the look of him, that does make sense. He's shorter than Kieran, but seems to be pure muscle, his biceps filling the short sleeves of his white shirt, his thick thighs stretching the fabric of his shorts.

When Kieran strolls to the baseline to start their warm-up, my stomach twists and lurches. Chewing my thumbnail, I have no idea how I'm going to sit through this entire match alone.

FLORA
Are you watching him?

IRIS
No, I have to watch the play on centre court
But I'll keep checking the score when I can 🖤

I feel so nervous
I want him to win so badly

For him or for you? 🐿️
If he wins, he stays in the flat longer, right?

He's rented the flat out
for the whole tournament

Tennis players don't tend to hang around
Wimbledon once they've been knocked out 😵

So if he loses today,
he might leave today??

Maybe

I hadn't thought of that
Do you think he can win?

If he wants it badly enough
Wimbledon always has a few surprises in store

Shit it's starting

God, he's beautiful to watch. Kieran's a breathtaking Adonis flying across the grass court, so effortless, nimble and fast, so fluid and powerful. You can see the fire in his eyes as he goes for the ball with a fierce expression of grit and determination, whipping it over the net in one swift, flowing swing of his racket that has become a natural extension of his arm.

At the end of the first set, I conclude that his opponent has no chance. Kieran won it 6–4, and he looks like he's barely broken a sweat. When the camera zooms in on his face as he finishes swigging a bottle of cloudy vitamin water, his eyebrows are pulled together, his mouth a straight line – he's giving away nothing, but surely he can accept that he's got this in the bag. I'm absolutely buzzing! Now that I've seen what he can do, the nerves have morphed into smug satisfaction and I've taken the opportunity to swap my glass of water out for a can of Pimm's.

When in Rome.

The second set begins and I'm lounging happily on my sofa, cheering loudly at every winner, groaning in irritation at a point loss – although I suppose he has to let the other guy have something. When he breaks Berger's serve, I jump to my feet and applaud him enthusiastically on the off-chance he can hear my lone clapping through the TV, and when he takes the game and the second set, I'm up on my feet, cheering and whooping along with the Irish in the crowd, dancing around the living room floor.

FLORA
He is SMASHING this!!

IRIS
Don't jinx it

He's two sets up!!

Sounds like he's playing brilliantly
But this is the test

What test??

The third set
He has to keep his head

Does he normally lose his
head in the third set?

When you get close to winning you start
thinking about winning rather than each point
You know?

Not really
But I'm sure you're making sense
I'm not worried
He's killing it

🖐🖐

Also Pimm's is DELICIOUS

Why don't we drink this all year round?
It's an important question
You should address it on your blog
Stop writing about championships and tours
I want to hear more about Pimm's
Give the people what they want
I'm glad you're getting into the spirit of things
I love this game!!

I hate this game.

I absolutely *hate* this game. How is this possible? How is this *happening*? He's just lost the third set 6–2! It doesn't make any sense!

My head in my hands, I watch as the camera zooms in on Kieran dabbing the sweat off his neck with a towel before he tosses it on the chair next to him. His right leg is shaking. Or rather, he's shaking his right leg. I wonder if he even knows he's doing it. His jaw is twitching, his eyes have darkened – he looks more angry than determined.

'Keep your head,' I tell him through the screen. 'You've got this.'

But he can't hear me. *I hate that he can't hear me.*

It's time and he pushes himself sluggishly off the chair while his opponent springs to his feet, racing down his end of the court.

'No, no, no,' I mutter, frowning at Kieran as he plucks pointlessly at the strings of his racket. 'Don't lose hope. You're still a set up.'

Not for long. As the fourth set slips away from him, his whole demeanour changes and the atmosphere on court sours. He starts yelling at himself whenever he makes a mistake and knocking at his leg with his racket in frustration. The microphones can pick up on what he's saying as he tells himself it's 'not good enough' and to 'sort yourself out'. During an end change, Kieran spends too long at his chair fishing out another racket from his bag and the chair umpire prompts him again.

'Yes, I'm coming!' Kieran snaps.

The umpire lifts his eyebrows – he doesn't approve of the tone.

When Berger wins the set point with a masterful forehand, Kieran watches it fly past from the other side of the court, powerless, and he closes his eyes and nods. It's like he's accepted the loss.

I'm worried now, but I won't lose hope, and I try to send all those vibes through the screen to Kieran, willing him to believe in himself. It's the fifth set and the crowd are as invested in this match as I am. It's already been a rollercoaster and could go either way. He wins his serve, but then swiftly loses the next game. As he steps up to serve again, I am sitting on the edge of my seat, leaning forwards with my elbows resting on my knees, my jaw aching from how tightly my teeth are clenched.

Do not lose this game, I'm thinking over and over. Because I can tell that Kieran's confidence is hanging on by a thread and if the other guy breaks his serve, I'm not sure he will find the strength to come back. *I* know he has it in him, but I don't think he does.

Kieran kicks the game off with a powerful serve, but Berger gets the return. They embark on an extraordinary rally, both playing as though everything rests on this one point. Kieran gets in what I'd assume to be a lethal slice drop shot, but Berger miraculously reaches it, tapping it over the net as he stumbles over his feet. Kieran lunges forward and manages to lob the ball back. Only just recovering from the drop shot, Berger doesn't give up, racing backwards with his racket outstretched and sending it soaring back over the net to the baseline. Kieran isn't prepared, but he goes for it all the same and manages a clumsy return. Now in full control, his opponent calmly measures up the ball and thwacks the ball diagonally across the court to the open space. It should be a winning shot.

But Kieran has guessed his play and he's there.

It's like slow motion, the way his body rotates, pulling the racket back and then swinging it through the air in one smooth, silky flow of movement. A bright yellow blur, the ball zips over the net and lands just inside the singles sideline of the service box.

He's won the point. Just before he launches into an animated fist pump in celebration, I see the flash of surprise cross his face. Berger is flabbergasted. That one little point was the confidence boost he needed and now, nothing can stop him.

He's back in the game.

FLORA

What type of cake do you think is more appropriate
to celebrate getting through the first round of Wimbledon,
chocolate or red velvet? Or could go Victoria sponge??
Instead of Champagne, I'm going for English sparkling wine
I thought that's kind of on theme,
because it's an England tournament
Although now I think about it,
they serve Champagne at Wimbledon
Argh do you think he'd prefer Champagne??
I'll stick to my guns, it's already in the basket
How cute is this, I found tennis-themed napkins!!
They have little tennis balls all over them.
I bought two packs of 20
Probably a bit excessive
Also they only had HAPPY BIRTHDAY banners
so I got one of those and I'll just scribble over it
Hello?
Are you there?
Cool cool just talking to myself

IRIS

Wow
I was updating the blog so have just seen these
How many Pimm's have you had?

★

Kieran enters the flat arguing with Neil.

'You knew!' he snaps, as he steps through the door, his sharp voice echoing off the walls, sucking every ounce of excitement right out of me and making my blood turn cold. 'You knew this whole time and you didn't say anything! You lied to me.'

'I didn't lie to you!' Neil protests.

'You didn't tell me the truth, Neil. That's lying.'

Kieran storms into the living room with a thunderous expression, Neil hot on his heels. I'm standing stupidly under the HAPPY BIRTHDAY GETTING THROUGH TO THE SECOND ROUND banner, ready to pull a party popper, but I quickly realise that this is not the time. Kieran barely notices me. He's rubbing his forehead with his hand, looking pained.

'Kieran,' Neil says pleadingly, 'I was trying to protect you.'

'Protect me?' Kieran growls, rounding on him, his nostrils flaring with fury. 'I was *blindsided*. I was on a high, Neil, and the rug was swept out from under my fucking feet by a journalist who seems to know more about my life than I do.'

'I didn't want it to affect your performance,' Neil explains calmly, looking him in the eye. 'I knew it would be a blow and I didn't think you needed to deal with it right before the tournament.'

'And dealing with it after the first round of the tournament is much better,' Kieran scoffs.

'I had no idea the press knew about it. I wasn't even one hundred per cent sure it had been confirmed. If I'd had thought for a moment that someone might ask you—'

'You should have told me, Neil,' Kieran states coldly. 'I deserved to know.'

Neil swallows, his eyes glistening with regret. 'It might not be that bad,' he says quietly, pressing his hands together. 'It could be nothing and—'

'*Nothing*,' Kieran hisses, recoiling at the suggestion.

Neil can sense his poor choice of words and hangs his head.

Kieran shakes his head at him in disbelief.

His eyes land on me and he manages to whisper, 'Sorry, Flossie,' before he exits the room. I jump at the bedroom door slamming. Neil exhales, his breath shaking.

'*Shit*,' he whispers.

'What happened?' I ask, aghast.

He glances at me, his lips pursed.

'We had a press conference after the match. It was going very well until one of the reporters asked him what he thought about the news that his father has written a book.'

My mouth turns dry. 'A book about Kieran?'

Neil nods slowly. 'Kieran, Aidan, all of it. It's a memoir.'

'Oh my God,' I utter, my chest swelling with an ache of sympathy for him.

'I don't know how much you know about the O'Sullivan family, but I can't imagine Kieran will come out looking like the son of the year. And obviously, anything about Aidan—'

His eyes fall to the floor.

I'm too shocked to speak, my heart too heavy to say anything useful.

Eventually, Neil clears his throat. 'I should go. I'll be back in the morning to pick him up for training. Lots of work to do.' He hesitates, giving me a pointed look. 'Probably best to leave him tonight. Let him cool off.'

I nod.

'Right then.' He takes a deep breath. 'Goodnight.'

'Goodnight.'

He turns to leave, shuffling out of the room and down the hallway, each step weighed down with disappointment and regret. The front door shuts and the flat descends into an eerie silence. I go quietly into the kitchen to put away the cake.

15

'Do you want to talk about it?' I ask carefully, sinking down onto a chair opposite Kieran at the kitchen table.

He taps his fingers on the side of his coffee mug. I was wide awake when he left the flat this morning to go for his jog and by the time he got back, I'd showered and dressed, and made him one of his fruit smoothies to greet him with at the door. I've watched him make them enough times now to know all the ingredients. Flushed and out of breath, he'd taken it gratefully and retreated to the bedroom. Now, freshly showered, he's come to find me in the kitchen, taking his place at the table silently while I made coffee.

'I'm sorry about last night,' he says eventually, his eyes fixed to the table surface. 'I needed some time alone.'

'I understand. If you want to be on your own now, that's okay, too. I want to make sure you're all right, that's all.'

'I'm fine. In a bit of shock, but fine.'

He lifts his eyes to meet mine. They're filled with pain and uncertainty, and it makes me want to throw the table between us over on its side and rush to wrap him in my arms and hold him tight. Instead, I clasp my coffee mug and take a sip.

'You've seen the news by now,' he states, no need to make it a question.

The reveal of Brian O'Sullivan's book has hit the press, but the bigger story is Kieran's reaction to it. Since he was told about it at a press conference, there were several cameras on him at the time. All of them captured the colour drain from his face before he snaps that the conference is over and storms out the room, his chair tipping backwards from the force of his abrupt exit. You can tell that he didn't knock his chair on purpose, but many of the tabloids have gone with the juicy Kieran-O'Sullivan-throws-his-chair-in-fury angle.

'I'm so sorry, Kieran,' I say, my fingers itching to reach out to his hand resting on the table. 'You must feel so hurt.'

'I can't believe he would do this,' he says, his eyebrows knitting together in earnest bewilderment. 'Does he want to destroy me? And, worse, Aidan's memory?'

'Nothing could destroy Aidan's memory,' I assure him. 'You knew your brother, you loved him, that's all that matters.'

He sighs, closing his eyes for a moment. 'My reaction yesterday won't have helped matters,' he says bitterly. 'The publishers can be sure of good sales now. Everyone will want to hear about a fractured relationship so fucked up that I threw my chair across a room.'

'You know those headlines are ridiculous. Loads of people on social media are calling the tabloids out on that and saying it's clickbait. People are on your side,' I tell him, leaning forwards. 'People are also saying that they'd like *your* memoir, not your dad's. It's your story they're interested in.'

He snorts. 'They'll never be getting that. And while that's all very well, it doesn't mean his book won't sell. It will.'

I take a deep breath. 'Kieran, do you think... maybe you should talk to him?'

'Who? My dad?'

'Yeah.'

'No way,' he states, shaking his head. 'He didn't even have the respect to tell me he was writing the fucking thing, let alone that it was going to be published. I have nothing to say to that man.'

'Maybe if he knew how upset it was making you—'

'He knows,' he snaps, dismissing my suggestion with a wave of his hand. 'He doesn't care. You know he messaged me yesterday before the match? He texted me to say that I was going to win and that he'd be watching. Getting that message—' he inhales deeply, his voice cracking with emotion '—it made me want to win *for him*. Even after all this fucking time, after everything we've been through, I'm still trying to make my dad proud. It's pathetic.'

'It's not pathetic,' I say, hot tears pricking at my eyes, threatening to spill over. 'We all want our parents to be proud of us, it's natural.'

'I don't want anything to do with him,' he says forcefully, as though trying to convince himself. 'I didn't need this, not now.'

'You're right,' I say, unable to keep my distance any longer.

He glances up on hearing the legs of my chair scrape back across the floor as I get to my feet. I walk over to the chair next to him and sit down, taking his hands in mine and looking him in the eye.

'You *don't* need this now. Because you're here to win Wimbledon. You have to find a way to shut out the noise. All of it. The only thing that matters to you right now is the next point, got it?'

Tiny creases form around his eyes as he offers me a small smile, a pool of warmth filling my belly as I gaze at him, wondering how anyone could ever hurt someone with eyes this searing and so blatantly vulnerable.

Damn it, Brian O'Sullivan, you really are a fuckhead.

'You trying to coach me, Flossie?' Kieran asks softly.

'Sure.' I shrug. 'If it helps you to stop listening to all the other crap. I watched your match yesterday. You were brilliant.'

'I very almost lost.'

'You won.' I squeeze his hands. 'And you'll win again. And again and again and again until you're holding up that trophy and thanking me in your speech.'

He lets out a small laugh. 'I wouldn't get too ahead of yourself.'

'You know, if you could have heard me through the TV screen yesterday, that's *precisely* what you would have heard me saying to you.'

'Not to get ahead of myself?' He furrows his brow. 'In what way?'

'You know my friend Iris?'

He offers a weak smile. 'The sports journo who thinks I still have some fight left.'

'The very one. She said something to me yesterday that seemed confusing at the time but the more I think about it, I get what she means. She was talking about how when you – and I mean, people generally, not you specifically here – when you get closer to winning, you start thinking about *winning*. What it will mean to win, to you, to your family, to your fans, to your country. Fucking hell, Kieran, it must make your heart race a million miles per hour when you let yourself think about that!'

'A bit.'

'That pressure. It's hell!'

He's watching me carefully.

'Easier to not have those expectations, right?' I continue. 'If no one expects you to win, including yourself, the pressure ebbs away.'

He hesitates, tilting his head. 'What are you getting at?'

'There were moments yesterday when I think you got in your own head. You got ahead of yourself, thought about winning the match, and then maybe the doubts set in. Maybe you listened to that voice telling you that you couldn't do it. But then that first point of the third game in the fifth set – it was magical. You really fought for it.'

'Okay. But that was just one point.'

'That point changed everything,' I inform him as though I know what I'm talking about, letting go of his hands to sit back in my chair and fold my arms. 'You weren't trying to win, you were just playing tennis. That's what you should do.'

The corners of his lips twitch as he suppresses a laugh. 'That's your advice, coach? I should… play tennis?'

'My advice to you as an expert tennis player who really knows her shit—' I press my hand against my chest as he sniggers '—is that you should play for each shot. Forget what everyone else thinks, drown out the voices in your head, mostly yours, and focus on winning the next shot. Done.' I shrug. 'Then come home and eat cake.'

He arches a brow. 'There's cake here?'

'I went with Victoria sponge. Was that a good choice?'

'Perfect. I'm not mad about all the fancy flavour cakes out there nowadays; I like the old favourites.'

'Okay, Grandpa, I'll keep that in mind.'

'And thanks, by the way, for the banner.'

'You may not have noticed, but it was originally a Happy Birthday banner.'

'No, really?' he says in mock surprise. 'But the way you'd altered it with a black marker pen was so subtle!'

'I am seriously considering producing banners for any occasion as a side hustle to my non-existent art career.'

He smiles, mirroring my position and sitting back. 'Unbelievable.'

'That I would consider myself a serious banner creator?'

'That you've… I don't know.' He sighs, his eyes searching mine. 'I feel lighter.'

The doorbell rings and he stiffens.

'That will be Neil,' he mutters without moving from his chair.

'I'll get it,' I offer, standing up. Halfway out the room, I pause. 'Kieran, I don't want to overstep the mark and it really is none of my business, I don't know much about your relationship, but – Neil is your coach. He wants you to win. I think he really was trying to protect you from this.'

'He should have told me the truth. He knows what's gone down between me and Dad. They used to be friends.'

'That's kind of my point,' I say carefully. 'He knows you, Kieran. Maybe he didn't want you struggling with this when you already had the looming pressure of Wimbledon. Judging from how upset he was yesterday, at a guess I'd say he really cares about you.'

Kieran presses his lips together, refusing to say anything further. I go to get the door, standing aside to let Neil and the assistant coach in.

'He's in the kitchen,' I inform them, following them down the hallway and then diverting into the living room to locate my art supplies. Flicking through to a fresh page of my sketch pad, I overhear their conversation.

'Are you ready?' Neil asks him tentatively.

I hear movement and assume that Kieran has got up and is gathering his things.

'Kieran,' Neil continues, 'about yesterday—'

'It's fine, we're good,' Kieran cuts in. 'Let's just focus on how to win Wimbledon.'

'Right. Fine by me!' There's a note of pleasant surprise in Neil's voice. 'How to win Wimbledon. Let's do this.'

Before Kieran leaves for his match the next day, I catch him heading out the door and hand him a folded piece of paper.

'Are we passing secret notes in class, Flossie?' he whispers conspiratorially, as Neil stands waiting by the car, pointedly checking his watch.

Last night his team came back with him again and we didn't get any time alone. By the time they left, it was late and I made my intentions clear, getting under my duvet on the sofa before anything could happen. I can't trust myself around him. His kisses have become burned on my brain, replaying over and over, torturing me slowly. But these are not just any tennis matches he's playing, it's fucking *Wimbledon*. He has to focus on his game; he can't let me become any kind of distraction.

So last night when I couldn't sleep, while my mind drifted to him being on the other side of the bedroom door and my body burned at the thought of the way he's kissed me, I tried my best to convince myself that I was doing the right thing and did a sketch to give to him today. Now that I've started sketching again, I feel like I can't stop. Last night, creating this drawing helped me to understand how I was feeling and what I wanted to say – by giving it to him, I'm hoping it might help him in some way, too.

'Sort of,' I admit. 'Don't open it now, but maybe have a look before the match.'

'Okay, I'll try to find the time around blowing the bubbles.'

'Don't mock it. Maybe you won the first round thanks to bubbles.'

'Oh, don't you worry, I'm being serious,' he assures me, holding up his hands. 'It is fully integrated into my pre-match routine. Can't mess with whatever worked last time.'

'Good.' I smile smugly as he gazes down at the piece of paper, his eyes full of intrigue. 'It's nothing special; a little something to help get you in the zone. I drew it last night after you'd gone to bed. It's not for the book or anything, it's just… for you.'

'A Flossie Hendrix original.' He brings his eyes up to meet mine. 'I'm honoured.'

'Kieran, let's go,' Neil calls out.

Kieran ignores him, looking up at me hopefully. 'See you later?'

'See you later.'

'I just have to go play tennis. I'll play each point and then come back to eat cake,' he says robotically as though he's memorised it from a textbook. 'That's my plan today.'

I give him a thumbs up. 'You're playing for you. No one else.'

'Are you sure you don't want to be my coach—'

'Kieran!' Neil cries impatiently.

'—because there may be an opening soon,' he finishes drily.

I chuckle. 'I'll think about it. You should go.'

'Okay.' He holds up the piece of paper. 'Thanks for this.'

'I hope it helps.'

Nodding, his eyes flicker down to my lips. He swallows. My breath catches as his body sways ever so slightly towards me.

'*Kieran!*'

He winces at the sharpness in his coach's tone and draws back, making his way down the steps to the car. He turns to give me a wave before sliding into the back seat. I shut the front door and lean against the wall in the hallway for a moment to gather myself. That brief intense moment, whatever it was, has made me giddy and I have no idea how I'm going to concentrate on anything else today but him. My hands have become clammy and I shake them out. I really hope he likes the drawing.

It's another sketch of the back of someone, but this time it's of a man in tennis gear, walking out from the tunnel towards Centre Court of Wimbledon, surrounded by all the tiny blank faces of the stadium spectators. With his tennis bag slung over his shoulder and his other hand in his pocket, his head is bowed.

The caption below reads: *Believe when no one else does.*

16

The way Kieran's looking at me is making my heart race and my breath catch. He's standing over by the fireplace, one elbow resting on the mantelpiece, and he's meant to be listening to one of the several people in his team who all seem to be talking over each other, discussing what he did right today, what he did wrong, what he needs to work on, how he's going to win the third round. But he's not listening to them. He's staring at me as I linger awkwardly at the back of the room, his eyes fiercely intense, his jaw locked, his chest rising slow and steady. He almost looks angry, but there's more to it than that. *Hunger.*

When he got home this evening, I was unashamedly ready to greet him in the hallway. After a shaky start, it was a brilliant match and he deserved to win. He was down three games in the first set, and I could see him getting frustrated, but he sat down between the end change with his eyes closed, taking deep breaths and muttering something to himself. When the umpire announced, 'Time,' Kieran's eyes flashed open and there was something different about the way he stepped back onto the court. It was like a switch had flipped and he'd decided he wasn't going to lose after all. He won in three straight sets.

As I heard the car pull up, I stood in the hallway in a cute red summer dress, impatient to see him, but when the door opened, a crowd of people spilled into the flat and Kieran was somewhere in the middle of them. Now that he's through to the third round, I guess things are getting serious and his team aren't going to waste a spare moment of preparation.

His entourage, in a frenzy of excitement after his win, accompanied him home to start prepping him for his next opponent. I had managed to say a timid congratulations that he'd heard and tried to respond to, but Neil was talking over everyone, telling them where they should be and what they should be doing. I've been hoping they don't stay late again tonight. I just want some time alone with Kieran.

I'd nominated myself as drink-bearer, offering beverages to his team as they took over the living room. Having brought some chilled soft drinks through, I've found myself stuck in the corner at the back, waiting while Kieran's fitness specialists organised the gym equipment so I can dart back out again.

But I realised his eyes were on me the minute I looked up. He'd been watching me, waiting for me to notice. I smiled at first. A warm, beaming, you-did-it type smile, but he didn't smile back.

He looked at me as he's still looking at me now, a searing gaze that makes my brain scramble and my heart flutter with anticipation, my belly filling with warmth and fluttering butterflies all at once. Without dropping my gaze, the creases in his brow deepen and he lifts his hand to rub his mouth, agitated, while his assistant coach is saying something and pointing at the screen of his iPad. Kieran doesn't bother to pretend to seem interested. My heart is now thudding so loud it's in my ears, and the rest of the room has been reduced to white noise.

Swallowing, I part my lips. His eyes flare.

'Everyone out.'

The room falls silent as his team all turn to look at him, startled by his abrupt instruction.

'Kieran,' Neil says, his smile faltering as he observes Kieran's expression, 'we have a lot to go through and—'

'We'll go through it tomorrow,' Kieran interrupts, his voice low and severe, his eyes still fixed on me, melting me to the ground.

'Okay, but surely you want some physio tonight or—'

'Neil,' Kieran growls, ripping his gaze away from me to glare at his coach, 'I have won a big match today and I would like to rest so I can win the next one. I'm very grateful to everyone here and, frankly, the team deserves the night off, too. So, everybody *out*.'

After sharing some looks, the rest of his team gather their things and, after congratulating him once again, begin to file out the room. Neil doesn't move, his hands on his hips, his expression terse as he studies Kieran closely.

'You sure about this?' he says quietly.

'I'm sure,' Kieran replies, no hesitation.

Neil's chin juts out, before he holds up his hands and says, 'Okay. Okay, if this is what you want. You did well today. You can have the night off. But I want you on top form, ready to go when we arrive bright and early tomorrow. We have a fight on our hands next round. You need to be prepared. Got it?'

Kieran arches his brow in response, amused that Neil might think he's the one in charge right now. Finally acknowledging that Kieran's not going to budge, Neil turns and glances at me accusingly as he goes, exhaling audibly down the hallway. The last one to leave, he slams the front door shut behind him and the flat falls into silence.

Kieran and I remain on either side of the room.

The air between us is so charged, I can practically feel the sparks crackling.

'You... you were amazing today,' I manage to say.

'Do you know how I pulled it back in the first set to win?' he says, his expression serious, his voice strained and impatient.

My mouth is so dry under his intense gaze, I have to lick my lips.

'I thought about *this*,' he says.

He reaches into his pocket with his right hand and pulls out a folded piece of paper that he holds up, neatly wedged between his middle and forefinger. It's the sketch I gave him this morning before he left.

'The anger I felt at myself seemed to lessen,' he says, taking a couple of slow steps across the room towards me. 'The tightness in my chest eased. The anxiety loosened its grip.' Another step. 'The fog in my brain drifted.' And another. 'The fear dissolved.' One more step. 'My heart rate slowed.' He's right in front of me now, the intoxicating musky scent of his cologne filling my lungs and making my body tingle. 'For the first time in a long time, Flossie, I felt I could win.'

I can barely breathe, my heart thrumming.

'And you proved today that you can,' I whisper, bringing my eyes up to meet his.

His jaw ticks. 'Before each point, I tried to shut out all the voices, but there was one I couldn't shake. Yours.'

He reaches up to trail his fingers along my jaw.

'You're inside my head, Flossie Hendrix,' he states huskily, making me shiver.

His hand is suddenly curled at the nape of my neck and he pulls me towards him, his mouth clashing against mine violently, devouring me without wasting another moment. As his other hand grips at the curve of my hip, a swirling heat erupts through my body, consuming every part of me. My hands grasp his broad shoulders and I arch my hips into his, causing him to groan into my mouth, a sound so hot it sends a shudder down my spine.

This kiss is everything. He is everything. Nothing else matters. The world could be on fire, I don't care. I need more. *I need him.*

My hands fall to the hem of his shirt, and grasping fistfuls of the material, I yank it up and he breaks the kiss to finish what I've started, pulling it up over his head and dropping it on the floor. I swallow the lump in my throat as I admire the curves of his smooth muscled biceps and his impeccably toned torso. *Fuck.* This isn't fair. He's so perfect, he should be on every billboard in the city. I'd buy whatever he's selling. As he grabs my hips and pulls me back towards him, his mouth finds mine again, and my hands splay across his warm, solid chest, my fingers impatiently gliding over his skin to his groin, indulging in every indent, ridge and flex of muscle.

He responds by nibbling down my neck to my shoulders, making me shiver. His hands travel round my back, desperately hunting for the zip of my dress. He finds it, yanking it down hastily and letting the dress tumble to the floor. It crumples in a circle around my ankles and I step forwards to kick it away. Keeping his hands on my hips, he draws back briefly to look at me, his eyes widening as they roam down to my matching black lacy bra and thong before coming back to lock with mine, his scalding gaze igniting something wild and feverish in me.

He just has time to breathlessly mutter, 'You're fucking unbelievable,' before our mouths smash together again. An impulsive moan climbs up my throat and I can't stop it. The sound sends him into overdrive, his hands dropping to grip the back of my thighs before he picks me up in one swift movement, winding my legs around his waist.

Without breaking the kiss, he carries me into the hallway as though I weigh nothing at all and he moves towards the bedroom, one hand clasping the back of my thigh, the other pressing into my back, holding me in place. I feel so safe and small up here, cradled in his arms. *I'd go with him anywhere.* I cup his face in my hands, kissing it all over, nipping his mouth, trailing my lips softly along the prickly stubble of his jaw. I'm intoxicated by him and I want him to know that. I run my tongue along the skin below his ear, gently tugging at his earlobe with my teeth.

'*Flossie,*' he growls, knocking his elbow into the doorframe of our bedroom as a thrill rolls in my stomach at having the power to distract him.

He lowers me gently onto the bed, my legs still locked around his waist as he kneels on the duvet between them. Urging me to let him free for a moment, I unhook my ankles from his back and he begins to strip away the rest of his clothes down to his underwear, his glazed eyes fixed on mine the whole time, his expression serious and steady. Leaving his black boxers on, he places his hands either side of the pillow and dips his head to kiss me. Sinking my nails into his shoulder blades, I can feel the muscles tightening and flexing as he hovers above me before he props himself on his elbow, easing his weight down on top of me.

As his tongue parts my lips once more, his fingers graze over the lace of my bra. I respond by inhaling deeply so that my chest swells into his hand, a move that seems to destroy his last shreds of resolve, as he yanks down the fabric and squeezes my breast urgently. His hand follows the fabric of the bra round to the clasp at the back and I arch my spine to make it easier for him to unfasten it, in turn pressing my hips into the hard bulge of his boxers and causing him to groan deeply.

'You're so beautiful,' he tells me, heaving a sigh as he pulls my bra off and tosses it to the floor. 'And so sexy. So unbelievably sexy. *Christ.*'

A ripple of shyness flutters through my body as he takes a moment to look at me properly. He must notice something cross my expression, because he lowers himself down to kiss me gently, whispering, 'Are you sure you want this? We can stop.'

Before I can stop it, a laugh bubbles up my throat. 'Are you *kidding?*'

His lips twitch into a mischievous smile, his eyes flashing dangerously at me before he tilts his head to kiss the edge of my jaw, his breath in my ear as he murmurs, 'Say it.'

'Say what?'

'Tell me what you want.'

Heat pulses between my legs as I feel his lips on my neck. 'You know what I want.'

'Say it.' His kisses move down to my collarbone.

'I want this,' I breathe urgently. 'I want *you.*'

'Good,' he mutters against my skin, his tongue circling my nipple, one hand resting on my hip. 'Very good.' His hand slides down to the top of my thong, his finger trailing along the seam. He's tormenting me and it's agonising. 'And can I touch you here?'

'Yes.' I'm losing my mind and he's toying with me, the bastard. 'Kieran, *please.*'

I shift beneath him impatiently and he chuckles softly, before he takes my nipple into his mouth and slides his fingers beneath the edge of my thong, gliding down the damp material between my legs.

A tortured growl escapes his mouth, vibrating against my skin.

'*Fuck,*' he rasps. 'You're so wet.'

I've never been so turned on in my life, craving him more and more every second. After what feels like an eternity, he slides a finger inside me and I gasp, tilting my head back into the pillow and closing my eyes, moaning as he keeps thrusting, adding a second finger while his thumb circles my clit, sending sparks dancing behind my eyelids.

'Is that good? Like that?' he's asking breathlessly, but I can barely concentrate on what his words mean, let alone form ones that make sense enough to answer him.

All I can do is utter 'yes' repeatedly through soft whimpers and moans, losing control beneath his fingers as they work faster and harder.

He groans into my neck. 'You look so fucking good like this, you have no idea.'

When he pulls his fingers out, my breath catches with disappointment, but before I have the chance to beg him not to stop, he's moved to kiss a trail down from my belly button to the top edge of my thong, making my stomach tighten in anticipation. He removes my underwear completely, peeling it down my legs and dropping it over the side of the bed. He starts to kiss along the top of my thigh, before he runs his tongue around my clit and thrusts two fingers inside me again.

I gasp with pleasure, my spine arching. He lets out a moan of satisfaction at my response and as I feel it vibrate through me it nearly tips me over the edge. I grip the duvet beneath me, jolts of electricity shooting through my body. I've never been so close with someone so quickly before. It's a heady mixture of him being the sexiest man I've ever laid eyes on and someone who knows exactly what he's doing. I'm writhing beneath him, grinding into the rhythm of his hand and tongue, willingly powerless under his control.

My legs begin to tremor uncontrollably, the pressure mounting.

'Kieran, I... oh God... I'm going to...'

He doesn't let up, increasing the pace of his fingers in coordination with his tongue, sending me into spasms as I squeeze around his fingers and cry out his name, a flood of turbulent pleasure unfurling through my body.

I lie in a daze, my head spinning, my breath erratic and shaking as my body slowly starts to regroup. He moves to lean over me, kissing my neck as I reach out for him, gripping his shoulders, wanting him close, *needing* him closer.

'Oh my God,' I whisper, slowly emerging from my haze.

'How are you feeling?' he mutters, his lips grazing against my skin.

I exhale, my heart fluttering. 'I want more.'

Running my fingers down his chest, I reach beneath the waistband of his boxers, and hear his breath catch as my hand wraps around his cock.

Wow. I can't stop my eyes widening at how big he is, taking a beat to imagine what he'll feel like inside me, before I start to softly stroke him up and down, thrills rushing through me as his breathing grows heavier. His groans are causing an intensity to build between my legs again and I grip him firmer, moving my hand faster until he gasps, reaching down to grab my wrist and make me stop.

'If you keep going like that, I won't last much longer,' he says through gritted teeth.

I smile up at him, biting my lip and rolling across to my bedside table, propping myself up to open the drawer and find the box

I'm looking for. Lying back, I hold out the foil package and he takes it, tearing the condom open with his teeth and rolling it on. When he moves to settle between my legs, leaning over me, his eyes are blazing with heat and it makes my pulse quicken that I can have this effect on him, this unbelievably hot, sculpted guy who I'd never believed would look twice at me. But if I want proof he's as turned on as I am, I only have to glance down. His chest is heaving, but he hesitates.

'Are you sure?' he checks.

Removing any lingering doubt, I cradle his face in my hands and bring his lips to mine.

'Yes, I'm sure,' I whisper into his mouth and he kisses me.

My breath hitches as he enters, slow and a little cautious at first as my body opens to take him in. He feels so incredible, I know straight away that I'll be able to come again. He pulls back achingly slowly and then slides back in, rolling his hips, thrusting harder and deeper, and filling my body with fluttering waves of ecstasy each time. As he groans into my ear, I grab the nape of his neck with one hand while the other grabs a fistful of the duvet, moaning loudly as he rocks into me faster.

'You feel so fucking good, baby,' he breathes, pressing his lips hard against mine.

I don't know if it was him calling me that in his low, raspy voice – as though, even if it's just for this one blissful, surreal moment, I'm his and only his – but something combusts within me. Heat rockets through my body and every muscle tightens and quivers. He feels it and I watch him lose control, his eyes glazing as he moves his hand down to rub the spot between my legs, sending my body into overdrive as the pressure builds.

'Fuck,' he grunts, 'I can feel you. Flossie, fuck, you're making me c—'

He sinks into me with a loud groan, and as I feel him pulse and swell inside me, I lose myself again, consumed by the ecstasy rolling through my body, trembling beneath him.

*

'How are you feeling about the next round?' I ask softly, once he's returned from the bathroom and has got back into bed. I'm nuzzled into the crook of his arm, my head resting against his bare chest, one hand lazily doodling patterns across his stomach.

He chuckles, tightening his arm around me. 'You want to go again? Give me a minute and I'm game.'

'I'm talking about Wimbledon.' I roll my eyes, but break into a grin, flattered at his enthusiasm. 'You remember winning your match today?'

'Oh, that, yeah, rings a bell.' He sighs, lifting his other hand to rest behind his head on the pillow. 'I don't know. A little nervous, I guess. It's still early in the tournament, but one step closer and all that.'

'What is it about Wimbledon? Why is that the one you all want to win?'

He takes a moment to work out his answer and in the quiet, I listen to the soothing rhythm of his heartbeat. I didn't want to assume that I'd sleep in the bed next to him tonight after everything that's just happened, but I was relieved when he asked me to stay. I'm not sure there's anywhere I'd rather be than here lying beside him, sheets draped over us, my leg wrapped around his, his arm cradling me against him, his fingertips resting lightly on my hip.

'There's something about playing on the courts there,' he answers eventually in a soft voice. 'You can feel the history, everything and everyone who went before you. Wimbledon has a lot of heritage and all the rules encourage you to respect that heritage and tradition, you know? It's the prestige of it. The biggest thing for me is the silence.'

I raise my eyebrows. 'What do you mean?'

'When you step up to serve at Wimbledon, it's silent. Complete silence.'

'That must be daunting.'

'Mm.'

We fall into comfortable silence and I relax against him, closing my eyes. I'm starting to drift off when he speaks again.

'Flossie?'

'Yes?'

'Will you come watch the match on Friday?' he asks cautiously. 'You can sit with my team in the player box of the stands. I'd like you to be there.'

'Sure, Kieran,' I say calmly, although my heartbeat quickens in my chest to an alarming rate. 'I'll be there.'

17

Kieran is looking to me. There are hundreds of people in this crowd on Court Eighteen watching him play and out of everyone here, all the faces looking down at him, he's choosing to look to me after winning that incredible point. I've been on edge for the entire rally, my fingers gripping the bottom of my fold-down seat, my nails digging into the plastic. It's not that hot today, but I'm sweating with nerves, the backs of my thighs sticking to the seat as the shorts of my blue playsuit ride up when I'm sat down. He fought for that point and he won it with a stunning forehand that soars to the baseline, too fast for his German opponent, Jürgen Keller, to return. The crowd erupts with applause, several up on their feet in appreciation of such beautiful play, and he turns to the box where his team are sat. He scans across and *he looks to me*. My heart somersaults.

My eyes locked on his, I nod sharply to him with just a hint of a determined smile.

That's it. More like that, please. You've got this.

He turns away, taking the towel offered to him by a ball girl and wiping his forehead before tossing it back to her. He collects three balls from a ball boy, selecting two of them and sending the third back. He steps up to the line to serve. The stands fall silent, eerily silent, just like he said they do. I practically hold my breath, I'm too scared to exhale and make a noise that might distract him.

He looks relaxed and controlled as he tosses the ball up in the air and brings his racket down over the top of it in a smooth, fluid motion. It's a deceptively powerful and accurate serve. Keller doesn't stand a chance. It zips past his outstretched racket.

Ace.

I breathe out as Kieran moves to the other side of the court to another ardent round of applause, the Irish spectators in the stands cheering loudly and waving their flags.

'Forty – fifteen. Set point,' the umpire mumbles into the microphone.

Kieran points to the ball boy who provided the balls for the last serve and he obligingly bounces two towards him. Kieran checks them and approves, before stepping up to serve again. Keller wipes the back of his hand against his forehead, squinting across at Kieran and crouching low to the ground as he awaits the shot. Kieran's chest rises with a deep breath as he decides where to place this next one, before he bounces the ball twice on the grass and then tosses it smoothly up into the air and sends it flying powerfully across the court. Keller only just manages to return it, stumbling off balance.

As the ball lands softly in the service box, Kieran is there, ready with his deadly forehand. The ball zips back in a blur, spinning so fast it hardly bounces.

'Set, O'Sullivan.'

The roar from the crowd is deafening. Everyone is up on their feet, clapping and whooping as Kieran chucks the spare tennis ball from his pocket across to a ball boy without reacting, and calmly goes to sit on his chair. That's two sets to one. He can do this, I know he can. But I'm not going to celebrate yet. I'm learning that at Wimbledon, it can all change with just a few points.

Talking to the assistant coach sat next to him, Neil glances down the row at me, but I pretend not to notice, adjusting my sunglasses and keeping my eyes fixed on Kieran. Despite being here with Kieran's team, I'm not *really* with the team. I'm very much an outsider and Neil has made sure that I know I'm not going to be let into the fold anytime soon. Which is fine by me. I appreciate I'm not important. I'm here for Kieran.

I think I'm beginning to understand that Kieran has spent a long time, on and off court, feeling like no one is really on his side, even those he pays to help him win. But I care about him, win or lose. No matter what happens, I want him to feel like he has someone in his corner. Someone who *chooses* to be in his corner.

'Time.'

At the umpire's announcement, he picks up his racket and gets to his feet. His eyes flash up at me.

Here we go.

I've not actually been to the Wimbledon tournament before. We didn't go last year and I've never thought to apply for the ballot to get tickets, but now that I'm here I feel like I've missed out. It's warm, the atmosphere is buzzing, and this is easily one of the most beautiful sports grounds I've ever seen. Everything at the All England Lawn Tennis Club is clean, bright and preened, with hundreds of hanging baskets, troughs and flower beds around the courts brimming with dark purple and white petunias, perfectly complementing the green foliage and courts. If you asked someone to imagine how a quintessential English country garden might translate to a sports ground, this would be it.

And the crowds are all on their best behaviour. There may be Champagne and Pimm's flowing freely, but there's no rowdiness or raucous activity. It's as though all the spectators know that they have to treat somewhere so well preserved with respect.

I'm enjoying milling around. I felt that, since I'm here, this is a good opportunity to experience Wimbledon properly, so I might as well wander around for a bit and take it all in.

After Kieran won the match, Neil told me explicitly that I was welcome to enjoy the grounds but that only Kieran's team could join him in the player's area. I had expected as much anyway.

It's not like I was planning on hanging around the men's locker room while Kieran showered and changed, although that would be *extremely* pleasant. So I messaged Kieran to congratulate him and then said I was going to hang around for a bit and he could let me know if he wanted to meet, or else I'd see him back at the flat.

I join the queue for the strawberries and cream stand. There's no chance that I'm coming to Wimbledon and not having strawberries and cream. That would be insulting the tournament and, quite frankly, the country itself. Having purchased my tub of strawberries, I proudly take a selfie of me holding it up and grinning, and send it to Kieran, having swapped numbers this morning before he left. We both found it amusing when we realised we hadn't actually got round to doing that yet.

Celebrating your win with strawberries on Murray Mound! I caption the photo.

Finding a spot on the hill in front of the giant screen that's on the side of Court One, I sit down cross-legged and start spooning the cream over the strawberries. I'm trying to scoop my first one onto the spoon when someone's shadow blocks the sun.

'Fancy seeing you here,' Kieran says, sitting down next to me in his Wayfarers and cap. He's not in his tennis whites, but navy shorts and a white shirt.

'Hey!' I exclaim, swivelling to face him as he rests his arms on his knees. I hesitate, a smile spreading across my face as I lower my voice and lean into him. 'Aren't you that famous tennis player who just got through to the fourth round of Wimbledon?'

'You must be mistaking me for someone else,' he whispers back.

'Congratulations, Kieran.'

'Thank you.'

'You played amazingly,' I gush, desperate to throw my arms around him, but I get the feeling that he doesn't want any fuss that might attract attention on this busy hill. 'It was incredible to watch. You did it! You're through to the next round.'

'It's hard to believe,' he says, unable to stop a wide grin breaking across his face.

'Not for me. How do you feel?'

He bites his lip and nods. 'Yeah, good.'

I wait for him to expand and when he doesn't, I snicker. 'Wow, Kieran, that was beautiful. The musical poet would be proud to express himself in such an eloquent manner. You're through to the *next bloody round of Wimbledon*. And you're feeling "good".'

He chuckles softly, his cheeks flushed. 'All right, fine. I feel...' He pauses, exhaling and turning his head to look at me. 'I feel like this is a dream and I'm scared to wake up.'

I smile, nudging his arm with my elbow. 'It's not a dream. It's all real.'

'Yeah. The magnitude of it is definitely starting to feel real.'

'Kieran,' I say, giving him a stern look, 'you're just here to play some tennis. Don't be a diva about it.'

He bursts out laughing, quirking his brow at me. 'Did you just call me a diva?'

'If you're going to be all dramatic and start talking about the magnitude of winning another round of Wimbledon, then you're in the wrong company.'

'That so?'

'I'm here to enjoy the atmosphere and eat some strawberries.'

He nods to the bowl in my hand. 'Are they as good as everyone says?'

'I'm about to find out. Surely you should be the one to tell me how good they are,' I remark, using the edge of my spoon to cut one in half since they're absolutely ginormous. 'I bet you're sick of these.'

He shrugs. 'I've never had them here.'

I stop what I'm doing. 'What?'

'I've never had strawberries and cream at Wimbledon.' He takes a glimpse at my expression and laughs again, his dimples prompting a warm swell in my belly. 'Why are you looking at me like that? I've never had the chance!'

'You've played in this tournament, like, a billion times!'

'Slight exaggeration. And how many tennis players do you see casually sitting on the court tucking into a bowl of strawberries and cream?'

'You're not sitting on the court now, are you?'

'True.'

I hold out the bowl to him. 'Come on, you have to have one. I think if anyone else overheard what you just said, you might be kicked out the tournament altogether. Time to lose your virginity. Here—' I use the spoon to nudge the bit I cut over towards his side of the bowl '—you have that half.'

He sighs, picking it up in his fingers. 'I guess it would be a crime not to.'

'*Sláinte*,' I say, holding up my half of the strawberry on the spoon.

'Cheers.'

We eat our halves at the same time, turning to look at each other after the first bite and nodding with approval in unison.

'Not bad,' he comments.

'A top-notch cuisine,' I say, already sawing away with the spoon to split the next strawberry.

I hold out the bowl to him again and he grins, gratefully taking his half and plopping it in his mouth while turning to watch the match being shown on the screen. For the next few minutes, we sit together watching the tennis, polishing off the bowl of strawberries. When they're done, I put the bowl to the side on the grass, and he stretches his legs out in front of him and leans back on his hands.

'This is it, isn't it,' he sighs wistfully. 'This is what they mean.'

'Who?'

'When people talk about Wimbledon, this is it,' he explains, his eyes fixed ahead on the screen. 'Sitting in the sunshine, eating strawberries, watching tennis.' He turns to look at me. 'It's perfect.'

I rest back on my hands too, stretching my legs out next to his. This playsuit has a cut-out detail below the tie knot that sits in between my cleavage and I notice him glance at the skin of my stomach on show, making me blush.

'Yeah,' I say. 'It is.'

He smiles at me and then goes back to watching the screen. A few moments later, I feel his fingers brush over my hand, before he interlaces his fingers through mine. My breath catches and my heart swells in my chest, my skin tingling at his touch. I keep staring ahead, just like him. Neither of us say anything. We don't need to.

'There you are!' Neil exclaims, appearing in our pathway as we make our way down the steps next to Murray Mound. 'I've been looking for you everywhere, Kieran. You don't answer your phone now?'

'Neil, have you ever had the strawberries and cream here?' Kieran asks breezily, unfazed by the sharpness in his coach's tone. 'They're delicious.'

Neil stares at him in disbelief. 'What are you talking about strawberries for? I've been trying to reach you. We had a post-match press conference, remember?'

'Slipped my mind.' Kieran shrugs, continuing to go down the stairs, ignoring the glances he's receiving from people he passes along the way as he's recognised.

I slow my pace, walking a step behind him. He didn't say anything to me about missing a press conference whilst we were just lounging on the grass doing nothing. My stomach knots at Neil's murderous expression.

I have an idea that I'll be the one fielding the blame for this mishap in his eyes.

'You can't do that, Kieran, it's not a good look,' Neil hisses, falling into step with him.

'I don't care how it looks. I'm here to play tennis, not win over the press.'

Neil sighs, getting out his phone. 'Yeah, I think they got the message. Nicole is concerned that your image is going to go from bad to worse if you keep up this attitude. We've said that you missed the conference due to concern about injury and you had to rush to the physio. We'll have to do some damage control at the drinks tonight. You can give some quotes to the reporters or something.'

Kieran stops in the middle of the pathway to address Neil. 'I'm not going tonight.'

Halting abruptly, Neil blinks up at him. 'What do you mean? You've been invited to drinks at the club with the members tonight. You have to go.'

'I can't. I'm busy.'

'Doing what?'

Kieran turns to me. Having stopped behind him, I've been pretending to look around at all the other people milling about as though I'm not listening to every word of the conversation.

'Flossie, do you want to go for a drink tonight?' he asks. 'We could go somewhere in the village. The Dog and Fox maybe?'

My mouth drops in surprise. 'Uh. Well, yeah, but only if you're not needed somewhere else.'

'I'm not,' he tells me. He turns back to Neil. 'I'm busy having a drink with Flossie at the Dog and Fox tonight.'

'Kieran,' Neil begins, his voice low and urgent, 'I don't think this is a good idea.'

'I think it's a great idea,' Kieran counters. 'Tonight is not important, Neil, and after a long day, I don't want to have to wear a tie and make polite conversation with a bunch of people I don't know. I promise I'll be at the All England Club chairman's big fancy do for the players tomorrow, okay? I've got my tux ready and everything.'

Neil takes a moment to respond, putting his hands on his hips and looking down at the ground, shaking his head. I glance up at Kieran nervously, but his mouth remains straight and serious. Neil eventually lifts his eyes up to him.

'Fine,' he seethes, his jaw tense. 'As long as you're there tomorrow.'

'Promise, coach,' Kieran says, reaching out and patting him on the arm.

Agitated, Neil's eyes scan to me and his nostrils flare.

'It's just one drinks evening, Neil, it's not a big deal,' Kieran reminds him, his lips twitching upwards into a small smile. 'It was a good win today. You should take my advice and have some strawberries. We've worked hard for them.'

Kieran reaches down to take my hand in his, interlocking our fingers and leading me away from Neil, who watches us go with a grim expression. My cheeks flushing with heat, I keep my head down as we walk down the path towards the exit, increasingly aware of the number of people noticing us and openly staring.

By taking my hand in front of Neil, it feels like Kieran is making some kind of statement, confirming Neil's dreaded suspicions. By continuing to hold my hand as we walk through the crowds of Wimbledon, it feels like he's telling everyone else.

And when he lifts my hand to his lips to lightly kiss my fingers when no one's watching as we leave the grounds, I'm hoping he's making a statement to me.

18

'This isn't a fair fight,' I groan, yanking my darts out of the wood surrounding the board. 'I'm an artist. You're a professional athlete!'

Kieran raises his eyebrows. 'We're playing darts, Flossie. Athleticism doesn't really come into it and it's hardly my area of expertise.'

I gesture to the scoreboard. 'I beg to differ.'

He shoots me a lazy grin. 'Not my fault if I happen to be good at darts.'

'Like you happen to be good at ping-pong? Seriously, is there anything you're not good at?'

'Many, many things. Small talk, art, public speaking, baking—'

'I mean, any *sport*,' I sigh, plodding back to him and heaving myself up onto the bar stool to the side while he stands up for his turn.

'You think because I'm good at tennis, ping-pong and darts, I'm good at all sports? You have no idea what I'm like at rugby or cricket or swimming.'

'Okay, what are you like at rugby, cricket and swimming?'

He grins. 'Pretty good. I like golf too.'

'Fuck's sake.'

'I'm also not bad on a horse.'

'Of course.'

He clicks his fingers. 'You know what, I'm terrible at ice skating.'

I snort. 'Okay. When did you try ice skating?'

'When I was about thirteen. We were skiing and I thought I'd have a go.'

'Let me guess, you're a really good skier,' I grumble.

'I'm all right,' he admits, with a slow, sly grin. 'Anyway, I was terrible at ice skating. Couldn't master the gracefulness.'

'You're pretty graceful on the tennis court,' I comment.

'You mean manly and rugged, right?'

'No, I mean graceful and elegant,' I confirm haughtily, as he holds up a dart to take aim. 'Powerful and aggressive, too of course. Good luck to your next opponent. I bet he's quaking in his little boots.'

He hits a triple twelve. 'I doubt it. He's a little scary himself. His backhand is specially terrifying.'

'Maybe picture him on ice skates,' I suggest. 'When I picture you on ice skates, it's pretty amusing, like Bambi on ice, limbs skidding about everywhere. So you can do the same with the other guy and he won't seem so scary anymore.'

'I am this close to sacking Neil and putting you in charge,' Kieran says, lining up for his next shot. 'Your pep talks are much shorter and much more effective.'

'Who says I'd accept the job?' I say, folding my arms as he hits the fifteen. 'I'm afraid I'm much too busy and important to squeeze in time to coach you.'

'Shame,' Kieran sighs, taking aim with his third and final dart. 'We would have made a great team.'

He throws and hits sixteen. With a smug smile, he saunters towards the board to retrieve his darts. I roll my eyes, reaching for the glass of wine he bought me. It's an Albariño, which Kieran recommended I try. It's obviously delicious. You know, it's really annoying that he keeps being right about things. At some point, I'd like to be the one who knows something about *anything*, so he can be impressed.

As I take a sip of my drink, my eyes flutter up to see a cluster of girls huddled nearby, giggling and whispering, with their phones pointed in our direction.

'We've been rumbled,' I inform Kieran quietly, as he returns to our little table in the corner by the board to have a sip of his pint.

He follows my eyeline and then turns back to me with a shrug.

'They're not the only ones. The two lads on the table to your left have been taking videos and pictures since we got here,' he says casually.

I glance over my left shoulder to find two more phones pointed at me. I scowl at them, swivelling back to Kieran and looking up at him, concerned.

'Should we go?' I ask reluctantly, unable to hide my disappointment.

I've been having so much fun this evening. On our walk to the pub, it started to cloud over and while the beer garden was packed with people, the inside wasn't so busy. Since Kieran knew it was expected to rain tonight, he suggested we grab a table indoors. We'd spent all afternoon outside, so I was happy to chill in here and it's been so nice and relaxed. He's letting his guard down with me and the more I get to see behind it, the more I want to spend time with him.

When he's at ease in a situation, he's chatty and funny and charming. When I first met him, I'd assumed that it was his looks and fame that made him so popular amongst all those celebrity women he'd been linked to, but now I can understand why just one night in the company of this guy here in front of me – the one asking me questions about my life, bantering over silly things, making me laugh with his quick-witted comebacks, flashing me dimpled grins that make me melt into the floor – would be enough for me to forget all my senses and throw myself at him. And with my slim experience of trying to go about my evening in the knowledge that I'm being watched and stealthily filmed, I can also totally understand why he'd be guarded, reserved and untrusting with strangers.

I shouldn't be surprised that people have picked up on

Kieran being here. Firstly, if you're around Wimbledon during the championships, you're going to be on the lookout for famous tennis players hanging around the vicinity trying to go unnoticed. Secondly, Kieran stands out just a tiny bit, what with his tall, broad frame and dazzling good looks. Thirdly, it turns out that our spontaneous rendezvous on Murray Mound wasn't as private as I'd thought – Kieran had, of course, been recognised by a couple of people sitting above us and they'd taken photos and uploaded them to social media.

That third point wasn't too good for Neil because he'd already told the press that Kieran missed the conference due to physio – but here was proof he'd actually been lazing around the grounds eating strawberries. When I tried to look at the comments as the photo gained traction online, Kieran insisted I put my phone away. I caught a glimpse. I was getting off fairly lightly so far. Most people just seemed to be wondering who the hell I am.

Anyway, I was glad for the incoming dark clouds that meant we could hide in here away from the busy beer garden, but the pub is now slowly filling inside.

'I don't want to leave,' Kieran says, his eyebrows pulled together and his mouth turning down as he ignores our audience. 'Do you?'

'No. It's just... distracting. You don't care that people are taking photos and videos of you without your consent?'

'I do care, but there's not much I can do about it. Best to ignore it.'

'I hope they don't post these pictures on social media,' I mutter, bringing my glass to my lips. 'They might catch me at a bad angle.'

He tilts his head at me. 'Not possible. You don't have any bad angles.'

I blush furiously into my wine. He said that as though it was fact, not opinion, and now he's continuing to speak as though he hasn't just said something so lovely that it's made my head spin and my whole body feel like it's on fire.

'Maybe if I was more approachable then people wouldn't feel the need to film me stealthily,' he's wondering out loud, placing the darts on the table next to his glass. 'That's what my PR team has tried telling me anyway.'

I wince and he gives me a strange look.

'What?' he says, a glint of curiosity in his eyes. 'What was that face for?'

'Nothing.'

'Flossie, I know when you're lying,' he informs me, quirking a brow.

'No, you don't.'

'I do,' he insists, stepping closer to me and waggling his finger in my face. 'Your cheeks go this adorable shade of pink.'

Placing my glass down, I bite my lip and press my palms against my burning hot cheeks. 'Are they all red? How embarrassing.'

He reaches out to wrap his fingers around my wrists and lower my hands from my face so I have no choice but to leave my cheeks on show for him to study, a small smile creeping across his lips as he does so.

'No, it's beautiful,' he says softly. 'Makes your freckles even more prominent.'

'When I was younger, I used to try to cover my freckles.'

'Why would you *cover* them? They're...' He trails off searching for the right word, knitting his eyebrows together in concentration. 'They're *you*. I like them.'

I smile bashfully, glancing over at the huddle of girls. 'You're making me go even redder for the cameras.'

'Don't think you've escaped my question, Flossie,' he says, taking a small step back, his voice returning to a lighter, more playful tone. 'Why did you make that face when I mentioned my PR team asking me to be more approachable?'

'I wouldn't fancy doing your PR that's all.'

He quirks a brow. 'Why not? I'm a great client.'

'You skip press conferences, you refuse to do interviews no matter what journalists are saying about you, so you let their narrative stick, and you have moments of... embellished infuriation on court.'

He tips his head back and cackles with laughter, a sound that makes me light up from the very centre of my core. 'Embellished infuriation! Now who's the musical poet?'

'I was trying to put it nicely!'

'You may have a point. It can't be easy for my publicists to turn embellished infuriation to my advantage in the eyes of the public,' he says, his eyes drifting over my shoulder. His eyebrows shoot up and he leans in conspiratorially to me. 'Although they may have it wrong about my approachability. Someone's coming over to me now.'

As he fixes a polite smile on his face, I swivel on my stool to face the incoming fan and find myself face to face with—

'Zoe!' I exclaim, my stomach knotting in horror.

'Hey, Flora,' she says timidly, glancing from me to Kieran and back to me again, 'I hope you don't mind me interrupting.' She beams up at Kieran. 'I'm just such a huge fan and I keep seeing you at the flat. We're bound to bump into one another eventually. I thought I'd take the opportunity to introduce myself.'

'You know each other?' Kieran says, his shoulders easing.

'Zoe lives next door,' I say in a strained voice, my face flushing with heat.

'Oh, right, hi, Zoe. I'm so sorry about the reporters on the road,' he begins, holding out his hand to shake hers warmly. 'I hope they haven't been bothering you too much.'

'It's no problem,' she says with a breezy wave of her hand. 'Congratulations on your win today. It was a fantastic match and you played so brilliantly.' She gives him a winning smile, her eyes bright underneath her full fluttering eyelashes. 'I've got tickets to Centre Court for the semi-finals. I have no doubt that I'll be watching you play then.'

He smiles modestly, glancing down at his feet and back up to her again. 'That's very kind of you to say, Zoe, thank you.'

'I... have to go to the bathroom,' I croak, sliding off my stool and making my way through the bar to the loos. It's getting very crowded in here now, as the rain grows heavier.

I glance back at Kieran and Zoe as I get to the door. They're already engaged in a lively conversation. My heart sinking, I push the door open and lock myself in a cubicle, slumping down on the toilet and burying my face in my hands.

Of *course* he's chatting easily to Zoe. She's a lovely person to talk to, warm and inviting, with her sparkling pearly-white smile and striking eyes. Bet he's noticed how good her figure is in that outfit too, her flawless skin and model figure on display in a burnt orange silk top and high-waisted white linen shorts. He's always dated models and actresses and amazingly glamorous women who were born to stand out. Women like Zoe.

Not like me.

I can't believe she waltzed over like that. Am I so small and insignificant that she thinks what she did doesn't really matter? Does she think that it's been a few months now, so we can shrug it off and pretend it didn't happen? I'm not okay with that. I know there were two people in that bed and it was Jonah who was in the wrong. He's the one who had the girlfriend, *he's* the one who broke his promises. It's not like she had any loyalty to me. Just because we'd had a few nice conversations didn't mean we were friends. But it still really hurt to know that she didn't insist Jonah break up with me first to spare me that betrayal. She willingly went along with it, in the full knowledge that I was being humiliated. She was part of the act that made me a fool.

For her to stroll up to us in a pub so brazenly fucking *hurts*.

I take a deep breath and remind myself how far I've come since January. She doesn't need to matter to me. But Kieran does, and sitting here feeling sorry for myself in a toilet cubicle isn't helping anyone. I can't be so intimidated by her beauty and style that I physically exclude myself from my own date. I *think* it's a date. He hasn't explicitly said that, but he did hold my hand on the way here. That has to make it a date.

Making my way back through the pub, my heart sinks when I see Zoe is still there with Kieran. They're playing darts together. Stopping a few metres away, I'm unable to approach any further. My feet won't seem to move. I watch Zoe step up to the mark at Kieran's encouragement, take aim and throw the dart. It hits bullseye. She shrieks and his jaw drops with amazement before she jumps up and down excitedly, throwing her arms around his neck in celebration. I feel a pang in my chest so sharp, my eyes well with tears. I have to get out. I push my way through a startled group of people huddled by the door, tripping over my feet and throwing myself out the door.

It's now pouring with rain and I don't have a coat, but I don't care. My chest feels tight and I need to be in the fresh air. Closing my eyes, I take a few moments to breathe slowly in and out, allowing the rain to soak through my clothes and dampen my hair. Then, hugging my arms across my body, I start to walk down the path out the pub.

'Flossie!'

I start at his voice, turning to find him right behind me, a confused expression across his face as he hunches in the downpour.

'Where are you going?' he asks, baffled. 'You're soaked! What's wrong?'

'I... I have to go home. You go back in, enjoy yourself,' I say bluntly.

'Flossie,' he says, grabbing my wrist and stopping me from going, 'I won't enjoy myself without you there. Please, tell me what's happened? Did someone say something to you? Did you read something online? I told you not to look at it.'

I shake my head, sniffing. 'No. It's nothing like that. It's... it's too embarrassing. I can't tell you.'

'Yes, you can,' he states matter-of-factly, raindrops trailing down his cheeks and through his stubble, dripping from his sculpted jaw.

Fucking hell, he's even more beautiful in the rain. His skin is glistening and his shirt is growing so damp it's plastered to his body, accentuating every curve of his defined muscles. I can guarantee that he's not thinking anything like that about me. I imagine my make-up is running down my face by now and I resemble some kind of wet, miserable panda.

My heart in my throat, I resolve to tell him. I mean, we're standing here in the rain because of me and he can tell I've been crying, so I'm not going to be able to pretend it's nothing. And I don't want to lie to him.

'Jonah cheated on me with Zoe,' I say quietly, unable to look him in the eye.

I hear him inhale sharply. 'That Zoe? The one I was just talking to? Your next-door neighbour Zoe?'

I nod dismally. 'Yes. I came home and found them together in our bed. She apologised and I know it was his fault, not hers, but... I'm not her friend.'

'Yeah. I can understand why.'

'I'm sorry for storming out like that,' I stammer, chewing my lip. 'I wish I could be stronger. But it's so hard when I compare myself to her.'

'Flossie, what are you *talking* about?' Kieran asks, and I hear something like amusement in his voice, which digs the knife even deeper.

Maybe he finds this so pathetic, it's funny to him.

'She's so bright and beautiful and fun and smart. She has everything going for her, and I know that it's hard not to be attracted to her because, hello, she's perfect, but I just didn't want to stand there and watch you... flirt with her. You're, you know, this famous tennis star slash model—' he snorts as though I'm joking, but I mean it so I don't laugh '—and it makes sense for you to be with someone like Zoe, in the same way it made sense for Jonah to want her. It makes me resort to feeling as small as I felt back then.'

'Flossie.' Kieran steps closer and reaches out to gently lift my chin with his fingers, so I'm looking up at him, the two of us blinking like mad through the rain. 'I'm so sorry for putting you in that position.'

'It's not your fault. You didn't know.'

'I was talking to her, not flirting with her. I only want to flirt with you.'

Shutting my eyes, another tear falls and I dig my teeth into my bottom lip. 'But Zoe—'

'Zoe is beautiful, yes,' he states, before using his thumb to sweep away the tear that's mingling with the droplets running down my cheeks. 'But that doesn't mean you're not. Because you are beautiful. You are so, so *beautiful*.' He pauses to swallow, his throat bobbing as I bring my eyes up to meet his. 'When you're in the room, Flossie, there's no one else.'

I'm crying again, but happy tears now.

Fucking-happiest-ever tears.

Salty tears that I can taste as he captures my mouth in a kiss so slow and deep, I finally understand what it means for someone to take your breath away.

Time stops still as we stand pressed up against each other in the pouring rain, his mouth moving against mine, his fingers tangled in my wet hair. His other hand slides around my waist and presses into my lower back, allowing me to lose myself entirely in this Hollywood-grade kiss and arch into him, tilting my head back as my arms wrap around his neck and his tongue brushes against mine, sending a roll of shivers down my spine and a surge of heat lurching through my body.

When we eventually break the kiss, we're grinning goofily at each other, our faces damp from the rain. He looks even more mesmerising with droplets on his eyelashes, his hair plastered across his forehead, the skin of his cheeks flushed and dewy. I have to kiss him again, and he reciprocates, moving his arms to lock around my waist and squeezing me tight as I cradle his face, crushing my lips into his.

'We should really get out of the rain,' I say eventually, wiping the drops from his forehead and running my fingers through his hair.

'Yeah, I think that would be wise.' He laughs, the rain only getting heavier and louder. He quirks a brow. 'So, what do you think? My place or yours?'

19

It takes us longer to walk to the flat than it should. Our fingers interlaced, Kieran stops every few minutes to draw me into another kiss, each one growing more passionate than the last. Rushing down our road, giggling, he stops to pin me up against a tree, propping one hand over my head and leaning into me as the other urges my hips into his. His mouth smashes against mine, his tongue demanding and urgent, a low frustrated growl from his throat vibrating against my lips. He's acting as though he's not going to be able to wait until he gets me home and it's so hot feeling this wanted, this desired, this needed. The road is empty, but even if there was anyone there neither of us would notice or care.

Right now, it's just the two of us, kissing up against a tree in the rain.

His fingertips move to swirl around the bare skin of my stomach on show before making their way down over my hip bone, continuing onwards to trail along the bottom hem of my playsuit shorts. His palm warms my outer thigh as he slips it underneath the fabric.

'Hmm, this outfit is making things difficult,' he notes, tugging at the shorts. 'Next time, wear a dress so it's easy access, please.'

I laugh lightly. 'You think I should base my outfit decisions on the off-chance someone wants me up against a tree?'

'Not just *someone*,' he grumbles, a hint of jealousy in his tone that makes my heart skip a beat. 'Me.'

'And what about the paps?' I remind him, arching my eyebrows.

He glances down the road. 'There's no one watching.'

'They're good at hiding.'

'True.' He sighs, leaning back and grabbing my hand to pull me away from the tree. 'Better get you back quick.'

Dragging me down the pavement to my gate, he opens the latch and holds it open for me so I can go ahead and open the door, my keys out of my bag and in my hand at the ready. He's behind me, kissing my neck, his hands roaming down my hips as I try to concentrate on opening the door, my hand slipping, the edge of the key leaving a scratch mark around the lock.

Finally I complete the task and we're in. He kicks the door closed behind us with his foot as he presses me up against the wall, his mouth urgently seeking mine, his hands roaming around every inch of my back, waist, hips, moving too quickly for me to know where they are at any given time. We're kicking off our shoes, I'm unbuttoning his sodden shirt, my fingers working the buttons as efficiently as possible while he kisses the breath out of me. He helps me with the last couple of buttons of his shirt, before he peels it off, dropping it to the floor where it lands with a heavy slap against the wooden panels, the rainwater beginning to pool around it. *Look at him.* This bare muscular chest, these broad solid shoulders, his smooth skin glinting with moisture from the rain. I brush the palms of my hands from the centre of his chest out to roll over his shoulders, digging my nails into the curve of his bicep. *Fuck.* I will never get over that I get to kiss this man, that I'm lucky enough to have him all to myself right now, that he's going to let me touch him, feel him.

While I shamelessly gawp at him, his hands move to the tie at the bottom of my playsuit plunge collar and I laugh as he grows muddled, his brow furrowed while he tugs at the ends of the knot.

'What the—' he says in bewilderment.

'It doesn't untie there,' I inform him, admiring how sexily cute he looks when he's confused, his eyebrows pulled together, the little creases in between them deepening.

'Then, how do you get it off?'

'Like this.'

He watches in wonder as, one arm at a time, I reach up to nudge the damp sleeve down my shoulder, pulling my arm free of it until the top of my playsuit is hanging around my waist. His eyes follow the slope of my collarbones to the curve of my breasts, lifted with the help of a lacy blue plunge bra. He swallows while I continue to undress myself, sliding my hands under the elasticated waist of the playsuit, widening it and shifting my hips to draw it down over my arse before I let it fall to the floor. Kieran's eyes darken as his pupils widen.

'There,' I say, my voice cracking slightly under the intensity of his gaze.

'Holy shit. That—' he begins in a low, gravelly voice, his warm hands sliding around my waist as he brings his lips to mine to talk quietly against them '—was unbelievably sexy.'

He crushes his mouth against mine and, after that brief interlude for a tutorial in taking off a playsuit, the kisses ramp back up to urgent, desperate, devouring. My hands thread around the sides of his head, grasping his hair, and I let him take the lead as he wraps his arms around my waist and manoeuvres us down the hall, stumbling into the darkness of the living room. Lost in the thrill of his lips, I'm not paying attention to where we are and find myself surprised when the backs of my legs hit the sofa. Before I can think about the next move, he lifts me up to wind my legs around his waist – *God I love how he does that so easily* – and lowers me onto my back across the sofa, positioning himself in between my legs. My breathing is coming out in short, shallow rasps, as he finds the light switch on the wall and turns it on. He leans over me, running a hand through my damp, dishevelled hair as it splays out on the cushion around my head.

He inhales deeply through his nose, his jaw tensing.

'You're so sexy with your hair wet like this,' he tells me, before he lowers his lips to graze the skin in between my breasts, nipping at the little bow at the centre of my bra with his teeth, and then slowly begins to kiss a line all the way down my stomach to the top band of my pale blue thong, the lightness of his lips covering my skin in goosebumps.

'You have no idea how beautiful you are,' he whispers against my skin, making my stomach tighten at the tickle of his breath. 'All day I've been thinking about doing this to you.'

'Uh-huh, sure, when you were playing in Wimbledon you were thinking about this,' I mutter, and then wonder why the hell I've chosen this moment to be sarcastic when I have the sexiest man on the planet in between my legs, kissing along my hips.

Don't question him now, Flora. He can say whatever the fuck he wants down there.

'Why do you think I won? I had to get the match to end. The sooner it was over, the sooner I could get my hands on you, the sooner we could do this.' He grins, his fingers inching under the flimsy fabric of my underwear. 'Simple.'

'Oh, so *this* is why you won.'

'*You* are why I won,' he corrects, and my heart somersaults. He groans as his hand slides lower and he feels how wet he's making me. 'Fuck.'

He swiftly removes my thong, dropping it on the floor next to the coffee table and a memory flashes across my brain of the last time this room had underwear strewn across it – when I was standing in my towel and I dropped my pants in front of his team. It almost makes me laugh how long ago that feels now, how much has happened since then. He notices me suppress the smile.

'What are you thinking about?' he asks intrigued.

'Nothing.'

'Come on,' he insists in a low, deep voice, moving up to hover over me. 'I know something funny just crossed your mind. You got that twinkle in your eye.'

'I get a twinkle in my eye?'

'When you're amused,' he says matter-of-factly. 'Your eyes go all mischievous. It's like you're sharing a joke with yourself.'

I break into a wide smile, my heart flipping, because I love that he's noticed things about me. Little things that others wouldn't see or understand, or bother to know. Like he sees me in a way that no one else does. I want him to be that person for me.

I want to be that person for him.

'So?' he prompts, kissing the corner of my mouth gently. 'What was it?'

'I was thinking about the last time my underwear was dropped in here – when I was in my towel and Neil came over. I think it was the second or third morning you were here.'

'The first,' he corrects without a moment's hesitation. He smiles at my look of surprise. 'I remember it very well. You standing in that towel, the water still dripping down your neck from the shower.' A sound of approval comes from his throat as he moves back to kiss my stomach again, just below my belly button, his stubble scratching across my skin, his hands gripping my hips. 'I was imagining what you looked like beneath it.' His lips move lower and heat floods through my body. 'And now I get to know. I'm the luckiest man in the world.'

As I stare up at the ceiling, my heart is hammering out of control. His lips explore between my legs, and he takes his time to tease me with light kisses before his tongue settles in the centre and with one stroke he sends jolts of electricity racing through my body.

Lifting my arm to grasp the cushion behind me, I shut my eyes and tilt my head back, letting out a moan as I lose myself. As he moves one of his hands from my hips to sink his fingers inside me while increasing the pressure of his tongue against my clit, the sensations are almost too much for me to handle and any inhibitions are lost as I gasp and cry out his name. He groans in pleasure at my response and escalates his rhythm, and my whole body starts to tremble, my mind spinning, as the swirling heat within me builds and builds.

'Kieran, stop,' I manage to gasp, biting my lip and trying to make my brain work, as he does what I ask. 'I want you. I want to come together. Please.'

He considers my request and leans forward to kiss along my collarbone and shoulder while I try to collect my senses after his lips sent them into a spin, before he leaves the room. My body is too flushed with heat for me to register how long he's gone, but when he returns with a glint of foil in his hand, I'm overwhelmed with gratitude to have him back and impatient for more. He's had his fun wielding the control, now it's my turn.

As he pulls down his clothes and rolls on the condom, I swing my legs off the sofa and stand up to press my hands against his chest, moving him back to sit down, his eyes widening as I stand over him. Gripping his shoulders for support, I lift myself up to straddle him, my knees settling either side of his hips. His hands rubbing up and down my waist, he leans his head back and exhales through his nose.

'Have I mentioned how beautiful you are?' he murmurs, his eyes locked on mine.

I smile, running my hands over his bare chest, savouring the smooth touch of his skin beneath my fingers. 'You're beautiful, too. I can't believe…'

You're mine.

I stop myself just in time before I say it, my face flooding with heat at how close I'd come to saying something that might have scared the crap out of him. He's not mine, not really. Maybe in this moment, maybe for tonight, but it's too early for me to have any kind of claim to him, no matter how I feel. And I *do* feel. I feel so much. It's stupid how my feelings for him are growing at an alarming rate, but with every second that passes in his company, I want more. I want to know everything about him, his feelings, his thoughts, his memories, his opinions, his dreams. Is it possible to fall this hard this soon? Am I kidding myself? Is this what people mean when they know full well that they should hold back just in case of inevitable heartbreak, but have absolutely no intention of doing so?

If he hadn't glanced up at me during that tennis match. If it wasn't me he was seeking out when he needed whatever he was looking for in that moment: support, confidence, courage, hope. Then, I might not let myself believe that this has the potential to *be something*. But I do.

When you're in the room, there's no one else, he said to me earlier tonight.

I hope he meant it, because I'm starting to think there might be no one else but him for me in any room ever again. It's foolish, dangerous, downright stupid. He's the sort of person who must have every woman he's been with thinking like that. But there's nothing I can do. I'm letting myself hope, because there's no better feeling.

I can't believe...

...*you're mine*.

...*we're here*.

...*I'm falling*.

So many ways of finishing that sentence that I have to hide from him. I wish I could read his mind, but I'm so thankful he can't read mine. He'd run a fucking mile.

Kieran doesn't ask me to complete the sentence, but his eyes are boring into mine as though he might have an idea. I can't let him see the truth, so I bow my head to part his lips with my tongue, deepening the kiss enough for him to moan with frustration into my mouth, his fingernails digging into my hips. I need him inside me. I straighten and then sink slowly onto him, using his chest to balance myself as I push up and then slide further down, my breath hitching at his size as it fills me.

'Flossie,' he gasps, his eyes blazing as I take him in. 'You feel incredible – *fuck*.'

Holding on to my hips, he helps me find a rhythm. I grow more confident – he makes me feel more confident, moaning and muttering about how sexy I am – and he moves one hand to my bra, dragging down the material to palm my breast, groaning as I tilt my head back and lose myself in… fuck it, lose myself in *everything*. No more thoughts about where this is going, what he means to me or what I mean to him. I don't want to get inside my head and overthink anymore; I want to be in this moment utterly and completely.

I lose myself in the way he feels inside me, full and hard and pulsing and perfect; the way he tastes when I kiss him; the way he looks at me with those bewitching eyes like I'm *it* for him, whether that's just for this moment or forever; the way he smells, the hazy scent of his cologne tonight, a scent I know will make me feel weak at the knees if I ever smell it on someone else again; and the way he's touching me, as though he desperately wants every part of me, nothing hidden, nothing held back.

'Oh my God, you look amazing.' His voice is rushed and heavy, and I see him watching me with his lips parted, his eyes burning with need. 'You're making me close.'

His hand slides down between my legs as his breathing gets heavier, and a flare of unruly heat is sparked in the spot where his thumb begins to work. I roll my hips harder and faster, encouraged by his touch and his words, and I wish I could tell him that I've never had sex like this before, the kind where I'm not worrying about what I look like or trying to disguise those fears with darkness or duvets. The way he looks at me and touches me – it's not just what he says, it's the way he shows me – he makes me feel so hot.

'Flossie,' he rasps, 'oh fuck.'

His eyes flash helplessly at me, and knowing he's so close makes me lose all control. As I tip over the edge, I can feel him come too, in rapid jerks of his hips as he pumps deep inside me. Groaning loudly together, the ripples of pleasure flooding my body are so consuming that I would lose my balance if he wasn't holding me in place, my limbs trembling, head spinning, heart hammering.

As we catch our breath, I collapse against him and eventually his mouth searches for mine, kissing me and breaking into a smile.

'What?' I ask, drawing back to look at him properly.

'I was just thinking… it sounds stupid.'

'Tell me,' I beg softly.

He sighs. 'I was just thinking, how lucky it was that I picked this flat, and how lucky I am that you decided to stay.'

20

When Kieran first tries to get out of the bed the following morning, I drag him back under the sheets, but he groans and tells me off for making it harder to leave, reminding me that he really can't be late on account of, you know, needing to practise before that fairly important career-defining game he's playing tomorrow.

'We should have woken up earlier,' he growls into my neck, my arms wrapped around his, my fingers threading through his hair and tugging it suggestively.

I sigh, reluctantly letting him go and snuggling back into the pillows. 'Wimbledon is so annoying. It keeps getting in the way of our fun.'

'Yes,' he agrees, leaning over me and propping himself up on his elbows either side of my head, 'but it's also because of Wimbledon that we met.'

'That's true. It's really a love-hate relationship I have with this tournament.'

He grins, kisses the tip of my nose then my mouth, moving his lips down to my collarbone and in between my breasts, before a small sound of frustration climbs up his throat and he forces himself up away from me, rolling out of bed.

I lie for a few minutes in blissful cosiness while I listen to the sound of the shower, letting my mind wander, imagining if this is what it would be like on weekend mornings if we were really together. I picture us lying together in bed lazily, holding hands as we go out for brunch in the Village, me complaining that he has to leave for training, bickering over his hours on the tennis court and the mind-blowing make-up sex we'd have after...

Uh-oh. I'm even daydreaming about *arguing* with this guy.

And this could be over in a week. The idea makes me shudder, so I swing my legs out of bed and go into the kitchen to put on the coffee, hoping that keeping busy will distract me from all the thoughts racing through my mind, good and bad.

Checking my phone while I stir the spoon around my mug, I gasp at a WhatsApp from Iris that reads:

He kissed you in the rain. IN. THE. RAIN. ARE YOU FUCKING KIDDING ME?! You are living a FANTASY. That picture is the best thing I've ever seen, like a snapshot from a movie. Call me and tell me EVERYTHING!!

It doesn't take me long to find the picture she's talking about. Someone must have been lurking nearby outside the pub and noticed us. I would be upset at the invasion of privacy and the pervy actions of a stranger thinking it's appropriate to take secret photographs of us kissing, but... it's a damn good photo. Iris is right, it looks like it could be a still from a movie, me tipped back in his strong arms, our eyes blissfully closed, our lips locked, his chiselled jaw glistening with moisture, my hair dripping wet...

I smile to myself. My very own Audrey-Hepburn-in-*Breakfast-at-Tiffany's* moment.

The photo has gone viral on social media and I see from clips posted that it's even made it onto morning shows as an 'uplifting' segment, presenters swooning over it. I bite my lip as I scroll through the trending tag #WimbledonRomance.

'You've seen it then,' Kieran grimaces, coming into the kitchen showered and dressed. He pads over to me with a concerned expression. 'I'm sorry.'

Putting my phone down on the counter, I stand up on my tiptoes to kiss him. 'I'm not. We look pretty good.'

He sighs, his hands resting on my hips. 'You do. But still. You must be upset.'

'Forget it,' I press, giving him a relaxed smile. 'I'm not going to let it ruin how amazing last night was. Are you?'

He shakes his head.

'Good. It's not important. I'll be back in a minute.'

He stands still, his head bowed slightly in deep thought, as I pull away to go to the bathroom and brush my teeth. When I return, he's chopping up some fruit. I lean against the counter in my pyjama cami top and shorts, sipping my coffee, my stomach filling with fluttering butterflies as I watch him make his smoothie, loving the way he knows his way around my kitchen.

'I have five minutes before the car arrives,' he tells me hastily. 'Want to go out into the garden for a bit?'

I lead the way and we place our drinks down on the small outside table, wiping down the garden chairs and sitting next to each other. He leans back, closing his eyes and as I watch him relax with the sun beating down on his face, the early birds providing our background music, I realise that this idyllic scenario is doing nothing to help put an end to my runaway daydreams about our future.

'I could get used to this.' He sighs, putting his hands behind his head, his biceps straining against the sleeves of his T-shirt.

I lift my eyes to the sky. *Seriously, God?* You're letting him say shit like that when I'm trying to be SENSIBLE here?!

'Me too,' I murmur, looking out at my tiny garden.

I'd put a bit of work into it recently, sprucing it up a bit so it looked nice for the photographs that were going to the letting agency. It's small, but it had actually taken quite a few hours of googling and hard work to make it look presentable. It's worth it, though. The sunflowers and sweet peas I'd planted along the raised borders are blooming. I'm very proud of them – although now I've seen the floral displays at Wimbledon, they don't seem all that impressive in comparison.

'It's so peaceful here,' he comments. 'You forget you're in a city.'

'Mm.' I take a sip of my drink. 'Do you ever get much time off?'

'We get some weeks away from the tour,' he says, opening his eyes and looking straight ahead, 'but I'm always doing some kind of training. It's always hanging over you, the tournaments, the strategy, your losses.'

'Your wins,' I add pointedly.

He sighs heavily. 'It's one hell of a career, and I'm lucky to have had it. But there's not much time for anything else.'

'But you love it, right?'

A muscle flinches in his jaw. 'I love tennis. The tour... it's tiring.'

We sit in silence for a beat, before he clears his throat and sits up. Swivelling in his seat, he rests his elbows on his knees as he leans towards me. 'I have a question to ask you.'

'Okay.'

'Are you busy tonight?'

'You want another game of darts? It's fine if you do, but tell me now because then I'll spend the day practising so I can kick your butt.'

He chuckles. 'I'd honestly prefer that, but no, I don't want to play darts with you. Actually I was hoping you'd come with me to the players' event tonight. It's at this posh hotel in Kingston and it's hosted by the All England tennis club chairman. I thought... I wondered if you'd like to come. With me.'

My heart jumps into my throat. 'Seriously?'

'Yeah, I mean, I can't guarantee it will be all that fun, lots of mingling and small talk. Definitely not as fun as playing darts down the pub, but I thought, you know, with you as my date, it would make things a lot better. And there will be free Champagne.' He hesitates, his eyes falling to the ground nervously. 'But if you don't want to, it's really not—'

'I'd love to.'

He brightens. 'Yeah?'

'Yeah.'

'Great. That's... great.' He breaks into a relieved smile, sending shivers of happiness down my spine. A thought seems to flit across his brain and he furrows his brow. 'It's black tie. Do you have a dress? Sorry, short notice.'

'It's fine. I'll get something new,' I say coolly, desperately trying to contain the delirious excitement he's set off in my body that makes my chest tighten and my skin tingle. I want to scream and jump up and down, dancing on the spot. Instead, I gaze out at my sunflowers. 'It's a nice excuse to go shopping. I'll message Iris and see if she can help.'

His phone goes and he checks the screen. 'Car's outside. I better go.'

Getting up from his seat, he moves round to stand behind me, leaning down and wrapping his arms around me, resting his chin on my shoulder.

'If you're buying something new for the occasion, then I'd like to pay for it,' he offers. 'It's the least I can do when I've dropped this on you last minute.'

'No, Kieran, that's not necessary.'

'I'd like to,' he says softly in my ear.

'Thank you, but I can't let you do that. I'm really happy to buy it myself!'

'Let me spoil you. Please,' he says kissing my ear, his lips driving all sense and stubborn protests out of my brain.

Letting out a heavy sigh, I run my hand along his forearm resting across my collarbones. 'If you insist...'

'Good. I do,' he states, straightening. 'Someone from my team will be in touch.'

I raise my eyebrows. 'Very VIP of you. Have your people call my people.'

'And don't hold back. Buy whatever dress you want,' he

says, his hands massaging my shoulders. 'You're going to look amazing. I'm excited to see you in it.'

'You have no idea what I'm wearing yet.' I laugh.

'Doesn't matter,' he says, leaning back down to kiss me on the cheek. 'You look incredible in everything. I'll see you tonight.'

With a final squeeze on my shoulders, he heads back into the house. I wait for him to call out goodbye and shut the front door behind him before I scrunch up my eyes and let out a squeal of pure joy, jumping to my feet and running inside to call Iris.

'The car is here,' Kieran calls from the living room.

'I'll be out in a minute,' I shout back, putting my earrings on and taking a step back from the mirror to look at my reflection properly.

I nervously turn at an angle to check the back of the dress. It's the most expensive thing I've ever worn: a floor-length fitted black gown with a plunge neckline and a thigh split. I'm not sure I would have had the confidence to choose this if Iris hadn't come shopping with me this afternoon. We'd gone to the type of shop I'd usually be intimidated by, but the staff were very welcoming and didn't blink when I said what I was shopping for, getting to work immediately selecting a variety of dresses.

'They've seen the rain picture,' Iris had whispered to me with a sly smile.

The photograph of Kieran and I kissing in the rain is front page of nearly every paper on the newsstand. People have lost their heads over it, calling it the most romantic celebrity moment of the year. I don't know about that, but I can confirm it was magical.

When I walked out the changing room in this dress, Iris's jaw had dropped to the floor and she'd slowly set her glass of Champagne down to shamelessly gawp at me.

'That's the one,' she'd said, the shop assistants nodding in agreement.

'It's not too... slutty?'

She'd tilted her head and given me an *oh-please* look. 'It's sexy as fuck, if that's what you mean. Don't you feel good in that thing? I mean, look at you!'

'I do feel good in it,' I'd admitted, blushing. 'I don't know when else I'd get to wear something like this.'

'Life is short, bitch, wear the dress,' Iris had stated, picking up her Champagne again.

'*Amen*,' the shop assistant next to her had muttered.

So, I didn't feel I had much choice in the matter but to allow Kieran to buy me this gown and then I'd bought some new shoes and jewellery to go with it – we'd gone for a pair of Christian Louboutin strappy heels and statement gold earrings. I've never spent that much money on shoes before, but this is a once-in-a-lifetime event. I have to go all out.

This afternoon I'd gone for a blow-dry and as one of the stylists curled my hair, the other hairdressers crowded round my chair to pelt me with questions about Kieran and the night ahead of me. When I'd tried to answer their questions best I could, one of them sighed wistfully and went, 'You're living a fairy tale.'

Standing here in this gown, I get what she means. In this dress, I don't feel like a nobody. I feel like a princess, getting ready to go off to the ball.

With a spritz of perfume on my wrist and neck, I grab my clutch bag and tentatively open the bedroom door, slowly making my way down the hallway and into the living room. Kieran is waiting by the fireplace, leaning on the mantelpiece in his tux. He looks devastatingly handsome in his tailored black jacket, crisp white shirt and silk black bow tie. With his designer stubble that shows off his chiselled jaw, and his dark hair that's perfectly styled without looking like he's spent too much time on it, he manages to look both suave and ruggedly unkempt at the same time. He looks up on my entrance and does a double take. His mouth parts slightly as his eyes roam down the dress and back up again. He swallows, walking over to me and exhaling as he stops in front of me.

'Is this okay?' I ask, looking up at him under my heavily mascaraed eyelashes.

'You... you look...' His brow creases as he trails off, unable to find the right word quick enough. I try and fail to suppress a smile. 'Jesus. That's quite a dress.'

'You look great,' I say quietly, my cheeks flushing as I reach up to straighten his bow tie. I lower my hands to rest against his solid chest, feeling it rise against my palms with each breath. 'Like an Irish James Bond.'

The corners of his lips twitch, before he leans forward to kiss me on the cheek, the musky and masculine scent of his cologne sending my head into an uncontrollable spin. His face lingers against mine, his stubble tickling my cheek. I feel the warmth of his hand through the thin fabric of the dress sliding onto my hip and round to my lower back.

'Maybe we skip the party tonight,' he suggests in a low, deep voice, his breath in my ear sending a shiver down my spine.

'We can't,' I whisper, biting my lip as he pulls me closer to him. 'Neil would kill you.'

'Happy to take the risk,' he murmurs, his lips lightly kissing down the slope of my neck and along my shoulder, before he takes the strap of my dress in his teeth and tugs lightly at it.

'Kieran,' I warn, giggling and pushing him away. 'We're going to be late.'

He sighs as he reluctantly steps back, the intensity of his eyes making my skin tingle.

'Fine, but let's make a quick appearance,' he says, as I turn round to lead the way out the front door. 'Five minutes there is all we need.'

I laugh, shaking my head as I wait for him to step out so I can lock up after us. 'Five minutes! After all this effort, I'm staying there longer than *five* minutes, Kieran. Do you know how much this dress cost?'

'Actually, I do happen to know.'

'Oh yeah. Thanks by the way.'

'The pleasure really is all mine.'

Standing close behind me as I lock up the door, he places his hands on my waist and nuzzles into my hair.

'We don't need to go out for me to make you feel that this dress was worth every penny,' he says in a low suggestive voice, sweeping my hair to the side so he can run kisses along my shoulder. 'Let's stay. Please?'

Smiling to myself, I turn round and give him a look.

'All right, we'll go,' he concedes, holding out his arm to help guide me to the car in these towering heels.

Kieran's driver Matthew is waiting by the door to the back seat, opening it with a warm smile as I carefully slide in with Kieran following in behind. As Matthew shuts our door, Kieran glances over at me and lets out a small groan.

'What is it?' I ask, frowning at him.

'This *dress*,' he mumbles as he sits close to me and looks pointedly at my legs. I realise that when I'm sat down, the split of the skirt opens widely to expose the majority of my thigh.

'Ready to go?' Matthew checks, getting into the front.

His eyes fixed on me, Kieran exhales through his nose. 'If we must.'

We pull away and after a couple of minutes, Kieran's hand slides onto my thigh, my skin prickling with heat beneath his fingers. My breath catches as he moves his hand up at an antagonisingly slow pace, slipping beneath the fabric of the dress, the warm pressure of his palm sending shuddering jolts through my body. As his hand slips between my legs, I witness his eyes widen with surprise.

He swallows, asking in a hushed voice, 'Are you... are you not wearing any underwear?'

Shooting him an impish grin, I shake my head.

'Christ,' he says hoarsely under his breath. 'Tonight is going to be torture. We're staying *five* minutes tops and then we're coming back.'

'I want to enjoy this fancy event, so we may stay there all night,' I tease. 'You'll just have to be patient.'

He quirks his brow. 'Oh really? You're happy to wait all night.'

'Really.'

'Hm.'

He's looking at me dangerously. I've set a very competitive man an interesting challenge. His hand hasn't budged from between my legs and, digging his teeth into his bottom lip, he runs his fingers along the top of my thigh before his thumb begins to lightly trace circles around my clit. I inhale sharply and he leans in to whisper in my ear, his warm breath tickling my skin and making me shudder.

'Soon, you're going to be begging me to turn the car around,' he murmurs.

I believe him.

My breaths come faster as he gradually increases the pressure of his thumb. When he slides two fingers inside me, my back arches as my hips instinctively rock into his hand. Heat flushing through my body, I clench my teeth, trying to be silent as he watches me closely, his gaze focused and intense. His fingers retreat and sink into me again, deeper this time, and I gasp, my fingernails sinking into the leather seat as he increases the pressure of his thumb. Oh God, he's *so good* at this.

'*Kieran*,' I breathe, my muscles tightening around his fingers.

My whole body is flushed with heat and my toes are curling in my stilettos, my legs naturally falling open wider as I almost forget we're not alone. He's making me forget.

The indicator clicks come on as the car slows, reminding me.

My eyes dart nervously to the driver and Kieran slowly draws his hand away, gripping my thigh. Wound up and whimpering, I reluctantly bring my knees together, wanting nothing more than to ask Matthew to turn the car around. *Damn it.*

'Here we are,' Matthew announces cheerfully, and I hope he's been oblivious to everything that's been going on back here, although I have to admit that it was too hot for me to really care.

Still watching me intently, Kieran tips his head back against the headrest, his Adam's apple bobbing. 'Matthew, would you mind driving around for a bit longer before we pull up to the hotel? I'm going to need a minute to... calm my nerves.'

'Of course,' Matthew replies, driving on down the road and taking a left.

Glancing down at Kieran's hands attempting to hide his erection isn't helping me pull my focus from the pulsing heat between my legs. I turn to look out the window, suppressing a smile. Matthew takes a long route round and when we approach the entrance to the driveway of the hotel a second time a good few minutes later, he checks with Kieran in the rear-view mirror. Catching his eye, Kieran clears his throat.

'Ready now, thank you.' He turns to me, arching his brow. 'So. Five minutes and then we leave?'

'Make it three.'

He locks his eyes with mine, a dangerous smile playing across his lips.

21

A grand Victorian manor house set in a sprawling secluded estate, the whole of Warren House Hotel has been hired for the event tonight. There's a red carpet but no paparazzi, just the official photographers hired by the organisers, and the ballroom looks spectacular with dozens of flickering candles and extravagant green and purple flower arrangements on display. A string quartet is playing in the far corner and staff are waiting on the entrance to greet you with long-stemmed flutes of Champagne. I gladly take one – I'm going to need as much confidence as I can get at such a glitzy event – while Kieran sticks to a soft drink, fourth round looming over him tomorrow.

From the moment we enter the party, Kieran barely leaves my side. Guiding me through the room with his hand resting protectively on my lower back, he stays next to me as I'm introduced to the chairman and her husband, before his hand returns to the base of my spine and he weaves a path for us through the crowd of glamorous guests to a spot by the window that looks out onto the lawn. Although I may not be a tennis aficionado, I'm still able to appreciate a few of the big sports stars in the room – Serena Williams is about a metre away from me, in conversation – but I'm soon distracted from my celebrity spotting by patrons of the club, keen to introduce themselves. Kieran's fingers brush against mine as they eagerly ask him questions and, while offering them vague and tentative answers, I notice him continually glancing at me.

At first I think it's because he's worried about the fact that

I'm out of my comfort zone and don't know anyone, so I make a huge effort to be as warm and friendly as possible, launching into conversations with other guests nearby in the hope that he's reassured – I don't want him feeling like he has to babysit me all night. But I gradually get the feeling that he actually wants to stay close to me out of choice. He's tense here and more reserved, and I realise that I have the rare privilege of seeing Kieran O'Sullivan at home, relaxed and at ease. Outside those walls, he gives the impression of the person he's expected to be: moody and cold. But I know now he's neither of those things, not really.

'Ah, Kieran, there you are,' Neil says, appearing next to us. He pats Kieran's arm, looking relieved. 'It's good to see you.' His eyes flicker to me and his jaw tenses. 'Flora, nice to see you, too.'

'Thank you for asking the chairman to let Kieran have a plus-one,' I say gratefully.

'Yes, well. I'm not sure Kieran gave me much of a choice,' he mutters, before clearing his throat. 'Anyway, lots of people I'd like you to chat with tonight, Kieran, so stay where you are and I'll find you in a moment.'

'Can't wait,' Kieran says under his breath, rolling his eyes once Neil has left.

'What did he mean by that?' I ask, watching him weave through the crowd, looking for someone specific. 'That you didn't give him much of a choice.'

'I said if he couldn't swing a plus-one for you tonight, then he shouldn't expect me to show,' he answers simply, taking a sip of his drink.

'Kieran! I'm trying to get him to like me! You throwing around diva demands on my behalf won't help matters.'

His lips twitch. 'That's the second time you've called me a diva, Flossie. I'm beginning to worry that the first time wasn't a joke.'

'Have you met you? You refuse to drink tap water.'

'I don't refuse. I just... prefer bottled.'

'Classic diva excuse.'

He smiles to himself. 'Anyway, Neil likes you. Who wouldn't like you?'

'Uh, you when we first met,' I remind him haughtily.

'I didn't dislike you.' He hesitates. 'Okay, maybe a little. But largely because you chucked wine at me. I got over that very quickly and then you just irritated me.'

'Aw, that's sweet. I feel so comforted.'

He arches an eyebrow, and lowers his voice. 'It still didn't stop me from thinking about you in that towel.' I feel my cheeks heat while Kieran gives me a meaningful look. 'Why do you care if Neil likes you anyway?'

'Because he's your coach. He's… important.'

I realise that I'm entering uncharted territory here. I don't want to lie to him and act as though I don't care what the people in his life think of me, but I also don't want to scare him off by acting like a girlfriend hoping for the approval of his friends and family.

'I just think it would be easier in general if Neil likes me,' I add. 'So if he doesn't want me to come to certain events, then maybe allow it.'

'I appreciate the suggestion, but I disagree,' Kieran replies with a shrug.

'He probably thinks I'm a distraction. A bad one.'

'Then he's an idiot.' Kieran frowns, before he peers down at me. 'If anything, you make me want to do better.'

There's something about that look he's giving me that's making my heart pound against my chest and sends a tingling warmth swirling through my veins. His gaze has softened now and he's almost smiling, and it makes me want to throw my arms around him and kiss him tenderly, and tell him that I'm proud of everything he's achieved. I'm here for him. I'll keep cheering him on. I'll hold him if he loses. Whatever he needs. I'm on his side.

Instead, I take a sip of my drink and say, 'You are playing fairly well at the moment.'

'Not too bad.'

'It's the pre-match blowing bubbles isn't it.'

He laughs lightly, nodding. 'The bubbles must be it.'

Someone accidentally knocks into Kieran's shoulder as they pass by.

'Sorry, mate – Kieran!' The man's apologetic smile falters.

Kieran stiffens, hostility oozing off him. I know the other guy is familiar but it takes a moment for me to realise that it's Chris Courtney, the Australian tennis player and Kieran's biggest on-court rival. The one who married Kieran's ex-girlfriend painfully soon after she and Kieran broke up. While it's safe to assume that the tabloids occasionally exaggerate or get celebrity private matters wrong, witnessing just one look between these two men is enough to tell me that all those articles about how much they dislike each other are spot on. They're both so tall that they're at the same eye level, serving each other the same hard stare. A couple of years older than Kieran, Chris has long, thick fair hair, hazel eyes and soft features. He's good-looking in a boyishly handsome way.

Easing his shoulders and breaking into an easy-going grin, Chris shoves one hand in his pocket and holds out the other to Kieran. Reluctantly, Kieran takes it and they shake hands. The air between them is so cold, it sends a shiver down my spine.

'How have you been, mate?' Chris asks, dropping his hand.

'Fine, thank you,' Kieran replies icily.

'You haven't been doing too badly this week. Still got a few surprises up your sleeve, eh? Guess we'll see how long it lasts,' Chris says, tilting his head. When Kieran doesn't respond, his eyes drift across to me and widen with intrigue. 'I'm sorry, very rude of me. I'm Chris Courtney.'

I politely take his outstretched hand. 'Flora.'

'It's a pleasure to meet you, Flora,' he says, his hand clasping mine for longer than necessary. He takes the opportunity to look me up and down. 'A real pleasure.'

'You too.'

Kieran's hand is on the small of my back again and I

instinctively lean into his side. Chris notices the gesture and looks bemused, putting all his attention on me.

'Tell me, Flora, what do you do?' he asks with a flirtatious smile.

'Oh, um, not much. I was working as a PA, and then—'

'She's an artist,' Kieran cuts in, nudging me with his hip.

'An aspiring artist,' I clarify, blushing.

Chris arches an eyebrow. 'I'm sure you must be very talented.'

'She is,' Kieran states.

'I bet.' Chris smiles, his eyes roaming down my dress and making my skin crawl. 'I'd love to see your work sometime. I've got a good eye for art, Flora.'

Kieran shifts, the pressure of his hand on my back increasing.

'Really?' I say, feigning interest but desperate for him to leave us alone.

'Around the time I won my first Grand Slam – you remember that, right, Kieran? I think you were there…' he pauses to wink at me, as Kieran's jaw twitches '…I bought a fascinating piece by a young artist who no one had heard of called Trent Bloom. Now, he's a major player in the New York art scene. His pieces are selling for hundreds of thousands.'

'Wow. That's… amazing.'

'If you wanted, I could introduce you to some people,' Chris suggests, taking a sip of his drink and sucking it through his teeth. 'I know a lot of big names. Just say the word and I'll set up a meeting.'

'Oh, uh, thanks, but I'm good,' I answer.

I hear Kieran exhale quietly next to me, his shoulders dropping.

Watching me curiously, Chris nods. 'You want to do it your way. I respect that.' He notices someone waving at him across the room, trying to get his attention and he smiles at me apologetically. 'Excuse me, I'm wanted elsewhere, but I hope we get to talk again, Flora.'

He leaves, swaggering through the parting crowd to his acquaintance. Kieran watches him go, burning holes into his back.

'Are you all right?' I ask cautiously, turning to face him properly and shield him from anyone else.

'Fine,' he says gruffly. 'He's... grating.'

I snort. 'One way of putting it. He's just what I thought he'd be. A smarmy wanker.'

Kieran's eyebrows shoot up in surprise and then he breaks into a wide smile. 'I know I shouldn't be pleased that you don't like him, because that would be petty, but...' he pauses, his eyes sparkling at me '...I'm really fucking glad you don't like him.'

I laugh. 'I get why you must hate him, but why is he so against you? Shouldn't he be really embarrassed about what happened with Rachel? Apologetic about how it played out, or at least being sure to stay out of your way?'

'That's not Chris,' Kieran says bitterly. 'He's fiercely ambitious, loves the spotlight and, most of all, hates losing. That's what makes him such a good tennis player.'

'You're all those things, too. Except the spotlight thing.'

'When I played him in the final of the Australian Open all those years ago, all the talk was about me,' Kieran recalls, his brow furrowing. 'Because I was so young and everything with Aidan – the press were all over me. Chris was near me in age, and had obviously done well to get to the final, but no one was talking about him. He hated that. He resented me for it. In his eyes, he was the young star, not me.'

'But he won, so why does he still have it in for you?'

'After that the press played us off against each other, telling us comments that the other one had made. We were both kids, so we'd snap back. He said nasty things about me. I said worse things about him. It was a vicious circle that the papers encouraged. We kept clashing; they kept printing and selling. Great entertainment I suppose. You can imagine how much they loved the drama of Rachel leaving me for him.'

'That must have been horrible.'

'One of the lowest points of my life,' he admits, before giving a weak smile. 'You have no idea how bad it was when the press came for me...' He trails off and his eyes glaze over as he loses himself for a fleeting moment in a memory, but he soon pulls himself back, clearing his throat. 'It's in the past. I moved on and learnt to keep my private life private. It became hard to trust anyone, especially when Rachel and Chris did so many interviews.'

'Ugh. It sounds like you dodged a bullet. And what does she even see in Chris? He seems to actually enjoy making you uncomfortable.'

'Yeah, our issues aside, I've learnt that Chris isn't exactly a decent person. Let's hope he gets knocked out, so I don't have to face him this tournament,' Kieran says wistfully, glancing over at Chris as the people he's with burst out laughing at something he's said.

Chris is laughing louder than any of them at his own joke.

'I thought enemies liked the challenge of facing each other,' I remark. 'Isn't that, like, a classic thing if you're an athlete? You have to beat the best so you know you're the best.'

Kieran arches his brow at me. 'Does all your knowledge of athletes come from movies?'

'Pretty much, yes.'

'I thought so.' He gives me a knowing smile, the crinkles around his mouth sending a flutter of butterflies around my stomach. 'I obviously would like nothing better than to beat Chris Courtney in a tennis tournament, but I also hate coming up against him. He likes to attack his opponents mentally.'

'Like trash talk?'

Kieran presses his lips together. 'Worse. He knows exactly what to say to make you lose your footing. He stoops low and he's not afraid to sting right where it hurts.'

His eyes darken as he continues to watch Chris from afar. I can only imagine the kind of comments Kieran has had to endure from someone like that. Finding his hand, I lace my fingers through his so he tears his eyes away from Chris and fixes them on mine.

'One more voice to shut out, then,' I say. 'You'll have to find a way to ignore him and not let those comments get to you. Hey, do you remember how you told Jonah that you don't like people who belittle others to make themselves feel bigger? Right before you pinned him up against the fridge?'

'I have a vague recollection.'

'Chris is doing the same. Throwing around insults doesn't make him some kind of big dog on the court. It's a sign of weakness. By going to the effort of making those cutting comments, he's letting slip his own self-doubts. He knows you can beat him; that's why he wants to bring you down.'

He considers my point, his eyebrows pulled together.

'Kieran!' Neil interrupts, sidling up to us accompanied by a very familiar face. 'I'd like to introduce you to John McEnroe.'

Kieran's eyes light up as he shakes his hand. 'It's an honour, sir.'

I might not be a tennis expert, but I know John McEnroe, one of the greatest tennis players of all time. I smile politely as they strike up conversation but, not long after Kieran has introduced me, I take the opportunity to place my drink down and excuse myself to go to the bathroom. It's obvious that Kieran is talking to one of his heroes – both of them joking about the perils of losing one's temper on court – and I didn't want to get in the way of such a momentous meeting. Neil was doing his best to edge me out the conversation anyway.

While I'm in the bathroom I wonder if I should use tonight as an opportunity to win over Neil. I'm sure if I'm charming enough and make it clear that I'm not here to distract Kieran from Wimbledon, he might warm to me.

Worth a shot.

Having checked my reflection and freshened my lipstick, I emerge from the bathroom and begin to navigate my way through the guests back towards Neil and Kieran. But when I'm halfway across the room to them, someone steps directly into my path.

'Flora, wasn't it?' Chris Courtney says, his hazel eyes flashing at me. They flicker down to my empty hand. 'You don't have a drink! Let's sort that.'

'It's okay, I have one over—'

He clicks his fingers at a passing waiter to get their attention, taking a glass of red wine from their tray and passing it to me. 'There you go.'

'I actually wasn't drinking red. I'd rather—'

'So, what's the deal with you and O'Sullivan?' he cuts in, raking a hand through his hair. 'What did he do to land a girl like you?'

My cheeks flush with heat. 'Uh, nothing. We met recently and it's been great getting to know him.'

He snorts. 'Great? Not a word I'd use for him.'

'Guess we'll agree to disagree.'

I go to step around him but he moves to block my way.

'The thing is, Flora, I'd hate for you to be under the wrong impression here,' he says, leaning in conspiratorially, forcing me to stumble backwards. 'Kieran isn't the sort of person you want to align yourself with. He's not a favourite, if you know what I mean.'

I glare up at him. 'I have no idea what you mean.'

'He's a loose cannon on the court. Impulsive and reactive. These are not good qualities.' He sighs, giving me a sympathetic look. 'You should be with a winner. Not a loser.'

Ignoring him, I try to step past him again, but he stops me.

'Look, I was serious about the art meetings I can set up for you,' he says in a low voice, his eyebrows raised. 'If ever you want to come over for a drink, my door is open.'

He reaches out to brush my arm lightly with his fingers.

I physically recoil, staring at him in disbelief. 'You're *married*.'

'She's away filming.' He shrugs with a sly smile.

'I really would like to get back to Kieran,' I mutter, not bothering to hide my disgust. 'Please move out of my way.'

'It's cool, we're just talking here,' he says breezily, giving me a strange look as though I've overreacted. 'I'm trying to do you a favour.'

'Everything okay here?' Kieran asks abruptly, coming out of nowhere and looming over me, his eyes filled with concern.

'It's fine,' I tell him hurriedly, aware that others are starting to look our way. 'It's nothing.'

'It didn't look like nothing,' he growls, rounding on Chris, his fists clenched at his sides. 'What were you saying to her?'

Chris barks with laughter, attracting more attention. 'Paranoid much, are you, Kieran? We were having a conversation. Is that allowed or are you that threatened by me? I'm married, mate, remember.' He sneers at him, before adding quietly so no one else can hear, 'I think you may know my wife. At least, you thought you did. Uh-oh, have I hit a nerve?'

'Kieran, leave it,' I instruct sternly, noticing his jaw tense. 'Ignore him. *Please*.'

'Do you want to know what Flora and I were talking about?' Chris says, relishing Kieran's reaction and pushing it for his own amusement. 'I was telling her what everyone else here knows. That you can't win. You never have and you never will. You may have had a bit of luck so far, but we all know it won't last. You can't quite go the distance, can you? Always fall at the last hurdle.'

'I'm warning you, Chris,' Kieran says in a voice so venomous it makes my stomach twist, his eyes burning with rage.

'What?' Chris raises his eyebrows, bemused. 'What are you going to do, Kieran? Lose your temper? That wouldn't come as a surprise to anyone, would it. We've all seen it countless times before. Every time I beat you, over and over and over, out comes the rage.' He tuts, before turning to me. 'You really want to be with someone who has a tantrum when things don't go their way?'

'Don't talk to her,' Kieran snaps, taking a step forwards so he's right in Chris's face.

The room has descended into quiet now as everyone tunes in

to the confrontation, except for the string quartet that heroically plays on, giving the drama a jarring classical theme tune. Panic rises in my throat as I notice Neil looking over in horror. This has turned into a scene and it's all my fault. I reach out for Kieran's arm, but he shakes me off.

Chris is smirking, his eyes lit up with the thrill of riling him. 'Ooh, you really do lose control, don't you, Kieran. You just can't bear the fact that I beat you. You've lost every Grand Slam match you've played against me and you lost Rachel. That must still hurt. Is that what you think about every time we play? You think about how you weren't quite enough so she chose me instead? How you couldn't give her what she wanted, but I could?'

Kieran's chest rises dramatically with a deep breath and then as he exhales, he lowers his eyes and shakes his head. As he turns away from Chris, I feel a wave of relief.

He's found the strength to walk away.

'My question is, why do you still bother playing when you know you can't win?' Chris sighs, raising his voice slightly so Kieran won't miss it. 'You know you can't take the pressure. It's in the O'Sullivan blood.'

Kieran freezes. His eyes widen and he hunches forward as though he's just been punched in the stomach and had all the air knocked right out of him. I know what's going to happen, I can see it in his eyes as they glaze over with rage. Before I can do anything to stop him, Kieran has swivelled back around to face him and, without a word, in the middle of the party, he punches Chris Courtney square in the face.

22

When I open my eyes the next morning, Kieran is placing a mug of coffee down on the bedside table next to me. He's dressed and ready in his sports kit, and he smells fresh and clean, so he must have already showered.

'What time is it?' I ask, yawning as I sit myself up.

'Early,' he replies, taking a seat on the edge of the bed and resting his hand on top of the duvet over my knee.

I reach out to take my hand in his. 'How are you?'

He looks down at his feet.

After he stormed out of Warren House last night, he refused to talk about what happened. He said nothing on the short journey back to the flat and when I asked him if he was okay, he said he just wanted to go to bed and not talk about it. I respected his wishes and prepared to sleep on the sofa, happy to give him his space, but as I began sorting out the pillows in the living room in my pyjamas, he came in in his boxers and, giving me a strange look, quietly asked what I was doing. His tone was much softer and calmer, the rage he'd been battling with on the drive having subsided.

'It's fourth round tomorrow – you need a good night's rest,' I'd said with a reassuring smile. 'I'm fine to sleep here. This sofa is really comfy.'

He'd come plodding over and wrapped his arms around my waist, resting his chin on my shoulder. 'Will you come sleep with me tonight?' he'd asked, his voice muffled in my hair.

'Are you sure?'

'Yes. I want you there.'

So I'd abandoned my sofa and climbed in with him into bed. He'd pulled me close to him and after we'd turned off the lights, he whispered sleepily, 'You're wearing the Snoopy.'

Which I was. I'd smiled to myself as his arm tightened round my waist and his hand clasped over mine. It's so funny how much he loves that stupid T-shirt.

I thought that after the drama of the evening, it would be difficult to fall asleep, but safe and snug, nestled into my Kieran cocoon, I found myself drifting off easily. *Everything will be better in the morning*, I thought. But now it's morning, I'm not so sure. From the look on Kieran's face, things certainly don't seem better.

'The flat is surrounded by paparazzi,' Kieran finally answers, his whole body deflating. 'They've taken over the road. Today is going to be hell. I'm so sorry.'

'They know what happened?' I ask, reaching for my coffee.

He nods. 'The general consensus is that I'm the bad guy, and Chris is the hero.'

My mug pauses halfway to my lips. '*Excuse me?* How is that possible?'

'His people got to work very quickly,' he explains quietly, deep creases etched between his eyebrows. 'The story that the majority of publications have run with is that, according to "sources"—' he uses his fingers to mimic the quotation marks and rolls his eyes '—I saw Chris talking to you, jumped to the wrong conclusion and punched him before he had the chance to explain that he was generously offering my aspiring-artist friend the chance to meet some of his contacts in the business. Apparently, he's forgiven me for the misunderstanding. Very generous of him,' he adds drily.

'Surely people won't believe you hit him just because you saw him talking to me. That's ridiculous.'

'Not that hard to believe when they see me lose my temper on court over a bad call.'

'That's different. And he said horrible things! He was pushing you!'

'Yeah, but the reporters don't know that.'

'Then maybe we should tell them. They should know the truth.'

He shakes his head. 'I don't speak to the press. Not about stuff like this.'

'But if they knew—'

'If I told them the truth, I'd have to tell them exactly what he said,' Kieran interjects firmly. 'I didn't punch him because he spoke to you, although, I'll admit, that made me *want* to punch him.' He hesitates, raising his eyebrows. 'Did he hit on you?'

'If I say yes, are you going to punch him again?'

'I'd hunt him down and kill him.'

'Then, no. He was, in fact, telling me how he thinks you're a real stand-up guy.'

'He did, didn't he? I am going to *kill* him.'

'I'd really rather you didn't.'

He sighs. 'If I promise you I won't, can you tell me what he said?'

'He may have implied that his wife was away and I should join him for a drink,' I say cautiously, wincing at the recollection. 'I knew he was an arsehole right from the off.'

Kieran's expression has darkened. He's too angry to speak, his mouth pressed in a thin, straight line. When he finally opens it, he utters, 'I should have punched him harder,' in a low, threatening growl.

'I think the punch you threw was good enough,' I say, attempting a light laugh to crack the tension. 'Kieran, it doesn't matter. He's a sleazeball – forget about him. You have to focus on the tournament. You're doing so brilliantly. I'm sorry that I caused all this mess. I'll make it up to you, I promise. I don't know how, but I'll think of something.'

He furrows his brow. 'Why are you sorry? Because of me, you

have reporters swarming the flat and prying into your life. *I'm sorry.*'

'If it wasn't for me talking to him last night, you wouldn't have punched him.'

'I've told you, I didn't punch him because he was talking to you. I punched him because of what he said about Aidan.'

I pause, frowning at him. '*Aidan.*'

He nods silently.

'I don't remember him saying anything about Aidan,' I admit, racking my brains and replaying the incident over and over in my head.

'He said I wouldn't win because I couldn't handle the pressure. Something that runs in the O'Sullivan blood,' Kieran says, looking pained.

'Wait, you think he was talking about Aidan?' I stare at him in disbelief. 'I just assumed he was talking about you and your dad or something, I didn't... surely he wouldn't stoop that low.'

'Yes, he would,' Kieran says gravely, a glaze of sadness over his eyes. 'He would, and he did.' He swallows, his forehead creasing as he looks down at his hands in his lap. 'Aidan had depression. Not many people know that. My dad didn't like to talk about it and he felt it was a family matter. He said he wanted to protect him, so we kept it quiet. Aidan had been on meds since his teens and... he'd struggled.' He pauses, sitting there quiet and pensive. When he speaks again, his voice is much softer. 'Most people know that he died of an overdose. They don't know that we're not sure it was an accident.'

I feel sick, my gut wrenching in pain.

'Kieran,' I whisper, hot tears filling my eyes, 'I'm so sorry.'

'There were always rumours surrounding his death,' he says, lifting his chin and inhaling deeply through his nose. 'Since his issues with mental health weren't widely known, a lot of people blamed what happened on the pressure of being in the sport. They think he couldn't handle it.' When he turns his head to look at me, his eyes are glistening. 'They're wrong. Tennis helped him. He came alive when he focused on the next match. He didn't mind the pressure. He enjoyed the competition. You should have seen him play, Flossie. He was born to play tennis. The one place he felt safe and in control was on the court.'

I sniff, giving him a watery smile.

'I punched Chris Courtney last night because he was implying Aidan couldn't handle the pressure, and that's why he did what he did.' Kieran's face crumples and he reaches up to rub his forehead. 'I shouldn't have risen to it.'

Unable to fight the need to hold him any longer, I shuffle down the bed and move so I'm kneeling next to him before I gently wrap my arms around him, clasping my hands over his far shoulder and resting my forehead on the one nearest to me. He doesn't say anything, but reaches up to place his hand over mine and dips his chin to rest on my forearm. We stay like that for a moment, and I lose myself in focusing on his breathing. It's shaky and uneven at first, but eventually becomes slow and steady. When I lift my head to look at him, I don't loosen my grip, refusing to let him go quite yet.

'Thank you for telling me,' I say quietly.

He turns his head and leans in, nudging his nose against mine before he kisses me, slow and gentle, his fingers brushing along my arm as his body slowly swivels towards me and then trailing around my shoulder and down to my waist. He pulls me closer as our kiss deepens and I bring my hands to rest on the nape of his neck.

When we break the kiss, he keeps his eyes closed and presses his forehead against mine. He lets out a small, contented sigh and a gratified warmth glows and swells in my belly as I interlace my fingers behind his neck, holding him there. No matter how close I am to this man, I want to be closer.

'Will you be at the match today?' he asks. 'If you're free, I'd like you to come sit with the team and watch the fourth round.'

I bite my lip. 'Kieran, I'd love to come, but after last night, I don't think Neil will be happy for me to be there. In terms of winning him over, it couldn't have gone worse for me.'

'I'm the one playing. Neil doesn't get a say in who I invite to watch,' he states firmly, getting up from the bed to go get his tennis bag ready. 'And with the headlines today, I'm going to need all the help I can get. I'd like you there.'

'If you really think it will help, then sure,' I say, unable to stop a smile at his insistence. 'I feel very honoured.' I hesitate, watching him carefully. 'Have you spoken to Neil yet? He looked mad when we left.'

'I'm sure he'll want to talk when he picks me up in a minute. I've had a lot of emails from Nicole, my publicist. I do not envy her this morning.'

'You certainly keep your publicity team on their toes.'

'Speaking of publicity, Nicole has mentioned that you and she might want to have a chat today about a few things.'

'What sort of things?'

'What to say to the press, what not to say—'

'That's easy,' I cut in, taking a large gulp of my coffee, 'I just won't talk to them at all. There. She doesn't need to come over now.'

'I think she'll also want to check you're... prepared.' He finishes zipping up his bag and throwing it on the end of the bed, before he puts his hands on his hips and gives me a hard stare. 'Last night changed things, Flossie. I couldn't go for a jog this morning, because reporters pretty much set up camp out on the road last night. They are all over this story, and a large component of it is you.'

'Me?' I clasp my mug, raising my eyebrows. 'But there's nothing to say about me.'

'They'll find something to say; they always do. God, what a fucking mess.' He sighs, lifting his eyes to the ceiling. 'I really am sorry, Flossie. We'll do our best to lie low and hopefully this will blow over soon. I don't know how I'm supposed to focus on the match today with all this shite going on.'

'You're just going to go play a bit of tennis, remember? One point after the other,' I say, trying my best to put him at ease. 'A few silly printed words don't need to affect your forehand. Nothing matters out there on the court but the tennis. Everything else is background noise.'

'I know. I could have done without the extra attention, that's all.'

'You're going to have extra attention anyway if you get through to the fifth round.'

'You mean, the quarter-finals.'

My eyes widen at him. 'Next round is the quarter-finals? Shit,' I blurt out, as he nods solemnly.

'I'm going into this as the major underdog and, thanks to today's headlines, I doubt the crowd will be on my side.'

'*I'm* on your side,' I state, pleased to have the opportunity to say it out loud. 'You won't feel alone today. Is there anything I can do to help lessen the nerves?'

'Oh I can think of a fair few things, but annoyingly I don't think we have time.'

I roll my eyes. 'I'm serious, Kieran. Get your mind out the gutter.'

'You can wear the Snoopy T-shirt.'

'You're obsessed with this thing,' I giggle, resting back into the pillows.

'Snoopy is one of my favourite cartoons,' he says matter-of-factly, checking his watch and swinging his bag over his shoulder.

'Wait, are you serious?'

'Yeah,' he says with a lazy grin. 'The moment I saw you wearing that on my first morning here, I knew I didn't stand a chance.'

'And here I was thinking I would wear my sexiest lingerie for later, but it turns out there's no need. I can just wear the Snoopy T-shirt.'

His eyes light up. 'I don't think there's any harm in a bit of variety.'

I smirk into my mug. 'That so?'

He comes round the side of the bed and leans in to kiss me on the lips. 'I'll make sure a car is arranged to pick you up to bring you to the grounds, okay?'

'Thank you,' I whisper, a thrill shooting through me as he kisses me again before he goes to leave. 'Good luck for today.'

'Why would I need luck when I'm just going to play a bit of tennis?' he calls back over his shoulder.

FLORA

Have you seen what they're saying about me?

IRIS

Have you seen you in that DRESS?
🔥🔥🔥🔥

'Rumoured property heiress'
That's what one paper has called me!!

I think that sounds quite cool

Yeah, it would be cool if I WAS one
But Dad's wife isn't exactly planning on
leaving me her family's empire
Have you seen all this stuff about Kieran?

Some people are on his side
Anyway ignore the stories
I believe your version of events
Most people know that the tabloids exaggerate

So embarrassing
My dad's PA called to 'check in'
He basically asked me wtf was going on

Don't tell me your dad isn't secretly excited
you're dating Kieran O'Sullivan

Maybe
He was always big on sports
Some people online are saying it's really romantic,
Kieran throwing a punch for me

Others are calling me a gold digger

Idiots

Don't they know you're a property heiress?

Stop reading the comments, Flora

Who cares what anyone else thinks?

Thank you for not writing
anything about this on your blog

It's not the story I'm interested in

I'm interested in Kieran's new lease of life on court

He's playing better than ever

What a time for a comeback

Everyone thought he'd retire but look at him!

He's amazing
I'm going to the match this afternoon

Of course you are

His lucky charm 🕸

Don't you start
It's got nothing to do with me

You sure about that?

I've tracked Kieran's career a long time

He started well and then things fell apart

He held on in there, but his spark had faded

Now it's back

Maybe he got tired of everyone
telling him he couldn't do it

Maybe he's found love

Shut up

I'm being serious

At the Australian Open this year, I would

have told you that his heart wasn't in it anymore

Watch him play this afternoon

You'll see

See what exactly?

He's playing with heart again

And it's making him unbeatable

*

Later, when Kieran wins match point, the court erupts with noise. Everyone is on their feet cheering and clapping, the Irish fans chanting support. I wait for him to finish shaking hands with his opponent and the umpire before he looks to me.

With a sly smile, I quickly unzip my jacket to reveal the Snoopy T-shirt underneath.

He tips his head back and barks with laughter, before nodding at me, a dopey grin on his face. I beam back at him, lifting my hands above my head as I continue clapping along with his growing fan base until he's walked back through the players' tunnel and out of sight.

23

Neil is waiting for me when I come down the steps off the court.

I'm on a high, flushed with excitement at Kieran's win. If the headlines today affected him, it was in a positive way – he was more determined than ever, going for every ball like it was match point. He even added a little showmanship in, recovering a drop shot by hitting the ball through his legs with his back to the net. It was a winning point and the crowd went absolutely wild. He'd smiled at the reaction, his eyebrows shooting up in surprise at his own brilliance. I don't know enough about the game and his career to make a call on whether he's playing with more heart, like Iris believes, but he was definitely more animated in this match than I've seen him before. And not in an angry way, but in a fun way. Like our spontaneous training session on the local park courts, I could tell he enjoyed today's match.

I'm not expecting Neil to be waiting for me. I know that I'm not wanted behind the scenes after a match, and I was planning on heading to the nearest strawberry stand to purchase a bowl for Kieran to celebrate his win.

'Flora,' Neil says through a fixed smile, sliding his sunglasses up his nose and putting his hands in his pockets, 'are you available for a quick chat?'

'Uh… sure,' I say, stopping in front of him, my beaming smile fading fast. 'What's up?'

'Maybe we can chat elsewhere,' he suggests, glancing at the

phones pointed in our direction as spectators coming off the court form a circle around us.

Neil is famous in his own right, as a former Wimbledon champion and now as Kieran's coach, but I think people are also starting to realise who I am, and we're drawing a larger crowd than I'm used to.

I nod and he gestures for me to accompany him as he walks towards the Clubhouse, a building reserved for players and their teams, and VIP ticket holders. When the doorman stands aside to let us in, I immediately feel underdressed. Of course I had to be invited into the VIP building on the day I'm wearing my Snoopy T-shirt. As Neil whips off his sunglasses and leads me up the stairs, I quickly zip up my jacket.

We walk down a maze of corridors in silence, Neil strolling while typing into his phone, me scurrying along behind him, admiring the framed pictures hanging on the walls of Wimbledon legends and the elegant vases of fresh flowers dotted around the pristine halls that fill the building with a soft, sweet fragrance.

Neil leads me to an exclusive bar where we're seated on the balcony overlooking the grounds. Sitting up straight as I perch nervously on the edge of my seat, I gaze out at the stretch of outside courts and the crowds of people milling around the pathways, making their way to various matches and soaking in the atmosphere.

'Champagne?' Neil suggests, glancing up from his phone at me when the waiter comes to ask for our order. 'We should celebrate Kieran's win.'

'Sounds great,' I say, swallowing the lump in my throat.

'Two glasses of Champagne, please,' Neil instructs to the waiter who hurries off. He puts his phone away and leans back, clasping his hands on his lap and looking out at the view. 'It's a great spot, this.'

'Yeah. It is.'

'Although, personally, I'm a big fan of the view from Henman Hill – or is it Murray Mound these days?'

'Both, I think.'

'M-hm.'

The waiter returns with two flutes of Champagne, placing them down in front of us and checking that we don't need anything else. Once he's left, Neil raises his glass.

'To Kieran.'

I pick up mine and clink it against his, taking a sip. It's light, crisp and delicious, but it burns down my throat and the bubbles only serve to heighten the swirl of nerves in my stomach. From the outside, this looks like a pleasant drink and a gesture of kindness from Neil, but the atmosphere is all wrong. It's cold and tense. I don't feel like a guest being welcomed into the fold. I feel like a burden that's being given a taste of the high life before I'm kicked to the kerb.

'Kieran played well today,' Neil remarks, setting down his glass.

'He did.'

'It's nice to come here and raise a glass to him.'

'Sure.' I hesitate. 'But won't he be expecting you in the locker room?'

'He has the rest of the team, and like I said, I wanted to have a chat with you.'

Cool and collected, he gives me a pursed-lip smile. I take a large gulp of my drink. I get the feeling I'm going to need all the courage I can get.

'What did you want to talk about?' I ask.

He inhales deeply through his nose. 'Kieran is through to the quarter-finals of Wimbledon, a goal he hasn't reached in quite a while. He is proving to himself, and everyone else, that he has what it takes. You see, Flora, I've always known that. I've been his coach for a long time and, when others thought I should have moved on, I stuck by him.'

'I imagine he appreciates that.'

'I hope so. I saw that something special in Kieran when he was an up-and-coming player. Everyone talked about Aidan, but for me, it was Kieran who could go the distance. That's why, even though it put my friendship with his father on the line, I offered to step in as Kieran's coach when their working relationship broke down.'

'Kieran mentioned you used to be friends with Brian.'

'Brian is... complicated. Ultimately, I respect him. He believed in his boys. His methods may have been tough, but he worked hard to get Kieran to where he is. Our friendship remains fractured, but he knows what I know: Kieran has the talent and ability to win Wimbledon. And many Grand Slams to come. The thing is, he's had personal issues that have distracted him from those goals.'

I nod sadly, lowering my eyes.

'Losing Aidan was a heart-wrenching tragedy that would destroy anyone,' Neil says, his brow furrowing and his voice sounding more human than it has been. The rest of this conversation has felt planned and drafted, but that he said with feeling. He takes a beat, shaking his head. 'And, of course, then came Rachel.'

I press my lips together.

'I wasn't his coach at the time, but as a family friend, I witnessed it all,' he continues, rubbing his chin with his hand. 'Kieran has been on a journey. After losing Aidan, he threw everything he had into tennis. You couldn't drag him off the practice courts. His hands blistered from playing so much. He didn't know what else to do, how to cope with his pain.'

'Tennis saved him,' I murmur.

He nods, his mouth curling into a smile. 'Exactly. He reached the finals of the Australian Open and became a superstar overnight. That was when it all went wrong.'

'Chris Courtney.'

'Not just Chris. Sure, he's a tough opponent, but with the fame came the pressure, and Kieran already wanted to win for Aidan.' He exhales loudly. 'Can you imagine having that on your shoulders? He was just a kid and he felt like he was playing in honour of his brother who had just died. Then you add the pressure of the whole of Ireland pinning their hopes on him, throw in the expectation of his father, his picture on every front page in the world – it was too much and he wasn't ready. And then that bloody interview about beating Aidan at Wimbledon. It broke him.'

'I found that article,' I admit, frowning at him. 'That was before that final, wasn't it?'

'He did that interview before Aidan passed away.' He nods. 'It published just after. He felt consumed by guilt. Imagine how it looked: telling everyone that he was the one to watch, not Aidan. It was brotherly banter – but it looked bad. He swore never to do an interview again after that; he couldn't trust journalists not to twist his words. His dad assured him that it was just one piece. It would be forgotten. Then, he beat the world number one in the Australian Open and that interview was fished out because there wasn't anything else for reporters to go on. His quotes were pulled from context and flashed everywhere. He thought everyone in the audience would have read it.'

'That must have been *horrible* for him.'

'But he kept fighting,' Neil says, waggling his finger at me. 'He kept going after that. He was bruised and volatile on court – a fucking nightmare sometimes, to be honest – but he didn't want to give up. His dad kept him focused and then he met the love of his life.'

'Rachel,' I say, twirling the stem of the glass round in my fingers.

'When she left him, it was the last straw. He broke,' Neil says, with a sorrowful sigh. 'He was all over the place. He couldn't focus, he lost his confidence, he hated everyone. Then he had to take quite a lot of time off because of an injury, and I remember thinking that he wouldn't come back to the game and maybe that wouldn't be such a bad thing. But he did. Tennis, it's all he knows. Of course, by that point, he and Brian were a disaster. Neither of them were listening to each other. It didn't work anymore.'

'That's when Kieran sacked him?'

'It was the year Kieran got through to the semi-finals of the US Open. I was there as a commentator, and I remember watching him play and thinking, "He's not completely out of it yet." I knew if he could get a grip on his mental state, he had the talent to win. And over the years he's proven to me that he has the motivation to get there, but then whenever he'd get close, he'd bow to the pressure. He'd pretend he wasn't serious. Go out drinking, lose his temper, piss off the umpires. He kept his expectations low.'

'Then he's not disappointing anyone if he loses, least of all himself.'

'Exactly, Flora. This year, he's back on form. It's fantastic. I couldn't be prouder.'

I watch him carefully. 'Neil, why are you telling me all this? Why am I here?'

He picks up his glass, takes a sip and places it back down again. 'That overview proves to you that Kieran has had his fair share of downs, as well as a smattering of ups in his career. The one most damaging was Rachel leaving him for Chris. Beneath that brooding exterior, Kieran is sensitive. She broke his heart and he stopped believing he could win.'

'What has that got to do with me?'

His eyes fixed on me, he lifts his chin. 'What happens when Wimbledon is over? Where does this thing between you two go from there?'

'Neil, we haven't talked about that. We've known each other for three weeks.'

'That's my point. But the tournament will come to an end, and Kieran is showing to everyone right now that he's not done with the tour. God, Flora, the way he's playing right now, he might actually win this thing. You think Chris Courtney wasn't thinking that last night when he pushed him to the brink?' He leans forward and jabs his finger against the table to accentuate his point. 'Kieran's career is taking off again. He does well here, he does well everywhere. He's not retiring anymore, I can tell you that much.'

I shift in my seat. 'I still don't understand what this has to do with me.'

He leans back, folding his arms. 'Do you know what the life of a tennis player is like?'

'Busy?'

He snorts. 'You got that right. Constantly on the move, travelling the world. It's a difficult life and maintaining a relationship is hard. Especially a new one. Trust me. I've been married three times.'

'Neil, I don't really—'

'He likes you, Flora,' he states, his relaxed smile fading as his mouth becomes a hard, straight line. 'I've seen him with girls he's dated before, but this is different.' I blush furiously, taking another gulp of my drink. 'So let me tell you what happens next. You two have this whirlwind romance because you're in this perfect Wimbledon bubble, and then as time goes on, reality sets in. It doesn't work out and Kieran loses the best shot he's had in his career at achieving all the dreams he's had since he was a kid.'

A lump forms in my throat. 'So what are you saying?'

'I'm saying that when it comes to matters of the heart, it's human to be selfish. But maybe you need to consider what it will ultimately cost him.'

'Why are you so certain that he wouldn't win no matter what's going on?'

'Because unlike you, I know Kieran very well,' he asserts. 'He pays me a lot of money to be the person to tell him what's good for him and what's not.'

'But you're not that person to me,' I remind him coldly.

He looks surprised at my comeback, before an icy smile crosses his lips. 'No, but perhaps I can offer you some advice as... a friend. Sometimes, Flora, it's best to step back before anyone gets really hurt.'

He takes a moment to pull out his phone and read a message that's just come through, his brow furrowing in concentration.

'I'm afraid I have to go,' he says, sliding off his seat. 'Feel free to stay here a bit longer and enjoy the view. The staff saw you coming in with me, so they won't mind.' He hesitates, clearing his throat. 'To be clear, Flora, none of this is personal. It's... business.'

'Actually, Neil, I think it's very personal,' I mutter, arching a brow.

He looks down at his feet for a moment before giving me a *what-can-you-do* shrug.

'I'd appreciate it if you kept this chat between us,' he says. 'Whether you believe anything else I've said, I'm not wrong that Kieran is a sensitive soul. He needs me right now.'

I press my lips together, refusing to give him the satisfaction of agreeing.

'Right, then.' He gives me a sharp nod, and turns on his heel, marching out of the bar.

My heart sinking, I turn to look out over the courts. Every now and then a cheer goes up from one of them as a player gets one step closer to achieving their dream. I knock back what's left in my glass and leave, my sunglasses hiding the tears of humiliation filling my eyes as I make my way home alone.

24

Kieran knows something is up. I'm trying my best to act as though everything is normal, but it's not easy when Neil's voice is in the back of my mind, telling me that I'm being selfish for even entertaining feelings for Kieran when he has the chance to achieve his childhood dream. I want that for him. And the reason I want that for him, is because I care about him and his happiness. As in, really care. I'll admit it. I'll hold my hands up and say it.

I'm falling for Kieran O'Sullivan.

When I'm not with him, I'm thinking about him all the time. And when I'm with him, I feel deliriously happy and safe and confident and important. All those things you're supposed to feel when you're falling for someone. My feelings for him are growing every single day and the idea of the tournament coming to an end makes my heart ache as I beg for time to please slow down. He makes me laugh, he's kind and thoughtful, he's smart and sexy, and he's opening up to me. He trusts me and I trust him.

So lying to him isn't coming naturally. Neil's advice had been painful to listen to at the time, but the cuts grew deeper the more I thought about it and heard what he was trying to say. He wants me to be the one to end it. But it's unfathomable. I *can't* end this. It's too good, too exciting, too perfect. But then the guilt comes creeping in. Am I being selfish? Have I thought properly about what comes next? Can this really work? Are we on the path of a doomed whirlwind romance that everyone else can see from a mile off?

My head was in a total spin that night, and I couldn't tell Kieran any of it. Neil may be a dickhead, but he's right about Kieran's sensitive nature. I know that by now. It's obvious that Neil's demands are already bothering Kieran, and if I told him about our drink, I don't think Kieran would be too happy about it. Driving a wedge between a player and their coach right before the quarter-finals would be a disaster. So I'm stuck in this alone.

When Kieran got back after his win, he was confused as to why I left the grounds without coming to see him after the match, so I had to tell him I had a really bad headache. Then he started fussing over me, being all sweet and attentive, which made everything worse. He'd just got through to the quarter-finals of Wimbledon for Christ's sake, and here he was running me a bath and waiting on me hand and foot. I tried to persuade him to go out, celebrate his win with his team, but he dismissed the suggestion and insisted he was exhausted and wanted to chill with me. I went to bed early just so I could close my eyes and not have to look at his beautiful torturous face, and then pretended to still be sleeping when he left the next morning for training.

He bent down and kissed my temple before he left.

As soon as the front door shut, I pressed my face into the pillow and screamed in frustration. I knew then that there was no chance I would do what Neil wanted me to do and break it off before it's really begun. Instead I just have to accept that I'm a selfish bitch who is potentially going to be blamed for the tanking of Kieran's career.

But I can't make such a painful decision when no one has any idea what the future holds. Neil could be wrong and this could last. Or maybe Neil's wrong about the way Kieran feels about me. He could be playing his part very well and I could be another fling that he'll dump as soon as Wimbledon ends. He'll go on to win all the Grand Slams in the world and I'll be the one left broken-hearted and embarrassed for thinking any of it could be real.

Either way, I don't want to end our story before it has the chance to play out.

So, I have to sit here on Court Two watching Kieran play in the quarter-finals of Wimbledon, knowing that his team, sitting right next to me, all think that I'm gambling his future on my selfish desires. Meanwhile, I've been acting strange around Kieran because, thanks to Neil, I now can't stop thinking about what the fuck we've got ourselves into.

'Silence, please,' the umpire tells the two-thousand-strong crowd, as Kieran prepares to serve at the start of the second set and some of his fans shout words of encouragement through the silence that settles over the court.

Thanks to reading Iris's blog this morning, I know that Kieran is playing Felipe Díaz, a Spaniard ranked number seven in the world, and a hot favourite to win Wimbledon thanks to his stunning performance on grass so far this tournament. In his last match, he won in three straight sets.

Kieran is currently a set down, the score 3–6. When Díaz broke Kieran's serve in the first set, I heard Neil mumble, 'He's being indecisive' to the assistant coach, and I could see Kieran's frustration with himself when he lost the first set, shaking his head with his hands on his hips as he walked to his chair.

I'm trying my hardest not to betray any emotion to anyone. My face straight and expressionless, helped in large part to my sunglasses, I'm here for Kieran, no one else. So when he looks to me just before he chooses the ball he's going to serve with to kick off this second set, he can see I'm looking straight at him. I tilt my chin up just a little bit.

You've got this. Forget everything else, just win this next point.

He selects a ball, shoving the other in his pocket and stepping up to the baseline. The crowd waits with bated breath. His shoulders relaxing, he tosses the ball up in the air and hits it with so much power and precision that the thwack of his racket connecting makes me gasp.

'Ace,' the umpire announces to rapturous applause.

Wiping his forehead, Kieran allows himself just the hint of a grin as he strolls to the other side of the line. I smile to myself. I don't know the game well enough to understand what Neil meant when he said Kieran was being indecisive in the first set, but I know Kieran well enough to know that he's just made the decision to win.

3–6 6–3 6–3 6–3

I beam with pride as Kieran's score is displayed on one of the screens in the grounds, while I hang around after the match. After a wobbly start, Kieran found his footing and seized on some unforced errors by Díaz to take the second set. From there, it was fairly smooth sailing as Kieran dominated the match, breaking serve early on in the next two sets.

As he walked off the court to an eruption of cheers from his Irish fan base, he looked up at me and nodded. Neil frowned at the gesture, but a giddy warmth flooded through me. This time, I wanted to hang around afterwards to congratulate him, rather than scarpering as I know Neil wanted me to do. He's through to the semi-finals of Wimbledon! This is HUGE.

I'm not going anywhere.

I send Kieran a quick message to tell him I'll wait before putting my phone away in my shoulder bag, lurking near the media pavilion as the grounds start to empty. The match on Court Two at the start of the day went on for a good few hours, which meant there was a backlog and Kieran's started much later than planned. Play on the outside courts has pretty much wrapped up and now we're into the second week, there's less going on as more players are knocked out. A tinge of sadness creeps in as I consider how fast these two weeks fly and the end of it approaches.

Suddenly, Neil appears in front of me.

'Kieran would like to see you.'

'Now?' I blink at him. 'He's already ready to go?'

'No, he's refusing to get ready until he's spoken to you,' he says in a strained voice. 'I don't know why, but I'd like us all to go home and rest, so if you wouldn't mind.'

He holds out a lanyard for me to put on and gestures for me to follow him.

I hurry to keep up as he marches towards a door guarded by one of the Wimbledon security team. He tells him, 'She's with me,' and I hold up the pass hanging round my neck, before darting in after him. We've entered an eerily silent carpeted corridor with pale pine doors leading off it that has the feeling of an exclusive health club. I try to smooth the creases of my dress out with my palm, suddenly feeling too informal in this white spaghetti-strap summer dress and tan gladiator sandals.

'Is this the players' area? It's so quiet,' I remark, my voice echoing off the walls.

'It's the end of the day,' Neil replies wearily, turning a corner and going down a flight of stairs. 'Most people have left by now.'

I run my hand down the shiny banister as I descend after him. 'It's so smart and clean.'

'This *is* the All England Lawn Tennis Club.'

'Congratulations on Kieran's win, by the way,' I say politely as we set off down another corridor. I don't know why I'm trying to break the ice. We didn't exactly leave things on a high note last time we spoke and he's made his feelings on my presence quite clear.

'Thank you,' he says, at least sounding genuinely sincere. 'We have a lot to work on.'

'Sure, but you can enjoy the win for now, right?'

He stops at a door and turns to face me with a hard glare. 'The semi-finals are a different ball game. The pressure is mounting, the competition is fierce, and the whole world is watching. Kieran is very much the underdog. He needs to focus on the tennis—' he looks me up and down '—no distractions.'

Fed up with his derision, I hold his stare. 'Neil, can I ask you a question?'

He narrows his eyes suspiciously at me. 'Yes?'

'Would you talk to me this way if I were a famous actress or supermodel?'

'I'm sorry?'

'It's a genuine question: would you? Because I don't think you would. I doubt that you spoke to Henrietta Keane like this. Even if you disapproved of him having a relationship right now, I think if you thought I was someone important, you might be a little bit more mannered. Maybe even kind.' I pause as he pulls his eyebrows together. 'I get that you're stressed and I also appreciate that you're trying to protect Kieran, but I'm human. Maybe not an important one in your eyes, but still.'

His jaw tenses and I wait for him to reply. Eventually, he nods to the door we're standing next to. 'He's in there,' he says, before he turns and walks off down the corridor.

Watching him go, I exhale, adrenaline pumping through my veins from the confrontation. I don't like being awkward, but I meant what I said. He treats me like a child who's playing outside the rules. He's welcome to treat Kieran that way, but he has no right to do so with me. I'm not the one who employs him to boss me around.

Shaking him and his sour attitude out of my head, I tentatively push open the door, aware that the plaque nailed into it is telling me that this is one of the men's locker rooms. It's a spacious room with walls lined with large wooden lockers, and benches dotted around the area. Kieran is sitting on one of them towards the back and he glances up when I step in. Apart from his shoes and socks, he's still wearing all his tennis kit.

He breaks into a smile. 'Hey.'

'Hey,' I say quietly, glancing around as I make my way across the room to him. 'Am I allowed to be in here?'

'No, but there's no one around so it's fine. I checked.'

'Congratulations, Kieran,' I gush, stopping in front of him as he stands to his feet. 'You're through to the semi-finals. You so deserve it.'

He places his hands on my hips and peers down at me. 'What's wrong?'

I give him a strange look, resting my palms of my hands on his chest. 'What? Nothing! I'm so happy for you! You *won*!'

'Thank you, now tell me what's wrong,' he insists, his brow creasing. 'You haven't been yourself the last couple of days. I'm worried I've done something. Talk to me, please.'

I sigh, looking down at the floor and smiling hopelessly, even though my head is a giant muddle. This makes me fall for him even harder. The way he cares so much. The way he notices things. The way he looks so helpless right now, as though he *needs* to know what's affecting me because it's affecting him.

'I'm worried,' I admit.

'About?' he prompts, his eyes searching my expression now that we're getting somewhere.

'About… this,' I say, gesturing to the gap between us. 'I don't know what it is and I don't know where it's going. It's happened so fast and I… I'm scared of getting hurt. Wimbledon has to end and then what happens from there? I don't want to lose myself in the moment and then deal with shitty consequences.'

There. I've found a way to say how I feel without throwing Neil under the bus.

'Flossie, I get that you're organised, but are you so organised that you have to plot out an entire relationship when you're only a week or so in?' Kieran says, with a hint of amusement in his tone.

'Don't make fun of me,' I huff. 'We're in unusual circumstances and I'm trying to protect both of us. I can't read your mind; I don't know what you're thinking.'

He reaches out and, resting his finger beneath my chin, he gently tilts it up so I'm looking into his deep blue eyes.

'I don't know what this is, but I know this is something,' he insists in a low, gravelly voice, the lightness in his tone banished. 'I can't see into the future and I don't want to second-guess what you want, but if I have it my way, this is going to go way beyond the end of Wimbledon.'

My stomach flips, my heart beating so hard it's going to explode from my chest at any second if he doesn't stop looking at me like that.

'Does that help clear things up for you?' he asks, his hand on my hip sliding round to my lower back and bringing me closer to him. My bag drops from my shoulder to the floor with a thud that echoes round the room.

'Yeah,' I croak. 'A little.'

'Hmm, sounds like you need a bit more persuading,' he growls, his gaze flaring, a coy smile playing across his lips.

The moment he bows his head to claim my mouth with his, a fierce desperation consumes my body. *Fuck Neil.* I've kept myself from Kieran for two days and it's felt like an eternity. Raking my hands through his hair, I arch into him and nip at his lip, and a groan rumbles deep in his throat, a sound that almost makes me combust on the spot.

As our kiss grows more urgent, I drag my hands down his chest, finding the hem of his shirt and pulling it upwards, allowing him to yank it off properly himself before I pull his mouth to mine again, craving every inch of him. Cradling my head in his hands, he kisses me fiercely, pressing his body against mine and manoeuvring us until my back is up against something cold and solid, and I realise he's pinned me against the lockers.

As he traces kisses down my neck, nudging the strap of my dress off my shoulder, he drops one hand to my hip and it finds its way under my skirt and into my thong. His fingers rub between my legs, knocking the breath right out of me, his lips returning to my mouth to capture my moan in his.

'Can't be too loud,' he reminds me with a devilish smile, his eyes flaring. 'We don't want to get caught.'

His free hand finds mine and lifts it above my head, grasping my wrist and pinning it against the wood. I'm completely at his mercy. He increases the pressure on my clit, winding me up until I'm begging to have him in hoarse whispers, my nails digging into the nape of his neck, feeling him hard against me. *I need you*, I hear myself say in his ear, too close to the edge to hold back what I want to say.

'Tell me you have a condom in your bag,' he growls, his fingers slowing so I have some chance at answering him coherently.

'Actually I do,' I admit, a shy smile creeping across my lips. 'It's in the side pocket.'

He pulls back to look at me, impressed. 'Did you put one in there this morning in the hope that this would happen?'

'Sure.'

His lips twitching, he exhales through his nose. 'I'm going to pretend to believe you.'

Leaving me breathing heavily leaning back against the locker while he bends down to grab it, I thank Iris over and over in my head for the time she made me put one in there when we were headed on a night out together.

'You never know what might happen and, trust me, when you're in that moment, you want to know you have protection handy,' she'd said with a wink.

Thank you, Iris. You were right, I think, hearing the sound of the foil ripping. *Thank you, thank you, thank you—*

He's in front of me now, pushing down his shorts, rolling the protection on and within a split second, his hands are under my thighs, lifting me up, my dress hitching up round my hips as my legs tighten around his waist. *Fuck, this is hot.* I've decided that this is my favourite place to be, up here in his arms, our bodies locked together, fitting perfectly.

My back pressed against the lockers, he balances me there with one hand, while he guides himself into me with his other, nudging my underwear aside and sliding in with a quick, deep thrust. I whimper and he starts moving quicker and quicker, his hips grinding into me, sending me into a spiral of dizzying pleasure. As he grunts into my neck, I tighten around him, brought back to the edge in record time. I gasp his name, my nails etching dents into the skin across his shoulders.

'Come with me, baby,' he says hoarsely.

The way he feels, how he's taking all my weight, the thrill of where we are, his gravelly voice in my ear, him calling me that name like I'm his – it's all too much. As soon as he makes that request, it's game over and the uncontrollable pleasure is rippling through my body while he drives deeper into me, groaning into my neck, unravelling in unison.

Our breath comes together in a chorus of short, shaking rasps, as Kieran carefully lowers me onto my feet. I grip his forearms for balance, my body still a melting, quivering mess. I close my eyes and slump back against the lockers, running my hands through my hair as he pulls his shorts back on. His chest rising heavily, he closes the gap between us to kiss me gently while I continue to catch my breath. Since I'm in no hurry to emerge from my blissful daze, he thoughtfully adjusts my dress for me, pulling it back down and checking the straps are in place on my shoulders.

Having faded into a blur, the world starts to return into focus.

I clear my throat. 'I should… um… go. I don't want to get you in trouble and you probably want to… celebrate your win with the team.'

He offers me a playful smile, tucking my hair behind my ear. 'I think we just celebrated pretty well.'

'Hm.' My cheeks flushing, I bite my lip.

He gazes into my eyes so intently that it makes my pulse race, just when I was starting to get it back under control. It's not fair him looking at me like that when he's still topless, his toned muscular chest and abs on show. My mind is drifting again.

'I really should go,' I say out loud, trying to persuade myself to take the first step away from him but finding it near to impossible. 'And you really should… do whatever it is you do once you've got through to the semi-finals of Wimbledon.'

'Okay.' He grins, amused by my awkwardness, dipping his

head to give me one final kiss before I finally manage to break free of his spell and make my way back to the door.

'Flossie?' he calls out as I reach it, and I spin round to face him. 'I'll see you at home.'

I nod, convincing myself to get out of there before the temptation to run back to him grows too much to fight. As I shut the door behind me, check down the empty corridor, and stroll as breezily as possible back towards the stairs, I feel proud of myself for finding the strength to leave him looking like that.

It's not until I walk into the flat later that I process what he said as I left.

He called it home.

25

'Flora broke my heart by DUMPING me for rich tennis hunk':
Ex-boyfriend of Kieran O'Sullivan's rumoured new love
FINALLY breaks his silence

'Kieran, you really didn't need to come back early from training,' I sigh, placing my hand on his arm as he comes to sit next to me on the sofa. 'You have the semi-finals tomorrow! This isn't important. I told you I'm *fine*. It's okay, please go back to practice.'

'It is *not* okay,' he counters, before turning to Nicole with a murderous expression. 'What options does she have to fix this? Can we get them to take down the article?'

From the armchair by the window, Nicole sets down her cup of tea. 'I'm afraid Jonah has every right to speak to the press and give his version of events. They use the word "allegedly" throughout, and all the stated allegations are quotes from him. There's nothing we can do but release Flora's own side of the story, if that's what she wants to do, but she's told me she doesn't want that.'

'I don't want that,' I tell him firmly. 'I'm going to leave it.'

'So he gets away with it,' Kieran snaps, jumping to his feet and stalking over to the mantelpiece, rubbing his chin, irritated. He spins round with an intense look of outrage in his eyes. 'He can say all these things about you and there are zero consequences!'

'You know the drill better than anyone, Kieran,' I point

out, frowning at him. 'It's best I do nothing. The things he said aren't *that* bad. Okay, it's not great he's made it out as though I dumped him for you and there are implications that I cheated... and lied, obviously, but he also says we had a loving three-year relationship. That's something.'

'A relationship that, according to his story, you viciously destroyed in favour of my riches and fame,' Kieran seethes, clenching his fists.

Watching him pace about the room all flared up, it occurs to me that he seems much angrier about this article than all the articles that came out about him after the incident at Warren House, and although I don't want him to be so upset and cross, there's something really quite sweet and old-school about how much he wants to protect my honour. I shouldn't like seeing him like this, all riled up and angry on my behalf, but I do. I can take care of myself, but it's sexy witnessing how much he wants to protect me.

'Kieran, this will blow over. Anyone can see that it's an embarrassing and desperate attempt from an ex-boyfriend to get publicity for his new play,' I point out, offering a weak smile when he glances over at me to try to reassure him. 'He mentions it, like, ten times in the interview. He's playing a jilted lover, so he was able to use his experience from our relationship to get into character.'

'He's shameless,' Kieran mutters bitterly.

'Yeah, and it shows. He's having his fifteen minutes.' I turn to appeal to Nicole. 'Wouldn't you agree?'

'Absolutely.' She nods, smiling encouragingly at me. 'I'm sorry that this has happened, but I agree that the best way to handle this is silence. We don't want to draw more attention to it by making it a he said/she said situation. We let it blow over and be forgotten.'

'How can he get away with such baseless lies?' Kieran fumes, running his hands through his hair. 'Don't they fact-check anything?'

'They asked Flora for comment,' Nicole informs him. 'That's their way of checking.'

'It's not like there's a written record of who cheated on who,' I say, slumping back on the cushions. 'And I highly doubt Zoe is going to come forward with the truth. I've told Iris not to say anything either, even though she's about as mad as you are, Kieran.'

'We hadn't even met when you two broke up!' Kieran seethes. 'If I see that guy again, if he dares come anywhere near you or this flat, I'm going to—'

Nicole clears her throat pointedly, giving him a look.

'I will... *talk* to him,' Kieran concludes through gritted teeth.

'I don't think he'll be coming anywhere near here anymore,' I say, getting up and moving over to him, taking his hands in mine. 'Kieran, I promise, I'm okay.'

He exhales, his shoulders dropping as he leans forward to press his forehead against mine. 'I hate that he's done this to you,' he murmurs.

'Me too. But, honestly? It hasn't hurt me like I thought it might,' I admit, pulling away so I can look him in the eye. 'He doesn't have any power over me anymore.'

He sighs. 'Good. I hate that guy.'

'Forget him. And see it this way – I'm going to have some really good ammo when we next play tennis and you lob a ball my way. I'll just think of him and this interview and BAM. A winning smash.'

Kieran breaks into a smile, tiny crinkles forming around his eyes.

'I think I'm all done here, then, if you're feeling okay, Flora?' Nicole announces, standing up and picking up her designer handbag.

We've only been properly acquainted for an hour, but I really like Nicole. She's a smart, no-nonsense woman in her thirties, and she reminds me a bit of Iris. As soon as you meet her, you know you want this person on your side.

'I'm fine. It was really good of you to come over to talk me through everything.'

'Any friend of Kieran's...' She smiles, walking across the room to the door. 'In a professional capacity, I can say that you're making a sensible decision by not responding to this interview. In a non-professional capacity and completely off the record, I'd like to say that your ex is an attention-seeking prick who never deserved you. You're well rid.'

I laugh. 'Thank you, I appreciate that.'

'If you need anything else or have any questions, just call me. Kieran, we'll talk later about the press surrounding the tournament.'

'Thanks, Nicole,' he says, showing her to the front door.

When she leaves, sunglasses on, head bowed, I hear the instant barrage of questions from the awaiting paparazzi. The door shuts and Kieran wanders back into the living room, leaning on the doorframe, watching me closely as I chew my thumbnail.

'Are you okay?' he asks gently.

'I've told you, I'm fine.'

'Yeah, but are you saying you're fine when you're not actually fine?'

I drop my hand and smile. 'What he said about me sucks and it's embarrassing, but I'll get through it.'

'I'm so sorry,' he says quietly, chewing his lip. 'You must have had such a shit day.'

'Actually, I did loads of sketching today. My book is really coming along,' I tell him brightly. 'I didn't see the article until lunchtime.'

Kieran's eyes drop to the floor and his expression saddens, the creases on his forehead deepening. 'This is my fault. One of the hazards of knowing me. Privacy intrusion.'

'Hey,' I say softly, walking over to him and cupping his face in my hands. 'This isn't your fault. Jonah is the one who decided to sell his story to the press.'

'It's because of me that your life is being pulled apart,' he mutters. 'They won't stop here. They'll keep digging and prying and hurting you. All because you know me.'

'Kieran, stop!' I insist, my heart aching at how defeated he seems. 'I don't mind.'

'I mind. *I mind*,' he repeats, his eyebrows pulled together. 'Until I came along, you didn't have to worry about anything like this. Now, your ex is airing your secrets and—'

'It's worth it,' I state firmly, holding his gaze. 'Okay? It's worth it to me.'

He doesn't say anything, his chest rising as he inhales deeply.

'I'm okay, I promise. We have to take the high road,' I continue. 'One day, Jonah will regret it. Please, let it go. You have to focus on the semi-finals tomorrow. I'm annoyed you left practice early. Neil must be fuming.'

'It's fine, we were almost done anyway. I'd planned... I'd planned on taking you out on a date, actually.'

I step back, raising my eyebrows in surprise. 'Really? This afternoon?'

'Yeah. It occurred to me that we haven't really been on one, and it's important to have some downtime and relax, take my mind off tennis for a bit. I thought it was the perfect opportunity to take you out properly.'

'But you've worked so hard today. Don't you want to crash on the sofa or play your little PlayStation? You should be resting and relaxing.'

His mouth twitches into a wry smile and he reaches out to put his hands on my hips and pull me towards him.

'I'm relaxed when I'm with you,' he says, as I wrap my arms around his neck. 'And when you say "little PlayStation", it hurts my feelings because you're demeaning it.'

'I apologise. I meant, your important, serious PlayStation.'

'Thank you. Apology accepted.' He grins, his dimples deepening. 'I have a plan for what we can do together. I think you'll be happy about it.'

'You have a big day tomorrow, Kieran. We can't go out and stay up late. You should stay here and relax.'

'We won't stay up late. You don't know what my plan is yet.'

'Are you sure we should do this? I don't want to get you in trouble or risk jeopardising tomorrow.'

'You're not jeopardising anything and this is my choice.' He sighs heavily. 'If I stay home for the next few hours, I'll sit around worrying and stressing – especially with this added stress from Danny Zuko. It's important to have a break. If you're worried, I can ring Neil and he will tell you that he's always saying shit like that to me.'

'I'm not sure he'd say that this time,' I mutter. 'But I'm going to trust you, and an outing would be fun. Although we'll have to get through the barrage of paps outside.'

'Matthew will drive us, I'll ask him to call when he's outside.'

'Come on then, what's this great plan of yours?'

'You'll see,' he says, his eyes twinkling at me. 'The question is, were you telling the truth?'

I tilt my head curiously. 'The truth about what?'

When the car pulls up to Battersea Power Station, I'm still not sure what Kieran has in mind. There are lots of cool places around here to eat, but none of them would cause that annoyingly smug smile on his face. It's not until we head up to level one and, my hand grasped in his, he starts marching towards Bounce with unabashed excitement that I understand why he's so pleased with himself.

'A ping-pong bar,' I say, my shoulders shaking with laughter.

'You told me you were good at it. Now, we're going to see if you were making that up to try to impress me.'

'I was *not* just saying stuff to impress you!'

He stops in front of Bounce and arches a brow. 'Guess we'll find out. Do you like it? Or were you expecting something a bit more glamorous for a first date?'

'Technically, it's our second date, if you include the pub darts.'

'Second date, then,' he concurs, grabbing me round the waist and pulling me close. He smells so good, it makes my heart flutter. Running my hands over his broad shoulders, I know that I will never get tired of him holding me. 'So, what do you think?'

'For a second date, I think it's… pretty perfect.' I give him a mischievous smile. 'You can take me somewhere glamorous for the third date, if there is a third date.'

'There will be a third date.'

'Cocky.' I grin, as he bows his head and his lips brush against mine softly.

It's the sort of kiss that relays a huge weight of meaning. It's not urgent or desperate or showy, it's caring and quiet and gentle. Like everything is okay. It makes my heart hum and my belly fill with a comfortable warmth and affection. It turns the busy world around us into stillness. When he breaks the kiss, I reach up on my tiptoes to kiss him again.

We head in to Bounce and, after the guy who greets us has a fangirl moment over Kieran, we're given a table and order a couple of mocktails.

'Shall we have a few warm-up rallies and then play to see who serves first?' Kieran suggests, picking up a bat and sauntering to the other end of the table.

'Sounds good to me,' I say, tossing the bat up into the air and letting it spin before I deftly catch the handle. It's actually a complete fluke but it looks bloody good.

Kieran raises his eyebrows, impressed. 'Whoa. Go easy on me, Hendrix.'

'Are you scared, O'Sullivan?'

'Never.'

We launch into a rally and quickly discover that, although I was telling the truth and I can play ping-pong to a fairly high standard, there can be no doubt that the professional tennis player at the table has a significant advantage. We have a few minor distractions from our game when a couple of the bar staff come over to ask for a picture with Kieran, which in turn alerts others in the bar to his presence. But we manage to forget about the people taking stealthy photos and videos of us, and have a really fun time.

Soon I'm shrieking with excitement when I manage to get one of his annoyingly sneaky drop shots. He's just as invested, yelling 'COME ON' to himself when he misses the ball or punching the air in celebration when he wins a point. We start to incorporate silly tasks into the next match – like, we have to do a 360-degree spin after hitting the ball, or hop on one foot while playing, or play with our left hand. The best one is when I announce that we have to incorporate our favourite dance moves in between playing shots, inspired by the loud music playing in the bar, and although he takes some encouragement, when he does the chicken head bop after serving, I'm doubled over wheezing with laughter. After I do an extremely impressive top spin forehand that he can't return, he's so proud of me that he tosses his bat on the table with a loud clatter, runs around to my side and lifts me up in the air, spinning me around.

I can't remember laughing this much.

After such exhilarating play, we take a break, sitting next to our ping-pong table and chatting over our drinks.

'Can I ask you a question that I've wanted to ask for a while?' I say, setting my glass down determinedly.

'We're on a date, Flossie, questions are part of it. Ask away.'

'I think it may be personal, so you don't have to tell me the answer if you don't want.'

He holds up his hands. 'It's grand. Shoot.'

I take a deep breath, holding his gaze. 'Why did you have to stay in Lingfield Road? Did you make that up to be stubborn when I wouldn't leave the flat, or is there genuinely a reason?'

He nods slowly like he'd already accepted that I'd ask this

someday. 'There's a reason. But it's a secret. So, if I tell you, then you have to tell me one.'

I smile. 'Deal.'

'Okay.' He drops his eyes to the floor. 'The first time I came to Wimbledon, it was because Aidan was playing in the junior tournament, but I was too young to qualify. He was knocked out first round and in the car on the way back to the hotel, I told him that I was sorry he lost. He shrugged it off and told me that he'd be back one day to win.' He takes a moment. 'He looked out the window and told me that one day we'd be living in a big house on that very road and we'd both be Wimbledon Champions.'

I reach for his hand, threading my fingers through his.

'We happened to be driving down Lingfield Road at the time,' he continues, bringing his eyes up to meet mine and giving me a sad smile. 'I was such a cocky little shit I told him that I'd be Wimbledon Champion first, and he just smiled and said, "Kieran, the only chance you'll have at winning Wimbledon is if I'm out that year due to injury." Our dad was driving and he roared with laughter. Aidan was so quick like that. He was really clever.'

'He sounds brilliant.'

He squeezes my hand and then collects himself, rolling his shoulders back and giving me a grin, his eyes brightening. 'So that's the reason that, if I have the chance to be on Lingfield Road, I'll take it. I wasn't talking bullshit.'

'It all makes sense to me. That's a good reason.'

He pulls his eyebrows together, looking pensive. 'I should thank him.'

'Who?'

'Aidan,' he says with a shrug. 'He brought me to you.'

My breath catches and my heart does too many somersaults to count.

He nods to the ping-pong table. 'Enough chit-chat. Another round or are you ready to surrender?'

'To you? Never,' I assert, swiping up my bat with enthusiasm.

He grins and I swear to God, every time I see those dimples,

I fall deeper and deeper. It's lucky he's forgotten to ask me for a secret in return. My biggest one is just how strongly I feel about him, and if I say it out loud, it will probably frighten him.

Because it terrifies me.

26

About five minutes after we get back from our date, the bell rings and I cheerfully head back down the hallway from the kitchen to open it and find Zoe standing nervously on the doorstep. The reporters that had been waiting for us on our return from Bounce have slunk away, having come to the conclusion that now we were home, it was doubtful we'd be going back out. She must have waited until they were gone to come over. Still in her work clothes of a white silk blouse, high-waisted black trousers and heels, she has her head bowed slightly and she's looking up at me with big doe eyes.

'Hi,' she squeaks, attempting a smile.

I stare at her, shocked at her presence.

'I just wanted to say that I had no idea Jonah was going to do that article,' she blurts out hurriedly, glancing at my hand that's still resting on the door, as though she's worried I'm about to slam it in her face and she has to get her words out all at once before I do. 'I swear, Flora, I didn't know. I think his lies are horrible and disgusting. I've sent him a message telling him that. I… I'm so sorry. About everything.'

'Oh. Okay,' I mumble, not sure what else to say.

She exhales heavily, her face crumpling. 'I'm so disappointed in myself, because I really thought… I built up this idea of him in my head. What I did was so wrong and I feel so, so bad, Flora. I thought I was in love with him. I'm such an idiot.'

Dropping my hand and leaning my shoulder against the door, I drop my eyes to the floor and press my lips together.

'I've been too embarrassed and ashamed to come speak to you properly,' she continues, sniffing. 'I should have done this sooner, but I didn't think you'd want to talk to me. And then at the pub the other day, I wanted to break the ice because… well, we live next door and I see you all the time. I wanted to play it cool and not ruin your evening, and then you left and I knew it was because of me.' She bites her lip as I force myself to look up at her. 'Flora, you don't have to forgive me or like me, but I wanted you to know that I really am sorry. You've always been so nice to me, and I'm the bad guy here. I was an absolute idiot who got caught up in the forbidden romance and I fell for a guy who didn't exist. Me and him are over. If you want—' she juts out her chin defiantly '—I will speak to the reporters and tell them the truth about what happened.'

I let her words sink in and let out a sigh.

'I don't want you to do that, Zoe. Thank you for the offer, but let's just leave it.'

She nods. After a moment of tense silence, she turns to leave.

'Thank you for the apology,' I say, stopping her in her tracks. She spins round to look at me hopefully. 'And… you're not the bad guy. Jonah was the one who broke his promises.'

'Still.' She shrugs dismally. 'I did a bad thing.'

'It doesn't make you a bad person.'

'I really am sorry.'

'I know.'

She offers me a small smile. I give her one in return.

'I'll leave you to your evening,' she says, hesitating as she turns to go. 'I'll be cheering Kieran on tomorrow.'

'I'll tell him.'

As she leaves, I shut the door and lean back against the wall to take a moment to process the conversation. Kieran appears in the hallway, having been lurking by the living room door. He raises his eyebrows at me.

'You okay?' he checks.

I nod, finding myself smiling. 'Yeah. I am.'

The doorbell goes again, making me jump.

'What more do you think she wants to say?' I frown, straightening.

But when I swing open the door, it's not Zoe waiting for me on the other side. It's a tall older man in a suit. He's got greying dark hair, a defined jaw and intense blue eyes. Even if I didn't recognise him from pictures, I'd know who he was from a mile away.

'Hello, Flora,' Brian says in a broad Dublin accent, as I hear Kieran inhale sharply behind me. 'Is my son in?'

Kieran and his dad seem to be having a staring match. It's only been a few seconds of silence, but it feels like this horrible uncomfortable tension has dragged on forever. Finally, Brian emits a pointed noise from his throat that breaks the silence.

'Aren't you going to invite me in?' he says.

He's looking at Kieran, but it's me who replies. 'Uh, of course. Sorry, come in.'

I'm not sure if that was the right answer, but I'm ready to explain to Kieran that whatever comes next, whether it's a blazing row or a surprise reconciliation, it's best if it happens inside the house rather than out on the street for anyone else to witness.

I stand aside and Brian steps in, politely wiping his shoes on the mat as I close the door behind him, my heart in my throat. I've never seen Kieran look tenser. The muscle in his jaw is twitching and his whole body has stiffened, as he stands frozen to the spot.

'What are you doing here?' he asks, his frown deepening.

Brian doesn't take another step forward, putting his hands in his pockets. 'I wanted to see how you are.'

Kieran snorts. 'Try again.'

'I'm telling the truth, Kieran,' Brian says tiredly. 'I wanted to check in and make sure you were okay. I felt like we needed to talk.'

'Did you?' Kieran says flatly.

I can physically see his guards coming up, that hard outer shell that I've been cracking through the last few weeks is piecing itself back together in front of my eyes. His mouth becomes a straight hard line, his eyes cold and untrusting. His defences are back, prepared for attack. With Brian blocking my path, I feel too far away from Kieran and the need to protect and comfort him is kicking in.

'Why don't we go into the living room?' I suggest, nodding encouragingly at Kieran.

He doesn't budge for a moment, but eventually heeds my advice and steps back into the room, allowing Brian and I to approach and follow him in. He remains standing, lingering by the fireplace.

'Would you like a drink?' I offer Brian, gesturing for him to have a seat.

He takes the one by the window. 'No, thank you.'

'He probably won't be staying long,' Kieran mutters.

Brian sighs. I don't really know what to do but I feel awkward standing, fidgeting with the hem of my cropped shirt, so I perch on the edge of the sofa. It suddenly occurs to me that I actually shouldn't be in the room, so I get back on my feet.

'I'll leave you guys to chat. Are you sure you don't want a drink?' I squeak, the croak in my voice betraying how uncomfortable I feel right now.

'You can stay if you want, Flora,' Kieran says, a brief but distinct flash of vulnerability crossing his expression. It's gone as quickly as it came, and he's back to fixing his dad with a hard stare. 'Anything he has to say, he can say in front of you.'

I slowly sink back onto the sofa.

'So,' Brian begins, fixing a smile, 'how have you been, Kieran? The semi-finals tomorrow, that's really—'

'Why are you here, Dad?' Kieran interrupts abruptly.

'I told you, I wanted to check in.'

'You could have messaged or called.'

'I knew you wouldn't reply or pick up.'

'So you... decided to fly over and knock on my door.'

'Something like that.' Brian shifts. 'Neil called me.'

Crossing his arms, Kieran smiles in disbelief, his eyes dropping to the floor.

'I was as surprised as anyone. We haven't spoken in a long time,' Brian continues, his brow furrowed as he watches his son carefully. 'He thought it would be a good idea if I came over to... talk. He felt, and I agree, that it's important to try to heal any rifts as the tournament gets serious for you. He doesn't want any distractions.'

I swear his eyes flicker over to me as he says that.

'Did he? I thought Neil knew me fairly well,' Kieran says. 'Turns out he doesn't know me at all.'

'Kieran, I want you to know that there's been a misunderstanding about the book,' Brian says, leaning forwards to rest his elbows on his knees and clasp his hands together in front of him. He looks remarkably relaxed given the circumstances. I can barely move, I'm so tense.

Kieran raises his eyebrows. 'You're not writing one?'

'I have written one, yes,' he says, before adding quickly, 'but it's not what you think it is. It's not a memoir.'

'I heard it was.'

'What, from the press?' Brian gives him a pointed look. 'You trust everything they say, do you? I hope you know better than that.'

Kieran doesn't say anything, pressing his lips together.

'It's a tennis guide, Kieran,' Brian says gently, appealing to him with a sincere look in his eye. 'There's a smattering of personal experience with you and Aidan in there, but it's a celebration of you both! Your talent and work ethic. People who read it will be inspired by our story. They'll realise that tennis is more than just a game. It can be a lifeline. You've always said that, haven't you? I wanted to write it to help inspire others. You can read the manuscript before it publishes, all right? There's nothing in there for you to worry about.'

Kieran watches as his dad rakes his fingers through his hair.

'I'm sorry that I didn't tell you about it,' Brian adds in a softer tone. 'That was wrong of me. I was trying to find the courage to contact you. It was cowardly of me. That, I'll hold my hands up to. I'm not here to cause trouble, Kieran, if you want me to leave, I'll leave. You need to be on your best form and I would never, ever want to do anything that jeopardised your chance at winning Wimbledon.' He sighs heavily, rising to his feet. 'The truth is, I'm happy Neil called. It's given me the nudge I needed to come over here and tell you to your face how proud I am of you.'

Kieran's jaw tenses as Brian cautiously approaches him.

'I'm so proud of you, son,' Brian emphasises, his voice hitching as he stops in front of him. His face angled away slightly, Kieran is blinking furiously, his eyes glistening. 'You should have seen me down the pub watching you in the quarter-finals. The way I was roaring and boasting, there's not a man in Dublin who doesn't know you're my son.'

Bowing his head, Kieran can't help but smile. Brian sees it and is encouraged, reaching out to place his hand on his arm.

'The whole country is behind you,' he tells Kieran, his hand tightening around his son's arm. 'No matter what happens now, you've done us proud. But I know you can go all the way – you know that too, don't you?'

Kieran swallows, giving a sharp nod.

'I know we've had our differences, but I'd like to stick around and help if I can,' Brian says. 'When we worked together, I was able to bring out the best in you. I haven't been there for you for a long time; I want to make that up to you. And I've been studying your form this tournament and there are a few things I think you can do to really knock this out the park. Just a couple of pointers for you. Neil is in charge, I respect that. Let me stand on the sidelines and see if I can help. If it doesn't work, you can send me packing.'

Kieran frowns, looking unconvinced.

'I've changed, Kieran,' Brian tells him firmly. 'I've worked through my issues and I've changed. My methods back then—' he shakes his head in disapproval '—they were all wrong. I want to make it up to you, son, if you'll let me.'

Brian looks at him hopefully. Taking a deep breath, Kieran finally allows himself to speak. 'You only have a *couple* of pointers?'

Brian breaks into a grin, chuckling. 'Maybe a few more than a couple.' He glances over at me and hesitates. 'Flora, I wonder if I could take you up on that offer of a drink. A cup of tea would be lovely. Milk and a sugar, if you have it.'

'Sure,' I say, getting to my feet. 'Kieran, do you want anything?'

He shakes his head. I leave the room with a feeling of uncertainty swirling in my belly. Brian seems sincere and I'm happy for Kieran if he's able to find a way to forgive his dad and work with him again, if that's what he really wants. But I also know the power someone like Brian can wield over his son, who will forever be searching for his approval. He's played his part perfectly, and I'm scared it's too perfect.

I can't hear their conversation while the kettle is boiling, but when it's come to a stop and I'm waiting for his tea to brew, I catch part of it. I creep closer to the door, listening to their voices float down the hall.

'—and you don't want to throw away your dream on something that might not last,' Brian is saying in a low hushed tone, but it's clear enough for me to hear every word.

'You don't know that, Dad. You haven't been here.'

'I know that you're *this* close to achieving what you've spent your whole life working towards and any kind of distraction, the tiniest of emotional pulls, can derail your path. This living arrangement – it's odd. And I get it, I get it. I know how you feel about this road, and Neil has explained to me what happened.

You've made the best of it – I can see that. But nothing is more important than this tournament, nothing. Kieran, do you really think you'll have another chance like this one? Be honest with yourself. This is it. I can feel it in my bones. I think you can feel it too.'

There's a beat of silence. I can't tell how Kieran responds.

'This is your shot, my boy. This is your chance, and together we are going to make sure that you take it. You owe it to yourself and your country. You owe it to Aidan. It's time to get serious. Don't let anything or anyone come between you and *your dream*.'

More silence, and then I hear Brian say warmly, 'Good lad.'

Which means that Kieran must have agreed.

It's good advice, after all. He shouldn't let someone come between him and his dream. If it was anyone else, I'd be heartily nodding along, rather than leaning against the doorframe like I am with a debilitating crushing feeling consuming my heart. Because it doesn't take a genius to know that the someone Brian was talking about… the someone getting in between Kieran and his dream, is me.

27

I'd volunteered to sleep on the sofa after Brian left. Kieran had acted as though he didn't understand and had tried to persuade me to stay in the bedroom.

'We both know that you need a good night's sleep,' I'd reminded him with an assuring smile. 'Imagine if I talk in my sleep or kick you or something. It would be so bad if I did anything to keep you up. This way, you can be sure of getting the important rest you need before tomorrow.' He hadn't looked entirely convinced, so I'd finished getting the duvet sorted on the sofa and then walked over to him to kiss his lips lightly. 'Everything's fine, okay? But nothing is more important than tomorrow.'

If he realised I was echoing his father's words from earlier, he didn't show it. He'd sighed and reluctantly agreed, before kissing me again. He'd pulled me into a hug, his hands travelling around my back and pressing me closer into him, his head nuzzling into my hair.

'I'll miss you, though,' he'd whispered softly in my ear.

A lump had formed in my throat and I hadn't trusted myself to speak.

The truth was, if Kieran had disagreed with what his dad was saying, he would have told him. He would have pointed out that he'd come this far and he was playing better than ever before, just like he told me in the locker rooms. He would have told him that he needed me. But he didn't. He didn't say anything at all.

With yet another person in his corner disapproving of what we had, I'm not surprised that he was starting to listen.

I knew I couldn't give up on us yet, but I accepted that I might have to take a step back and wait in the wings until the end of the tournament. If distance was what Kieran needed to win, then I wouldn't hesitate. So, when Brian eventually left to go to his hotel, I'd already decided I would sleep on the sofa. I don't want to make things even more complicated or confusing for Kieran than they already are. This way, he doesn't have to make a choice. He's already got enough on his mind. I'll make the hard decisions for him.

Of course, I've barely slept.

When I hear Kieran head into the bathroom, I'm wide awake, staring at the ceiling. Forcing myself out of bed, I whip off my pyjamas and pull on some high-waisted ripped mom jeans and a T-shirt. I'm fully aware that his team will arrive any minute and I'd rather I wasn't caught in my pyjamas or a towel this time. I'll shower once they've left. I'm tying my hair up into a loose bun when, bang on cue, the doorbell goes.

'Good morning,' Neil says, sweeping in ahead as I answer it.

'Morning,' I reply as a few more people from Kieran's team come trundling in.

The rear is brought up by Brian, who gives me a strained smile as I shut the door behind him. 'How are you both this morning?'

'I'm fine, thanks. I haven't seen Kieran this morning, so I can't speak for him.'

'Ah.'

Strolling into the living room, I start moving my things out of the way. I notice the look shared between Brian and Neil as I fold up the duvet and pillow from the sofa to put away in the chest. Closing the lid, I straighten and fold my arms across my chest.

'Flora,' Neil begins, leaning towards me conspiratorially with a solemn expression, 'I really think it's for the best that—'

'I know what you think,' I snap, and it comes out a lot sharper than I'm expecting. Neil's eyes widen in surprise at my tone and Brian arches his brow. I take a deep breath and mutter, 'I want Kieran to be happy, so I want him to win. I'll do whatever he needs.'

Neil nods in response. 'Thank you, Flora. And I imagine you don't want to talk about it, but I'm sorry about that stuff in the paper about your parents. If you need to speak to Nicole, then please don't hesitate to give her a call.'

I snap my head up. My blood turns cold.

'What?' I whisper, before I start looking around frantically for my phone. I sweep it up from the coffee table and google my name.

'Oh, you haven't seen it,' Neil says, sounding panicked. 'I didn't realise...'

He trails off at the sight of my expression. Most of the articles about me are either fluff stories about our cute date night at Bounce, using the footage captured by others in the bar, or the ones relating to Jonah and his sad story.

But there's a new one that comes up as the most recently published:

From a traumatic childhood to a whirlwind Wimbledon romance: How Kieran O'Sullivan's love interest Flora Hendrix overcame troubled teen years with an alcoholic mother and an absent father to find happiness with the bad boy of tennis.

As I scan the article, I feel like I can't breathe. They don't have many of the facts, and have managed to make a few nuggets of information into a full-blown rambling article – in reality, readers learn very little about me here. But the journalist writes about my mum's 'devastating addiction issues' before her tragic death; they detail when my dad left and his subsequent marriage; they even have a line about how I'd 'find solace' in the Lake District with my grandmother. As I get to the quote from Jonah about how I 'never liked to talk about' my childhood, it all becomes clear. I can't believe he mentioned this to a reporter.

'Are you okay?' Neil asks, and he sounds genuinely concerned.

I must look really bad for him to be worried about me. My brain springs into action.

'Don't tell Kieran,' I say urgently, looking up from my screen. He frowns. 'But—'

'I mean it, he can't know about this,' I say, keeping my voice hushed and grabbing Neil's wrist. 'You have to keep it from him today. Don't let anyone mention it to him. If he sees this, he'll get really upset and it could affect how he plays. Please.'

Neil rubs his forehead. 'Flora—'

'We'll make sure he doesn't see it,' Brian assures me, understanding instantly.

My shoulders lower in relief. 'Thank you.'

Neil eventually nods, seeming a little torn. I can understand his initial reluctance. The last time he kept something important from Kieran, he got an earful and I know the last thing he wants to do is risk fracturing his relationship, but he knows it's for the best. I know that Kieran will blame himself for this, and that guilt, however misplaced, would be near to impossible to shake in the lead-up to this afternoon's match. He'd be distracted and angry. We can't risk it. I can't put this burden on him today.

'Maybe it's best, Flora, if you… keep your distance today,' Brian suggests. 'We don't want anything that will distract him from such an important match, and if there's lots of attention on you, he might lose focus.'

My heart sinking, I nod.

When Kieran appears in the doorway, his bag slung over his shoulder, Neil brightens, strolling over to him with gusto.

'Right, big day ahead,' he declares, rubbing his hands together. 'How are you feeling?'

'Fine.' Kieran looks straight past Neil at me. His face eases into a smile. 'Hey.'

'Hey,' I reply, glancing at Brian.

Kieran follows my line of sight and his smile fades. 'Dad. You're here.'

'Raring to go,' Brian nods, taking a step forwards so he's flanking Neil.

I bow my head, retreating.

'Everyone out, let's go, the cars are waiting,' Neil announces. 'Kieran, I think you'll be happy with the schedule we've set up before the match. You'll have a couple of treatments and then warm-up and we talk over strategy, okay?'

'Yeah, fine,' Kieran says distracted. 'Flossie, Matthew will come and pick you up before the match. We're playing second, so it depends on how long the previous match goes on, but I think my match will probably start around four – what do you think, Neil?'

'Actually Kieran, I… I don't think I can be there today,' I say.

The room falls silent. Kieran stares at me, his eyebrows pulled together. Neil drops his eyes to the floor. Brian lifts his chin. My words go against every gut feeling I have. I want to be there in that box watching him. I *need* to be there for him. And with my childhood being bandied about for entertainment, I need to feel close to him today especially. But this isn't about what I want or need. This is about what's best for Kieran.

'You're not coming,' Kieran says slowly, as though saying it out loud will help him to understand it.

'I have… an interview,' I say, my brain scrambling for something believable. 'A job interview. It's late this afternoon and I won't be able to make it to Wimbledon in time.'

He tilts his head. 'You can't reschedule?'

'No, it's super competitive. This was the only time they could do.'

His eyes bore into me and although I try to hold his gaze, I can't. I look down at the floor.

'This is my first time playing on Centre Court,' I hear him say in a small voice.

God, this hurts. This really fucking hurts. He's telling me

he needs me without telling me he needs me. Something in me falters. Maybe everyone has got this wrong. I open my mouth to speak, but Brian jumps in, stepping round Neil to pat Kieran on the arm.

'And you'll have me and Neil and all of your team in your box, there for you. You've got the support network you need. She can't drop her life to fit around yours, Kieran. If she's got a job interview, then she can't miss it. She'll be cheering you on from afar, right, Flora? This is the Wimbledon semi-finals, Kieran. You shouldn't be thinking about who's in the box, but how you're going to play. Who you're up against. Forget who's in the box and who's not. Focus on you.'

Kieran lowers his eyes.

'Good, let's go,' Brian says, nodding to Neil.

As they file out of the room, I stay where I am chewing on my thumbnail. Everything about this feels unnatural, and even though I want to do what's best for him, I can't let him go to Wimbledon without saying goodbye at least. I rush forwards into the hallway just before they open the front door.

'Kieran!' I say, prompting all of them to turn to look at me. He cranes his neck to see me past his father. 'I... I just... have you got the bubbles?'

His hopeful look fades.

'Wouldn't leave without them,' he says, patting the side of his tennis bag.

I smile at him, but he doesn't see. He's already turned away and is busy putting on his cap, lowering the visor over his face in preparation. My eyes begin to sting.

'Okay, everyone, heads down,' Neil instructs from the front, before he opens the door and the waiting paparazzi swarm around the gate at the bottom of the steps.

I stare at the closed door a long time after they've all gone through it. I feel like I've somehow let Kieran down, and it's an emotion that weighs down on my heart so heavily, it's hard for me to move. I finally force myself to traipse into the bathroom to get ready for the day, but I feel like a zombie, going through the motions without any purpose.

At least the story about my sad childhood doesn't get much traction. The story making waves is that Brian has, against all odds, made his way back into Kieran's inner circle.

When my dad's office calls the first time, I ignore it.

My eyes are glued to the TV screen. Kieran's match is underway and he's two sets down. This match has been the hardest to watch and I'm almost glad I'm not in the box so I can bury my face in my hands and groan loudly whenever he makes a mistake.

The support on Centre Court for him is amazing: there is a huge amount of green scattered around the vast stands – green jumpers, green shirts, green caps – and many Irish flags waving in between points, his fans making themselves hoarse as they cheer when he wins a point. But there haven't been all that many of those. He's up against Denmark's Arne Jensen, who, Iris told me, favours grass and is number-eleven seed. Jensen seems much more focused than Kieran today, and it doesn't help that Kieran has started to lose his temper. He also received a time-wasting warning from the umpire in the second set for taking too long on his serve. He tried to protest, marching over to the chair and shouting at the umpire that it was an unfair call, but she didn't budge. It's been painful to watch.

Brian has been sitting in the box next to Neil, shaking his head and flinging up his arms in exasperation whenever Kieran glances up in their direction. The commentators have already remarked on how Kieran seems to be making a lot of unforced errors: 'This is Centre Court for you,' one of them said a moment ago. 'Some players can't take the pressure and they get inside their own heads.'

When he sends what should have been a winning forehand straight into the middle of the net, he yells out in exasperation and hurls his tennis racket on the ground. He's getting a warning from the umpire, standing at the bottom of the chair with his hands on his hips, shaking his head, when my dad's office calls again. It's actually nice to have an excuse to mute the TV. I'm not sure I'll be able to watch much more of this.

'Hi, Andy,' I say breezily on picking up. 'Sorry I missed your call.'

'Flora, hi. It's me.'

The sound of Dad's voice immediately makes me sit up straight.

'Dad! Hi!' I exclaim, feeling flustered and nervous. I'm used to speaking to his PA, not him directly. Every time we speak, I've forgotten how to act. 'Is everything all right?'

'Yes, fine,' he says in his formal clipped accent. 'I was actually calling to ask you that question.'

'Oh.' I swallow. 'That's... uh... nice of you.'

There's a beat of silence before he speaks again. 'I'm sorry I haven't been in touch more regularly recently.'

'That's okay. I know you're busy.'

'Yes. It seems you've been busy, too.'

'I'm so sorry if reporters have been bothering you and Camila. I haven't told them anything and I'm hoping if we keep ignoring them, they'll get bored and give up on trying to find the story.' I hesitate, raking a hand through my hair. 'I don't know if you've seen the most recent one today about... my childhood...'

'Yes, that's why I was calling. My team brought it to my attention this morning.'

I bite my lip, my face flushing with heat. 'It's all nonsense. I think... God, this is embarrassing, but I think my ex-boyfriend maybe gave them a few titbits of information to run with. Is it going to affect your business?'

He sighs heavily. 'Flora, I'm not calling so that you can apologise to me. I'm calling so that I can apologise to you.'

I falter, stunned into silence. He clears his throat and continues. 'I can understand why you'd feel that I... abandoned you at a difficult time in life, and I'm aware that I haven't been present as you've grown up—'

'Dad,' I interrupt, 'I didn't leak anything to the press. That article isn't my opinion.'

'Nevertheless, I wouldn't blame you if it was,' he says. 'One might say that reading the article this morning was a bit of a wake-up call. Moving forwards, I would like to work on our relationship, Flora.'

I bite back a nervous laugh. It's not that I don't appreciate the call or what he's saying, but it's the way he's saying it: formal and business-like, as though he's speaking to a client about a deal, not his daughter about her life. I've learnt to accept that my dad is not a father figure in my life. I've come to see him as more of an acquaintance who feels guilted into having to look after me financially when I need it. There was a time when I wanted my dad to take notice of me, but somewhere along the way, I accepted what we were. It made everything easier. He's this important businessman who I'll always be slightly intimidated by because I never won his approval, and I'm the artistic daughter from a doomed marriage that he never quite understood. We work by keeping things polite, emotionally restrained and distant. The truth is, Dad doesn't really know how to be a dad.

Hence the phone call that makes working on our relationship sound like his next strategy outline.

'Okay,' I say, glancing at the TV to see that it's 6–6 in the third set.

'Good. I've spoken to Camila and we'd like to fly over to see you this summer.'

I raise my eyebrows. 'You want to come to London?'

'You can show us your flat and the area, and perhaps we can meet your boyfriend.'

A lump rises in my throat. 'My boyfriend.'

'Kieran O'Sullivan.' He pauses. 'The reason I'm calling now is because I noticed you weren't on Centre Court. I was worried that perhaps this article about your mother… as I said, I wanted to check you were all right.'

I find myself smiling into the phone. 'Thanks. That was thoughtful of you. I'm fine. You're watching the match then?'

'I had a glance at it. Unfortunately, I won't have time to watch the rest, but I've always been a fan of O'Sullivan,' he says, his tone lifting into something like excitement. 'I watched him in the US Open early on in his career and you could tell there was something special about him. I was delighted to hear you were dating him.'

I've never heard my dad so enthusiastic before. He sounds almost relaxed, as though he's actually enjoying the conversation, which I'm not used to at all. It throws me.

'Oh. Uh, yeah, it's been a bit mad.'

'Yes, well, I'm afraid I don't have long to chat now because I'm in the office, but another time we can catch up and you can tell me about him. How you met, et cetera.'

'Right.' I nod. 'I'll fill you in on all the… et cetera.'

He pauses and I can hear him exhale. 'I'm sorry about what they've written in the article about your mother.'

'Yeah, me too,' I say quietly.

'She did love you, you know.'

'I know.'

'I wasn't always very kind about her.'

I smile weakly. 'She wasn't always that kind about you either, Dad.'

'No, I can imagine.' He takes a deep breath. 'I do want to work on our relationship, Flora.'

'Yeah. Sounds good. I mean, I want that, too.'

'Good. Right, anyway, I'm afraid I have to go to a meeting,' he says brusquely.

'Yeah, me too. Well, not a meeting, but… I have to go.'

'Oh look, he might have had a stroke of luck there.'

'Who?'

'Kieran,' he informs me. 'The other guy has gone down during the third set tie-break. Looks like an injury.'

I spin round to face the TV. The camera is focused on Jensen who is sitting on the ground gripping his calf, his face scrunched up in pain.

'Let's hope he takes this opportunity to fight back,' Dad enthuses. 'As I said to Camila when we watched his last match, tennis is all about your own psychological warfare. You have to refuse to back down, even when things seem hopeless.'

'I… agree.'

'Hmm. Well, perhaps we can come to Wimbledon next year. It might be fun for us to do together. Me and you, I mean.'

I nod slowly. 'Yeah. It might be.'

'Very good. I will discuss with Camila and we can propose some dates to you for our trip this summer,' he concludes. 'Speak soon, Flora.'

'Okay. Speak soon, Dad.'

He hangs up. Feeling completely bewildered from the call, I reach for the remote just in time to hear the roar from the crowd as Kieran wins the third set.

28

'—and with this kind of attitude, Kieran, you're not going to win tomorrow. Chris Courtney will embarrass you on Centre Court in front of the world. Is that what you want?'

Brian's voice echoes around the flat the moment he steps through the door on Saturday afternoon, his aggressive remarks making my stomach lurch. I start gathering my sketches sprawled across the table into a neater pile, setting down my pencil and going to the sink to wash the dark smudges off my hands.

'You have to go on the attack, Kieran,' Brian instructs, his voice coming closer as they walk towards the kitchen. 'You're not playing like you really want it. Do you want it?'

'Of course I want it,' Kieran snaps, appearing in the doorway.

I turn off the tap, glancing up at him as he comes in. 'Hey.'

'Hey,' he replies, before his brow furrows even deeper and he heads straight for the fridge to grab an energy drink.

Ignoring my presence completely, Brian lingers in the doorway. 'You're floundering because you're letting your emotions get the better of you. You have to stay focused. Don't let your mind and your emotions take hold of your performance. Be more…'

He searches for the word.

'Be more like Aidan?' Kieran suggests, his tone mechanical but cutting.

My breath catches.

Brian breathes out slowly, his expression darkening. 'Be more controlled is what I was going to say. Jesus Christ, Kieran.' His eyes flicker to me before he clears his throat. 'Get some rest for the next couple of hours. I'll be back this evening to analyse your play from today. We'll go through our strategy. Chris has plenty of weaknesses that we can home in on. You've got it in you, Kieran, you need to find the strength to fight for what you want.'

Kieran doesn't say anything, his expression inscrutable as he takes a swig of his drink.

Brian shakes his head and turns, stomping down the hallway and out of the flat. I feel like I can only breathe once he's left, but his presence still lingers here somehow, as though he's managed to make the air in here chillier. Kieran doesn't move, his body tense, his mouth straight, his eyes glazed over.

He's different. His expression, the way he's holding himself, it's all different. Ever since the semi-finals, he's felt distant from me. That's what I wanted, it was for the best. But I've been grappling with an aching heart as I've had to stand by and watch him withdraw into himself the last couple of days. I don't know how it must feel to reach the final of Wimbledon, to have what you've always dreamed of just within your grasp, but I can imagine that it's hard to keep focus beneath the staggering pressure, and it seems as though the way Kieran is handling it is to turn numb to everything and everyone around him.

The whole world is talking about it. It's a sensational story: Kieran O'Sullivan and Chris Courtney facing each other in the final of Wimbledon. Two fierce rivals, neither of them youngsters on the circuit anymore, both of them desperate for this one title. Chris is a Grand Slam winner but he's never got Wimbledon. According to the media, the atmosphere in Ireland this weekend is electric. Kieran's face is plastered everywhere around Dublin. The pubs are crammed with revellers eager to celebrate their local boy's surprise ascent to the top once again. On Sunday, the entire country will be watching without fail, cheering him on.

But in the flat, the atmosphere is bleak.

Brian and Neil came home with him after the semi-finals and I only just managed to congratulate him before they started outlining the strict routine they had for him. When they left, he lingered in the living room with me and neither of us seemed to know what to say.

'You're through to the final,' I'd managed to blurt out stupidly.

He'd nodded. 'Not sure I can believe it.'

'I can.'

He'd lifted his eyes to mine and his eyebrows had pulled together, his jaw tensing.

'Flora,' he'd croaked, 'the article about your parents...'

'It's nothing. I was hoping you wouldn't see it.'

'It was shown to me after the match. You must have thought I didn't care.'

'No, that's not... I didn't think that. I'd rather forget about it anyway.'

He'd bowed his head. 'I'm so sorry.'

'We need to stop talking about this and talk about the fact that you're through to the Wimbledon final! This is amazing, Kieran. I'm so proud of you.'

'I got a free pass,' he'd said, his expression clouding over. 'Everyone knows that if it wasn't for his calf cramp, then he would have won. He could barely run in the last set.'

'That's not true. You would have won anyway. That's what I think.'

When he didn't reply, I'd taken a few steps towards him and tentatively put my arms out, pulling him into a hug. His hands slowly came across to my lower back, pressing me into his body, as he lowered his head and exhaled into my hair, as though he was breathing out more than air. He was breathing out the stress, the anxiety, the chaos of the day, and he was finally still. We'd stood there for a few seconds and I'd felt my resolve fracturing as I melted into the warmth of his chest, felt the safe solidarity of his arms around me, breathed in his freshly showered scent that sent tingles down my spine.

I'd so badly wanted to talk to him then. I'd wanted to ask him how he felt and tell him how I felt, talk to him about his day, tell him about my call with Dad. But it wasn't fair to burden him with all of that when he'd just played in the semi-finals. He was exhausted.

So, I'd pushed away and told him that we should go to bed.

He'd remained quiet and pensive as I'd got the duvet and pillows ready for the sofa.

It was for the best.

But looking at him now, as he remains still against the counter, sipping at his energy drink like a robot that's been programmed to play tennis and then completely switch off in between, I'm not sure it's been for the best at all. The last couple of days, I've left him at the mercy of Neil and Brian, with no one else to talk to. They're hardly a barrel of laughs. I doubt he's had a moment of light relief and, considering this is the biggest event of his career, that might be what he needs. The worst thing is that he knows I lied to him about the job interview. What a stupid excuse.

'You've been working on your book,' he says suddenly, jolting me from my thoughts. He puts his energy drink down on the counter and gestures to the pages piled up on the kitchen table next to my sketching pencils.

'Yes, it's been going well actually.'

'You didn't do any drawing yesterday, though.'

I blink at him. 'Oh. Uh, no I didn't. You noticed. How did you—'

'You leave your pile of sketches out. The top one was still the same yesterday as it had been on Thursday.'

'You're not supposed to look at my drawings,' I say lightly.

He shrugs, allowing a weak smile. 'Can't help it.'

'The inspiration wasn't flowing yesterday. Or today, to be honest. I tried to get a bit done, but I'm not sure it's any good,' I admit. 'Not my best work.'

'I'm not surprised.' His eyes drop to the floor. 'You've had to contend with your life being splashed about for everyone to see. I can't imagine that's good for creativity.'

I watch him carefully. He looks troubled and tense, and I want to help him.

'Kieran, are you okay?' I ask gently, my fingers twitching, aching to reach out to him. 'Is it your dad?'

He glances up at me, a frown creasing his forehead. 'What about him?'

'The things he was saying when you came in. I don't know, they seem a bit harsh.'

'He wants me to win.'

'I know, but does he need to be so mean about it? That stuff about Chris Courtney embarrassing you tomorrow, it's a little unnecessary.'

'He's right, though, isn't he,' Kieran says in a low, defeated voice. 'The way I played today, I embarrassed myself.'

'I'm sure you weren't that bad.'

'You weren't there,' he snaps.

I press my lips together. He's frustrated with himself, I can see that, but there was something else that crossed his expression then. Hurt, I think.

'Kieran, I'm sorry about the semi-finals,' I say, stepping back and gripping the counter behind me for something to do with my hands. 'I wanted to explain about why I made up that stuff about the job interview to miss being there for the match.'

He bows his head. 'It's okay, you don't need to explain. I know why you couldn't be there. Why you shouldn't be there.'

Shouldn't. One tiny word. Or two words, if we're getting technical. Two little words, meshed together with an ability to cause a blow so considerable it knocks the breath right out of you. It changes everything that word. It tells me that he agrees with his dad and Neil. I think part of me hoped he'd fight for me to be at the final, even if I was the one to take the step back. It's natural, isn't it, to want someone to fight for you?

'You do,' I say, my heart sinking.

'I'm sorry that I put you in this position,' he says quietly. 'I wasn't thinking straight. I was being selfish.'

'Me too. I want what's best for you.'

He nods. 'And I want what's best for you. It's better this way,' he croaks, his voice strained and unnatural. 'It would be worse to end it further down the line.'

I blink at him. 'End it?'

'I want you to know that I never set out to hurt—'

'Kieran, wait.' I stare at him in disbelief. 'You... you want to end it completely? Me and you. You... you're ending it.'

He watches me in confusion, his eyebrows knit together. 'That's what we were saying. That's what you've been talking about.'

'No! Not... really. I just thought I needed to step back a bit for the end of the tournament,' I say, the words tumbling out of me as I become desperate to explain myself, desperate to clear up any miscommunication. 'I had to let you focus on the tennis, rather than... us. I've been a distraction. That's why I didn't come to the semi-finals. No one thought it was a good idea, and I didn't want to be the reason you lost your chance, so I thought...' I trail off, my head spinning. 'You really want to end it? As in, properly end it?'

His lips part, his jaw set. 'I... we have to.'

'No, we don't.' My heart is thudding so loudly against my chest, it's making my ears ring and my breath shake. 'Kieran, did your dad and Neil tell you to end it?'

He flinches. 'What? Why would you ask that?'

Because they told me to, I want to shout. But in spite of everything, I'm still not able to bring myself to reveal their meddling ways the day before the Wimbledon final. No matter how I feel, he needs them. He has to be able to trust them. I can't affect that.

'Did they?' I press.

'They don't get to tell me what to do in my personal life.'

'Really?' I say curtly, folding my arms across my chest.

He glowers at me. 'Really. I can make my own decisions.'

'Neil has been against me from the start.'

'Yes, and I've told him to fuck off,' he says tersely.

'Okay, so ending it now is what you want.'

'It's not about what I want,' he growls, his eyes falling to the floor. 'It's about doing what's right. This isn't going to work. The last couple of days have shown that.'

'Kieran, if this is about me ducking out of the semi-finals and sleeping on the sofa, I've told you that I wanted you to be able to focus on the tennis. I knew the team felt that way, and so I was trying to do what's right.'

'Exactly, and that's what I'm trying to do now.'

'I don't understand. We can see where we are after Wimbledon. We can give things a go. I want to give things a go.'

'Flora, we have known each other for a few weeks and look what's happened,' he says, scrunching up his eyes and rubbing his temples. 'Look at what being with me has done to you. The paparazzi everywhere. The news stories about your family, about your past. It's crushing, all of it is crushing. I can't... I don't want this for you anymore.'

A flicker of hope alights in my heart. He's protecting me. It's not that he doesn't want me, he's trying to protect me. That has to be it. *Please let that be it.*

'I don't care about that stuff,' I say, my voice raspy and soft. 'I can cope with it.'

'They don't give up. They keep going after you.'

'I'll handle it. Kieran—'

'No.' He's shaking his head, his cheeks flushing. 'You haven't been able to work because of it. It's affecting your drawing. I'm getting in the way of your dream. Things will only get worse. It won't work. It's for the best.'

Grabbing his energy drink, he pushes himself off the kitchen counter and, taking a large swig from it, he storms out the kitchen heading towards the living room. He needs a break from this conversation, but he's not getting it. I'm not going to let him.

'That's what I've been telling myself the last couple of days. It's for the best,' I say, following him in as he moves to stand by the window. 'But it wasn't, was it. Kieran, I watched your match. I think... I think you needed me there.'

'I needed to be better. I got inside my head.'

'You let your dad inside your head,' I correct stubbornly. He stares at me, stunned at my comment, but I plough on regardless. 'I could see the effect he had on you. You were playing differently.'

'I was too emotional.'

'And what's wrong with that?' I challenge, taking a step forwards. 'The best times I've seen you play are when you play with your emotion, Kieran. You play with passion and fun and love of the game. That used to be your style, didn't it? You played with flair.'

'I was never good enough.'

'You *are* good enough,' I tell him sternly, pointing my finger at him. 'You're more than good enough. You're the best and you're going to win Wimbledon tomorrow.'

He gazes at me, his chest rising and dipping with each haggard breath. 'And if I do, then what? I keep going on the tour, travelling the world, trying to win again and again?'

'If that's what you want.' I hesitate, watching him as he turns away from me. 'Is that what you want?'

He doesn't say anything. He's standing motionless now, staring at his shoes.

'I don't think that's what you want, Kieran,' I begin cautiously. 'I think that's what everyone else thinks you want. The Grand Slams. The tour. The wins.'

'I want to win Wimbledon,' he states firmly.

'I know. And I think you will. But you don't have to win to feel… happy. I've seen you light up when you're playing this game, this game that saved you when you felt so lost and alone, the game that gave you purpose. *Tennis* makes you happy, not the winning. You don't have to shoulder all this pressure. You can do something else.'

He rubs his forehead. 'Flora—'

'I'm just saying, don't get bogged down by what comes next. You get to choose.'

He sighs, exhaling and closing his eyes. It takes me a moment to realise that he's called me Flora, and not Flossie. He's pulling back. I know it before he speaks.

'I'm sorry,' he says. 'I can't... I can't do this to you. It won't work. It never does.'

Hot tears prick behind my eyes.

'So you're giving up now,' I say, swallowing the lump in my throat. 'You're not even going to bother to try. You're throwing something good away because you're scared.'

'That's not what this is.'

'That is what this is,' I retort, a tear rolling down my cheek. My chest tightens as it grapples with confusion and hurt and anger and sadness all at once. 'You told me that you knew this was something, you promised me a third date, but now you're doing what you always do, even in tennis. Giving up before it gets real. Saving yourself from the pressure. You're pushing me away to protect yourself.'

'I'm trying to protect *you*,' he argues, his eyes ablaze. 'For fuck's sake, Flossie, it shouldn't be this hard! We've barely even started out and look at us!' He throws his hands up. 'This is how it goes. And if I win tomorrow, then it only gets worse. The distance, the pressure, the spotlight. Everything heightens and so everything cracks.'

'This might not!' I cry, the tears flowing freely now.

'It will! Of course it will!'

'You think you don't deserve to be happy. I don't know if it's because of guilt over Aidan, but for some reason, you think you don't deserve to win Wimbledon. But you do, Kieran. You deserve everything. You just have to take the chance.'

He exhales and rubs his face with his hands. 'Look, I'm sorry, but I can't. I just... I can't. Not with you. I can't do this. I'm sorry.'

The room falls into silence.

'That's it then,' I whisper.

Unable to bring himself to look at me, he gives a sharp nod.

After a wave of emotion, I suddenly feel numb. I've been here before. Rejected, unwanted, foolish for believing it might just work. I'm not going to beg him to reconsider. I've tried to make him see, and he doesn't want to.

So, as I said. That's it then.

My body seems to know what to do, though my brain and heart are in freefall. My feet take me out of the room and to the coat hooks, where I find my bag that has my sunglasses in. My fingers trembling, I fish them out and rest them on top of my head. I crouch down to take my trainers from the shoe stand and I falter when I see his trainers on the floor next to it. He must have kicked them off when he came in out of habit. Previously, he's enjoyed teasing me about how long it takes for me to notice his shoes lying around and put them neatly on the stand.

Our little in-joke doesn't seem funny anymore.

I don't put them away. I leave them where they are. Sliding my feet into my shoes, I check my reflection in the mirror. My eyes are red from crying. My skin is pale from the shock. Reaching for my phone in my back pocket, I order an Uber. There's one two minutes away. During the championships, they tend to hang around the Village.

Waiting for it to turn onto our road, I inhale deeply and shuffle to the doorway of the living room. Kieran hasn't moved from where I left him. His head is hanging forwards now, and he's folded his arms tightly across his chest, his shoulders slumped.

He hears me come back in and he looks up.

'Before I go, I just wanted to clear up something,' I say so softly that I realise I'm going to have to speak up for him to hear me across the room. 'You said earlier that you're getting in the way of my dream. That all the nonsense that's been going on the last couple of days—' I gesture to out there, beyond the front door '—has affected my work. You think, because of you, I stopped drawing.'

He stares at me, tight-lipped.

'But you forgot that you were the reason I started drawing

again in the first place,' I say, mustering a regretful smile. 'Good luck for tomorrow, Kieran.'

I don't wait around for him to respond. I walk down the hallway to the door, sliding my sunglasses on and opening it. My exit takes the paparazzi by surprise, but they don't take long to spring into action, swarming around me as I come through the gate. My head down, I ignore their questions and practically throw myself into the back seat of the waiting car, slamming the door shut behind me.

The driver sets off, taking me away from Lingfield Road.

29

COURTNEY vs O'SULLIVAN

Why the gentlemen's singles Wimbledon title is all to play for
By Iris Gray

When I started this blog two weeks ago, I was asked by my editor to give my prediction on who I thought would make it to the final. I made a shortlist and I published it, and the majority of comments I received were in agreement.

Neither Australia's Chris Courtney nor Ireland's Kieran O'Sullivan were on that list.

But here we are, the day of the final when Courtney or O'Sullivan will walk away as Wimbledon Champion. It's true what they say, then: at Wimbledon, anything can happen.

I won't be bothering to predict who will be the new king of Centre Court, but I can say with absolute certainty that we are in for quite the match. Here we have two experienced players, both in their thirties, both delivering a remarkable comeback this tournament.

Let's start with number-eighteen seed, Chris Courtney, the Aussie who had a meteoric rise in his twenties, winning three Grand Slams: the Australian Open, and the US Open twice. Once admitting in an interview that it was his 'fear of defeat' rather than the joy of winning that spurred him on, Courtney remains a top-tier player, although in the last two years has found himself coming up short more than once. Having had a good run at Queen's in June, this tournament has seen his ambition return and he has had a spectacular two weeks, proving his mental resilience and remarkable power. Woe betide anyone who underestimates this fierce and dynamic player.

Is there a reason he's back in the forefront? Well, perhaps he's playing to match the recent unforeseen rise of his long-rumoured rival...

Kieran O'Sullivan. The unseeded Irishman who, against all odds, has reached the final of the Wimbledon Championships. I'm calling it now: this is the comeback of the year.

Two weeks ago there were whispers about his impending retirement, but he's been, undeniably, the most exciting player of the tournament. Catapulted into international stardom as a fresh-faced teenager who beat the then-world number one to reach the final of the Australian Open, O'Sullivan rendered spectators speechless with his abundance of natural talent, smooth style and exquisite precision – he had, as one commentator at the time put it, 'a serious spark on the court'. He subsequently faced a number of challenges in his professional and personal life, not least the tragic death of his older brother, Aidan, and his career has had its ups and downs. He's struggled to find his balance amongst the top players, becoming more recognised for his flaring temper than his ATP wins.

But something has changed in O'Sullivan this tournament, and we have had the privilege of watching something extraordinary: his spark is back. We can't know for sure what – or should we say, who – may have caused this change, but what we do know is that he is playing with more heart than we've seen from him in the last decade and it's making him a force to be reckoned with.

Two great players who have earned this shot at the most coveted trophy in tennis.

May the best man win.

I peer at Iris over the top of my phone as she sets down a mug of coffee on the table next to her parents' sofa.

'What?' she says defensively, moving my feet so she can sit down.

I clear my throat and read out loud: '"*We can't know what – or should we say, who – may have caused this change, but what we do know is that he is playing with more heart than we've seen from him in the last decade.*"' I lower my phone. 'Are you serious?'

'He is! There's nothing in there that implies it has anything to do with *you*. I could be talking about anyone! Maybe I'm talking about Neil. Maybe his dad.'

Tilting my head, I arch my brow. She rolls her eyes.

'Okay, so maybe it could be interpreted in a way that suggests his falling head over heels has impacted his performance on the court.' She offers me an apologetic smile. 'In my defence, I wrote that yesterday and it was on a timer to publish this morning. I forgot to edit it.'

I sigh, reaching for the mug. 'I'll forgive you because you've brought me coffee. And without you, I would have been homeless last night.'

'*Mi casa es su casa.*' She hesitates. 'Or rather, my parents' house is your house.'

I smile into my drink. 'It's so kind of them to let me show up without warning and crash on their sofa.'

'It's really no problem; they love having you. Mum's been using you as an excuse to yell at Dad for turning the second spare room into a gym that he never uses. I do feel bad you being on the sofa. You should have slept in my bed with me.' She pats my leg under the duvet. 'I'm a very good sleep partner. I don't snore or anything.'

'I would have kept you up, tossing and turning. My brain wouldn't let me sleep. Anyway, I've become accustomed to sleeping on the sofa recently.'

She looks at me, her eyes filled with concern. 'Are you okay, Flora?'

'Yeah, of course,' I say. She looks unconvinced. 'I'm fine, really. It was a whirlwind romance, a summer fling, and now it's over. We're adults. We move on.'

'It seemed more than a fling, though,' she says carefully. 'Maybe you shouldn't give up on it quite yet. The pressure of Wimbledon, it would cause even the most level-headed person to spiral. He might have been having a moment yesterday.'

I shake my head, picking at the handle of the mug. 'He made his feelings very clear, Iris. There's no hope. And even if I think we have a shot, I don't want to have to persuade someone to love me back. If he's giving up, then I'm not fighting for it.'

She's looking at me strangely, her teeth digging into her bottom lip, her eyes glistening.

'What? What is it?' I ask, puzzled by her expression.

'Oh, Flora. You said you don't want to persuade him to love you back,' she says softly, giving me a half-smile. 'You love him.'

I stiffen. 'No, I... I didn't mean...'

My sentence trails off as the realisation sinks in that there's no point in protesting something that we know to be true. My heart jumps into my throat and I start to feel sick, an uncomfortable feeling sinking into my stomach.

'I can't,' I whisper, looking at Iris in a panic. 'I haven't known him that long.'

She shrugs. 'When you know, you know. And it has been an intense few weeks for you two. You've been through a lot and you've been living together. Besides—' she raises her eyebrows at me '—I don't think there's a rigid rule about how long you need to know someone to fall in love with them.'

I press a hand on my chest in an attempt to steady my erratic heartbeat. 'I admit, I've been falling for him. I mean, who wouldn't?'

She nods solemnly. 'He has the body of a Calvin Klein model, he has an Irish accent *and* there's only one bed in your flat. Obviously you fell for him.'

'Exactly. Obviously.' I chew on my thumbnail, frowning. 'But I didn't think I'd fallen, you know, all the way.'

'And now you know you have,' Iris says slowly, looking at me as though this is a test.

I take a moment to seriously think about this. It might have been a slip of the tongue earlier. I can still back out; I can still claim that I spoke without thinking. But that's the thing. I wasn't thinking when I said it. I wasn't concentrating on the exact words, choosing the most appropriate and considered ones. I spoke how I felt. I spoke from the heart.

I love him.

It suddenly seems obvious, almost insignificant. Of course, I love him. He's the most wonderful person I've ever met. He's kind and thoughtful and smart and fun. Beneath his moody and guarded shell, he's soft and warm, loving and loveable. He's unquestionably good-looking, but when you get to know him, he's breathtakingly beautiful. Think of the way his eyes light up when he gets passionate about what he's talking about, or the way his dimples show when he grins broadly or properly laughs, and the tiny creases that appear between his eyebrows when he's concentrating.

When he makes a smoothie for himself, he makes one for me, too. When he discovered my love of drawing, he patiently encouraged it, but didn't push it. He cooked for me, he bought me wine I liked, he shielded me from the paparazzi. He used a coaster when he knew it annoyed me, and he left his shoes in the hallway every day just so he could tease me affectionately about it when I had to go put them away. He's a secret comic book nerd, he loves Snoopy, and he is adorably baffled by playsuits.

But it's the way he made me feel that made it impossible not to love him. Everything he did – the conversations, the tennis lesson, the way he looked at me, the way he kissed me and touched me – made me feel happy and confident and sexy and powerful.

He made me feel loved.

And now it's all over. The most magical four weeks of my life. Iris is right. We went through it all. From the moment we met it's been bewildering, chaotic, ridiculous, intense, fun, awful and wonderful. Now it's run its course and I have to let him go. I should have known that was coming. It's happened to every other woman he's ever been linked with. He doesn't let them get close. Ever. I don't know why I was stupid enough to think I was any different. It's embarrassing.

My heart feels like it's splintering. It's an all-consuming invisible agony that makes my stomach cramp and my chest tighten. I feel like I haven't earnt the right to feel this way, because I haven't known him long enough for him to make this kind of impact. But suddenly I can't imagine how I'll ever be able to go home if he's not there, waiting for me.

'Flora,' Iris prompts softly, studying me as she reaches over to take my hand.

'It doesn't matter how I feel,' I say hoarsely, as tears begin to trail down my cheeks. 'Whatever it was, whatever we had, it's done.'

'I'm so sorry,' she says, squeezing my fingers.

'It's fine. I'm fine.' I clear my throat and wipe the tears away with the back of my hand, before taking a glug of coffee. 'Anyway, let's talk about something else. What is new with you? How have you been? What are you up to today?'

She grimaces. 'I'm… covering the Wimbledon final.'

'Right.' I close my eyes, chuckling at my own stupidity.

'I can call in sick,' she offers. 'Someone else can cover it and we can hang out, do whatever you want.'

'You write the blog, Iris, you have to go! Besides, you already spent the first bit of the year looking after me as I emerged from a break-up, I'm not going to let you hold my hand through this as well. You've done your bit.'

She rolls her eyes. 'That's not how it works, Flora.'

'You have to go do your job. It's important! And I hear it's a highly anticipated match.'

'I'm going to assume you don't want to come?'

'No, thanks. The absolute last place I want to be today is at Wimbledon.'

'I can try to get you a press pass. We can hurl strawberries at him while he plays.'

'We'd get kicked out and you'd get fired.'

'It would be a cool story for the blog, though.'

'Thanks for the offer, but I'm good,' I assure her.

She sighs, tilting her head back. 'Argh, I feel bad leaving you here all day on your own.'

'I'm not on my own. I'll hang out with your parents; they seem cool.'

'Ah. They're coming to Wimbledon. Sorry. They got ballot tickets.'

'Oh. Well, that's fine. I can go for a walk and stuff, check out the area,' I say as brightly as possible, having another sip of my drink. 'Putney is very nice. There's loads to do here. Don't worry, I'll keep myself entertained.'

'You're very welcome to hang out here if you just want to slob around.'

'Maybe I'll check out your dad's gym.'

'Yeah, he set it up a year ago and the equipment has never been used,' she says, easing into a grin. 'Seriously though, make yourself at home. They've said you're welcome to stay as long as you like.'

'That's really kind of them, and if they don't mind, I'll stay one more night. But then the rental is up and the flat is mine again. Win or lose today, he'll be gone tomorrow.'

I keep my smile fixed as though my heart isn't sinking.

She nods. 'I'm going to go shower and get dressed. You okay to get ready after me?'

'Great, thanks. No rush. Although since I left in a bit of a hurry last night, I may need to borrow some things.'

'Sure, what do you need?'

'Just a couple of toiletries, like if you have a spare toothbrush that would be amazing. And I'll need to borrow some toothpaste obviously. And some cleanser, if that's okay, and then maybe your make-up bag, too. A phone charger would also be really handy as mine is on low battery. And also a clean top if you don't mind, since I had to sleep in mine from yesterday. Oh, and underwear please.'

She blinks at me. 'So... everything.'

'Not everything. I brought my sunglasses.'

She chuckles, getting up and then bending down to give me a hug before she leaves. As she pulls back, she cradles my face in her hands.

'You want my professional opinion?' she asks.

'Sure.'

'If he wins Wimbledon without you,' she sighs, 'it will be a fucking miracle.'

Iris leaves for Wimbledon bright and early, and I shower and get dressed – she has lent me a clean T-shirt that I've tucked into my high-waisted shorts. I put on a brave face while her parents are still here, answering all their questions about what I'm hoping to do for work and smiling as they express how great it is I'm passionate about drawing. Neither of them mention Kieran, and I'm grateful to Iris who, no doubt, warned them. As soon as they wave goodbye and the front door has shut behind them, I collapse onto a sofa in a heap.

I will allow myself today to wallow. It's actually a blessing that they've all gone to Wimbledon because I have my own space to sit with my miserable thoughts and be sad without worrying about bringing anyone else down with me.

Nothing can push him from my mind. I try to distract myself by scrolling through social media, but Kieran, or something that reminds me of him, keeps cropping up amongst the cute dog videos and funny memes. Everyone is talking about Wimbledon today. They're posting smiling pictures of themselves in the grounds, or they're at the pub, or they're watching it on one of the big screens around the city, a glass of Pimm's in hand. With each post I glimpse, the pang gets sharper and the ache grows stronger.

When my phone is down to ten per cent, I put it on power-save mode and set it down on the table, pleased that Iris doesn't have the right charger for it and I have a reason not to torture myself anymore. I get up, make myself a coffee and go stand in the garden, admiring all the colourful flowers cared for by Iris's dad. It's a grey, cloudy day, but it's not cold. I inhale deeply, my heart that little bit lighter from the fresh air, before it sinks again as my mind drifts to strolls in the park with Kieran.

I return to wallow on the sofa and turn on the TV, by which point of course, the first thing that pops up is coverage of Wimbledon. I turn it off and toss the remote aside with a dramatic cry of exasperation. After taking a moment, I turn it back on, knowing full well that I have the ability to change the channel and watch something else.

Having watched a couple of episodes of a reality TV show that just makes me feel worse about the world because everyone is screaming at each other, I switch to the Wimbledon coverage just to check in.

He's lost the first set and he's losing 1–2 in the second, with Chris about to serve for the next game. The camera zooms in on Kieran as he makes his way onto the court, his head bowed as he wipes the sweat from his forehead with the back of his hand.

I turn it off.

After sneaking into Iris's room and scanning her bookshelf, I select one and settle myself back downstairs, trying my best to lose myself in the story and not let my mind wander to him, even though that's what it keeps trying to do.

My phone rings. I'd ignore it but it's Iris, the one person I'm happy to talk to.

'Hey,' I say on answering, 'I haven't burnt down the house.'

'What?' She sounds shocked. 'Why would you burn down the house?'

'I thought that's why you might be calling, to check I haven't burnt down the house.'

'No, Flora, I'm calling because you need to turn on the TV.'

'Why?'

'Turn on Wimbledon.'

I groan. 'Iris, I really don't want to watch it. I'm reading and—'

'You've got to see this, Flora. Turn it on.'

'Do I have to?'

'Trust me, you're going to want to see this,' she says, and I can hear that she's smiling. 'He's doing the strangest thing and I have a feeling that you might know why.'

'Okay, let me find the remote, hang on.'

I turn it on and Kieran fills the screen. He's two sets down and he's sitting in his chair at the side of the court in the break. The crowd is tittering with laughter, the commentators are snickering and wondering aloud what's going on. I gasp, hardly daring to believe what I'm seeing.

'Have you got it on?' Iris asks eagerly. 'Can you see him?'

'Yeah, I see him.'

'What is he *doing*?'

I break into a smile. 'It's obvious isn't it? He's blowing bubbles.'

He's in the middle of the Wimbledon final on Centre Court, being watched by thousands of people in the stands and even more on screens around the world, and he's holding the bottle of bubbles I gave him, and serenely blowing bubbles, smiling softly as he watches them float up into the air and pop one by one.

'Yeah, I can see that he's blowing bubbles, Flora,' she sighs. 'But what does it mean?'

Our conversation plays out in my head. I remember it all. If ever I saw him blowing bubbles on Centre Court, I'd said...

You'll know I'm thinking of you, he'd finished.

'Flora, do you know what it means?' Iris repeats when I don't say anything.

'Yes,' I whisper in a daze. 'It means I have to get to Wimbledon.'

30

'Iris, if I come now to Wimbledon, will you come meet me and help me get in?' I ask her urgently, jumping up and rushing to the front door to find my trainers.

She gasps in surprise. 'Really? You're coming? Yeah, let me see what I can do. I'll meet you at Gate One.'

'Okay, I'll be there in—'

My phone makes a low battery sound before promptly dying. *Shit.*

WHY didn't I grab my charger last night before I stormed out of the flat?! I can't order an Uber now, so I rush out the house, shut the door behind me and race onto the road. It's empty and residential, with no cars trundling down it, let alone any cabs. It's also starting to drizzle and I don't have a jacket or umbrella. *Fuck.*

Sprinting as fast as I can to the main road, I turn round the corner and stop to catch my breath, desperately looking both ways and praying for that beautiful yellow light of a free black cab. When one comes into view, I squeal with joy and wave him down with two hands to make sure he doesn't miss me.

'Wimbledon please!' I cry, hurling myself into the back and out of the rain that's getting a little heavier. 'The tournament, I mean.'

'You're a little late, aren't you?' he remarks, setting off.

'You have no idea,' I breathe, slumping back and biting my lip. 'As quick as possible if you can.'

'Sure, it's only an eight-minute drive from here, won't take long,' he assures me, glancing in his rear-view mirror. He squints at me and as we come to the traffic lights, he swivels round to peer at me through the glass. 'Hey, don't I know you from somewhere? Are you famous?'

'Uh... no.'

'Huh. You look familiar.' He shrugs, turning back to watch the road as the lights go green. 'I feel like I've seen your face somewhere.'

I sigh, deciding to own up. You can always trust London cabbies in my experience.

'I've been dating Kieran O'Sullivan,' I admit.

'That's it! He punched that other fella over you.'

'Not exactly, but I was there.'

'And you had that kiss in the rain.' He beams at me in the rear-view mirror. 'Great picture, that.' His face falls. 'So how come you're not at the final watching him play, then?'

'We... we had an argument.'

'Oh. Sorry to hear that.' He quirks a brow. 'You were being stubborn were you, after your fight? Saying you wouldn't go watch him today?'

I look down at my hands in my lap. 'He said he didn't want me there and I believed him. But I think we were both wrong.'

He chuckles. 'Have I been there. Sometimes the missus speaks in riddles – she says one thing, but really she wants me to do the opposite. I've learnt over the years that the words don't really mean much; it's the actions that count, isn't it.'

I nod.

'So you racing to be there for him now, that will count for a lot,' he adds.

'I hope so,' I say, my heart hammering. 'I'm going to put up a fight anyway.'

'That's the spirit.' He smiles warmly. 'Let's hope he starts thinking that way on the court, too. He's letting the other guy walk all over him. Maybe seeing you will help give him that oomph he needs. By the looks of this weather, they're going to need to close the roof soon. The rain is light but it will make conditions slippery.'

'You don't think it's going to stop and clear up?'

'It's forecast to continue for the rest of the afternoon. Typical! We've had quite good weather for Wimbledon this year, but it had to rain on finals day.'

Something suddenly occurs to me that makes me sit bolt upright, my stomach flipping. 'I don't have any money!'

He pulls his eyebrows together. 'What's that, love?'

'My phone died, which has my cards on it, and because of my argument with Kieran, I stormed out of our flat without my wallet! I don't have any cash to pay you! When we get there, if you just wait, I'll ask my friend who's meeting me if she has her cards on her.'

'You know what, it's on the house,' he says, turning the running meter off.

'What? No! I owe you for the journey!'

'You've made my day. I get to tell everyone I was the cabbie who raced you here to declare your love to Kieran O'Sullivan...' He pauses. 'That is what you're planning on doing, right?'

A warmth swells in my belly and my heart feels so full it rises into my throat, making it hard to breathe. 'Yes,' I breathe, unable to stop a smile. 'That's the plan.'

'And I get to be a part of that story. It's like a bloody movie!' He chuckles. 'It's an honour to be your driver today, miss.'

'Thank you so much,' I gush, pressing my hand to my chest.

As we reach the main gate and he indicates to pull over, he winds down the window when I jump out and shut the door, thanking him profusely.

'Go get 'im!' he calls out as I impatiently wait for passing cars before I can cross the road, my hair becoming damp and scraggly from the rain.

There's no queue – there's no play on outdoor courts today and anyone who wanted to watch the final on Murray Mound is already in, huddled under umbrellas – and so I race towards the gate, spotting Iris already there, chatting to one of the security women, holding her umbrella over both of them.

'There she is!' Iris cries, waving me over.

'Iris, I don't have any money!' I announce breathlessly as I reach them.

'Peculiar thing to shout out on arrival,' she comments, sharing a look with the other woman. 'Flora, this is Selma. Selma, this is my friend who I told you about, who apparently doesn't have any money and likes to tell people about it.'

'I don't have my cards or cash on me, so I can't buy a ground pass,' I explain.

'Yeah, I couldn't get you a press pass either at the last minute without accreditation,' Iris says with a sly smile, 'but I've had a word with Selma here and I think we're good.'

'I trust Iris,' Selma says, her eyes sparkling at me as she lets out a wistful sigh. 'Plus, I'm a big romance fan. I'm not getting in the way of your Wimbledon fairy tale.' She leans forwards and lowers her voice. 'Courtney is a prat. I'm Team Kieran all the way.'

'You know, Chris Courtney once asked Selma if she knew who he was when, as part of her job, she had to search his tennis bag on entry,' Iris informs me.

'He yelled right in my face and there was nothing interesting in his bag anyway,' she adds, grumbling. She checks the time on her watch. 'Right, I'm just going to look this way for a moment and if anyone runs in while my back is turned, hey ho.'

Winking at me, she turns away and Iris grabs my wrist to pull me through the gate.

'Thank you!' I call out over my shoulder as we start racing to Centre Court, Iris attempting to hold the umbrella high enough to cover both of us.

'Where are we going?' she asks, and I realise I don't know the answer to her question so I slow down to a complete stop. 'Flora, what's going on? What are you going to do? Why did you change your mind about coming? And what is it with the bubbles?'

'Iris, I'll explain everything later, but I need to find a way to talk to Kieran.'

She emits a squeal of joy, grinning at me. 'Oh my God, the bubbles were for you, weren't they? I knew it! I knew you had to see it.'

'Iris, focus! Where in the stands can I go to get his attention while he's playing? The press box? I could try to get into the box where his team sits if—'

'Flora, Flora,' she interrupts, waving her hand in my face to get me to stop rambling, 'he's not on the court.'

'Oh my God.' I clap my hand over my mouth. 'Is it over? Did he lose?'

'No!' She gestures up to the sky. 'Play is paused while they close the Centre Court roof. The rain is due to last all afternoon. Even the weather is on your side.'

I inhale sharply, hope bubbling up my throat like lemonade. 'Where do the players go while the roof closes?'

She shrugs. 'I don't know. The locker room, maybe. I know Courtney has moved into the fancy dressing room, but I'm not sure where—'

I don't hear the end of her sentence because I've turned on my heel, already running as fast as I can to the outdoor entrance to the men's locker room, the one Neil led me to just a few days before, although that feels like a lifetime ago. I finally reach the door with Iris in tow, flustered and out of breath. The security man standing beside it looks me up and down.

'Hey!' I wheeze, clutching my side. I really need to do more cardio. 'Remember me?'

He studies me. 'Maybe.'

'I was here with Neil Damon, Kieran O'Sullivan's coach. He gave me a pass and you let us in?' I say hurriedly, desperate to jog his memory.

'Oh yeah.' He nods, breaking into a smile. 'I remember you!'

'Great!' Iris exclaims, grabbing my arm. 'So can she go in?'

He chuckles. 'Absolutely not. This is the players' area.'

'Yes, but you know me. I'm not a randomer, I'm with Kieran O'Sullivan.'

'Uh-huh, it's nice to see you again. Do you have a pass for this area?' he asks, amused.

'No, but—'

'I'm sorry, but I can't let you in,' he states with an apologetic smile.

'Come on, she needs to speak to Kieran!' Iris pleads. 'He sent her a secret message through the TV and now she's here to tell him how she feels!'

He quirks his brow. 'That's nice. I still can't let you in.'

'Please! Look, the cab driver gave me a free ride and the security guard at the gate let me in without a pass, just so I could talk to him!' I plead, biting my lip. 'Where's your compassion? Your sense of romance? This is important!'

He narrows his eyes at me. 'Did you just say one of our security team let you in without a pass? Because they really shouldn't have done that.'

I blink at him. 'No. No! Of course not. Don't be silly. I have a ground pass somewhere, I must have lost it. I—'

Suddenly a movement behind the glass of the corridor catches my eye and I see Neil on his phone, looking flushed and impatient as he tries to make a call.

'Neil!' I shout, waving my arms madly at him, because even though he's the last person who would let me in, he's my only hope. 'NEIL!'

He glances up and his face lights up as though I'm the answer to his prayers. Jumping towards the door, he swings it open and ushers me in quickly. 'She's with me,' he tells the security man, who instantly stands aside to let me in.

'Told you,' I hear Iris mutter, before she cries out after me, 'Good luck, Flora!'

Once I'm safely through the doors, to my utter surprise, Neil pulls me in for a hug. I'm too shocked to hug him back, but he doesn't seem to mind. When he steps back, he keeps his hands on my arms, and breaks into a relieved smile.

'Am I glad to see you,' he breathes, before he starts marching down the corridor at speed, encouraging me to keep up with him. 'I was trying to call you but it's going to voicemail.'

'My phone died,' I explain, hurrying round the corner after him.

'Listen, I owe you an apology,' he states, glancing over his shoulder at me so I can see the sincerity of his expression. 'When I'm wrong, I say I'm wrong. Flora, I was wrong about you and Kieran. You weren't getting in his way, you were getting him here. I'm sorry.'

'It's okay. I get you were trying to protect him.'

'Yeah, thanks to me, it's been one fuck-up after the other,' he says through gritted teeth as we descend the stairs. 'But I still think he can win today. Now you're here, I'm almost certain of it.'

He stops at the locker room and gives me a pointed look. 'You don't have long, maybe ten minutes. The roof is closed. They're waiting now for the air conditioning to acclimatise in there.' He nods at the door next to him. 'I'm not allowed in there; technically neither are you. But I'm hoping that even if you're sent out right away, at least he'll know you're here. That will be something.'

'Okay.' I nod, raking my fingers through my damp, knotted hair. 'Thanks, Neil.'

'Good luck,' he whispers, before he carefully and quietly opens the door just enough for me to slip through.

31

An official is sitting on a bench to the left, staring at the lockers opposite him, his eyes glazed over with boredom. Kieran is seated on a bench at the other side of the room with his head in his hands. Hunched over like that, he looks defeated.

I start walking towards him with purpose. The official notices me and springs to his feet. 'Hey!' he says, bewildered. 'You're not allowed in here!'

Kieran's head snaps up. I hear his sharp intake of breath.

'I have to talk to you,' I tell Kieran, as he jumps up.

'You need to leave!' the official orders, looking panicked.

'You're here,' Kieran says, ignoring him and striding over to me.

We stop in front of each other, while the official hovers to the side, his eyes darting between us. 'Excuse me, miss, but you really can't be in here.'

'This won't take long, and I'm not here to coach or comment on the game, I promise,' I insist, giving him a hopeful smile. 'Thank you so much for understanding.'

'What? No, I don't—'

'Flossie, I'm so sorry,' Kieran cuts across him, his face crumpling. 'I'm so sorry about everything. I convinced myself I was trying to protect you by ending it, but as soon as I walked out on that court today, I realised I'd lost what I'd been looking for this whole time. You were right about me. I pushed you away because I was scared. Scared to let someone else in again, scared to get hurt again, scared to hurt you. Because you're so precious, Flossie. You're everything, and I couldn't hurt you.'

Blushing, the official clears his throat. 'I really must protest—'

'But last night I couldn't sleep,' Kieran continues brazenly, looking down and shaking his head. 'I thought I was doing the right thing, but how could it be the right thing when nothing else seemed to matter? Winning Wimbledon has meant everything to me, and here I am in the final, and as I walked out on Centre Court today I realised—' He pauses to take a deep breath and bring his eyes up to meet mine. 'I realised that, without you here, winning doesn't seem to mean that much at all.'

His eyes glistening, the official gulps, before quietly saying, 'You're not really allowed—'

'I'm so sorry, Flossie,' Kieran concludes, his throat bobbing, his brow creased. 'I'm sorry for everything. I hope you'll find it in you to forgive me, but I understand if you can't, and I want to thank you for what you gave me the last few weeks. For the first time in a long time, I felt that someone really saw me. You reminded me to have faith in myself.'

The room falls into silence as I process his words. A warm, tingling sensation is flooding my body and I feel like I'm floating, like none of this can possibly be real. Everything around us seems to have faded into a dreamy haze and it's just me and Kieran. He's looking at me so intently, so earnestly, that it's difficult to remember to breathe. I could happily lose myself in those eyes all day long, forever more.

I forget that we're not alone until I hear the official emit a small whimper, moved by Kieran's speech. 'This shouldn't... this shouldn't be happening,' he reminds us in a hushed tone, but turns to me expectantly, willing me to answer.

I take a beat, my heart thudding against my chest.

'You forgot to ask me for a secret,' I say.

Kieran looks puzzled.

'When we were playing ping-pong, you told me a secret – the one about Lingfield Road – and then I was supposed to tell you one in return, but we never got to mine,' I begin to explain. This wasn't how I planned this to go at all, but my brain is insisting on taking us in this direction, so I'm going with it. 'My secret, Kieran, is that I'm writing a graphic novel.'

He frowns. 'I… I know that one.'

'Yes, but you don't know what it's about. No one knows. I've been too scared to tell anyone because when you put your heart into something – your whole heart – it takes a lot of courage to show it to others. So, here goes.' I clear my throat. 'It's a romance, about a girl at school who feels… lost. She doesn't have much family or many friends, and she's never felt like she's fit in or understood what her purpose might be. She's kind of muddling through hopelessly. She loses herself in books, because she doesn't feel alone when she reads. But then a new boy starts at the school. He's not particularly warm and friendly, he's got that sexy brooding thing going on—' I notice Kieran's lips twitch here and the official nod with approval. 'He keeps himself to himself, doesn't talk much or attempt to make friends. They get partnered together for a school project and they clash. But slowly, as they're forced to let each other in, they begin to understand each other. She sees him play tennis and she can tell that's where he comes alive, where he's truly himself. He lost someone close, you see, and tennis… it saved him. And his motivation and kindness inspires her to write her own stories. Slowly, these two lost, hopeless outsiders both start to feel that they are found.'

The official sniffs.

Kieran's eyes are gleaming. 'And how does it end?' he asks softly.

I shrug. 'I haven't worked out the ending yet. But I think their story will continue way past the end of the book.'

The corners of his mouth twitch. 'There's a sequel?'

'I hope so.'

'Me too.'

'Kieran,' I say, reaching forwards to take his hands in mine, our fingers entwining, 'I've never really felt like I mattered to anyone, but you've changed that. So, really, I should be thanking you. Not the other way round.'

He bows his head to press his forehead against mine and closes his eyes.

'I love you,' I whisper. 'Win or lose today, I'll be waiting for you after.'

He exhales slowly. 'Then it sounds like I've already won.'

'Oh my,' the official sighs, wiping his eyes. 'I'm so happy!'

A knock on the door makes the three of us jump.

'It's time,' a voice declares.

'Coming!' the official calls back in a shrill voice, before looking up at Kieran. 'All right, Mr O'Sullivan, it's time to go back on court. Please follow me.'

He turns and marches over to the door.

I place my hands on Kieran's shoulders and offer what I hope to be an easy, nonchalant smile. 'Shut out the noise, remember?'

'I'm just going to play a bit of tennis,' he says, his smile widening and the dimples turning my insides to mush.

'And then come home for cake.'

'Victoria sponge?'

'Of course.'

'And there will be a banner, right?'

'I'm going to put my all into it. It will be the best one you've ever seen.'

The official clears his throat pointedly and, taking one last deep breath with me, Kieran goes to pick up his tennis bag and sling it over his shoulder. I beam at him as he strides to the door. He looks taller somehow.

He quickly turns back to me. 'You'll be there watching, right?'

'Are you kidding?' I grin, putting my hands on my hips. 'I wouldn't miss it.'

'Good,' he says, whipping his cap out a top zip in his bag and putting it on. 'I'll look out for you.'

With a nod to the official, the door is opened and he walks

out, on his way back to play in the final of the Wimbledon Championship.

The official hisses, 'You were never here,' over his shoulder at me and winks, before hurrying out after him.

This is it. I'd better go find a seat.

3–6, 2–6, 6–1, 6–4

Standing at six all in the final set, it has gone to a ten-point tie-break.

The tie-break score is currently 8–8.

I feel like I can't breathe. My stomach is knotted, my heart in my throat, my body so tense that my fingers are trembling. I have to sit on my hands.

Kieran is readying himself to return as Courtney requests another ball from the ball boy before he serves.

This is unbelievable. *He* is unbelievable. The way Kieran's fought back has been nothing short of miraculous and the crowd are absolutely loving it. I've never been anywhere before with such an electric atmosphere. There are thousands of people in here but at the start of a point, it's so silent, you could hear a pin drop. One tiny cough echoes through the whole stadium, especially with the roof on. Then as the rally begins, the volume of the chorus of gasps begins to increase until it erupts with noise when the point is won. And Courtney has a solid support base, but Kieran is stealing hearts with every stroke that he makes. It started out so one-sided, they must have thought it was nearly over, but he's given them the sort of match that the Wimbledon final deserves: it's nail-biting, thrilling, dramatic, entertaining, *epic*. And they love him for it.

Everyone likes an underdog.

Bloody hell, I've never been so sweaty in my life.

I don't know how Neil is sitting next to me so calm and collected, his mouth a straight thin line the entire time. I feel like my heart is thudding so hard, Kieran might be able to see it pounding through my skin every time he looks up.

His glances to me have not gone unnoticed.

My face has been beamed up onto the big screen a couple of times, and the first time, when I'd just entered the box to take my place next to Neil, there was a ripple of intrigued whispers around the crowd. I flushed furiously. But when he won the third set and a shot of me appeared on the big screen again, I barely noticed. I didn't care one jot. I was too busy cheering him on. Brian acknowledged me with a curt nod when I came to sit in the box with Kieran's team, but he's sitting too far away to speak to me.

That's probably for the best. I don't really have anything to say to him.

Kieran's fight back to level with Courtney has been astonishing, and Courtney looks like he can't believe that he's here battling for the Championship with a tie-break. Frustration is creeping into Courtney's game as he faces Kieran's relentless aggression. He looked dumbfounded at the start of the fourth set, and by the end, seemed consigned to the fact that this was going to lead to a tie-break: he double-faulted twice in his last service game. In between the third and fourth set, Neil passed me his phone to give me a glimpse of Iris's blog as she keeps her followers updated with constant posts:

O'Sullivan is finally playing like he's just remembered he really wants to win. He believes now, and so do we.

As much as I dislike Courtney, I have to admit that the standard of tennis is unbelievably high on both sides. This really could go either way.

Okay, Courtney has selected a ball for his serve and he's stepping up to the line.

'Silence, please,' the umpire requests.

Centre Court abides.

It's a powerful serve from Courtney down the middle, but Kieran's reflexes are on fire and he's there with a backhand, reacting fast to return the serve to Courtney's backhand. Courtney sends a beautiful shot cross-court, before rushing towards the net. Kieran gets there to send it back hard and flat, to try to pass him down the line but Courtney reacts with an incredible lunging volley. Rushing forwards, Kieran just reaches it, lobbing it high over his head to the back of the court. The crowd gasps in unison as Courtney races back. The ball bounces a foot in front of the baseline. Courtney closes the gap sprinting back and manages to twist, swiping a messy forehand lofting over the net. Kieran has time. He gently slices the ball, taking the pace off and it drops just over the net, rolling to a standstill.

There is a moment's silence of disbelief at the skill displayed, before the stadium breaks into astonished applause, cheering and whistling. At the back of the court, Courtney throws his racket in fury.

Oh. My. God.

Kieran just broke his serve. He's taken the lead. He's winning. *Championship Point.*

Kieran is serving for Championship Point!

You wouldn't think it from the look of him. While the audience is up on their feet, congratulating him on his last point, he's busy checking the tennis balls in his hand, selecting two and storing one in his pocket with an inscrutable expression. He makes his way to the baseline, and the umpire asks the crowd to quieten down, issuing Courtney with a warning.

'Fucking hell,' I hear Neil mutter under his breath beside me.

Swiping the sweat off his brow with the back of his hand, Kieran glances up in my direction. I give just the hint of a smile. A smile that tells him that it doesn't matter what comes next. Either way, I'll be here. A smile that says, *always.*

He responds with a fleeting frown. It's gone as soon as it arrived, but I caught a glimpse of it and I wonder what thought has just flitted across his mind. Whatever it was, he sets it aside to focus on the next point. A rather important one.

As he bounces the ball in front of him, the silence is deafening.

I hold my breath, my heartbeat thundering in my ears.

He tosses the ball up into the air. It's a powerful serve across Courtney's body, forcing Courtney to respond with a backhand that soars across the court. Kieran backhands it down the line and chalk flies as it brushes the inside of the white paint. But Courtney is there with a mighty forehand back across the court. Kieran's wrong-footed and manages to just reach and return a floating ball down the centre of the court. Courtney races in towards it and hits another superb forehand into the back right corner of the court and follows his shot up to the net. Kieran instantly reacts, sprinting to the right and lunging to reach the ball. He hits an exquisite forehand straight down the line. Courtney is rooted to the spot, helpless as he watches the ball soar past him out of reach.

It all happens in slow motion.

There's an explosion of noise as Centre Court erupts in a roar of celebration. I spring up from my seat, my heart leaping. Kieran collapses to his knees on the ground, burying his face in his hands, his body trembling with sobs of joy and disbelief. The stadium seems to shake beneath the thousands of people jumping to their feet. Even with the roof on, the applause must echo for miles.

'He's done it! *He's done it!*' Neil is yelling next to me, hugging the assistant coach and hopping up and down on the spot. He spins round to pull me into him, holding me close and whispering, 'Thank you, thank you, thank you', repeatedly in my ear.

When we break the hug, both of our cheeks are wet with tears of joy.

Serenaded by thunderous applause, Kieran rises to his feet and goes to shake hands with Courtney, who is forcing a congratulatory smile through a sour expression. After reaching up to shake hands with the umpire, Kieran turns to wave at his adoring audience, overwhelmed by emotion. He tips his head back and closes his eyes to soak in this glorious moment. The Irish in the stands are giddy with excitement, their flags vigorously waving, their chants of his name reverberating through the stadium and piercing my heart. It is as if they all know him personally and couldn't be prouder. When he opens his eyes, they are glistening and he sets them straight at me. I lift my hands, stinging from the amount of clapping, high above my head and grin at him, tears streaming freely down my face.

He jogs across the court towards the box and begins to climb the stand to get to us.

The cheering has a new lease of life, another loud wave erupting as his fans watch him make his way up to the player box, people clambering forwards to clap him on the back as he goes. Neil is ready to greet him with a tight embrace, his eyes red and watery as he holds Kieran close and tells him he earned this, he deserves this, *he knew he had it in him*. The rest of Kieran's team join in on the hug, all of them crowding in with their arms around each other, Kieran somewhere at the centre of it all. As he breaks away, Brian is there with a brief hug and a clap on his back. Over the noise of the crowd, I can't hear what he says, but I hope he's finally telling Kieran he's proud of him. But I'm not sure Kieran is even listening, because he's craning his neck to look for someone else.

His eyes meet mine and he smiles, forging his way through the parting group surrounding him to get to me. As he wraps his arms around my waist and lifts me up, the crowd goes wild. It sounds as though they're as invested in our story as we are.

'You won Wimbledon!' I laugh into his ear. 'Kieran, *you won Wimbledon!*'

'I forgot to tell you something,' he says breathlessly, putting me down and gazing down at me. 'I remembered just before I served for the final point that in the locker room, I forgot to tell you that I love you, too.'

My breath catches, the booming noise of Centre Court drowned out by the thudding of my heart, aching with love and hope and happiness. All those things you dream of.

As he leans down to kiss me, I forget the world is watching. It's just me and him. Nothing else matters. And I smile against his mouth as I realise that everything that came before – all the mess, all the pain, all the chaos and joy – it was leading us to this one perfect moment.

It was leading us to each other.

Epilogue

One Year Later

'What do you think?' Kieran asks, putting his hands on his hips.

Taking my sunglasses off, I move to stand beside him and look out at the view. Surrounded by mountains, the lake stretches out before us, the water sparkling in the sunshine. As the breeze whips my hair around my face, I take a deep breath in and nod.

'Perfect,' I declare, much to his satisfaction.

He shrugs his backpack off, unzips it and reaches in for the folded picnic blanket, shaking it out and laying it on the floor before kneeling down to get out the half-bottle of Champagne, two glasses, a box of strawberries, a carton of cream and two spoons.

I sit down next to him and slide my sunglasses back on, stretching my legs out and leaning back on my hands. The Lake District is vast but at the height of summer it can still be tricky to find a secluded spot for a picnic. Kieran took the task very seriously and, after asking around, he decided to take his chances on this particular place by Rydal Water. I couldn't have hoped for better.

He pops the Champagne cork, pours me a glass and passes it over, before pouring his own. After clinking our glasses together, he sits back and joins me in admiring the view. I take a tiny sip and balance the glass on the grass by the edge of the blanket.

'I can't believe we're here.' Kieran sighs, lowering himself back on his elbows. 'It's been such a long week, I thought this break would never come.'

I reach over to place a hand on his leg. 'You so deserve this break. The ball last night couldn't have gone better. I'm so proud of you.'

'I didn't do it alone,' he says giving me a pointed look. 'It would have been a disaster without your superior organisation and planning skills. It still feels like a dream. I can't believe we pulled it off.'

I shrug. 'I can.'

When Kieran had the idea to throw a huge black-tie ball to raise money for his charity, Head in the Game, I knew it was going to be an ambitious job but it would be worth it. It had the potential to not only raise a lot of money, thanks to Kieran's sports contacts, but also give the charity a huge awareness boost, and it had done just that. This morning, official photos from the event, hosted at The Hurlingham Club, were across all the papers and social media, thanks to all the famous faces that showed up. We didn't just have big tennis names rocking up in their ball gowns and tuxedos, but glamorous stars across every sport you can think of, who'd all bought tables to be there.

We raised an astounding £1.25 million.

I thought I might burst from pride when Kieran, looking utterly shellshocked, announced the total raised to rapturous applause last night. He has spent the last year putting everything into this charity, which provides free sports sessions – like tennis, football, ballet and swimming, to name a few – to children aged between six and eighteen who have suffered the loss of a close family member. As Kieran knows all too well, sports and exercise can help when it comes to coping with grief, encouraging focus and a sense of purpose, and it's now his goal to make sure it's accessible to any child from any background who is suffering anything like what he went through. When he has the time, he's been offering some coaching sessions himself. The kids love him. No surprises there.

His passion and hard work is going to change so many lives for the better. I didn't think I could be prouder than when he lifted that trophy at Wimbledon last year, but last night somehow managed to trump even that.

Amongst the celebrities were family and friends. Iris was there, as were Neil and several members of Kieran's former team, including his publicist Nicole who I've grown close to. Even Brian flew over to attend. He and Kieran had a tense moment on his arrival, but they both managed to behave themselves and Brian donated generously – the charity means a lot to him too, since Kieran launched it in honour of Aidan's memory.

Brian's book came out last Christmas and Kieran hasn't quite forgiven him for several of the chapters that detailed personal family incidents, and in particular, the chapter that revealed how destroyed Kieran had been by that interview he gave being published after Aidan's death. Kieran is such a private person that he hated the world knowing his business, and it took him a while to speak to Brian again.

Despite his assurances, Brian's book wasn't a tennis manual, it was a memoir as had been originally reported, and he never sent it to Kieran in advance. He did, however, edit it heavily after Kieran's win at Wimbledon last year, which was why publication was pushed back to December. Rumour has it that the previous draft was a lot more negative about Kieran, and the more cynical amongst us might assume that he felt the need to change it now that he wanted to be back in the good books of his son, the reigning Wimbledon Champion.

I was glad he came last night, though, and that they're building bridges. Now that Kieran is out the game, Brian doesn't need to be his coach; he can just work on being his father. It will take time, but, as Kieran said yesterday, Aidan would have wanted them to both be there at the event, slowly making amends.

My dad and Camila were also there, having a great time milling amongst the famous faces at the ball. I shouldn't have been surprised at how many people they knew – apparently they've met several of the celebrities who were there before on the New York social scene. It's been nice getting to know them a bit better this past year. Dad kept his promise and flew over at the end of the summer and we spent some time together then. I wouldn't say the conversation flows with ease between us, but he's making an effort and checks in much more often. I often tease Kieran about the fact that Dad and I have managed to rebuild our relationship purely because we finally found something to talk about that we're both interested in: him.

Last night was emotional for both Kieran and I. Getting this charity off the ground has been a lot of hard work, and we've done it whilst moving into our new place, a dream home in Wimbledon Village. There wasn't anywhere else either of us wanted to live. After the championships last year, Kieran took a six-month lease on a flat in the area, since we both agreed that maybe we should do the dating thing for a while, rather than live together straight away. But six months was more than enough for us to realise that this was the real deal. He moved back into Lingfield Road as soon as his temporary lease was up. I'll be sad to leave the flat, but it's time for a bigger space of our very own.

I watch Kieran as he admires our tranquil surroundings and reach up to run my fingers through his hair. He closes his eyes and heaving a relaxed sigh, lies down on his back, gesturing for me to join him. Removing my sunglasses, I nuzzle happily into the crook of his arm, his fingers trailing circles lightly on my shoulder.

'You know, I think this is the first time I've seen you relax in a year,' I remark, my nose brushing against his neck. 'It's a strange sort of retirement you've taken.'

'I'm not sure early retirement was ever going to suit me.'

'I think it suits you very well,' I counter. 'Look at what you've done in a year.'

'And what about you, Miss Bestselling Author?'

I burst out laughing. 'It hasn't even been published yet! Don't say it will be a bestseller – you can't jinx it. I need a publisher to pick it up first.'

Every spare moment I've had has been dedicated to my graphic novel and I finally finished it two months ago. Even though he'd been integral to the process from the start, I was terrified to show Kieran the final book, but I also knew that I'd created something I could be proud of. I've never felt more vulnerable than when I sent it to agents and waited anxiously for their responses. After three rejections, I got an agent who was interested.

The day I signed with her, Kieran bought me a cake and stuck up a HAPPY BIRTHDAY SIGNING WITH A LITERARY AGENT DAY.

The execution wasn't the best, but he got a gold star for the effort.

'Your agent said she's confident the book will be snapped up as soon as it's out on submission,' Kieran reminds me. 'Which will be when, by the way?'

'Next week.' I bite my lip. 'I'm nervous. I hope a publisher somewhere out there likes it. If it's not picked up, it will be a little embarrassing.'

'There's nothing embarrassing about finishing a graphic novel, signing with an agent and getting it out on submission. That is a huge achievement already, no matter what comes next,' he insists, shifting his body to turn and face me, his arm still trapped under my head.

He takes off his sunglasses, sliding them into the pocket of his shorts, and I gaze into his piercing eyes, admiring his features, my heart fluttering as he smiles affectionately at me. *I can't believe he chose me.* You'd think after a year I'd be used to how beautiful he is, but he still has the ability to take my breath away.

'What if it isn't picked up?' I mutter nervously.

'It will be.'

'But what if it isn't?'

'Then you start work on your next one,' he says, before offering me a mischievous grin. 'You're in the right place. I hear it can be very inspiring here for authors.'

I arch my brow. 'Is that right?'

'You can understand the hype, though, right? It's pretty special here.'

'It is. It's very special.'

This feels like the right time. Since I took the test this morning, I've been waiting for a good moment to tell him, and lying next to each other, feeling like there's no one else in the world but us… well, I'm not sure I'd find better.

'Kieran,' I say breezily, as his eyes flutter closed.

'Mm?'

'You know that bottle of Champagne you brought today.'

'You want a top-up?'

'No, I don't. In fact, you're going to have to drink it on your own.'

'Why?' he asks lazily. 'Are you planning on going somewhere?'

'I'm not going anywhere. It's just, I won't be drinking for the next nine months.'

His eyes flash open and he moves his arm so he can sit bolt upright.

'Are you… are you…' he begins, flustered, his breath shaking as he leans over me.

Smiling coyly, I sit up and nod, my eyes filling with tears.

He inhales sharply before drawing me into his arms and holding me so tight, I wonder if he ever plans on letting go. When the blue plus sign appeared on the test this morning, it felt surreal. As it sank in, I felt a little bit of everything: absolutely terrified and deliriously happy all at once. But I know that I can do this, and I feel so lucky to have him at my side through whatever comes next. When Kieran pulls away, he cups my face in his hands, his watery eyes locked on mine.

'We're having a baby?' he checks hoarsely, as though hardly daring to believe it.

'We're having a baby,' I whisper, my jaw aching from grinning.

Breaking into a wide beaming smile, he dips his head to press his mouth against mine, a kiss so intense and meaningful that my heart skips a beat. He breaks the kiss to say in a raspy, breathless voice, 'I love you so much,' before gently pulling me against him again, his hands sliding around my hips and tightening around my waist.

As I rest my chin on his shoulder and hold him close, I exhale slowly, gazing out at the lake, the sapphire blue water flaked with gold as it shimmers under the warm afternoon sun. It's beautiful here, but really, it wouldn't have mattered where we were when I told him.

I close my eyes, smiling to myself as he whispers in my ear, promising me he's going to spend the rest of his life making me and our child happy.

It feels like a long time since I had my heart set on coming to the Lake District to write my story. But it turned out my story was in Wimbledon all along.

And there's still so much more of it to come.

Acknowledgements

SPECIAL THANKS to my extraordinary editor Kim, who has believed in Flora and Kieran from the start, and made me feel like I could actually write this book. So much of this story belongs to you, thank you for all your guidance and advice. I still can't quite believe how quickly we turned this round, but here it is – we did it!

Huge thanks to Holly, Shannon, Yas, Becky and the wonderful team at Head of Zeus for all your brilliant work on the book and getting it out into the world, and to the amazingly talented cover illustrator Sofia and designer Meg for giving me the DREAM cover. I could not love it more, thank you.

To Lauren and Callen, thank you for everything you do. Without you, I'd genuinely be lost and I'm forever grateful to work with you both. What adventures still to come!

Thank you to my husband, family and friends for cheering me on and for sticking with me even when I'm a stresshead because of all the deadlines. Special thanks to my dog, my constant companion, who always sits at my feet as I write.

I have to take a moment to thank Red Bull. You were right there with me for those long nights and early mornings. Thank you for tasting so delicious.

Lastly, I would like to thank anyone who reads this book. I loved creating this story and I hope you enjoy escaping into it. I hope you smile, laugh and fall in love along with the characters. And I hope you feel inspired, too. *Believe when no one else does.*

About the Author

KATHERINE REILLY is the pseudonym for an author of several young adult and adult novels, published globally. Katherine lives in London with her family and rescue dog.